F...

"*Familiar Angel* is fantastic… a transcendent love story… Harry and Suriel are heroes to die for, and their love is a lesson … I can only have faith and desperately hope she will keep turning out more tales like this!"
—Cindy Dees, NYT and
USA Today Bestselling author

"Both striking and sensual, the thought-provoking novel pays equal attention to love, sacrifice, the divine, and family."
—Publishers Weekly

Red Fish, Dead Fish

"The passion in her words of love and family somehow come through like no other author I know."
—Paranormal Romance Guild

Regret Me Not

"*Regret Me Not* is a wonderful holiday read, with just enough angst and Christmas cheer to satisfy most readers… Highly recommended for anyone who just needs a sweet happily ever after."
—Joyfully Jay

"It's what I come to expect from this author when she's not trying to rip my heart out. A little fluff, a little drama, a little sex, and a lot of romance!"
—Love Bytes

By AMY LANE

Behind the Curtain
Beneath the Stain
Bewitched by Bella's Brother
Bolt-hole
Christmas with Danny Fit
Clear Water
Do-over
Familiar Angel
Food for Thought
Gambling Men
Going Up
Grand Adventures (Dreamspinner Anthology)
Hammer & Air
If I Must
Immortal
It's Not Shakespeare
Left on St. Truth-be-Well
The Locker Room
Mourning Heaven
Phonebook
Puppy, Car, and Snow
Racing for the Sun
Raising the Stakes
Regret Me Not
Shiny!
Shirt
Sidecar
A Solid Core of Alpha
Tales of the Curious Cookbook (Multiple Author Anthology)
Three Fates (Multiple Author Anthology)
Truth in the Dark
Turkey in the Snow
Under the Rushes
Wishing on a Blue Star (Dreamspinner Anthology)

BONFIRES
Bonfires

CANDY MAN
Candy Man • Bitter Taffy
Lollipop • Tart and Sweet

Published by DREAMSPINNER PRESS
www.dreamspinnerpress.com

Published by DREAMSPINNER PRESS
www.dreamspinnerpress.com

BONFIRES

AMY LANE

PB
Rom

Published by
DREAMSPINNER PRESS

5032 Capital Circle SW, Suite 2, PMB# 279,
Tallahassee, FL 32305-7886 USA
www.dreamspinnerpress.com

Bonfires

Cover Art

Mass Market Paperback ISBN: 978-1-64108-079-8
Trade Paperback ISBN: 978-1-63533-340-4
Digital ISBN: 978-1-63533-341-1
Library of Congress Control Number: 2016915172
Mass Market Paperback published March 2018
v. 1.0

Printed in the United States of America
∞
This paper meets the requirements of
ANSI/NISO Z39.48-1992 (Permanence of Paper).

For Mate and Mary and anyone who is looking at themselves in the mirror with their spouse by their side and saying, "I can't possibly be this old—we only met yesterday and you're still too beautiful for words."

Running in the Sun

AARON GEORGE adjusted the collar of his uniform and checked his graying blond hair in the rearview mirror—and then felt foolish. He was forty-eight years old, for sweet Christ's sake. But Larx was running down Cambrian Way again, and he'd taken his shirt off in deference to the afternoon heat, and something had to be done.

His shoulders gleamed sleek and gold in the late-September sun, and his body—lean and long, although he was around Aaron's age—moved with a longtime runner's grace.

Aaron had been working hard to keep off the fifty pounds that had hit his waist when he turned thirty. He was about halfway successful, because diet and exercise weren't as easy when you drove an SUV up and down mountain roads as they had been when he was flatfooting around the city.

But Aaron's wife had died ten years ago, and he'd had three kids—two of them out of the house now. It had felt easier, somehow, to take a deputy position in Colton. The city—even Sacramento, which was a small city by most standards—was a young man's game. Colton, population 10,000 or so, was a little more laid-back and suited for raising a family.

Which had apparently been Larx's idea too, since he'd brought his daughters to Colton after his divorce.

Or that's what Aaron had heard. Mr. Larkin— Larx to his students and staff—had moved to Colton seven years earlier. Aaron's youngest two had taken Larx's science class and pronounced him "way cooler than anyone else in this hick burg." When the older administration retired, Larx had put up quite a fight to not be the principal.

Aaron hadn't been there, of course, but his youngest, Kirby, had been an office TA his junior year. He'd heard the battles raging in Nobili's office, and the staff room, and once, he'd told his father salaciously, in the middle of the quad.

In the end, Larx had conceded to be principal on three conditions.

One was that he got to teach AP Chemistry during zero period in the morning, before school, because he'd worked for five years to make the AP program flourish and he was damned if he'd give the class to the two-year rookie who was the only other teacher at the school qualified to teach the class. (Kirby told his father there had been much rejoicing with this cave-at, because Mr. Albrecht was, by all accounts, a power-hungry little prick.)

The second condition was that his best friend, Yoshi Nakamoto, be promoted to the VP's spot. Yoshi was in his early thirties and had taught English at John F. Colton High School for six years. As far as Aaron had heard, he was a solid teacher and a nice guy, and probably the exact person a new administrator would want to have his back.

The third condition was that Larx still got to coach the track-and-field team year round.

It was the one condition he hadn't been granted, because (and, again, with Kirby as his source) Mr. Nakamoto had insisted Time-Turners were only real in Harry Potter books, and Larx just didn't have the hours in the day.

Which was when Larx had started fucking with Aaron's nice orderly life in a big way.

Because every day at 4:45 in the afternoon, Larx would appear on this stretch of road, right when Aaron was wrapping up his rounds of the county. He would run from the school down Cambrian, turn right on Olson—which was barely more than a tractor road—and cut through to the highway, which was squirrely as shit and had no shoulder. He'd run the highway for a mile, turn right on Hastings, which was *also* squirrely as shit and had no shoulder, and then turn right and run back to the high school on Cambrian.

The first time Aaron had seen him do this, his heart had stopped. Literally stopped. Because he'd seen the headlines scrolling behind his eyes: *Local Principal Killed by Own Stupidity. Entire High School Runs into Road Like Wild Ducks in Protest and Mourning.*

And then, just when his heart had started beating again, he'd seen—really *seen*—Larx without his shirt.

Aaron was forty-eight years old. He'd known he was bisexual in high school, but it had been easier to date girls than boys back then, so he'd gone with it. He'd loved his wife with all his heart, hadn't looked back once from the day they'd met, and had been busy as hell over the past ten years trying to raise his children.

Aaron's libido had mostly closed up shop since his wife died, with occasional openings during tourist season when the kids were at their grandparents'. One glimpse of that glistening, tan back, those rangy shoulders, the sweat-slicked black hair, and his libido woke up and started to pray to Cialis, goddess of horny middle-aged men.

He'd gunned his motor that day and passed Larx in a haze of confusion. He was desperate to get the hell out of there before Larx caught him staring open-mouthed at a guy trying to be sweaty, glisteny roadkill in the red-dirt shade of pine trees up near Tahoe National Forest.

The next day his libido told him he'd been a fool to pass up that chance to watch Larx run, and that if he passed him again, he should slow down a tad and take in the view.

Aaron had done just that, slowing down a little, giving Larx a wide berth, smiling and waving as he passed. They knew each other from parent meetings, board meetings, community events. If given a chance, Aaron would gravitate to talk to Larx in a crowd, because he was funny and smart and a born smartass. So it was only natural that Larx waved back, friendly-like, and Aaron tried not to spend the next few hours of paperwork and gun and fishing permits grinning like a teenaged girl.

He'd had two of those. They weren't rational creatures, and he had no intentions of turning into one.

Larx had a narrow, mischievous face, a rather sharp nose and chin, and wicked brown eyes with deep laugh lines at the corners. He looked more like a hell-raiser than an authority figure, and when he grinned and waved, he gave a couple of dancy little steps to help keep in rhythm on the side of the road.

It made him look like a perky little lemur, except human, and with glisteny tanned shoulders and laugh lines and a nearly hairless chest and an ass you could bounce a quarter off, barely covered in nylon running shorts.

But no. Aaron was in no way turning into a teenaged girl.

That hadn't kept him from making sure he adhered religiously to his own schedule, the one that had him driving by Larx just when he started to sweat the most. Today, though, was going to be special. Today, Aaron was actually going to *talk*.

What could it hurt? Larx didn't have to know about Aaron's little crush. And even if he *did* think Aaron was hitting on him (which he most absolutely was positively not), Aaron knew for a fact that Larx had not only allowed but encouraged the GSA on campus. So even if he *thought* this was a come-on, and was not, in no way, absolutely not interested in men, hopefully he wouldn't go screaming for the hills, holding his shirt to his magnificent chest in maidenly horror.

Or that was Aaron's thinking, anyway.

He pushed his mirrored sunglasses up his nose, rolled down the passenger window, and slowed to a crawl, grateful the road was long and straight enough to give any car coming up behind him a chance to slow down.

"Good afternoon, Principal," he said laconically, trying to keep his smile genial.

Larx turned enough to salute and kept up his steady jog. "Howya doin', Deputy? Everything quiet, I hope."

"It is, it is indeed. But I gotta say, you been giving me a lotta bad moments, running on the side of the road these days. You never heard of a *track*?" Ooh— good one! The friendly neighborhood PSA, because nothing said come-on like irritating the fuck out of the object of your interest.

"Well, sir, I have heard of a track," Larx told him, his voice tightening. "However, the football team is running practices out there, and I really hate being the old man running laps."

He was lying. Aaron knew it.

"And the cross-country track that wraps around the back of the school's property?" Aaron knew for a fact Larx used to run with his cross-country kids, even during the off-season.

"Yes, sir, I may know a thing or two about the cross-country track as well." Stubborn shit wasn't even winded.

"Well, I'm glad you're so well-informed," Aaron sallied. "May I ask—and humor me here—if you are aware of other routes on which to run besides places that routinely turn the local wildlife into street waffles, then what in the holy hell are you doing on the side of the goddamned road?"

In response, Larx sped up.

"I'm *driving*, jackass!" Aaron hollered.

"What's that, Deputy? I can't hear you! Old man going deaf here!"

Larx held a hand up to his ear even as he poured on the speed. Ha! Guy thought he could out-stubborn Aaron? Two. Teenaged. Girls.

Aaron had this down.

They were nearing Olson, which was mostly a forestry service road, and Aaron stepped on the gas just enough to pass Larx up and turn right. He pulled up short and hopped out of the SUV.

When Larx rounded the corner, Aaron was leaning against the side of the unit, arms crossed, head turned toward the road.

"You gonna be civilized about this discussion," he asked, "or are you going to make me try to keep up with you? I warn you, I was slow in high school, slow in the military, slow in college, and I ain't got much faster since."

Larx scowled and kept running. "Try."

Aaron had lied, actually. He ran every morning. He wasn't as fast as Larx—or for as long—but he was ready for this, even in his boots.

He locked the SUV, pocketed his keys, and caught up with Larx.

"You're faster than you think," Larx muttered after a few uncomfortable moments.

"Well, I do run myself," Aaron panted. "But usually in the morning, on the old forestry service track out beyond Highway 22. You know that one?"

"Yeah?" Larx sounded impressed. "Yeah. I live out near there."

"I know you do." Three years ago Larx's oldest, Olivia, had gotten a flat tire driving home from a drama rehearsal. Aaron had helped her change the tire and followed her to make sure she got home. Olivia had since graduated—she was a year behind Aaron's middle girl, Maureen—but she'd been sweet. A little scattered, like a ladybug in a windstorm, but sweet.

"So maybe, now that you've proven your point about having enough time to coach the team, you could give an old man a break and run on the home track instead of out here where everybody can see you."

Larx stopped dead and stood, hands on his hips, scowling. "Is that what you think I'm doing?"

Aaron stopped gratefully and rested, hands on his thighs. "Isn't it?"

Some of the iron seeped out of Larx's body, and he shivered. Without self-consciousness, he pulled at the T-shirt around his neck and put it on. On the one hand, this relieved Aaron considerably—he was standing just close enough to smell Larx's sweat and become supremely aware that his bare skin was a reach-out-and-touch-me distance away.

On the other, the shirt was soft and comfy and was almost more intimate on than the bare skin.

"I just… needed to get off the property," Larx said after a moment. "I didn't want that fuckin' job."

Aaron had never heard a school official swear before.

He couldn't contain his grin. "That's the most amazing thing I've ever heard," he breathed. "Do you say the other swear words too?"

Larx rolled his eyes. "Please. Our staff room sounds like truckers and fishwives—the English teachers get really creative. You'd be surprised."

"Well, not anymore. You've plum taken the mystery out of it for me." Aaron winked, and Larx shook his head.

"Do I have to?" he asked plaintively. In those four words, Aaron heard the weight of the job on his shoulders. "I've got a shit-ton of messages on my phone right now, and if I don't get off campus, I am morally obliged to answer them."

Aaron took off his Colton County Sheriff baseball cap, smoothed back his blond hair, and tucked the hat back on again. "There is no law that says you can't put your life at risk, Larx. That's not what this is about."

"Then what's it about?" Larx stood, hip cocked now, and Aaron wondered if he'd been a resentful and rebellious teenager back in the day. And if anyone had told him it wasn't "in the day" anymore. Larx still had a kid in high school too—a junior, but in the AP class. Maybe he took lessons from her on how to be rebellious. In any case, Aaron had always thought Larx must have been a fun dad—and a good one. His ex-wife lived down in Sacramento, if Aaron remembered right, and Larx had the kids up here in the hills. Whatever their reasoning, Larx had custody, and that was a big deal.

He was a good man.

Aaron cleared his throat. "It's about your friendly neighborhood deputy wondering if he's going to have to tell his son that they need to hire a new AP teacher this year."

"Argh!" Larx ran his hands through his hair and stomped his foot. "I just… you ever want a grown-up to talk to who *doesn't* work with you?"

Aaron blew out a breath. "That's what my wife was for," he said apologetically.

Larx grimaced, probably in sympathy. "I'm sorry about that," he said, from reflex.

Aaron was tired of sympathy. "It was a long time ago, and you didn't drive the car. And it's beside the point."

"Yeah, I get it. The point is, you'd rather not have me set a bad example by running on the side of a shitty road. I get it."

"Well, the point is also that you could run on that forestry track, and that if you give me fair warning, I could run with you!" A part of Aaron was aghast. *Retreat! Retreat! Retreat! His gaydar might engage, and then you're fucked!* But a part of him was exhilarated. *Ballsy move, Sheriff George. That might just get you laid!*

Larx squinted at him. Aaron usually saw him wear sunglasses outside, but apparently he didn't feel the need when he was sweating. "Really?" he asked skeptically.

"My property is right off the back of it too," Aaron said, not sure if Larx knew this. "I'm about two miles away, if you follow that track."

"I did not know that." Larx confirmed his suspicions and scratched the back of his head. "You do seem a bit faster than you claimed to be."

"Well, I do run a few times a week. Only around three miles, but if you loop around, you could go longer after you pick me up and drop me off. It's better than running here." That was nonnegotiable.

Some of the starch and defiance seeped out of Larx's posture. "Yeah. Sure. That's… nice. Nice of you to ask. Thank you."

"So I usually leave the house at six thirty for work. We could meet at five?" That would give him half an hour to eat a granola bar and shower. And an hour to run if he went an extra two miles with Larx. It would be cold, so he wouldn't get to see Larx's glisteny chest, but he would get the man's company. Those brief conversations at football games and board meetings lingered in Aaron's mind. When he wasn't fighting the system, Larx was damned funny, a thing Aaron had appreciated even before noticing his muscular shoulders and tight, stringy glutes.

Larx nodded. "I've got headlights," he said, which was a good idea, because the days were getting shorter and running in the dark was a good way to get lost—or twist an ankle.

"Well, good. I don't. I usually go in the evening before dinner."

Larx cocked his head curiously. "So why are you changing now?"

Crap. "Kirby likes you," Aaron said. "Would hate to tell him I had to shovel your body off the pavement."

Larx tilted his head to the exact opposite angle. "You sure do believe in keeping your population safe. One person at a time, even."

Aaron had blue eyes and fair skin, and he fought against the heat building in his face. "Well, it's a small town. We'd feel it if you became roadkill—can't deny it."

Larx pulled a corner of his mouth back in a cynical smile. "Then don't try."

His eyes were brown, and his mouth wide and mobile. Aaron stared at that mouth just long enough for the moment to become uncomfortable.

"Tomorrow morning, Sheriff?" Larx asked, breaking the silence.

"You want a ride back?" Aaron asked courteously, pretty sure that would be the worst thing ever at this point, given how acute the attraction.

"No, sir. I think I'm going to finish my run."

Aaron nodded and repositioned his baseball cap. "Suit yourself."

He turned then and strode back to the SUV, resisting the urge to look back and see if Larx was gazing after him. He was pretty sure he felt eyes boring into his back, but he damned well wasn't going to turn around and check.

He managed to keep the little encounter to himself as he returned to the county office and filled out his dailies. He briefed the chief on his activities—how he was pretty sure the mom-and-pop weed operation they'd spotted a month ago had escalated and they might need to call the DEA, and how the high school's request for a sidewalk lining school property should be backed by the sheriff's office as a matter of general safety. He *didn't* mention Larx, but Larx wasn't the only idiot who thought he was immune to traffic.

Sheriff Eamon Mills nodded, asked if Aaron's report had been filed, and then, just as Aaron turned away, stopped him. "Uh, George?"

"Yessir?"

"I know this isn't your shift, but there's a home game coming up in two weeks. It's from one of those schools out of county—you know…." Mills grimaced. "We're a small town, mostly, and this is a big-city school. I'm sure *their* kids are going to be just fine, because I know the coach, and Foster runs a tight ship. It's *our* parents we need to worry about, you understand?"

Aaron grimaced. Yes, he did. Kids these days, with the internet and cable—they had a view on diversity and the wider world that was both boggling and gratifying. The adults in the family? Well, that wasn't always the case. Two years before, a school bus driver from a city school had gotten freaked out by a snowflake. Terrified at the prospect of driving in the snow, he'd left his students stranded in front of Colton High after they'd won a playoff basketball game. Aaron and Larx had managed to round up sheriff's vehicles and parent volunteers to get the kids back to their home school, but Aaron could still remember how afraid those kids had been, huddled together against the gym, surrounded by a hostile population of rednecks who were *not* happy to lose to a big-city team.

"You're looking for some more uniforms at the game?" he asked, not reluctantly. Not at all. Larx would be at the game. Game nights were part of a small-town officer's duty, and Aaron had worked his share. When Larx had been teaching, Aaron had seen him occasionally, because it *was* a community event, but not always. The principal *had* to attend the game, though.

Larx would be there. They'd have over a week of running under their belts. Aaron would drag Kirby there, Larx's youngest daughter would probably attend—it would be fun.

Platonic, single-parent fun.

Uh-huh.

"Yeah, son. That would be helpful. Maybe you and Larx could spend some time in the opposing team's bleachers laughing, giving out free concessions, letting our people know we're all friends here. That okay?"

Eamon was African American and in his sixties, probably ready to retire. He'd spent a few years in the military, a few more in 'Nam, and a few more "getting lost in New York," as he liked to say. He was both as homegrown and redneck as they came, and surprisingly educated and cosmopolitan in his own way.

Aaron loved him like the father he'd wished he'd had. "That's fine," he said, smiling a little. "I'll bring Kirby—nobody can be mean to that kid when he bats his brown eyes at 'em."

Eamon nodded. "I appreciate it. And definitely bring the whippersnapper along. That kid needs to spend more time here filing. Last time he went into the archives, he actually solved two cases."

Aaron grimaced. "Yessir, well, I'd just as soon he not get quite so excited about law enforcement as a career. He's a danger to himself *without* the firearm." Caroline had been sort of a charming klutz too, and that kid did take after his mother.

Eamon chuckled. "We'll keep the cabinet locked, don't you worry. But maybe don't actively keep him away, Aaron. You know kids. The more you say no, the more the kid wants to find ways to make that a yes."

"Two teenaged daughters," Aaron said grimly. Eamon had been there. Hell, Eamon had been there when Aaron's oldest, Tiffany, had to be taken home in a squad car when she'd been busted having sex with her boyfriend under Cofer's Bridge. He'd been there when Maureen had been busted getting drunk with the other drama kids after they'd taken down the stage of their senior production. Name an embarrassing moment in a parent's career and Eamon had been there to give advice, his hand on his deputy's shoulder.

"I remember," Eamon said now. "How *are* Tiff and Maureen?"

"Well, Tiff is on track to graduate in two years, because she just changed majors at the last fucking gasp and needs to take almost her entire four years over again."

Eamon whistled. "Pricey."

"It is indeed. I told her she'd have to work through part of that, and she called me a tyrant. I told her the only reason she didn't have to earn *all* of it was that her sister was on track to graduate a year early and join the Peace Corps so she could go teach children to read in India. Tiff called her sister a name, which I will not repeat, and Maureen called Tiff another name, which I will not repeat, and by the time they both went back to school, neither of them was speaking to the other."

"Or to you?" Eamon asked kindly.

"Well, Maureen was speaking to me. Which only cemented her identity as an 'ass-kissing little pussy'— in her sister's exact words."

Eamon grunted. "Son, you can't take that to heart. Kids...."

Aaron sighed and scrubbed his face with his hand. "I know. She'll get over it. She almost always does. I just… I have a brother I haven't spoken to in years. He just lives on the other side of the country, is all. I wanted so badly to have the kids grow up and give a damn about each other."

"Aaron, you've done your best. And you know, you've got Kirby. That kid can bring those girls together in a heartbeat."

Well, truth. Kirby had been sending the girls a letter a week over the past six weeks, each one on a little note card, each one updating the other on what her sister was doing. If anyone could play peacemaker there, it was Kirby. "I'm hoping so," Aaron agreed. That sounded like a good place to leave, so he turned away, only to be brought up short.

"Aaron?"

"Sir?" Aaron turned back.

"I almost hate to ask this, as a meddling old man, but I *am* old, and I haven't made it a secret that I may decide not to run in the next election. And if I don't, you know I'm going to ask you to step up and run."

Crap. This. "Yessir—and I'm honored." Aaron did know how Larx felt. There was not much he hated more than the thought of being the only grown-up left for other people to look to.

"Well, don't be. It's a shit job and you get no sleep. But it sure is easier with a helpmate on the home front."

Aaron grimaced. "Yessir. I have been aware of that for the last ten years."

"I know you have. And yet you've never looked for another Mrs. George."

Oh God. His whole body washed in a prickle of sweat at the prospect of lying to Eamon—or even dodging the question. You just did not *do* that to a man whose wife had cooked for your family once a week on the pretext of "just making extra." You didn't do that to a man who had kept cookies at his desk for ten years in case his deputies' children should be forced to do their homework in the police station. It wasn't right.

"Or Mr. George," he said, lungs feeling like they were being pressed between a Volkswagen and a sheet of steel.

Eamon's eyes opened wide, and he gaped a few times.

Aaron smiled weakly.

Eamon snapped his mouth shut and shrugged. "Is that so?"

"It's a toss-up, sir."

"Well, a missus would be easier, but that's not my call to make. I'm just saying that you don't have to do it alone."

Aaron closed his eyes to try to keep the burning behind them from getting out of hand. "Thank you, sir," he said quietly. "I should get home now."

"Gail's making cookies tonight, son. She'll have some ready for Kirby tomorrow."

Aw, dammit. Aaron had to turn away, because he was not at his manly best at the moment. "That's right sweet of her, sir. I'll have Kirby draw up a thank-you note."

"We look forward to them every time."

Kirby tended to draw cartoons on his thank-you notes. The last one had featured a pig rolling around in hearts and daisies, snuffling with happiness over a steaming plate of cookies.

"I'll tell him that."

Aaron kept walking. He just could not handle another hit in the feels this day, and that was the truth.

When Aaron got home, Kirby was at the kitchen table working dutifully on his homework, some sort of chicken/veggie/Thai disaster cooking in the small kitchen behind him.

"You're late," Kirby said without looking up. He was a stickler for things like that.

"I was talking to my boss." *I was coming out to my boss in case I could possibly maybe someday bang your principal.* Nope. That last part was staying subtext.

Kirby looked up as he walked in from living room, and the familiar shock of seeing Caroline's brown eyes, surrounded with a thick fringe of lashes, peering back at him zapped a little path of sweet pain through Aaron's heart. "What about?" Kirby worried. He had an active imagination, and in the same way Aaron couldn't watch Larx jogging down that horrible road without picturing the worst, if Aaron was so much as five minutes late, Kirby imagined him dead.

"About going to the football game next Friday night."

Kirby grimaced. "You're on redneck patrol, aren't you? To make sure we don't embarrass ourselves because we haven't ever seen big-city folk before."

"Pretty much. Want to come make some new friends?"

Kirby perked up. "People who have spent the last ten years of their lives somewhere that hunting season isn't considered a legit excuse not to go to school? I'm there."

This was Kirby's last year of high school, and Aaron could sense that need in his boy to get the hell out of this tiny town. Not that he blamed him—Aaron would miss him is all.

"Thanks. Eamon asked about you. He's sending cookies tomorrow." Aaron strode into the kitchen and poured himself a glass of protein juice to fortify himself for his run. Stuff tasted like shit, but Kirby had mixed it up for him the year before, and it really worked. Anything to keep him from eating cookies after his shift.

Kirby grimaced. "Dad…."

He walked back toward the battered wooden table so he could let Kirby see his actual sympathy. "Yeah. I know." Gail was the loveliest woman, and her casseroles and side dishes were amazing. But her cookies….

"We have chickens who will love them," Aaron said diplomatically.

Kirby shook his head. "That's why I drew the pig last time."

"Well, if it hadn't been so darned cute, maybe she would have gotten the hint. How's dinner?"

"Ready when you're done with your run," Kirby responded promptly. "So maybe get out of my hair and let me finish my chemistry. Larx'll be pissed if it's not perfect."

"Deal. But I'm going to start running with Larx in the mornings from now on, so however that fits into your plans."

Kirby squinted at him as though he had sprouted another head. "You're going to *what*?"

Aaron fidgeted with his empty glass. "I, uh, you know. Me and Larx are going to go running. In the morning. So he doesn't have to run on the side of the road. That sort of freaked you out."

Kirby blinked slowly. "Yes. Yes, it did. But I didn't expect you to go out and invite him to run. That's like, super deluxe up close personal service there, Dad. I'm not sure you can go above and beyond for every citizen in town—even this town."

"Well, Larx isn't just everyone," Aaron said, soldiering on. "He's the principal."

Kirby's face had been sweet and round as a child, but he'd developed a strong jaw and high cheekbones as he'd grown. He had dark blond hair like his father, and he'd be a fine-looking man someday, but right now he was a *beautiful* adolescent. The kind you thought angels modeled their own faces after.

Right up until his "bullshit" line arced between his eyebrows.

Like it was now.

"There are secret adult machinations at work here," he pronounced. "I'm not sure how or why, but this does not bode well for any involved."

Aaron fidgeted with his empty cup and then walked back into the kitchen. "Uh, watching a lot of science fiction there, son?"

"Yes, Dad, with you. So don't pretend you don't know what I'm talking about."

"Not a clue. Gonna change and go running. Back in half an hour. Bye!"

It wasn't pretty, but retreats seldom were.

That night he fell asleep remembering Larx squinting at him in the dusty sunshine, the iron out of his spine and some sweetness in his smile.

He dreamed he'd moved forward, taken a step, until he could feel the heat from Larx's exertion, until he could feel Larx's breath on his face.

He dreamed of their lips touching in a simple kiss.

Chromic Acid and Alcohol

"OKAY, BOYS and girls, quick review. Are we ready?"

"Ready, Larx!"

Larx looked up at his class and grinned. They'd said that in tandem, and he loved it when his kids played with him. "Good to hear it! Okay, what are the four measurements we use to evaluate chemical substances?"

A forest of hands shot into the air.

"Kimmy!"

"Particles!"

"Isaiah!"

"Moles!"

"Christiana!"

"Mass!"

"Kirby!"

"Volume!"

"Way to go! Now, Kellan, what do we use for qualitative analysis?"

"Coulomb's law, sir!"

"Excellent—and according to Coulomb's law, what is the formula that tells us about electrostatic force?"

And the drill went on.

On Monday they'd do the experiment where they charged the metal balls, used a laser pointer to measure the distance they repelled each other, and applied that to electron movement, but today they needed to know what they were learning when they did that. After the experiment and the lab write-up, they'd have the test to show if the kids could pair up the stuff they learned from the book with the stuff they learned in real life—and that would be one more step to passing the AP test.

"Very well done," he praised as the drill ran down. "Now, I want you guys to set up your lab reports with the info from the textbook so we're ready to run the lab on Monday. You've got about twenty minutes, so I need to see your lab books out, and any talking you do needs to be about my class and my class only. Are we clear?"

"Yes, Larx," they all said, like Larx didn't know they were about to spend twenty minutes talking about the football game, the dance, and who was dating who.

Didn't matter. What mattered was he gave them the time. How they used it made the difference between responsible students and last-minute slackers.

Larx had pretty much been the latter, so he had all sorts of understanding for that.

Still, he wandered from table to table, checking to see if anyone had any questions. He had to gird himself internally when he passed Kirby and Christiana's table. Aaron George's son and his own daughter were looking at him with grim mischief in their eyes.

"So, guys, any questions?"

"Yeah, Larx," Christiana said perkily. "I've got one. What do two middle-aged geezers talk about when they go running in the crotch of dawn? Inquiring minds want to know."

Larx glared at her, wishing she looked like her mother, because then he could dig his heels in against her like he had with Alicia during their entire marriage. But no, she looked exactly like Larx's late older sister, who had died of leukemia when Larx had been in college. Larx had adored Lila—wanted to be just like her, had lived for her visits to his dorm when he'd been confused and lost in a place he never thought he'd get to go to.

When Christi looked at him with that darkly arched eyebrow and those sparkling brown eyes, Larx didn't have a chance.

"We talk about our ungrateful offspring, of course," he replied smugly. "And how we think they should be getting better grades and doing more chores so we can eke every last nanojoule of value out of them before we fund their launch into the great wide world."

They both rolled their eyes so hard he was surprised they didn't get headaches.

"You're funny, Dad," she sulked. "Very funny. You were gone for an hour this morning."

"Well, that means I'll be home an hour earlier tonight, Christi-lulu-belle—doesn't this make you happy?"

"No," Kirby whispered frantically to her. "Tell him it does *not* make us happy. I was using that half hour to study and now my dad wants to know about my day!"

Larx looked directly at Kirby as he responded. "Tell your friend that this makes his father *very* happy, since he only has one child left at home and would like that kid to come back to his house after college."

Kirby grunted—a sound much like Aaron's, whenever their morning conversation got too personal. "Tell my father I am not a brain-dead skank like my older sister, and I recognize that he's been a superlative parent and an all-around good guy, so I would appreciate he not give me the third degree every time he walks into the house. I'm *trying* to study!"

"I just run with the guy," Larx protested. "I'm not his family counselor. Do we have any *other* questions?"

"Yeah. Do you think we're going to win tonight?" Kirby's brown eyes were narrowed as though he knew exactly what tonight's game was going to be like if the Colton Tigers didn't win.

"I got no idea. I hope everybody has a good time." And on that, Larx turned to his next table—and two of his favorite students.

"Isaiah, Kellan, tell me you're ready for tonight!"

Isaiah Campbell—six feet three inches of still-growing boy—smiled quietly at Larx with limpid brown eyes through a thick fringe of lashes. "I'm ready, sir," he said, ducking his head shyly. Isaiah was *not* the stereotypical football player. An honor-roll student, a member of the drama club, and an all-around sweet kid, Isaiah was one of those superstudents that happened maybe once every two or three years. Larx had been teaching for twenty-four years, and the thrill of having a kid like this—kind, smart, talented in a thousand areas—still hadn't faded. There were very few jobs that let you actually launch superlative human beings into what would hopefully be an extraordinary life.

"I thought so," Larx said warmly. He turned to Isaiah's shadow—five feet eight inches of bouncy, out-of-control energy that flinched like prey while wearing the body of a football-throwing predator. Kellan Corker, family whipping boy and lost soul, was the quarterback. From what Andy Jones, the head football coach, said, the only thing that kept a bundle of ADHD like Kellan focused on the field was Isaiah. Apparently when they were freshmen, Kellan had almost washed out of the game—which would have been too bad, because the coach was good at making football a sanctuary for the kids who needed it most. Isaiah had actually been more interested in drama club, but Jones had seen Kellan's almost slavish devotion to his friend and had decided to use that. He'd made Isaiah a receiver, and now, when the two of them were on the field, they were unstoppable.

"How 'bout you, Kell—you take your Adderall this morning?"

Kellan cackled. "Oh yeah—got permission to take another dose tonight. I'll be up until oh-dark-thirty, but I can get 'er done!"

"That's not good for you," Isaiah said, poking Kellan with a gentle elbow.

"I'm totally all over it." Kellan nodded, his black, cowlicked hair flopping everywhere. If Larx had ever had a son, he would have looked a lot like Kellan Corker—black hair, green eyes, a spazzy little ball of too much energy and too many ideas. Larx adored Isaiah, but Kellan was the kid he could do the most for.

"Well, remember it's just a football game," he said, winking at Isaiah. "Don't fry your brains out for one game—what would your buddy do without you?"

Kellan's expression went sulky. "He's got a girlfriend. He won't even notice I'm a drooling zombie."

"She asked *me*!" Isaiah protested. "It's the homecoming dance next week. You can get a date too!"

"Yeah, because girls love it when I forget what they're saying in the middle of a sentence. I was *gonna* go stag, and so were you, but that girl—"

"Which girl?" Larx asked, wondering who could possibly come between the dangerous duo.

"Julia Olson," Kellan blurted.

Larx couldn't help it—his eyes got big and he breathed sharply through his nose. "Oh… oh… *Isaiah*."

Isaiah grimaced. "Yeah. She… I guess she's had a crush for a while, and she, like, blindsided me. And it was in the middle of lunch and everyone was watching and… if I said no, it would be like, totally…." He bit his lip.

"You didn't want to embarrass her," Larx said, but he had a bad feeling about this. Julia Olson—great-granddaughter of the man who had donated his property for the school and had a road named after him—was a scary, scary kid.

Her grandfather had made a fortune by selling another batch of land to developers who created an entire tourist village in the north end of town. On the one hand, it allowed a small colony of artisans and craftsmen to run businesses in Colton, because the four-month flux of tourists between May and August sustained them for the entire rest of the year. A lot of those people came back before Christmas and brought friends, which meant campers and people renting cabins in that area also helped keep the town alive.

But that made the Olsons *very* rich, and *very* powerful. Julia's father had been a spoiled, arrogant little fuck, by all accounts, and he spent a lot of his time abroad, leaving Julia home with her former beauty queen of a mother.

Julia's mother had poured her heart and soul into living her life through her daughter.

Beauty pageants as a child, acting and elocution lessons as an adolescent—Julia was a perfectly turned-out doll of a girl who had been told her entire life that her pretty face and family connections trumped what any other adult told her. Without *her* family, the town wouldn't *have* a goddamned school, thank you very much!

Crossing Julia because he wanted to spend time with Kellan did not bode well for a shy football player who would rather run around backstage during the spring play than catch a football in front of the entire town.

"She's lonely," Isaiah said, shrugging. "It makes her mean. I… I didn't want to make that worse, but…." He bit his lip. "I'm… I mean, it's just a dance, right?"

"Yeah," Larx said. "Sure." Back in Sacramento, he'd watched a kid like Julia almost destroy a teacher's career. When the kid led a witch hunt to get Dana to change the girl's grade, the administration had caved, which had pissed Larx off. When the Colton board of education made him principal, he'd vowed he'd *never* let a kid like that, with powerful parents, fuck with anyone else's life.

"Just…." God. How did he explain the foreboding here? "Isaiah, just be careful. Every time she talks to you, asks you to do something you don't want to, send an email to Kellan, okay? Document it. If she makes you uncomfortable, or threatens to spread rumors, document it. I know you were trying to be a nice guy, but—"

"She's not nice," Kellan muttered. "She's crazy. I mean… *crazy*. You know she's the one who dumped perfume on Mrs. Pavelle's snake, right?"

"Bruce?" Larx felt an unexpected pang. Nancy Pavelle, the biology teacher, had kept a pet garter snake for three years. They'd fed that snake every Friday afternoon, watching carefully to make sure poor Bruce could eat the mouse put in his cage. Bruce hadn't been that bright, but he'd been affectionate and gentle—and dead, after someone had dumped perfume all over him. He and Nancy had spent hours trying to wash the substance off Bruce's skin, but in the end it hadn't worked. The perfume was toxic, the snake had absorbed too much, and he'd died. "She killed Bruce?"

"Mrs. Pavelle gave her a shitty grade, remember?"

Yeah. Larx remembered. Nancy was a chubby little woman with cookie-dough cheeks and a habit of rescuing God's least-loved creatures. Snakes, lizards, a butt-ugly fish that had it out for anything that ventured near its tank—Nancy took them in. She'd been surprisingly firm standing up to old Nobili—and unlike poor Dana back in Sacramento, Nancy had the documentation to back her up. They'd thought the perfume was an accident—a kid playing around who didn't want to fess up. But to find out it was deliberate?

"Why didn't you tell anybody?" he asked, appalled—and mourning Bruce the snake all over again.

"Because she's *crazy*!" Kellan sputtered. "Because she could screw us up with a nasty rumor, and nobody in the school is going to say shit against her. The only reason Mr. Albrecht passed her is because she threatened to tell her parents he grabbed her ass!"

Larx stared in horror. Goddammit, Nobili couldn't have waited until Julia had graduated to bail, could he? "Did he?"

"No!" Isaiah almost laughed. "Are you kidding? Mr. Albrecht can hardly look girls in the eye when they're wearing tight T-shirts. If he accidentally touched a girl, he'd probably wet himself and faint."

Oh thank God. "I sort of hoped that was the case," he muttered. "Okay, so, Isaiah, you're going to the dance with a really… frightening girl. You need to take Kellan with you. Kellan, you need to take a girl you like and trust, agreed?"

Kellan grimaced. "Yeah. Okay. Just as friends."

And later, Larx would feel stupid, because nothing pinged until just that moment. He thought he should have seen it—should have figured it out right then.

But he didn't, and he'd feel crappy about that for a long time.

He looked at the two boys again, both of them leaning on their science tables with a sort of earnestness he treasured in kids. Most of them were just like most people. Good. With good intentions and hopes. These were two of the best.

He opened his mouth to say something—anything—and then two students with an actual problem called him, and he rapped sharply on the desk in front of Kellan.

"Keep me posted," he said, and moved on.

But after the class, and on into his day as principal, he would think about those two kids and worry.

Something about them—about the way Kellan looked at Isaiah like he couldn't see past the boy's brown eyes, and the way Isaiah followed Kellan into whatever he was doing just to keep him grounded….

Something.

It reminded him of a sheriff's deputy jogging next to him on the red-dirt track of Olson Road in waffle stompers, asking him nicely not to get hurt.

"LARX? LARX! *Larx!*"

Larx shook himself and focused on Yoshi, which was hard because for a moment his face was just a big beige blur against the oppressive paneling of the principal's office. He finally got a bead on Yoshi—whose bird's-nest hair and chia beard did *not* make him look any older, like he hoped—and tried to remember what they were talking about before he'd wandered off. He could almost remember… homecoming floats… business and open-topped cars… he almost had it….

And then he yawned. "Sorry, Yosh. Getting used to running in the morning instead of the afternoons."

"How's that going? You and George getting along okay?"

Larx had to smile. Running with Aaron was actually sort of a kick. In full running kit, Aaron wasn't nearly as slow as he'd claimed, and Larx had fun pushing him, just a little faster, just a little harder. When he'd had enough, Aaron would smack him on the head with his baseball hat and Larx would pull back, and then, often, they'd begin to talk.

Kids, at first. Because they had them in common. Larx missed Olivia something fierce now that she'd gone away, and Aaron sounded like he had his hands full with his oldest.

"Do you text her?" he'd asked. "You know, when she's at school?"

"Text her with what?" Aaron asked breathlessly. "I think someone's poaching fish and I have to call Fish and Game?"

"Send her cute kitten stuff," Larx told him, their footfalls and panted breaths falling with comfortable evenness in the gray light of dawn. "Works like a charm."

He'd turned in time to see Aaron smile like a little kid learning about lizards for the first time ever, and his chest… it still hadn't recovered.

"We're getting on fine," Larx said, shaking himself awake over his desk. "Coffee—I need more coffee."

"Like I need my mother telling me to marry. Have a fruit juice, dammit!"

Larx scowled at him. Yoshi was gay, and closeted to everybody but Larx and the shy artist he lived with. Tane Pavelle was Nancy's younger brother—after high school he'd escaped the small town that had served as his prison, but after a series of misadventures he never spoke about, he'd returned to town to run one of the small tourist galleries that kept Colton going.

Yoshi had interviewed for an open teaching position the fall after Tane returned. Larx—trusted by both Nancy *and* Yoshi after the first year—was one of the few people who knew. And in return, Yoshi knew almost every detail of Larx's divorce from his wife—and it hadn't been pretty.

Yoshi was probably the one person Larx could tell about Kellan and Isaiah. Or the stupid way his whole body lit up as Larx jogged toward Aaron's little two-story house on the forestry track.

Larx didn't feel like talking about that second thing yet, though.

"Yosh, what do you know about Julia Olson?"

Yoshi sucked wind in through his teeth. "I can't think of a name bad enough. And I speak three languages." French, Spanish, and English.

"Kellan told me she's the one who killed Bruce the snake."

Yoshi's broad, boyish face contorted in grief. "Bruce? She killed Bruce? I need to ask my

grandmother if she knows anything in Japanese, because I'm telling you—"

"Yeah. Bad. She's got a crush on Isaiah Campbell—asked him to homecoming next week. You
know...."

Yoshi grimaced. "He's too smart for that shit."

"Right? But I've got a bad feeling—he said yes
because he didn't want to embarrass her, but—"

"Yeah. I get it. Don't feed the trolls."

"She's a Grade A troll."

Yoshi shuddered. "Let's hope she doesn't crap all
over the woods. And you dodged the question about
Deputy George. What's he like?"

"You've met him. Solid, friendly. Nice eyes." *Crap.*

"I *knew it*!" Yoshi crowed.

"What? I was kidding. I mean, he's got nice
eyes"—blue, clear, laugh lines at the corners—"but I
was just mentioning them. Like, comic relief. It was
nothing. I'm innocent. *Stop looking at me like that!*"

Yoshi broke up over his egg salad sandwich. "You
like him."

"We're running buddies! I know you resist all
physical exercise—"

"I do Pilates," he returned mildly.

"Whatever. You don't flirt when you run. It's a
rule." *The sound of their feet in what was almost a
dead sprint, and the whoosh of Aaron's hat as he tried
to tag Larx to make him slow down. Larx pulling back
just a smidge, just enough to let the hat brush his arm
on the next pass. So they could run side by side again.
So they could talk.*

"This is a really shitty office," Yoshi said, seemingly out of nowhere, but Larx knew better.

Larx looked around at the oppressive sixties-style paneling, the green carpet, the terminally uncomfortable visitor chairs. "I didn't choose the décor," he said.

"I was just wondering." Yoshi took another bite of his sandwich and chewed steadily, then swallowed. "What was the principal's office like when you went to school?"

"Those beige thumbtack walls," Larx said promptly. "A cheap Formica desk. Stacks of files everywhere."

"Bet you practically lived there." Yoshi licked his fingers after the last bite of sandwich.

"I had a cot. Why are we talking about this?"

"I'm just saying, you are such an incredibly crappy liar I can't imagine you got away with *shit* in high school. Forget a cot—you probably had a washroom and a closet and a plaque."

Larx glared at him, although Yoshi wasn't far off regarding Larx's impromptu camp in the principal's office. However, toward the end of his senior year, mostly he hung out there from a sense of nostalgia. He and Johnny Erikson had become buddies by then, because Erikson had talked him off the spazzy boy's adolescent ledge of hating the world before it hated him back. Larx had learned to love the dedication that had gone into saving him from himself.

He'd lived to give back.

"What, exactly, am I lying about?" he asked Yoshi now.

Yoshi shrugged and opened a bag of barbecue potato chips, offering Larx one. Larx took it automatically and then cursed himself because he suddenly craved the whole bag.

"You said he has nice eyes. He does. He has very nice eyes. But you weren't kidding—you meant it. You like him—admit it."

"He's becoming a friend." That was no more than the truth.

"You ever stop to think about, you know. Why now? You guys have been running into each other at football games, parent-teacher meetings, back-to-school nights—why would he suddenly ask you to go running now?"

Larx shrugged. "Because I just started running on the side of the road?" And like Johnny Erikson, who hadn't wanted to see Larx get lost in his own stubbornness, Aaron had stepped in.

"Or maybe because you both have just a little ways to go before your kids are out of the house, and suddenly, you can live for yourselves again."

Larx wrinkled his nose and automatically checked his phone. Olivia texted him like seven times a day—sometimes wanting his attention *right that moment* in spite of the fact that they both had "adulting" (her word) to do.

"You, my friend, have a highly romanticized idea of what children leaving the nest is really like," Larx told him grimly. Seven times a day was a few texts down from the maybe twenty frantic, needy texts he'd gotten per day when Olivia had first gone to San Diego in August.

"And you, my friend, need a sex life. Or a love life. Or any life that doesn't involve this school and your kids."

"Are you high?" Larx asked without heat. "I mean, that looked like egg salad, but you never know. Has Tane been mixing paint again?" He smiled conspiratorially. "Did you get lead with your egg salad, Yoshi? Because I could have sworn you just told me to make a pass at a probably straight man—a *sheriff's deputy*—in this teeny tiny redneck little town. As the school principal. I may be bi—"

"Bi?" Yoshi asked grumpily. "Really, Larx? Bi?"

"I like women," Larx responded mildly. Because he did. Just not quite as much as men. A thing he bitterly regretted telling his ex-wife—not because of how much she hated *him*, but because she had taken it out on their children. Family-court drama—blessedly kept confidential—but Larx had been more than happy to take his kids and move the hell away from Sacramento and the judgmental administration that would rather fry its teachers than support them.

"Stow it, Principal Larkin," Yoshi snapped. "I'm your best friend, remember? And you just said this guy had nice eyes."

"Well," Larx muttered, stealing another chip. He'd forgotten his own lunch and probably would not get to eat until he stole a hot dog from the PTSA stand that night. "Even straight men would agree. You don't see that shade of blue just anywhere."

Yoshi threw a chip at him and Larx caught it—and ate it. Yoshi threw the whole bag, intact. "Eat. And I'll go get you a fruit juice. You need a keeper, Larx—I swear to God, I have enough trouble making sure Tane remembers he lives here, on earth, and not in some divine place of inspiration. This guy can keep you. Don't blow it."

"Don't we have a homecoming parade to plan?" Larx muttered, but Yoshi was already stalking off to the vending machine, leaving Larx to eat his potato chips.

Mm. Larx could live off barbecue alone.

Games

"HOWDY!" AARON nodded to the family walking in the gates as they were looking apprehensively at all the white faces on the home side. "Welcome to Colton. Principal Larx right there will make sure you're more than comfy!"

He smiled reassuringly, and the father in the family showed his teeth back on pure reflex, eyes flickering guardedly from Aaron's badge to the field, shoulders squared in resolution. Goddammit.

Aaron flirted hopefully with the little girl, who stared back from grave brown eyes before hiding her face in her mother's shoulder, the bright plastic clips in her myriad hair twists rattling against her puffy pink coat as she did so.

"I promise," he said quietly, "we'll make this a fun game."

Dad nodded, Mom nodded, and the whole family looked to Larx, who smiled and gave them a free raffle ticket for the usual halftime giveaway.

"C'mon up, folks, to the visitors' side of the bleachers. We've got a hot dog stand, popcorn vendors, and somewhere around here the science club is selling hot chocolate to fund our trip to Monterey. I'm the principal—folks call me Larx—and if you have a question or a concern or want to gloat 'cause your boys won, I am here at your service!"

And the family relaxed and laughed, and Larx made a show of finding them a spot on the bleachers. He bowed to the little girl, shook Dad's hand, and winked at Mom, and suddenly all was well.

He came back in time to greet the next family, and Aaron turned to the one after that and did his best, but it was slow going.

"It's not you, you know that, right?" Larx said, appearing at his elbow after an entire family had just drifted by like he wasn't there. "It's that scary bling on your chest. Freaks people out."

"You appear to be okay with it," Aaron shot back dryly, and Larx rolled his eyes.

"Hey, when you were as rotten as I was, if you weren't on first-name basis with the po-po, you were *not* a happy boy."

This was not the first reference Aaron had heard to Larx's misspent youth. "You talk a good game, Larx, but I'm starting to think that's all it is."

Larx tilted his head back and laughed, the sound doing strange and awesome things to the pit of Aaron's stomach. "Someday, Deputy, I shall awe and terrify you with all of the awful, immoral things I did as a boy."

"I don't believe it!"

Larx turned to the new speaker and grinned. "Anthony!" he said, genuine warmth in his voice. "Deputy, let me introduce you to an old friend, Anthony Spano, who knew me as a green student teacher, long before the seasoned bureaucrat I am now!"

Anthony Spano was five six, maybe, but he had a military bearing that made him look a few inches taller. Dark hair, blue eyes, and a body that had possibly been athletic in his youth but was now comfortably beefy—he wasn't bad-looking, really.

Aaron's stomach chewed itself into a knot.

"Anthony, what are you doing here? Where's the wife and kids—God, they must be...." Larx shuddered.

"Teenagers," Anthony confirmed. "It's terrible. I can't even."

Larx looked at him in the frosty night air of fall in the mountains, lips twitching. "Can't even what?"

"That's a complete sentence nowadays. It drives me fucking insane. I can't even." Anthony rolled his eyes and Larx doubled over laughing.

"So what are you doing here tonight? Did you transfer?"

Anthony shrugged. "Place wasn't the same without you, Larx. And Johnstone was such a fuckin' weenie. Yeah, I transferred. This school's got a young staff—all optimistic and shit. Reminds me of you when you first started."

Aaron watched as Larx almost melted. "Oh my God—Anthony. *Dude*—it's so good to see you!"

They hugged fiercely, Larx's lanky frame draping over the smaller man like an adolescent puppy's. "You gonna sit with me?" Anthony asked. "And where's the principal—I heard he was a new asshole, all progressive and shit. Probably your kind of guy."

Aaron burst out laughing, not jealous anymore. This was an old friend—he had guys from the service he'd greet like this—and the shit-eating grin on Larx's face told Aaron everything he'd ever need to know about his past. The rebelliousness obviously hadn't stopped when he'd made it through high school.

"No…," Anthony said, eyes big. "No! They didn't! Some idiot made you God? That's fucking horrifying, that's what it is!"

"Oh, he didn't go easy," Aaron added, nodding to the next family troupe through the gates. This one actually smiled at him and moved to the visitors' side. "They had to drag him kicking and screaming into it. It was legendary—the kids would come home and report to us adults so we'd know how the campaign was going."

Anthony grinned at Aaron, delighted. "*That's* the Larx I know. What was the attrition? What concessions did they have to make?"

Larx was looking at Aaron in surprise, and Aaron winked at him. "They had to let him teach AP Chem," Aaron said, struggling to keep his face straight, "and he had to have his best friend as VP—"

"Who hasn't forgiven me yet!" Larx informed them.

"I don't blame him," Anthony chortled. "I'd fuckin' kill ya. What else?"

"I didn't get it," Larx muttered, shooting Aaron an amused look.

"Yeah, but what'd he try for? I need to know this is Larx we're talking about."

"He wanted to coach the track team," Aaron said. "Yoshi—his VP—called a kibosh on that, though, on account of Wonderboy here being human."

"Something about not enough hours in the day," Larx added, shrugging like Aaron hadn't seen him working through the time he used to go running.

"Yeah, that was you from the very beginning. You should have seen him after his first kid was born. He'd get in early to plan his lessons, teach all day, coach the track team, supervise a dance, and then go home to take over baby duty. It was *insane*. I used to ask him what he was teaching that day and he'd say, 'I dunno, Tony, whatever comes out of my ass!'"

Aaron laughed, and Larx? Larx actually looked embarrassed.

"I knew," he said, darting his gaze to Aaron. "I knew what I was teaching. It's just… you know… easier to articulate, I guess, when you're in front of the kids."

Aaron's heart thundered hard in his throat. Something about the way Larx was blushing, looking from Aaron to Anthony, made Aaron's breath shorten. *He wants me to think well of him.*

"I get it," Aaron said reassuringly. "Thinking on your feet."

Larx grinned and Aaron had to look away. In doing so he realized the press of people had slowed down to a trickle.

"Larx, they're gonna start—you need to go up to the booth and make opening remarks, 'kay?"

Larx nodded. "Yeah. I'll go over there, run up to the booth, and join you guys ASAP—Aaron, I got a radio, but you can always tag me on my cell if it's less dire." He turned to trot through the crowd to the booth above the home side, and then paused. "Aaron—hey. If you see Christiana or Kirby, ask them if they need more supplies. There should be another big thermos and a few more boxes of hot chocolate mix in the concession stand." Larx's face darkened. "And those PTSA assholes in the concession stand better not be taking my hot chocolate—I bought that mix with the science club funds."

On that note, he started cutting through the crowd at speed, and Aaron gestured to Jim Parks, one of two other deputies on football duty.

"Jim, you want to maybe close that gate? Then you can take home side, I'll take visitors' side, and Percy can get the gate for the last few stragglers."

Jim nodded and picked up his radio to call Percy Hardesty from the home side, where he was apparently talking with his family. Percy was homegrown, and frankly he was exactly the sort of redneck Eamon had been afraid of when he'd asked Aaron to supervise. Aaron had sent him to the home side on pretext—the farther that guy stayed from the visitors' bleachers, the better.

"Jim?" Aaron asked tentatively.

"Yeah—I'll keep an eye on him. Asshole never met a civilian he couldn't harass."

Aaron grunted. Well, yeah. But Percy was what they had to work with. Aaron turned to Anthony with a smile, liking him already.

"I'm sorry," Anthony said as they turned toward the bleachers. "I didn't get your name."

"Aaron George. Larx has got the manners of a sixth grader—it's not your fault."

Anthony laughed. "Yeah, well, it's why he's so great in the classroom. He's always been one of the kids. I'm frankly surprised they managed to get him in administration at all. He's always been more fight the establishment than join it."

That did not surprise Aaron in the least. "Well, they blackmailed him with the worst second choice in three counties. I think that's why he caved." Aaron gestured for Anthony to precede him up the middle section of the bleachers. "I've got to stand here on the track," he said, "but if you take the first row, we can gossip like old women."

Anthony laughed. "Oh, you must be good for him. He's a great guy, but God, worse than the kids, you know? He's always needed a grown-up in his corner."

Oh yeah. Aaron knew. "I think Larx just requires a little more room than most folks," he said diplomatically. "Like my oldest daughter. Has to spread her wings and not have people telling her what to do."

Another laugh, this one a wee bit cynical. "Yeah—until suddenly, they *totally* need people telling them what to do. Larx always needed a little bit of help with control. Man, he almost decked an administrator once, defending a teacher from the guy. Guy was a fuckin' *prick*, and Larx? He had sort of a soft spot for Dana…."

Aaron listened avidly as Larx's old friend told him stories of another Larx, someone younger and more idealistic, with a fiery temper and—Anthony's words—a "smartassed fuckin' mouth."

Then the man himself started to speak over the intercom, and suddenly it was time for the band to march out onto the field and play the national anthem. Anthony watched them in admiration as they retired to the home bleachers, the better to pound out "Go! Fight! Win!"

"Hey, those guys are pretty good. I mean, we have a decent drum core and all, but that was the whole shebang. I think I saw an oboe out there!"

Aaron nodded. "My middle girl played the bassoon—that was something to see. But yeah. They're one of the best in this part of the state. Larx told me the football coach got pissed 'cause they went out of town for a competition during a Saturday game. Larx told the guy he was just pissed 'cause the band has a better chance of winning than the team. He said it almost started a bloodbath."

Anthony cackled, and Aaron tried not to gloat. Yes, he had Larx stories too.

The whistle blew and Larx trotted over to them. It was slow going. He stopped and talked to people on the home side, waved at kids, shook hands with parents. By the time he got to the visitors' side, half the first quarter was over, and blessedly, all appeared to be quiet. But then, nobody had scored yet either.

"So," Anthony said lowly, watching Larx's stop-and-start progress. "Any reason we've got a deputy and a principal—"

"And the vice principal," Aaron said, giving Yoshi a salute across the bleachers. Yoshi waved back from his spot between Mrs. Pavelle, the biology teacher, and her brother. Nancy waved too, but Tane ignored Aaron completely, and Aaron wondered who Tane thought he was kidding. Everybody knew he and Yoshi were living together, and Aaron would place money on the guest bedroom being full of art supplies with no bed. But then, you just didn't talk about things like that—not in Colton.

"So," Anthony continued, "any reason at all we've got the upper-level staff over on this side of the stadium?"

"We are just trying to make a good impression, sir," Aaron said dryly. "Given that your side of the stadium is a bit cosmopolitan for our people, we thought that giving you all a full-court press welcome, complete with raffle tickets and hot chocolate, would impress you and let you feel neighborly toward us."

Anthony grunted. "Twenty years working in a culturally diverse school, junior. You were afraid of the brown people. Am I close?"

Aaron looked him in the eyes. "Not even a little," he said sincerely. "We've played your school before—and we know your coach and your kids have been nothing but gentlemen. We're not afraid *of* you, we're afraid *for* you. We wanted to make sure that if you won, you got the friendliest reception possible from our crowd, and that included as many of us in your stands as possible."

Some of the flint softened in Anthony's eyes. "Oh," he said. "Yeah. That sounds more like Larx. Okay." He thought for a moment. "Hey—*you're* the one who helped us out two years ago, right? After the basketball game? I wasn't there, but the coach told me the sheriff's department and some of the teachers helped to get the boys home."

Aaron nodded. "That was me and Larx and Yoshi right there." He let some of his own guard down in return. "We've got good kids here," he said. "But the parents need to be pulled kicking and screaming into the twenty-first century. We're doing our best."

"Yeah," Anthony said. "Same here."

They were quiet for a minute, and Larx managed—finally—to push through the crowd. He came to a stop near Aaron, and for a moment the two of them stood side by side, immersed in the game.

"So," Larx said, close enough and soft enough that Aaron had to tilt his head. "Anthony tell you all my dirty secrets?"

Aaron grinned at him, fighting the sudden urge to… oh hell, *nuzzle* his cheek. God. The things he must never do in public! "He told me you haven't changed much in the seven years since you moved here," he said, winking.

To his dismay, Larx looked hurt. "I've changed a *little*," he said sadly. "I mean… I don't know if you'd need to pull me away from a fistfight anymore."

Aaron gave a little shrug. "Don't know if you need to put *all* your fire out, Larx. I think it serves you well."

And this time it wasn't his imagination. He *felt* the heat waft off Larx's body.

He was blushing. Underneath the jacket and the stocking cap and the blue-and-white school-colors scarf, Larx was blushing.

"That's kind of you, Deputy," Larx said, and like that, the hurt went away.

For the first time *ever*, Aaron wanted to know why Larx had gotten divorced. Something had made him embarrassed about the person he was.

"So," Aaron said, changing the subject, "how do you think they're playing?"

Larx eyed the field critically. Like a lot of teachers, he didn't really believe in the *game* so much as he followed the students.

"That MacDonald kid is playing rough," he said, scowling. "And the kids are starting to notice. Kellan is throwing exclusively to Isaiah—it's like he doesn't trust anyone else out on the field. The defensive tackles are out for blood, when the other side's offense is mostly playing a fast long game. I am not liking this, Deputy. I am not liking this one single bit."

Aaron nodded. "I can see it. What about the home side?"

Larx looked at him and shook his head soberly. "We won't get a lot of help from them."

There was a sudden gasp from the crowd, and Larx and Aaron gaped openmouthed at the field. Aaron wished furiously for an instant replay of a real-life moment.

"Did you see that?" he asked dumbly.

"Did I see our quarterback tackle his offensive end? Yes, yes I did."

And both of them started jogging for the field.

When Larx got there, the coach was mediating a hot dispute between Kellan and MacDonald. Both kids had ripped off their helmets, and the look Kellan shot Larx was filled with such relief and gratitude that Aaron stepped back to watch the man work.

"Uh, Kellan?" Larx said, smiling genially. "I, uh, take it there's a reason you did that?"

Kellan nodded furiously. "He's using bad words, Larx. Mean ones. The other team's getting riled. He's being an asshole, sir, and it's not right."

"You just said 'asshole,' fucktard!" Curtis Mac-Donald snarled, and Kellan got back in his face.

"It's not the same thing and you know it! You get the folks in the bleachers all stirred up by screaming racist shit and nobody won't come here and play us no more!"

Oh!

Larx turned to MacDonald and was about to say something when the ref walked up to him. Great. And reffing for the home team was Lloyd Albrecht, the power-hungry prick of a two-year teacher that the school had used to leverage Larx into being principal.

"He was just trash-talking," Albrecht said. "Boys do it, Larx. Wasn't no harm."

"Sure, if you think a fucking riot is just a garden walk, wasn't no harm at all. Baiting the other team like that should get a player expelled, Albrecht. You shouldn't leave it to the kids to do your fuckin' job." Oops—his language was slipping. Aaron could hear, more and more, the Larx who probably hung out with Anthony Spano in the staff room. Larx turned to Mac-Donald. "Curtis, go get your bag. You're out of the game."

Coach Jones gaped at Larx. "Are you kidding? He's one of the best offensive tackles we have!"

Larx glared at him. "Well, then, if we needed him that much, we should have taught him some manners. One more instance—one more. I don't give a shit what it is—if it's a word, if it's a sound, if it's a gesture or a face—one more word about the color of the opposing side's skin and I will forfeit this game, do you understand me? I will go up into that booth and apologize to the away team, and tell them that we couldn't be around decent folks, and then I'll have the sheriff's office and the goddamned band escort those nice people to their cars while our parents sit and wonder why their perfect little angels turned into racist fuckers on the football field. Do you understand me?"

Aaron stared at Coach Jones and wondered if he was going to blow an artery right there on the field. Jesus, he'd known Larx was a firebrand, but this? This was serious warrior shit.

But apparently that much passion went a long way.

Jones nodded fiercely. "MacDonald, get your shit. One word out of you, you're off the team, no more games. Everyone else, we're using a time-out—team huddle at the benches!"

Larx turned to follow MacDonald, and paused. "Kellan?"

"Yessir?"

"You did good. I'm damned proud of you. Don't let anyone tell you being shitty to other folks is okay."

"Yessir!"

Kellan's face then shone with pride. He turned to the players coming into the field and, natural-like, fell in next to his wide receiver, Isaiah Campbell. In spite of the height difference, they jogged to the bench in perfect synch.

Like Aaron and Larx in the mornings.

Larx was heading for the sidelines, and as the home crowd booed and hissed, he grabbed Curtis MacDonald's arm and frog-marched him to the gate, pointing furiously to the boy's father in the crowd and gesturing for him to come meet them.

Aaron was torn. He should go back and stand by the away team—but Curtis MacDonald was a big, blond farm boy built like a tractor. His father was a big, balding redneck built like a freight train. He made eye contact with Jim Parks and pointed to the sidelines of the away team and followed Larx. Larx might have been a spitfire, but Aaron didn't like those odds.

They stood behind the ticket booth, Curtis stewing like a crucible of iron and Larx bouncing on his toes, while the game resumed.

"Larx," Aaron said quietly to him as they both watched Billy MacDonald charge down the bleachers.

"Yeah?"

"That was really fucking impressive. I just want you to know that. Don't worry about not changing or anything. You kept the good stuff."

Larx grinned at him, all his teeth, and Aaron felt another one of those uncomfortable twists in his stomach. A friend. Yup. A colleague sometimes. Okay. Fellow community member? Definitely. A running buddy. Sure.

That's how Deputy Aaron George felt about Principal Larkin.

Aaron had a sudden thought—an obvious one, silly actually—but before he could ask Larx about it, Billy MacDonald crashed through the gate.

"What in the mother of fuck happened out there!" he snapped.

"Your boy was shouting racist epithets at the other team," Larx said solidly. "We don't play that way. He does it again—in any context—and he's off the team. Right now he's just going home."

The elder MacDonald's eyes bulged out. "*That?* You pulled my boy for *that?*"

Larx leaned forward, lowering his head and waiting until Billy leaned forward too. When he spoke, he spoke quietly. "Do you want to be responsible for an on-field brawl, Billy? 'Cause if that happens, we have to forfeit the game. Do you want to be responsible for a riot? There's women and children in those stands—I don't give a *damn* what you think you should call them in your head, but they are *women* and *children*. Your son starts a race riot in *my school* and I will have him arrested for every bruise, every broken nose, every broken bone. What if someone gets more hurt than that? What if someone gets killed? You want him on trial for murder because he's a racist asshole whose father doesn't know any better?"

Larx's voice rose, and he paused and took a breath. "Do you?" he asked, quiet again.

Billy MacDonald was not impressed. He looked around them, as though realizing they were standing in a relatively private spot, and then he caught Aaron's eyes.

Aaron cocked his head and raised his eyebrows in an unmistakable challenge, and Billy spat in the dirt.

"You watch your back, you pansyassed little faggot. Nobody pulls my boy from a game."

"I just did. Now get out of here. And Billy?"

Billy turned back to look him in the eye.

"He don't come back to school for a week. That's the homecoming game and the homecoming dance he just missed. You can blame yourself for that one. Now go."

"Dad!" Curtis whined, and Billy grabbed his arm and dragged him into the darkness.

"Can you really suspend him for the week for what his father did?" Aaron asked.

"I can if his kid was flipping me off the whole time," Larx muttered. "I just wanted Billy to think the next time he opened his damned mouth."

Aaron chuckled. "Larx? You are hard-core."

Larx smiled, and some of the starch melted from his sails. "God," he muttered, looking at his hands. "I'm shaking. Jesus."

"Adrenaline comedown?" Aaron asked, holding on to the urge to take that shaking hand in his and calm him.

"Probably blood sugar," Larx admitted. "I think I had Yoshi's potato chips for lunch and quit there."

Aaron groaned. "You're *killing* me, Larx! You go sit down by your old buddy there and crow about what a badass you are. I'm going to go get us some hot dogs. Anthony want one?"

"Is Billy MacDonald a bigoted prick?"

Aaron just stared at him, unimpressed mostly because he'd taken the man's threats seriously.

"Too soon?" Larx quipped, but Aaron didn't back down. "Okay, okay—yeah. Better get us all two—yourself as well, if you haven't had any." Larx reached into his pocket, but Aaron waved him off.

"My treat this time," he said, because hey, even on a deputy sheriff's salary, he could afford some hot dogs.

"Well, next time I'll take you out to a real restaurant—my treat."

Aaron jerked, surprised and pleased, and then flushed. *He didn't mean that like a real date.*

He looked at Larx and gave a smile like a lame horse, but Larx didn't smile back. He was nodding to himself like he was having that conversation all over again and confirming that was *exactly* what he meant to say.

Aaron turned uncertainly and then got hold of himself and strode for the snack bar to get six hot dogs and a couple of giant sodas—and hopefully to find his kid to help carry every damned thing, because he couldn't do it alone.

He found both kids, because their shift with the science club's hot chocolate booth had just ended, and he bought them hot dogs too. They all trooped to the bleachers while Aaron and Christiana shared good-natured complaints about how Larx didn't eat.

"And he'll come home and be *starving*. Olivia started cooking first, right? He didn't ask her to, but he'd get home at, like, seven o'clock and just start throwing stuff in a pot willy-nilly, and we would eat some of the most *heinous* crap known to man. Like, my favorite was one of those frozen packages of honey-coated chicken thrown into pasta with a can of mushroom soup."

"Oh my God!" Aaron laughed.

"See, Dad!" Kirby spoke up from his other side. "Makes my Thai noodle shit look good, doesn't it?"

"And oh my God! Spaghilli!" Christiana cried. "Like, he was making spaghetti, but he was exhausted, so instead of spaghetti sauce, he threw in a jar of salsa instead? And then tried to fix it with a can of chili."

"Did you eat it?" Aaron asked, vastly amused.

"Oh God no. That was the night Olivia took over. We were sitting at the table, trying to choke it down, and he…." Her voice dropped like now that she was older, she realized this wasn't as fun a story as it had been seven years ago. "Well, he started crying, and Olivia, she gave him a hug and said, 'How about pizza, Daddy?' And Mike's had just opened, and they delivered."

"Ah." Aaron nodded, another piece of the Larx puzzle dropping into place. This piece was maybe his favorite—he could identify with "vulnerable father" on *so* many levels. "Well, I know he lucked out in the kid department. You two are the apple of his eye."

"I don't understand them," Aaron complained as their footfalls and breath grew regular after their sprint. "It's like they turned twelve and the unholy goddess of puberty took over their bodies. I mean, Maureen is one thing—she's going for the good-kid award. I get it. Tiff rebels, Maureen steps into the good-daughter footsteps. But I don't get why Tiff suddenly hates me."

"She doesn't hate you," Larx said gently. "I mean, it probably feels that way, but, you know. You were a guy raising her without a mom. She probably resents the no mom thing more than she resents you.*"*

"Did your girls?" Aaron asked dispiritedly.

"No," Larx said, and for a moment Aaron thought that short answer was going to be the end. "Alicia wasn't… she didn't leave the girls with a good impression. Sometimes I worry that they're such good kids because they're afraid the love is going to be yanked away, you know?"

"Well, Dad's pretty awesome," Christiana said now. "Even when things were really crappy with my mom and stuff, he never once made us feel like we weren't exactly the people he wanted in his life." She laughed shortly. "And he did, eventually, learn to cook."

Aaron wanted to pry—so help him, he wanted to pry. But not now, when they were nearing the bleachers. Larx was looking decidedly pale too, and Aaron figured it wasn't a moment too soon.

THE REST of the game passed uneventfully—although listening to Anthony and Larx comment on the plays on the field was a treat.

The Colton Tigers won, but only because the West Sac Wombats' star receiver pulled up short with a cramp before he could score what would have been the winning touchdown.

Anthony was furious. "A banana!" he snarled. "A fucking banana and a glass of water! Foster goes over it with them again and again and again—food, water, and sleep! Fucking Jesus!"

Aaron remembered Larx talking about how the English teachers swore like longshoremen and caught Larx's eye.

Larx winked and then went back to nodding and reassuring Anthony that yes, that kid was as dumb as a fucking box of hammers. Christiana was sitting next to her father, smirking as the obscenities hit the air, and Kirby was looking a little shell-shocked.

"Geez, Dad," he whispered. "I don't think *students* swear like this."

Larx overheard him. "Anthony's old. He's had more practice," he said dryly, and then turned to his friend, who had no shame at all.

The game ended and the band filed out, followed by the football players. Aaron had to run out to mind the parking lot and make sure no fistfights broke out as the players boarded the bus. "Could you find me with Kirby later?" he asked, trotting down the track before Percy could start roughing up somebody's little brother who was there with his friends.

"Deal!" Larx called, and Aaron counted on him for that.

The parking lot was—well, usual. Kids in high spirits, adults who snuck beer and were in higher spirits than necessary. Cheerleaders in uniform, football players out of it, showered and freshly clean for dates.

He saw the quarterback and wide receiver for the Colton team running quietly toward someone's truck in the shadows, and thought they had the right idea—get out of the crowd before anyone waylaid them. He saw the band kids getting into cars with their parents—or their friends—out of uniform and hopefully going for ice cream.

There were three places in town that would serve food after the game: Mike's Pizza, Lindburgers, and Frosties and Fries. Aaron was pretty sure each place would be packed with whatever clique ruled there this year, and he made a mental note to drive by each place on his way home. He wouldn't be in the police-issue SUV, but he still had his uniform on, and it would help keep things calm if he was visible.

Things were about three-quarters clear when Christiana and Kirby came walking out, Anthony at their heels.

"I've got Dad's keys," Christiana said, drawing near. "He said me and Kirby could go out for ice cream if it was okay with you, as long as you could give him a lift."

It was like hearing angels sing the perfect chord. Him and Larx? Alone?

"I can do that," Aaron said, hoping he was keeping his voice even. "Anthony, you on your way out?"

"Yeah—I asked to walk the kids out. It's been a while since Christi and her uncle A got to chat."

"Dad," Kirby muttered, "they *swear* together!"

Christiana burbled, and Aaron thought about how much she looked like her father. "You think Larx didn't teach Olivia and me every swear word we know?"

They continued to chatter as they walked toward Larx's old Dodge Caravan. As soon as they were ensconced, Anthony turned back to where Aaron was keeping an eye on a group of kids trying to get their shit together in a paper cup.

"Where do you wanna go?"

"I don't know, where do you wanna go?"

"Do you wanna go to…?"

"No, too many people, how about…?"

"No, my dad'll be there."

"Should we go to…?"

And so on until Aaron wanted to shout, "Give it up, assholes, we all know you're going to the vacant field by the school to get drunk, get laid, and add to the condom collection under the bushes!" Somehow he didn't think that would go over well with parents, though, so he held his peace.

Anthony watched the social clusterfucking with similar cynicism. "You think someone's parents aren't home? That could knock up some prom queens in the group."

"That's the band. Those kids use rubbers, 'cause they have college to go to."

Anthony laughed, then extended his hand. "Deputy, it's been a pleasure to meet you."

"You too, sir. It's good to meet a friend of Larx's."

Anthony paused then, uncertain, and then dropped his head and his voice so Aaron would have to move in. "Look, if I'm overstepping here, tell me to fuck off. But Larx—he's a good guy. His ex was a piece of work, and he needs someone to take care of him. You could be good for him, is all I'm saying. Be good for him."

Anthony broke off and then shook Aaron's hand again before trotting into the darkness to find his car.

Aaron was left to chivy the kids to their preferred party destination and warn them to drive safe.

AN HOUR—it took an hour for Larx to finally leave the stadium. He was the last one out, and the bright lights hovering over the field had been turned off but still glowed redly in the dark as he trotted through the gate and locked the chain.

Aaron had moved his car up to the entrance, and Larx waved as he approached.

"Thanks for waiting for me," he panted. "That took way longer than I thought!"

"Yeah, well, it's a big circus—lotsa monkeys."

Larx grinned. "And the big gorilla doesn't have a chance," he said before making oo-oo noises and scratching his pits.

"C'mon, big gorilla—let's get you home."

"Aw, man. I'm still hungry. Aren't you still hungry?"

Aaron had to think about it. "Two hot dogs," he said, as though Larx hadn't been there.

"But… ice cream! And coffee! C'mon—Frosties and Fries is still open, and most of the kids'll be gone. Whatya say?"

More time in Larx's company? Not running? Not in the company of teenagers or old friends or an entire town?

"Sure. No ice cream for me, though. I'm still trying to lose twenty-five pounds."

Larx looked disappointed for a moment, and then he perked up. "You can have some of mine. I'll make it a double."

Aaron had to laugh. "You're incorrigible." He clicked the lock of his SUV and gestured at Larx to get in. After Aaron had started the car and the heater—because the temp had dropped to the low fifties—Larx resumed the conversation like it had never paused.

"You heard Anthony—I'm the rebel without a cause. Incorrigible is in my job description."

"Sure it is." Just like charming and funny and dedicated.

"I don't know what I have to do to prove to you I'm a bad boy," Larx opined. "I mean, I'm a terrible fraud: friends with the sheriff's deputy, principal, father, and underneath it all is a street punk with an attitude. It's tragic!"

Aaron laughed at his foolishness and then thought about it. Maybe this wasn't all foolishness. Maybe this was Larx trying to say something important.

"Why?"

"Because green peas," Larx said quickly.

"Your kids must have been hellaciously confused," Aaron chuckled. "Why is it so important that I believe you were a bad boy?"

And just like that, Larx's irrepressible energy tamped down.

"Well," he said like he was choosing his words, "because. Because if you tell someone something about yourself and they don't believe you, they're... they're getting to know someone who's not really you."

Aaron sighed. "How about if I tell you I'm not that bright and just ask you to give me bad-boy details. Will that work?"

Larx laughed. "I was angry," he said after a few moments. "My dad split, my mom was working all the time, and it was just my sister and me. But she got sick in my freshman year of high school, and God. I hated the fucking world. My grades dropped, I pissed off all my teachers—got arrested a few times. Petty theft, vandalism. Usual kid shit, you know?"

"What happened to change it around?" Aaron ached for him. Sure, it was a long time ago. But a long time ago, Aaron had met a pretty woman and fallen in love. He still missed her, even though he'd lived almost as long without her as he had with her.

"Two things, actually," Larx said promptly. "One was that my sister went into remission in my junior year, and once she felt better, she began to kick my ass."

"Did it stick?" Aaron asked, hoping.

"No." Larx looked out the window as the highway sped by, the shadows weaving together under a clear sky. "She passed during my first year of college. And we knew it might happen. So I just spent those two years *not* being an asshole so all the time I had with her—that would be good time."

"I'm sorry."

Larx looked at him, and his teeth flashed whitely in the dark. "You didn't invent cancer."

"What was the second thing?"

"My high school principal. Johnny Erickson. Great guy. Must have saved my ass from expulsion a dozen times. He'd bring me into his office and talk to me—just talk to me. Like a human. And he started to promise that if I stayed out of trouble, I could be an office TA and we could spend more time talking and less time with him chewing my ass."

"Good guy," Aaron said.

"The best."

"So why'd you fight so hard not to be principal?"

"What?"

Aaron caught the double take from the corner of his eye and grinned. "You obviously admired the guy—why didn't you want to be just like him?"

"'Cause I couldn't," Larx said, like it was that simple. "Erickson, he was the best. I couldn't measure up. I mean… just, no way. And every administrator I ever had, I fought tooth and nail. You know the drill— they're all 'test scores, numbers, rules!' I was all 'feed the kids, teach the kids, and the rules can go fuck!'"

"How'd that work out for you?" Aaron asked, voice soft.

"I'd rather not talk about that right now."

Aaron's stomach went cold, and every instinct as a law enforcement officer started to whisper that here—*here* was where the real story was.

But they were close. Their conversation in the car—this was one of the most intimate things Aaron had experienced in ten years.

"So what about you?" Larx asked into the quiet. "Law and order all your life?"

"Not that it did me much good," Aaron acknowledged. "Out of school, into the military, folks were so proud. Got a wife, had kids, folks passed away, wife died in a car wreck—and following the rules got me three kids who are probably worse for having me as a father."

"No!" Larx protested, and some of the passion was back in his voice. "That's not true. Kirby adores you. I know Maureen thought the world of you. Don't give up on your oldest. She's just… you know. Like me. Angry. She's going to regret every bad thing she says. And you need to keep stretching out the olive branch, because you never know when she'll take it."

"I sent her like twelve kitten videos," Aaron said. "Nothin'."

"Well, you know. Maybe try puppies. Or alpacas. Or bunnies. Or, you know, anime."

"What-i-may?"

"You know—Japanese animation. Christiana is nuts about it. I'll get her to send me some pictures you can forward."

Aaron had to laugh. "You know, not that your help isn't appreciated—"

"I'm not giving up," Larx said, eyes gleaming in the darkness. "Seriously. We can't have our steadfast Deputy George feeling defeated! Where would the town get its hope?"

"From its dedicated principal, of course," Aaron said gallantly, and Larx's belly laugh was his reward.

"So you'll keep trying?"

Of course he would. "As long as you keep running with me in the mornings," Aaron said, because hey, he was a shameless opportunist.

"Deal. Tomorrow too?"

Aaron groaned. "God, don't you ever sleep in?"

"Well, I'll be honest. If I don't run tomorrow, I'm pulling up my summer garden, so it's probably more responsible to let you get some shut-eye."

"I work late shift tomorrow night anyway," Aaron admitted. "We all sort of spread out during the weekends so nobody sacrifices all of the family reunions and such."

"And you probably go to church on Sunday." Larx sounded dispirited.

"Nope. Do you?"

"God no!" He giggled then, probably getting the irony of the blasphemy after he said it. "No. No church for the Larkin family. I'm surprised about you, though."

Aaron thought about it carefully. Religions made or broke relationships sometimes. "It's not that I don't believe," he said after a few moments. They came to Frosties and Fries, and he pulled in to park, making sure they had a good half hour before closing time so he could at least finish the conversation. "I mean, there's a higher power. There must be. I saw it in my wife's eyes, you know? In our children. But I get tired. I get tired of people using their symbol—and I don't give a rat's ass which one—like a get-out-of-asshole-free card. That thing around your neck does not give you a free pass to judge while you go around and kick kittens and smack orphans, you know?"

"I do know," Larx said. "But wow."

"Wow what?" Aaron looked at him, hoping not to see censure or criticism.

Larx's smile reassured him. "I was just going to say my family was Methodist when I was a kid, and they didn't have a church up here, so I didn't feel comfy to go."

Aaron laughed. "Well, that too, except Unitarian."

"Oooh—even your church was fancy."

Aaron sighed and decided for a little more honesty. "Besides. Once my wife died, I… I was angry too. Not so much anymore, but like you said. Not feeling it."

"Well, good to know. Want to come help me with my garden if I'm not done?"

"What's my reward?"

Larx appeared to think about it. "Well, I've got the last of the squash, and some tomatoes, and I think there's some tubers I haven't mined yet. And you say your chickens are still laying, and I traded some canned tomatoes to that little artisan dairy that serves at the B and B's—"

"Bessie's?"

"That's the one. Anyway. I've got fresh cheese and hamburger that remembers when it was a real cow. I don't know what all that will become, but between me and Christiana, it should be something that doesn't suck."

"So no spaghilli?" Aaron asked, getting out of his car while Larx howled in outrage.

"Who told!"

CONVERSATION—WITHOUT the running, without the children. It was just as good in the Frostie as it was in the car. Aaron ate a couple of spoonfuls of Larx's ice cream, just to humor him, and evaded talking about his days in the military with Desert Storm.

"Bad?" asked Larx seriously.

Aaron shrugged. "I learned how to use a gun," he said.

"Sorry."

Aaron raised his eyebrows. "Why?"

"Because. I don't think you're a violent man. That must have been a… a difficult transition."

Aaron closed his eyes. "My wife never got that," he confessed. "She kept saying what a hero I was. I didn't have the words to tell her. You don't feel heroic. You just feel…."

"Afraid?" Larx asked.

Aaron opened his eyes and saw Larx leaning forward, arms crossed on the table in front of him, brown eyes open and compassionate.

"Yeah."

"I'm sorry you were afraid, Deputy," he said softly. Then he grabbed the spoon and fed Aaron another bite of soft-serve across the table. "It's the only remedy I got."

Aaron washed down the ice cream with a mouthful of coffee and looked around. The place had definitely cleared out—their little red booth was the only one with people still in it. JoAnna, the owner, and her two high-school-aged helpers were wiping down all the other tables and sweeping the white-tile floor. He'd gotten a text from Kirby a half an hour ago that said his son was safe at home. Larx had gotten a similar text about ten minutes later, and he'd raised his eyebrows meaningfully. "So, nobody planning to make us accidental grandparents, for which I'm grateful."

They'd laughed then, but Aaron was suddenly acutely aware of his duty to eventually drive Larx home and deliver him safely to his daughter.

"We should get going," he said now.

Larx sighed and scraped out one last bite of caramel-covered ice cream. "Yeah. Time and gardening wait for no man."

"Hey, you need to garden so I can come over Sunday."

Larx's smile had gold on the edges, it was that brilliant. "Deal."

But the conversation that had flowed so easily on the way to get ice cream and in the little red booth sort of died on the way to Larx's house, and Larx kept looking at him, strained.

"What?" Aaron said as he pulled into Larx's driveway.

"Nothing," Larx said, sounding defensive. But he made no move to get out of the car as Aaron came to a stop.

Aaron started to fidget. He put the car in Park and turned toward Larx, surprised when he saw Larx had twisted and was in the process of taking off his seat belt.

They were suddenly face-to-face in the frosty darkness.

"What?" Aaron croaked, mouth dry, heart thundering abruptly in his ears. Larx was *right there*.

"Why?" Larx asked, his own voice coming none too steadily.

"Why what? Why are we sitting here in the dark? Why did I eat that ice cream? Why—"

Larx's finger on his lips was mesmerizing. He shut up immediately and concentrated on the feel of that rough skin of Larx's finger pushing into the soft skin of his mouth.

"Why did you ask me to run?" Larx asked. The pressure against Aaron's mouth lessened, but the finger was still there. It took a few moments, a few even breaths, to realize it was stroking the curve of his lips.

Everything—nipples, ears, chest, all forgotten points south—tingled.

For a moment, Aaron was going to tell the "I was afraid for your life" lie again. But Larx was… oh God. *Right there*.

"Your chest," he confessed in a rush. "You took off your shirt, and your back and your chest were all sweaty and—"

Larx's mouth on his tasted of the sweetest heaven.

Lord, how long? How long since someone had kissed him like this? Like a seeking tongue could find the intimacies of the soul. Aaron opened his mouth and let Larx in, welcoming him, the curious sweep of his tongue, the way he invaded Aaron's mouth.

Aaron groaned, sliding his fingers back along Larx's scalp, tangling them into Larx's long hair. *Hold still, dammit. Yes. Just right there.*

Larx tilted his head back in compliance with Aaron's hand in his hair.

And he moaned.

Aaron plundered that moan. Took it from Larx's lips, made it his own. All of this—this kiss, this press of their hot bodies in the confines of the car—this was glorious, intimate, sinful, in ways Aaron hadn't had since his wife died, the quickies during tourist season notwithstanding.

Ah—ah ah…. Larx pulled away, cupping Aaron's neck so he could have some leverage.

"Deputy, that was… unexpected," Larx panted.

"The kiss?" Aaron asked, befuddled. "I've been wanting that for a while."

"How much I wanted more," Larx breathed, resting his forehead against Aaron's. "God. You couldn't have waited until our kids were out of school to make that move?"

"You're the one who took off his shirt for a month!"

Larx laughed helplessly. In front of them, the porch light came on at the bottom story of the house, and they both pulled back with alacrity.

"You've got to—"

"I've got to—"

Larx stopped, his hand on the door handle, and reached out to brush Aaron's hand where it rested on the seat. "We've got to see where this goes," he said, nodding. "See you Sunday, Aaron."

"See you Sunday, Larx. Wait—"

But Larx had already slammed the door. He stopped at the porch and turned and waved, leaving Aaron to lean his head helplessly against the steering wheel.

"Dammit, Larx," he complained to himself. "What in the hell is your first name?"

Last Taste of Summer

"SURE YOU don't want to stay?" Larx asked Christiana. "There's heat, there's dirt, there's bugs—all the finer things in life." He'd spent the day before in the garden, but it hadn't been enough. If he worked hard, he could get it all done this weekend, and then the burn pile would be seasoned for the next.

His daughter rolled her eyes at him, but she laughed, and that was his intention. "Let's see... help you in your garden, or go spend the last warm day of the year at Jessica's pool. Hm... decisions, decisions...."

"Fine," Larx said meanly. "Just remember, snakes *love* pools this time of the year."

Christi's eyes went flat. "You suck, Dad. You're totally the worst. I'm giving you no grandchildren—not even a cat."

Larx looked at the porch, where Olivia's one cat and Christi's *three* cats tried to be ultracasual in the sun. The fact was, they were watching to see if any mice were going to run out from the pile of paper feed bags Larx was setting in the burn circle—a game Larx and the girls had played with great enthusiasm over the last seven years.

"Sure," he said now, mouth twitching. "You're going to go out in the big world and live without a cat. I see that happening like I see the sun turning green."

But Christi was no longer even listening to him. "Sh!" she commanded, waving her hand. "Watch. Do you see it, Trigger?" she said to her ginger tom. "Do you see it? It's in there... it's in there... it's a-comin'...."

Both of them stopped and focused on the feed bags rustling in the gold light of the late-September sun.

Larx and Christi exchanged gleeful looks. It was coming. The varmints were getting ready... it was all happening....

Trigger's ginormous ears perked up, and his green eyes shot open from somnolent rest. Every muscle in his body went on high alert, and like the vicious predator he was, he lowered into a crouch, the better to slink across the yard to the den of his quarry.

"Ooh... not gonna let him beat ya, are you, Toby? Not gonna let Trigger get all the mice!"

Toby, the long-haired tortoiseshell, took Trigger's left flank, and Trixie, the delicate black calico, took his right. The only cat uninterested in the carnage about to go down was Delilah, the old, deaf, half-blind Siamese cross Olivia had dragged home their first year in Colton. Larx, desperate to give his daughters some of the normalcy that had been stolen from their lives, had taken that cat in and promptly spent all of the little family's extra money making sure she lived as long as possible. Seven years ago the vet had given her a year. Larx figured she was entitled to sleep through the games of the youngsters and have herself a good laugh at the vet's expense.

But the younger three—Christiana's "oh, Dad, it just followed me home!" kittens—they were on their *game*.

Asses wiggling, whiskers twitching, they moved with the precision of a crackerjack squad of assassins.

Trigger went first, darting to the pile and leaping in the air, landing on top of the bags and flushing their prey into the open.

Toby and Trixie were in position, paws flying as they caught, broke, chomped, and killed mouse after mouse. Trigger leaped off the pile of bags and pounced into the melee, claws flashing as he disemboweled furry bodies and snapped little necks with bloodthirsty glee!

Oh, the carnage!

Oh, the mouse-anity!

"Oh, you incompetent little shits!" Larx cried. "You let one get away!"

Sure enough, one of the mice—one of the bigger ones, but apparently wily—had slipped between Toby and Trixie's barrier of death and was making a break for it. There he went, straight toward the house.

Christi, who was closer to the porch, ran straight on an intercept vector, then turned and crouched in wait like the warrior princess she was.

The warrior princess who leaped into the air and squealed like a guinea pig when the critter ran over her sandal-clad foot.

"Aw, Christi!"

"Eww! Little feet little feet little feet—Dadeeeeee! Little gross feet on my bare *skin*!"

"Christi, the mouse!"

"Oh! Crap!" The young recovered quickly, and Christi spun on her heel and went tearing to the porch…

Where Delilah opened one eye at the nearly victorious mouse and took it down with a casual paw.

"Oh!" Christi screeched to a halt. "Delilah, way to go!"

Delilah yawned and lifted her paw just as the mouse was getting away and smacked it again. She raised amused eyes to Christi, then repeated the process—and probably would *continue* to repeat the process until the furry little prison-breaker stopped moving forevermore.

"Oh," Christi said again. "Delilah, you sadistic pussy. I'm impressed." She reached into the back pocket of her cutoffs and snapped a picture, then fiddled with the screen.

Stacking grain bags—one of the mice was nice enough to sacrifice himself to your aging goddess.

Larx's phone buzzed in his back pocket, and he knew he'd gotten that text too—along with any of the follow-up conversation. He was smiling when Christi turned back toward him, flushed and happy and having forgotten any threat to deprive him of grandchildren.

"Well, now that the entertainment's over with," she laughed, "I've got some rays to catch." She headed toward her bike, one of three that lived on the porch, and started to put on her helmet. She'd left a towel and a water bottle on the picnic table, and she tucked those into the basket behind the seat.

"You'll be back by dinner, right?" Larx said apprehensively. Once the sun went down, the roads went from squirrely to downright unsafe. Everybody's bike had reflectors and headlights, just in case, but it was his job to worry.

"Definitely," she said, winking. "Is Kirby coming?"

"I'm not sure. Aaron said he was whining about homework." Then, because he *was* the dad: "Why? You got a crush on Kirby?"

This elicited no outrage. She'd heard the question about boys—and girls—most of her life. "Nope," she replied cheerfully. "He's nice and all—like his company. But, you know, I've known him for seven years. Kissing Kirby would be like drinking caffeine-free Diet Coke."

Larx laughed, because she'd used this one before. "Pointless and icky?"

"Yup." Christi stopped fiddling with her helmet and grew suddenly sober. "But, uh, Dad?"

Larx swallowed. This sounded serious.

"Yeah?"

"I... if Kirby's *dad* is, you know, your flavor of soda?"

"Oh God."

"Yeah. Pour yourself a glass with some ice and enjoy, okay?"

"I promised you—" And he had. He'd been totally honest with the girls from the beginning. Why their mother had wanted the divorce, why she'd suddenly turned on his children as well as on him. And he'd promised that nothing he did, *nothing*, would touch their lives, their stability, ever again.

"Yeah, 'cause we were little!" Christi laughed. "But I'm going to school in two years, and you're going to be alone here." She bit her lip. "And I don't want you to be alone."

Oh charming. Charity. "I have friends!" he retorted, stung.

"Yoshi has his *own* boyfriend!" she replied. Then she got serious again. "Just think about it, okay, Daddy? You guys don't have to get all gross and serious all at once, but . . . you know. Think about it."

Like he'd been thinking of anything else since that day on Olson Road. "Christi. . . look, whatever you're. . . wanting me to think about, you've got to do me a favor, okay?"

"Sure."

"Don't tell—"

"Olivia? 'Cause we totally texted about this all yesterday. She thinks you should go for it because Kirby's dad is a total DILF."

Larx should be used to this feeling by now—twenty years of fatherhood should have prepared him for feeling like he was on the deck of a small ocean vessel that had just gotten undercut by a whale. "Uh, that's not awesome, but I was going to say don't tell *Kirby*." God. Because kids talked, right? And if Kirby didn't know, or suspect, or if Aaron wasn't as up-front with *his* kids as Larx had been with Christi and Olivia. . .

Bad. Just all the bad.

"Oh!" Christi looked like she hadn't thought of that. "You think he hasn't figured out his dad is crushing on you?"

"He's crushing on me?" Larx couldn't help but ask, pleased.

"Dad—dude. You were like talking to Uncle Tony and watching the game, and he was staring at you like you were water. It was totally obvious."

He couldn't help the shy smile that seemed to be taking over his face. "Really? Like I was water?"

She smiled back. "After a trip through the desert. Yeah. But if Kirby doesn't say something first, I won't dish. Deal?"

Larx nodded, hoping the embarrassment flush could be confused with sun exposure. "But... uh, look. Do me a favor and don't talk about, you know, why we left Sacramento. Okay? I need to tell him first."

"You didn't do anything wrong!" she said, dismayed.

Larx felt his third or three millionth pang of anxiety about this subject. "Not everybody agrees. Aaron's pretty law and order, hon. This might be the deal breaker."

Christi wrinkled her nose. "I don't think so. See you at dinner!"

"Wait, that's it? You don't think so and you're leaving?"

"Yup! Have fun while I'm gone!" She laughed wickedly as she swung her leg over her bike and took off, and Larx was left with his fallow garden and a field full of dead mice and fat, self-satisfied cats.

HIS BEMUSEMENT faded and he got to work after that. He harvested the last of the vegetables from the live plants and uprooted the dead ones and added them to the pile. By the time his pocket buzzed

again, he was hot, sweaty, and covered in dirt but almost done. Just one more plant—wait, let's pull up the
stakes and put them next to the porch for next year,
and the tomato racks too. And oh no! Almost forgot
the green-bean vines—the wood will rot under those
if they're allowed to stay past the rains.

And so it was, he was *still* almost done when Aaron came walking around from the front of the house,
one hand in the back pocket of his jeans, his T-shirt
stretched across his broad chest. He was smiling in-
dulgently, and Larx's heart stopped for a moment, just
seeing him, beautiful and confident in the long shadows the lowering sun cast through the pine trees.

Shit.

Was it that late?

"Oh my God!" he yelped, tossing one last handful of dead green beans into the pile. "I'm so sorry! I
got caught up! Oh shit! I was going to be cleaned up
before you got here!" He picked up the giant basket
full of squash, potatoes, and tomatoes and scrambled
forward, dodging little mouse carcasses as he went.

Aaron laughed and took the basket from him and
then, quite naturally, kissed him on the cheek.

Time stopped. Larx's heartbeat froze. The world
ceased to whirl, the shadows ceased to stretch, and for
a moment, everything was still.

Larx turned his head slowly in that moment and
captured Aaron's mouth for another kiss, this one on
the lips, with a little bit of tongue.

Larx pulled back and time started again, and he
and Aaron regarded each other soberly.

"Don't worry about being late," Aaron said, voice
soft. "I'll wash the veggies while you clean up."

Christiana was right. He was looking at Larx like *water*.

Larx nodded wordlessly and opened the sliding screen door, gesturing Aaron into the house while he kicked off his mud-covered flip-flops and stomped the dirt from his bare feet.

"Welcome to Chez Larkin," he said as he followed Aaron. "You passed the garage on the way around the house—we keep old craft supplies, Christmas decorations, and gardening tools in there."

"But not your car," Aaron observed.

"No, no—that's why we built the carport leading up to the garage. Because, you know, snow."

"Yes, yes I do know. The kids and I were sure we were going to *die* the first time it came down."

Larx nodded in perfect understanding. "It's white, it's from the sky, it's got to be evil magic. And it *happens every year.*"

It hadn't snowed in Sacramento in over forty years—it was nice to meet someone who had trouble with that transition too.

"So, in the house, from the backyard, we've got this useless anteroom that leads to the kitchen."

Aaron looked around, nodding. "You'd *think* it was a dining room, but you've got that—" He gestured to the completely fuel-inefficient double-sided fireplace that blocked the view to the living room.

"Yeah. It's not great. Anyway, we have friends over for Thanksgiving sometimes, and we bring in the picnic table from the porch and it fits here. Or the girls do their homework at the little desk in the corner—also handy."

Aaron raised an amused eyebrow. "I take it *you* have an office?"

Larx grimaced. "Not so much. I *did* have an office, and then it became a playroom for the girls, and then it became a cat room and a gaming room, and, well, it's sort of that right now." He gestured to the now-clean kitchen table and the stack of paperwork and the laptop tucked on the floor by the built-in china hutch next to it. "Behold, my office."

"Handily located near the refrigerator." Aaron groaned and patted his stomach. "This is why I converted the guest room pretty much after we moved in. I'd eat the house."

Larx grinned. "Who says I don't?" he taunted, and Aaron grimaced in return.

"That's mean. Just mean. I so much as look at ice cream and I gain ten pounds."

"Yeah, but that's the job," Larx said seriously. "I was put on paid leave a few years back and I packed on twenty in a month. Made me appreciate how much of my ass I really did run off."

Aaron arched his eyebrows, and Larx took the basket of veggies from him. Well, better now than after dinner, right? If Aaron suddenly decided he had to go home, Larx would know where they stood, and they could pretend two kisses and a few weeks' worth of running had never happened.

"Paid leave?" Aaron asked carefully.

Larx sighed. "Do you want to wait until after I shower before we have this conversation?" he asked carefully.

Aaron brushed some of the sweaty hair back from Larx's forehead—a curiously tender, intimate gesture that twisted Larx's heart. Oh… so much promise here.

"Tell me now," Aaron said. "Then you can go shower, and I'll cut up the veggies."

"I'm supposed to cook for you." Larx gave a weak grin, but his stomach was a mess of knots.

"Does this have anything to do with your divorce?"

Larx looked determinedly at the sink and set the veggies on the counter.

"See," he said, plugging the sink and starting the water, "I was a horny little bastard in college—fucked everything that moved. Girls, boys…." God. This didn't sound awesome, considering Aaron had been risking his life for his country at the same age. "Lila had just died," he said nakedly. "Mom passed away about a month later—"

"You were alone," Aaron said, turning off the faucet. "I get it."

Larx nodded and picked up the veggie brush and a potato. "So I started teaching and knocked up Alicia just about the same time. We got married, because… *kid*, right? And for a while, it's good. We had Olivia, and Christiana, and then…." He sighed. "And then Alicia miscarried. And we were both sad for a while. But for her—well, hormones are shitty things when you're a woman, you know?"

"I remember," Aaron said, his voice rumbly and comforting. He took the almost-white potato out of Larx's hand and gave him another. Larx had scrubbed the skin off and all.

"So no sex—for a long time. Almost a year. And I didn't cheat, 'cause I'm not geared that way. That's not…."

"Not what good guys do," Aaron supplied.

Larx gave him a quick smile, grateful. "I try. But I had a lot of time to *fantasize* about sex, and I realize, 80 percent of my fantasies are guys. And it hits me—I don't really *want* to have sex with Alicia, not really. But she's my wife, and she's sad, so I keep trying anything to make her happy again."

"Larx, that's the cleanest potato in the world. Take another one."

Larx gave the clean one to Aaron, who rummaged around the cupboard under the counter by intuition, apparently, and came up with a drainer to put them in.

"So finally there's sex again, but I know. I know I'm more attracted to men than women, and I have to fake it with my wife—but we're in it together. We've got the girls, and it's our job to make sure they're happy, right?"

He looked at Aaron then, trying to search inside his soul, maybe, through his pretty blue eyes, wanting to make sure they shared this one core value.

"Most important job in the world," Aaron confirmed.

Larx nodded nervously. "I always thought so." He grabbed the rest of the potatoes in the basket and threw them all in and started with the scrub brush again. "Anyway, so about eight years ago, this kid comes into my room during lunch. And he's a mess. He's crying, he's got cuts on his arms—his grades have gone down the toilet, and he's just like a breath away from ending it all, you know?"

Aaron nodded like he knew.

"So he comes into my room and tells me he's a freak who doesn't deserve to live, because he's gay.

And you know what the climate in this country was back then, right?"

"All the politicians who wanted to kill gays with fire? Yeah. I remember." He sounded grim, like there was a story there.

"Yeah." Larx closed his eyes and gave up on the potatoes. He turned around and leaned against the sink, crossing his arms. "So I told this kid I was bi. That it was okay. That he deserved a happy ever after and that the bullshit of high school would go away, and I was living proof."

"That was ballsy," Aaron said softly.

Larx shook his head. "Dumbest fucking thing I ever did." He grimaced. "The kid went home and told his parents he was gay, and when his dad threatened to kick him out of the house, he said it was okay, because *Larx* was gay, and that made him not a freak."

"Oh God," Aaron said hollowly.

"And I get called up and told to meet my union rep, and then I meet the head of human resources and my administrator, who was the same prick who liked to let the kids lead witch hunts on the teachers that crossed them. And they read this letter threatening to prosecute me for pedophilia."

"Oh my God—*Larx*!"

Larx shook his head, waving off his sympathy. "I was put on paid leave. It's what they do when they don't know what to do to you. They had to *prove* I'd done horrible things to this kid, and they had to *prove* I'd made him gay—which is what the parents were claiming—and they couldn't prove any of that, but God, they certainly couldn't have me teach, right?"

"So what did you do?" Aaron asked, and Larx still couldn't look at him.

"Well, I had myself some great union lawyers, who both assured me I wasn't a pervert. One of them got me a settlement, the other one saved my credential—but it took a while. I got my administrative credential in the year and a half it took them to resolve the matter." Larx shrugged. "I wasn't living at home by then anyway."

Aaron put a hand on his shoulder, but Larx couldn't let himself be comforted. Not now.

"'Cause I came home and told Alicia what I'd done, and she kicked me out. Which would have been… I don't know. Not fine, really, because…."

"Because you'd stuck with her when shit got bad," Aaron said.

Larx managed to meet his eyes. "I thought so." He stared at his tile floor again, aware there were some holes where the tile had cracked. "But apparently I was foul and evil and gross, just like she said… whatshername? I forget? That one bitch who was running for president?"

"Bachman Palin Overdrive?" Aaron quipped, and Larx appreciated the joke.

"Yeah, that's the one. Like she said. Anyway, so Alicia was home with the kids, at least, and I got to see them on weekends. But then I started to notice—the kids aren't looking too good when I get them. Olivia had this really long hair, and it's got rats in it—every time." He'd had to take her to have it cut, and they'd both cried, because it had been long and dark and lovely. "They're growing out of their clothes, and every time I come get them, they're *starving*. And I start asking questions and it turns out that Alicia—she's not caring for our kids. She told them straight-up that they're a faggot's kids and they don't deserve to be cared for—"

"Oh my God!" Aaron's horror felt like a balm to his soul.

Larx swallowed. "I don't think… I think she never got over that one we lost," he said, that soul-searching pain awakening again. "And when the world came crashing down on our heads, she was like, 'Oh! A sign! It's all Larx's fault and I should repent!'"

"That's horrible," Aaron snarled. "That's—it wasn't your fault. None of it."

Larx smiled at him, lower lip wobbling. "Well, yeah. But my kids, Aaron. She was taking it out on *my kids*. So I got my union lawyers to rec me a shark, and I used my settlement to go after Alicia in family court. I mean, it shouldn't have worked, right? But apparently enough of my old colleagues liked me. They got subpoenaed to come testify. It was really fucking human of them, because I wasn't allowed to make contact. So they don't see me for a year and a half, and suddenly they have to show up in court. And they all, to a one, said I was one of the best teachers and fathers they knew. And the prick administrator had moved by then, and… lawyers. Alicia's lawyers didn't even think to ask all the people who'd tried to kill me with fire by then anyway."

"So you got your kids," Aaron said, nodding like he understood.

Larx nodded back. "I did. And I got the job up here, and me and my girls, we got—"

"A family."

Larx met his eyes then, his throat thick with confession, his chest sore and aching with what it might
mean. "Yeah. A family."

Aaron leaned against the counter with Larx and
wrapped a beefy, secure arm around his shoulder.
"That was hard for you," he said. "Telling me."

Larx nodded and leaned into him. "You've got a
kid at home, Aaron. My girls, they know everything. I
told them why their mother was mad, I told them who
I was and what I'd done. We don't have any secrets.
I knew Olivia was fooling around with her boyfriend
before you caught her—I took her in for the pill. But
I don't know about you and Kirby. I don't know what
Kirby knows. You... you and me do this, and we can
keep it quiet for as long as you want. But you have to
know, sometimes that's not even as long as you think
it's going to be."

Aaron kissed his temple. "So you thought you'd
get this out in the open now?"

"I just thought it was fair."

Aaron's arms tightened, and a puff of air feath-
ered through Larx's hair. "Go get washed up, Principal Larkin. I'm going to decide what to do with all of
these lovely veggies, and we're going to have dinner.
And maybe, if your kid promises not to look out the
window, I'll kiss you good night before I leave. And
tomorrow we'll go running some more. Because I like
your company a whole damned lot. How's that?"

Larx turned, thinking he'd pull back so they
could talk some more, but Aaron kissed him, softly
at first, then harder, tongue charging, hands on Larx's
hips, body turning to press Larx back against the
counter. Larx groaned, seven years of repressed sex

drive breaking loose as he reached behind Aaron and grabbed himself a double handful of surprisingly taut backside, sinking into the kiss like a man dying of thirst sank into a pure mountain lake.

Like drowning would save his life.

He wanted. He wanted so much he was sobbing for it, and when Aaron pulled away, he mewled with need.

"Sh...." Aaron bumped Larx's cheek with his lips. "It'll happen, Larx. But my kid's coming for dinner, and your kid—"

Larx jerked back and looked outside, seeing that the lowering shadows had almost faded into an orange sky. "She'll be here soon," he muttered. "Oh God. Sorry. You're right. I gotta go wash up, and then we can make dinner and—"

"Larx!" Aaron laughed, framing his face for a quick, hard kiss. "Don't worry about it. We're good. You and me are good. Dinner can be a little late. Your kid can get home and direct me around the kitchen. We'll manage, okay?"

Larx nodded and let out a breath. "Good," he said, chest still aching from confession time. "I'll just go—"

"Go pull yourself together. Remember that I'll be back in the morning. It'll be okay."

Larx managed a shaky smile and ran off to let hot water restore him to normalcy.

It *did* take care of the dirt and the oily hair, and it helped restore his composure, but as he toweled off and dressed in jeans and a comfy T-shirt, he realized something.

Aaron had kissed him. Had comforted him. Had promised not to run.

Normal was a whole new thing now—not bad, but new, the way Christiana and Olivia felt about the world kind of new—and Larx needed to figure it out again.

He walked back downstairs and into the kitchen with some hope and a real smile.

Christi was there already, and she and Aaron were in the process of cutting potatoes and sautéing vegetables, talking about the best way to use what they had. There was a knock at the door as he passed it, and he let Kirby in, then led him through the living room in order to bypass the chaos in his rather small kitchen.

"They're busy," he explained. "You and I get to set the table."

Kirby laughed, and Larx thought that while his and Alicia's children looked more like him, Aaron's children were a pleasing mix of their big blond father and a woman who had, by all accounts, possessed a delicate, fine-boned sort of beauty. Kirby was a positively *angelic*-looking boy, and his sisters were stunning as well.

Larx was glad for Aaron. He seemed to have loved his wife with all the purity of his heart. It must have been comforting to see her growing up in their children.

"So, uh, do I have to tell the world I ate dinner at the principal's house?" Kirby asked, standing awkwardly by the table and waiting for Larx to give him something to do.

Larx rummaged through the drawers of the china hutch and pulled out a stack of placemats that he handed to Kirby before moving to the silverware drawer.

"Only if you think it will enhance your street cred. You know, 'cause Principal Larx is more badass than a motorcycle gang, right?"

Kirby relaxed a little and took a handful of forks and butter knives. "Uh, yeah. Sure. That's what we're saying."

Larx grinned. "I knew it! Did you hear that, Aaron? I'm badass!"

Aaron looked at him sardonically before chopping another potato into thin slices. "Sure, Larx. That's what you are. A badass public educator. You'll have your own film deal next."

"Damned straight." Oh, he liked having people to play with. He remembered the first time Olivia had sassed him back as a kid. "Gee, Dad, I don't know where I got my sarcasm. You got any ideas?" She'd been ten, and he'd been tickled because it meant he was raising a person he could talk with as an adult too.

They continued to play. The badass public educator does paperwork—a madman with a computer and a pen! The badass public educator teaches student leadership! Can he fold paper carnations fast enough? The badass public educator teaches freshmen! What will give first, his temper or their idiocy? This time he may have met his match!

They were all still laughing when Christiana said, "Ta-da! The main dish is ready, so if the table's set, we're good to go!"

"What's the main dish?" Kirby asked suspiciously. "It doesn't look like anything I've eaten before."

"My people call it 'fuud,'" she enunciated pertly. "And it comes in many forms. Dad, do we have any of that Panera dressing? The Asian stuff? 'Cause Aaron made a salad too, and that's my favorite."

Larx rooted through the ancient fridge for a couple of bottles—because he liked the Asian stuff, but ranch was pretty universal—and walked back to the table, noting that Christiana and Kirby had sat next to each other on one side, leaving him and Aaron side by side on the other.

He cast Christi a glance chock-full of irony, and she gave him a bland smile in return and then looked to where Kirby and his father were having their own telepathic conversation.

"That's it," Larx said out loud, startling everybody. "From now on, all conversation at the dinner table has to be verbal. Nonverbal communication may be used only if we're kidnapped by aliens and are forming an escape plan. Are we clear?"

"But Larx," Kirby complained, "how else am I supposed to whine about my homework?"

"Out loud, of course," Larx told him seriously. "That way I can gloat like all good AP teachers, knowing I have done my job."

They kept up the banter all through dinner, which was a delicious sautéed blend of squash, potatoes, tomatoes, hamburger, and garlic, and even through dessert.

Only Larx had to know that Aaron kept his knee pressed solidly against Larx's the entire time, the heat of his thigh searing straight through their jeans.

KIRBY LEFT shortly after cleanup, and Christi went upstairs to "shower and chill," which was often code for finishing homework she hadn't gotten to during the weekend. Larx and Aaron were left to linger over coffee and to talk about... well, anything at all.

"Your son looks a lot like you," Larx said softly. "But he looks like your wife too."

Aaron took a sip of coffee and regarded him with sober blue eyes. "My wife. She was beautiful," he said, shrugging. "I mean, I thought so. I mean, I wish you could have had what Caro and I did."

"Good?" Larx needed to know this too.

"It was. I knew I liked men too, but it wouldn't have been a hardship, only loving her for the rest of my life."

Larx nodded. "That's good," he said after a moment. He'd been hoping for what? More dirt? More blood? But Aaron wasn't geared like he was, to babble and play and talk. Larx would have to be more patient if he wanted to know what was going on in Aaron George's heart.

"Good?" More quizzical blue eyes over a coffee cup.

"You know what love is," Larx said simply. "You had some happy. I'm jealous, actually. You and your wife—I'm sorry she's gone. I am. Even if it means you wouldn't be here in my kitchen. But you were happy with someone." He didn't want to state the obvious.

He had never had that kind of happy, and he wanted it desperately.

Aaron just nodded, and then, surprisingly, he covered Larx's hand with his own. "You are good for me," he said, no smile. "There's a lot of cheerleader in you for a principal," he said at last, biting his lip shyly.

Larx grinned. "Go, Deputy, go!"

They laughed quietly together and turned the talk to friends they'd had back in Sacramento a long, long time ago.

Larx walked Aaron out to his SUV at nine, because they both had to be up early in the morning. Running stopped for neither man nor date, right?

"So thank you, Deputy, for coming over and sharing our fall harvest," he said formally. "But I want you to know, I still owe you a dinner after the hot dogs."

Aaron opened his door and then turned, grabbing the waist of Larx's jeans and pulling him forward until their groins were touching but they had enough space to talk. "A date," he said. "Someplace out of town."

Larx nodded, mesmerized. He would have said yes to a hotel hookup with an assumed name and a borrowed car.

"But not," Aaron clarified, pulling him out of half-realized fantasies and James Bond plans of covert ops dating, "because I'm ashamed. Or I want to keep us secret forever."

Larx's only response was an indrawn breath. Oh. This was actually better than Bond.

Aaron nodded and licked his lower lip slowly. "We're new," he said softly. "But when I'm sure I want to grow old with you, Larx, don't worry. I'll tell my boss. I'll tell my kids. We'll make plans."

"Okay," he whispered, not wanting to think about the school board, but Aaron read his mind.

"Don't think I don't know what you're risking too," he said softly. "So when you risk it, I want you to risk it for something you can hold up to the world and say, 'This! This is us!' And then we can do it together."

Because last time he'd done it alone. He'd done it more than alone. He'd done it alienated and reviled.

"Thank you," he said, so moved he couldn't smile.

"Don't thank me yet," Aaron whispered. "Wait until after the kiss. It's only polite."

Aaron's lips were soft and strong on Larx's, and Larx opened for him, pure and welcoming. This man was so real against his body, this kiss as much communication as desire. He kissed back, telling Aaron about arousal and wanting, about needing and fear. Aaron cupped the back of his head and held him still and plundered his mouth, talking about safety and kindness. Talking about tender carnality, the gentleness of a fever-pitch fuck.

Larx moaned, plastering himself against that solid wall of muscle while Aaron leaned back against the car, opened his arms, and became a rock harbor for all of Larx's storms. Larx bucked against him, his cock swelling, his body tingling, the memory of sex a buzz in his chest that he couldn't seem to still. Aaron slid his hand down the back of Larx's jeans and kneaded, locking him in place while Larx ground against him, a whine slipping out when he realized they were separated by jeans and nothing else.

"Impatient," Aaron whispered into the curve of Larx's ear.

"Augh!" Larx groaned and buried his face in Aaron's shoulder. This bowed his back, moving his groin out of contact, and oh, blessed holy touch, Aaron slid his hand around to the front of his shorts and… oh…. "God," he sighed as Aaron wrapped a strong fist around Larx's erection. "Oh… please…."

"Been a long time?" Aaron taunted, stroking. "You needed this a long time, haven't you?"

"Yesssss...." Larx couldn't think—couldn't even reciprocate. His knees were weak, and he clung to Aaron's hips with both hands, bucking in that sure grip while his body... his body remembered what sex was *about*. Years. Not since Alicia, and not with someone who—"Oh...." Because Aaron skated his thumb across Larx's cockhead. "Oh wow." He stroked some more, slip-sliding in the precome that drizzled over the top, and Larx was nearly in tears. "You're good," he whispered.

"It's my first time with a guy," Aaron confessed, squeezing his base hard.

"Wha... oh God!" Larx bit him on the shoulder, confused and on the brink of climax.

"Said I was bi—didn't say I'd ever been with a man," Aaron teased, and his stroking grew harder, faster, until Larx groaned, fucking his fist, shameless in his front yard as he hadn't been since college. When his climax exploded behind his eyeballs, he couldn't breathe, couldn't think, and if Aaron hadn't covered Larx's mouth with his own, he would have disgraced himself by crying out loud enough to wake the cats.

As it was, he half sobbed into the kiss, body shaking, eyes burning with the intensity of orgasm, with emotion, with the shock of no longer being alone.

Eventually his breathing stilled and he collapsed against Aaron's chest, dazed.

"I... uh...." He pulled back and squinted at Aaron's smug expression through the deep twilight. "I just got a man-virgin hand job in my own front yard," he said with a sense of honest surprise.

Aaron's teeth glinted in the light from the rising moon. "Just wait and see what can happen if we get a bed," he chuckled. Then, while Larx was still lost in what they'd just done, he straightened and pulled his hand from Larx's pants, wiping it on the inside of Larx's underwear as he did. He gave Larx a quick, hard kiss on the mouth before sliding into the SUV. "See you tomorrow, bright and early," he said, closing the door on Larx's stunned expression.

And then he drove away, leaving Larx to go inside and run up for a second shower before bed.

Tinder

LARX TEXTED him before he left the house, and Aaron was outside waiting in the dark as he swung by.

Aaron would recognize the thud-thud-thud of Larx's tennis shoes on the red dirt of the forestry road in his sleep. The mornings were cold in early October, and Larx ran in a baseball hat with a hooded sweatshirt, but Aaron swore he knew the man's knobby runner's knees.

As Larx drew near, Aaron could taste the aura of his heat and the clean smell of runner's sweat.

Every fiber of his being, every blood vessel, ever corpuscle, *knew* Larx, saw in him a friend, an ally, a potential mate. The last time he'd felt this hum in his chest and his groin? Had been when Caro had looked at him after a long, lazy day in bed and said, "I think we should get married, right?"

Of course he'd thought so. She'd been, well, a lot like Larx, actually. Kind, impulsive, tart-tongued, busy.

Beautiful.

Watching Larx approach, his runner's stride smooth and rhythmic, Aaron felt that same affinity. That same joy.

I held his cock in my hand.

And he also felt hard and aching and horny. God, when had his last hookup been? Two years ago? The kids had all gone to Six Flags in Vallejo, and he'd reserved a room for them down there so the girls didn't have to drive back up in the dark.

Funny—he could remember where the kids were, but he couldn't remember much about the woman he'd been with that night. But then, she hadn't sought him out either, afterward, and he was pretty sure she had a two-month cabin rental that year.

Looking back on it, he could remember every community event, every parent meeting, every football game, every school event he'd ever been to during which he'd had a chance to talk to the kids' teacher, Mr. Larkin.

Every one.

Aaron knew Larx. His body remembered Larx's body like he remembered the landmarks of home.

"Gonna just stand there?" Larx baited, hardly out of breath.

Aaron finished his last stretch and joined him, running down the track, past the last of the residential area, and into the trees. This was the part of the run they bundled up for, because the woods stayed dark until around noon and grew dark again around four. In the chill of the morning, they could see their breath against the panoply of shadows.

"So," Larx asked conversationally, "did you sleep well last night?"

"Like a baby," Aaron lied. He'd fallen asleep aching, lost in a misery of want.

"Yup. Me too."

A few hushed footfalls fell.

"So, no men," Larx said into the quiet.

"Knew I wanted them," Aaron replied equably. He'd followed his best friend slavishly through grade school, devastated when the boy had fallen in love in ninth grade. He'd dreamed about the high school quarterback sucking his cock. He'd yearned quietly for a boy he'd met during basic training. Aaron knew what gay was, and knew what bi was, and knew enough to know he wasn't curious. He wanted.

"So… me?"

"I wanted you bad enough to let you know I wanted you."

Larx stopped dead, putting his hands on his hips and glaring at him. "I dumped my heart out to you last night, goddammit. Be square."

Aaron sighed. "I've known," he said, panting too. "But… Larx. 1988—that's when we graduated from high school."

"1990," Larx muttered.

"Swell. AIDS—do you remember that?"

"I do, but—"

"But I liked girls too. I liked them enough that it wasn't a hardship." Aaron kicked a rock in front of him and watched it disappear into the shadows. "But… but not talking to you? Not getting to know you better? That would have been a hardship, okay?"

Larx nodded and started running again, struggling for a few steps to get his stride. Aaron kept pace, wondering how long he stayed mad.

"I've never been with a virgin before," he said, managing to chuckle evilly in spite of their exertion.

Aaron smacked him in the arm. "Shut up."

"No, seriously. I'm going to have to be gentle with you."

"Stop it."

"Like, you know, if I give you a blowjob, are you going to freak out? Imagine me with breasts just to keep up your manhood?"

"You are not that cute," Aaron grumbled, relieved that he was okay.

"I must be. 'Cause, you know. I'm your closet-door opener." Larx bounded a few steps ahead and turned, his arms spread in classic Vanna pose. "Ta-da!"

Aaron growled and turned on the gas, intent on getting to him and pummeling him or kissing him or something in the middle, and Larx turned and sprinted off, leaving Aaron to try desperately to keep up.

Oh *hell*—Larx was *winning*. He was going to *lose* Aaron, abandon him to soldier on the damned lonely path by himself. And just when Aaron was going to holler and call him a weenie coward for running away, Larx spun around again, barely visible in the darkness.

"Catch me now," he said, and *ran off the road*.

Aaron followed him, shocked, as what appeared to be a random turn actually became a small path, probably used by rangers and forestry workers. About twenty yards into the woods, a small service building loomed, most likely full of surveying equipment and emergency supplies. Aaron got there just in time to watch Larx disappear behind it.

Aaron slowed down enough to peer into the shadows. "Larx? Where'd you—?"

Larx's hand shot out and grabbed him by the collar, hauling him against the building while Larx's mouth crashed down on his with stunning heat.

"How'd you know—?"

"This was here?" Larx tugged on his lower lip. "Saw it last week. Looked it up."

Aaron had no more questions as Larx plundered his mouth, taking Aaron's surprise and using it to take over completely.

For once, someone else was in charge.

Aaron had no idea he needed that until it happened. Larx took over the kiss, took over his pleasure, made the decision to steal time from life. Larx moved his hands confidently under Aaron's shirts, ignoring the sweat and instead kneading at Aaron's pecs. Wow. Oh wow. You didn't usually grope your own chest during masturbation—Aaron tended to go for ground zero. Larx's attention made him weak, until he was leaning back against the building, lost in the haze of the kiss and letting Larx do… whatever he wanted.

What he wanted to do was shove up the shirts and pull away from the kiss to lock his lips around Aaron's nipple.

Aaron had to put his all into staying upright, and he knocked Larx's baseball hat off in an effort to tangle his fingers in Larx's hair. Oh… oh man. Yes. That. That right there.

"Larx!" he whispered.

Larx moved to the other nipple, lips pulling, tongue and teeth playing, and Aaron bucked unconsciously, pretty sure he could come right then and there, even if it meant running back to his house with come in his shorts.

"Oh God. Larx, I'm going to—oh!"

Larx sank to a squat, pulling Aaron's sweats down with him.

Aaron stared at him for a moment, shocked to be naked and open in the air. Larx leaned forward and licked the head of his cock gently, then looked up at Aaron, a serious expression on his face. "We can wait for a bed, virgin," he said quietly, every word puffing against Aaron's damp skin.

"Then I'd have to kill you," Aaron breathed, sagging against the building. This was ludicrous. They were grown-ups—Aaron was a *law enforcement officer*. Larx was… oh God. Didn't matter what Larx was. He had his mouth open and was wrapping his lips around Aaron's cockhead and—

Larx was the maelstrom, the fire, the passion Aaron had been missing from his life.

"Ahhhh…."

Larx had pulled back and was playing a dangerous, teasing game with his tongue and his breath and the careful edges of teeth, inflaming Aaron, drawing out this sudden lightning strike of arousal until Aaron could weep from it.

"Larx," he begged. "Please… fast this time. We'll go slow next time, I promise—ah!"

Down to the root. Larx took him down to the root, mouth clamping tightly as he pulled back in a long, slow pull.

It had been so long. So long since Aaron had felt any hands on his skin but his own. So long since a person he *wanted*, had *yearned for*, had touched him.

So long since he'd met Mr. Larx, the kids' science teacher, and thought, *Damn.*

Larx raised a hand to tickle his balls and Aaron was lost.

"Damn!"

It was the only warning he gave, but Larx? He didn't even hesitate, swallowing hard and fast and consistently until Aaron was drained, shaking, and dazed, watching in wonder as the sun peeped through the base of the trees.

He tugged Larx's hair gently, grateful when Larx pulled up his sweats and his underwear as he stood. Larx leaned in and regarded him with anxious eyes, and Aaron smiled, tilting his chin and taking his mouth.

He recognized the taste of his own come—Caro had liked that maneuver too. But Larx was still new, and the taste of his come in Larx's mouth gave Aaron a surprising satisfaction.

His. His come. His man. It was such a basic thing.

Larx pulled back. "Was okay?"

"Sh." Aaron turned him around and draped his arms over his shoulders, pulling Larx back against his body. "Sh. No worries. Look. The sun's coming up. Let's watch."

The hush of the new day swept over the forest, and Aaron clung to Larx as tightly as he dared.

THEY HAD to hurry after that, because they both cut a pretty fine line between their exercise time and their leaving-the-house time.

Kirby had already left by the time Aaron got home, a note that said *Must go faster* on the table next to a cooling bran muffin.

Rotten kid. Aaron ate the muffin as he ran out of the house after his shower, still coming down from the high of what had happened that morning.

Inspired by Kirby's note, when he got to work, he scrolled through *Jurassic Park* memes and came up with one about T. rexes and Mondays, and sent it to Tiffany in hopes it would make her laugh.

How passé.

Well, it wasn't *Dad, you're an asshole*, so he was taking it as a win.

But while he was looking at his phone, he decided to go full-on sentimental. He sent Larx a text with a smiley face and a *Good run this morning*. Inane, and a vicious understatement, but it wouldn't get Larx fired or outed either.

I thought so, Larx returned, and Aaron had to squint at the series of symbols that followed.

"Huh. Eight, equals, equals, D, squiggly line, greater than, zero?"

That made no sense. He pulled the phone back and squinted again.

8==D~~>0

And saw something that looked damned obscene.

Oh my God. I didn't know you could illustrate a blowjob with ASCII art.

Creative minds have no barriers. Want to do it again?

More than I want to breathe. When?

Got no idea. At this rate, we may have to wait until Thanksgiving vacation.

NOOOOOOOOOOOOOOO

I thought we were grown-ups who could wait for time and opportunity.

I am old. Old and decrepit. I may die before I see you naked. That would be a tragedy.

I agree. But I have no solutions. Give me time though. I used to be good at finding ways to get laid.

I like this skill. You should acquire it again.

I shall endeavor to do so—oops, there's the bell!

Aaron stared at his phone for an embarrassing amount of time after that, until Eamon came out of his office and claimed his attention.

"George, do you object to doing football duty again?"

"For homecoming? Not at all." At least Larx would be there—not to mention their kids, for easier supervision. "Do you expect anything big?"

Eamon grimaced, passing a hand over his close-cropped, gray curls. "Not necessarily. It's just that Mr. Olson is out of town again, and Julia's mother… she hasn't been too, shall we say, authoritative on laying down limits for her girl. If she decides to drive into Tahoe like she did last weekend, there could be one hell of a party at that really expensive house."

Aaron stopped staring moonily at his phone and paid attention. "Those parties have been getting bigger and bigger," he said grimly. And the rumors coming out of them—Kirby had actually looked through social media to make sure there hadn't been any atrocities committed. Too much had hit the news about kids being assaulted while they were unconscious for Aaron to just assume everything was okay at the Olson house because nobody had complained.

"I'll ask Kirby if he's heard anything."

"And Principal Larkin too," Eamon said seriously.

"Yeah, Larx too. He'll know."

Aaron put his phone in his pocket and turned back toward his list of morning inquiries.

Eamon didn't move but instead stood there, regarding him thoughtfully.

"Uh, anything else you needed?"

"No, not really. I just heard good stories about how that boy handled himself Friday night. Everyone said you were right by his side, but he did most of the talking."

Aaron tried to think if he'd mishandled himself. "Well, sir, it is *his* school."

Eamon smiled. "It is indeed. Don't mind me, Aaron. I'm just… I'm relieved for the school is all. High schools are getting more and more complicated these days. Nobili was a decent man, but he retired none too soon. I think you and Larkin will have a good partnership there."

Aaron fought the flush that threatened to creep past his collar. "Thank you. Some people you just… you know, click with."

Eamon looked at him sharply and raised his eyebrows. "Oh," he said neutrally.

The flush won. "Oh what?"

"Nothing, son. Just you and Larkin… you two be careful. That's all. Just… you know. Be careful."

"We will be, sir," Aaron said, not even pretending not to know what he was talking about.

"I'll back you, son. I'm ready to retire, and you're who's good for this town. Do let me know."

It was all he could ask for. "We're new," he said quietly.

"You won't be secret for long," Eamon said. Then he chuckled. "Not with that blush. My God, boy, how old are you?"

Eamon walked off, still laughing softly, and Aaron kept his seat for a moment, trying not to hide his face like a kid. Apparently you were never old enough.

"YEAH, I'LL keep an ear out," Larx said the next morning during their run. "That kid gives me the heebie-jeebies anyway—shades of my ex-wife, I shit you not."

Aaron shuddered, angry all over again. The thing that had twisted him the most was Larx finding a reason for his ex's behavior. Forgiving her as much as he could.

When you're young, you think being good is all about duty and honor and loyalty—and Larx had shown that. But he'd shown compassion too, and Aaron was in awe.

Such a good man. Some people thought they didn't exist.

And what his wife had done…. Aaron frowned. "You think Julia's that bad? I mean, I know about the parties, but—"

"The thing is," Larx said before he could flail any longer, "that people assume students are innocent. That they can be misunderstood by teachers—and sometimes that happens. They think that if maybe the parents got some classes or quit drinking or stopped working so much, the kid would just pop up magically and be a decent human being."

Aaron smacked him in the arm. "And sometimes it happens." Because Larx claimed *he'd* been that kid.

"Yeah, but that took work on my part. It's what keeps us *working*, believe it or not—the hope that the kid will learn. But sometimes the damage is fucking done. Think about it—we spend what, fifty-five minutes a day with between fifteen and forty kids? How much can we really *do* in that time?"

Aaron had never thought of it that way. "About as much as the kid'll let you?" he hazarded.

"Right? And they pop out of Mom with some of the basic hardware already dialed in. Is this kid anxious? Timid? That can be worked on, but the kid came out with that. Is the kid aggressive? Physical? Well, yeah—sometimes Mom and Dad make that happen, but sometimes Mom and Dad work on a kid who's physical in the first place. Olivia is majoring in theater. Christiana is majoring in science. They both like cats."

Larx was working up a head of steam here, and Aaron was just as glad he was the one talking. For once Aaron could actually keep up with him. "So what's that have to do with—"

"Julia Olson?" Larx kicked at a rock in the path and missed, spinning around in an effort to keep his balance. "She's a fucking psychopath. Vanity and arrogance working on a weak mind—or something like that. It's a Jane Austen quote. Olivia was a fan. But it's like the quote—Julia had the raw materials of a psychopath, and her parents refined that ore to pure grade."

Aaron shivered in spite of himself. "You've run up against that ore cart before?"

"A friend of mine," Larx confirmed. "She had…
well, a shitty year. I can't put it any better than that.
And the administration really *did* have it in for her. I
mean, they weren't subtle—the principal used to stalk
her class just to see if she'd slip up."

"Scary." Aaron had worked for bosses like that
before, in the military and out.

"Yeah. And her grades weren't in order—not her
fault. Her computer was a mess; the IT department
hadn't updated it in years. But this kid Ashley. Man,
this kid scented blood. And she went in for the kill.
Dana hadn't done anything wrong, but the way this
kid went on? It was frightening. Between the admin
and Ashley, it was a fucking witch hunt. They might as
well have started the bonfire in her classroom so they
could burn her at the stake."

"What happened?"

Larx grunted. "In the end? Not much. Dana
changed the kid's grade because hey, she needed the
job. The kid graduated, because that's what they do.
The asshole principal was there to fuck with people
another year. But Dana was a wreck. For months she
hardly smiled at her classes. She spent her own money getting her computer updated. She taught only the
textbook and none of the awesome stuff that made her
so good to begin with. And I'm pretty sure she developed an ulcer. So on the one hand—nothing. But on
the other hand—"

"Lotta damage," Aaron conceded. They reached
the part of the track where they looped around the
trees and ran through the edge of a meadow. The sun
hit them here, and Larx—a little ahead of Aaron—was
bathed in gold.

Larx turned and met his eyes, and his expression changed. Suddenly neither of them were thinking about Julia Olson and the way a spoiled, self-indulgent narcissist could mess with someone's life.

"Yeah," Larx said, answering a question Aaron hadn't asked. "Yeah."

Aaron grinned at him, his feet pounding, his lungs working, his blood pumping, and his heart… falling.

They ran in silence for a moment, and then Aaron brought himself back to their conversation with a sigh. "So what do we do?"

Larx grunted. "Do? Well, the dance is a closed system. The kids need to get there by eight, and it ends at eleven thirty. They can leave early, but homecoming king and queen are crowned around eleven, and believe me, Julia thinks she's got a chance, so she's not missing that shit."

"Nice," Aaron said sourly.

"I'm saying. Now, the party could happen later, not going to lie, but usually…."

He turned enough so Aaron could see him waggling his eyebrows. "Everyone wants to get laid on homecoming," Aaron deduced.

"Bingo. Again, no guarantees, but that's been the way the kids have done it since I've gotten here. Every school has its traditions."

"I hear ya. Some schools it's senior ditch day, some schools it's getting knocked up during prom—"

"Here they get knocked up during homecoming and get it over with. You understand."

They were rounding the bend for Aaron's house now, and Aaron was irritated. Watching Larx's mind work was pretty awesome, and Aaron wanted more.

"I understand. So the game on Friday?"

"Well. There's the school bonfire after the game and the homecoming dance the next day. The bonfire is across Olson Road at that clearing—"

"I know it," Aaron said grimly.

"Yeah—Baby Lane. Anyway, I can do two things. First is send out a mass voicemail to all the senior parents about how serious infractions against school policy can keep a kid from graduating. I'll throw in being drunk or disorderly or arrested or caught in morally compromising positions—" Larx actually had to catch his breath here. Lots of big words.

"Yadda," Aaron panted, "yadda."

"Right." Crunch-thud, crunch-thud. "So I can do that, and I can give an extra call for supervisors. If we set up an entrance and a perimeter, kids can't come and go from the bonfire, and nobody can go to the party and come back to the bonfire or the dance to collect his buddies. Now some kids are gonna break the rules 'cause kids are dumb. But not all kids are dumb. We put the fear of God into the more timid ones, and we can manage the troublemakers."

It was a sound plan, one that indicated a lot of experience dealing with mob psychology. Well, that was the job description, right?

"That'll help," Aaron agreed, slowing down considerably because this here was his cooldown. Larx traditionally slowed down here too, and then ran the next mile and a half to his house before cooling down again. Aaron wasn't sure what that did to his workout, but he knew he was very grateful for Larx's company.

"Well, shit." Larx stopped pumping his arms and put them on his hips for the last two hundred yards.

"'Well, shit' what?" Aaron asked, grateful to not be running anymore.

Larx looked away, toward the sun-glowing horizon and his house. "We missed our make-out window," he said with no irony at all. "I was...." He scowled. "You know. Looking forward to it."

Aaron laughed weakly. He'd done the same. "Well, I don't know what to—"

"Christiana is staying with a friend Saturday night," Larx said in a hurry. "I know the parents—Schuyler's a good kid—so I'm not just abandoning her to Julia Olson's phantom party. She hates Julia Olson anyway."

"Oh!" Aaron said, surprised.

"I don't know how late you let Kirby stay alone or—"

"I have to work nights sometimes," Aaron confessed. "Kirby is usually okay. He's not going to the dance, so I can just, you know, be late."

"We're, uh, having our own bonfire Sunday," Larx said, shy all of a sudden. "So, like, if you guys wanted to come over again—we're toasting hot dogs and marshmallows and stuff."

"I...." Aaron paused. Would he? He didn't know. He hadn't *dated* anyone he liked. "Someday I want to stay the whole night," he confessed.

Larx squeezed his shoulder sympathetically. "We may have to wait a year," he said, sounding depressed. "I get it. Kids and coming out—not so much fun."

"There should be a holiday for it," Aaron said. "All the amusement parks should be half-price, and we could wrap a rainbow ribbon around our kids' arms, send them down to Six Flags, and we could stay home and get busy like grown-ups."

"We're going to have to settle for college," Larx said. And then—probably on impulse—he paused, grabbed Aaron's arm, and pulled him in for a quick kiss on the corner of his mouth. "Have a good day, Deputy. Let me know if you or Eamon have any questions, okay?"

Aaron closed his eyes, wanting him closer with a ferocity that hurt. "Larx?" he asked, suddenly troubled.

"Yeah?"

"You… God. I'll do what I can Saturday night, okay?"

Larx smiled. "'Kay." And then he was off, trotting down the road like he'd never broken stride.

Aaron walked up his driveway and through his front door, wondering when he got to tell his son he was having a sleepover.

Somehow he didn't think that would go over very well.

Sparks

"So, GUYS, do we have our lab reports all typed and ready to go?" The bell had rung, and Larx stacked the pile of papers on his desk and put a nice big paperclip on them. Tomorrow, Friday, was the test, and then, hopefully, the kids would have the weekend to relax. Larx had never been the kind of sadist who assigned big stuff after school events. How was that fair? Especially when football and cheerleading and drama were some of the things kids came to school *for*.

The two boys approached Larx's desk uncertainly, their work clenched in shaking hands. Fact was, the two of them hadn't been looking good. Pale, heavy-eyed, with the weight of the world on their shoulders, they had dragged themselves into Larx's class all week with the air of two staunch patriots being carted to the guillotine.

Larx was pretty sure that what was going on with Kellan and Isaiah couldn't be solved with a lab report and a winning score in a football game, but damn if Larx wasn't going to hope anyway.

"Yeah, Larx. Here." Kellan handed him two lab books and the accompanying typed notes, and Larx thanked him.

"These look good," he said sincerely. Well, Isaiah wouldn't accept anything but best effort from Kellan. "You guys, uh, ready for the weekend?"

They did something then that Larx recognized from his married days. Olivia would want a treat, and Larx—ever the pushover—would be all for it, but Alicia had been the last word. What would follow would be an eyeball consultation, Larx to Alicia and back. If the answer was yes, Alicia would give it. If the answer was no, Larx would.

In this case, the answer was no.

"Yeah, all ready!" Kellan replied with false brightness, and Larx prayed for patience.

"Guys. Is everything okay?"

That silent conversation again, and for a moment it looked like no would win again.

"Uh, guys—I've got all period. I'm the principal, remember?"

"Mr. Larx?" Kellan said finally.

"No," Isaiah hissed, nudging his arm.

"It's scaring me," Kellan insisted. "She's… she's saying all sorts of things."

Larx bit the bullet. "What things?"

"I told her we'd be going to the dance as friends," Isaiah said, cheeks burning. "She said…." He glared at Kellan. "She made it sound so ugly!"

"Rumors about us," Kellan said, and the way he looked at Isaiah told Larx all he needed to know.

"Those rumors shouldn't hurt you," he said, knowing that they would, but knowing that they *shouldn't*. "If they're not true, you know it. If they *are* true, then she can't make that truth ugly. Do you understand? All the ugliness—it's in her soul. It's not in you guys unless you let it be."

A sort of hope flickered across Kellan's face, and he turned it to Isaiah. "That's true," he said wistfully.

Isaiah blinked hurt brown eyes at him. "My dad…."

"My folks are…." Kellan shivered. "They'll be a mess too. But it's like he said. It's only bad if we let it be bad to *us*."

Isaiah looked at Larx for the first time in the conversation. "It's not just the rumors," he confessed. "She says it like… 'if.' 'If you guys are like this, then I'd have to gut you like a fish.'"

They both looked ill.

"It's violent," Kellan said bluntly. "I mean…." He smiled like he needed to remind Larx of this. "We're football players. We get hitting and charging and power stuff, right?"

"But not this," Larx said, appalled. "Okay. Guys, look." He glanced around at the empty classroom and thought hard about how to handle this.

First things first—the girl was bullying, and that couldn't be allowed.

"I'm going to email the district psychologist to come talk to her—and her parents. I'm leaving your names out of it, but it needs to go beyond me. Has she put any of this stuff in print?"

"No," Isaiah said. "But she's said it to both of us—we did what you said, Larx. Neither of us has been alone with her."

Larx's stomach muscles were tightened against the upset. This was not good—not for these guys, not for Julia, and not for the school.

"She'll know," Isaiah said, but not like he was afraid. "She'll know it was us."

"That she will. Which makes what you two do next *very* important."

They looked at him hungrily, and he pinched the bridge of his nose.

"You've got two choices. Choice one: skulk around, act ashamed, stop talking to each other, and live your lives afraid that everything you do is going to draw attention to you in ways you don't like. And that's whether the rumors are true or whether they're not, do you understand?"

They both nodded, and he breathed a sigh of relief. Nobody had said it. Nobody had used the words *gay* or *bi* or *two boys in love*. But they were all on the same page.

"What's choice two?" Kellan asked, obviously not liking choice one at all.

"Choice two is that you own it. Do you guys think there's anything *wrong* with what she's saying? Or is it just the way she's saying it?"

"I hate it that she makes it dirty," Isaiah said, a level of hatred and desperation in his voice that Larx could well agree with.

"So if you want to own the rumors before she lets them loose, you could take all her power away," he said, voice level. "Right now all she's got is things she can say behind your back. If you can find some 'Straight but not narrow' T-shirts, go for it. I understand Target is selling. Join the GSA and talk about how to make people not afraid. We need straight people there, right?"

He smiled at them, stomach still clenched.

Kellan's eyes grew bright and red-rimmed, and he wiped at them with the palm of his hand.

Isaiah grabbed Kellan's other hand and pulled in a shuddery breath. "Larx?"

"Yeah?"

"We're not straight."

Larx nodded and shrugged, his own eyes a little bright too. "Good for you," he said, sincerity in his voice. "Good for you both."

Isaiah used his free hand to wipe his face, and Larx took the box of student-donated Kleenex and offered it to them both.

"Pull up a chair," he said. "We can talk. I'll write you a pass to your next class."

They ignored him, because they were kids. Kellan turned in Isaiah's arms and began to sob like a child.

Larx very quietly got up. He paused by the boys and said, "Come get me in my office when you're ready. I'm going to shut the door."

He hated himself for that. Because he wanted to be in that room, hugging and protecting—the father in him demanded it.

But he couldn't protect them if he was called to the carpet on sexual assault charges, and of all people, Larx knew that was a real possibility, especially if the boys' parents weren't on board.

Larx had never really considered himself a grown-up before, but as the door snicked shut behind him—locked from the outside but not from within—he heard the cynical sound of covering his ass.

"YOU DID what?" Yoshi asked, appalled.

"I let them get their shit together," Larx muttered. "The door was open, right? 'Cause it was a nice day outside. So I closed the door and left them alone."

The guys had come in a half an hour later, pale but composed, and asked for a pass to their next class.

"Do you want to talk?" he asked delicately.

"No, sir," Isaiah said, looking at Kellan for confirmation this time. "We have a plan. Don't worry. You've...." He swallowed and smiled with all the bravado in his young soul. "You've been a big help. We've got the rest of it handled. We can carry ourselves like men, don't worry."

Larx opened his mouth to say... *everything*. That there was nothing cowardly about not wanting the world in their business. That their lives were their own. But he knew that was wrong—wrong that it wasn't true, wrong to let them think that's all it was. But Isaiah and Kellan had just shaken his hand and walked away. For a moment Isaiah squeezed Kellan's shoulder, and Kellan leaned into him, and then Isaiah dropped his hand and the moment was gone. Two football players off to win the big game.

And now Yoshi was—rightly—reminding him that he might have done too much.

"I told them they could live in fear and act like they did something wrong or they could own it. I went in with the assumption that they were straight!" he said, defensive, hating himself because he'd been hoping they would come out, hoping it would make things better in the long run.

Knowing his own life would have been both easier and harder if he had.

"Look, I'm not saying you were *wrong*, Larx. I'm saying did you do anything that left you unprotected?"

"No," Larx said adamantly. "The door was open until I left them. I told them nothing personal. All of my statements were predicated on them being straight until they said otherwise." If anyone knew what he could be legally held accountable for, it was Larx.

"Did you hug them? Squeeze a shoulder?"

"Draw them into an ancient gay naked tribal dance?" Larx snapped. "No, Yoshi! I can't protect them if I don't keep my job!"

"I'm sorry," Yoshi said, rubbing his hand over his mouth. "I'm sorry. It's just so dangerous—I don't care what the law says. Laws like that are being overturned every day."

"Look, you're missing the point. The point is that girl is making physical threats—"

"Against two big football players!"

"Against two guys who play by the rules!" Larx protested. "I *ran* with the bad kids, Yoshi. Don't let your sexism blind you to this girl. Kids like her are dangerous—kids who feel powerless especially." That's why it was often the girls—misogyny did horrible things to people, and being told you had no power or no say in your life led people to learn tricky, underhanded behaviors to pull whatever power they had.

Julia was a classic case, which was no consolation at all when she was threatening two kids Larx wanted to ship off to Gaytopia so they could grow up safe and happy.

"What are we supposed to do about her, Larx? Lock her up?"

Yes. Lock her up so she can't take her ugly, spoiled heart out on the innocent children I'm supposed to be caring for.

"I've called the district psychologist and contacted Heather—"

"Perkins? The head of the board?"

"Yeah. I told her that the Olson kid is threatening to spread rumors about two football players if one of them didn't date her, and asked for permission to address bullying at the in-school rally tomorrow."

"Really?" Yoshi asked, running his hands through his fine black hair until it spiked up, filled with static. "How'd that go over?"

"Well, Becky is coming in tomorrow morning for a meeting with the kid and her mother. And Heather said she's getting back to me. If she doesn't get back to me by the rally, I'm taking it as a yes."

Yoshi let out a growl. "God, Larx, you're going to lose your fucking job!"

Larx grunted. "Yeah. Yeah, I just might. But you know what? At least I know the consequences. At least I know what I'm playing for, right?"

Yoshi sank down in the seat across from him, burying his face in his arms like a fifth grader. "You shouldn't have to do this again," he said after a moment. Yoshi had rather dense black eyebrows, and they looked like they were having a war over his eyes.

"You know my friend? The one who got caught in the witch hunt?" Larx asked, remembering this with such clarity it was like it got beamed into his head by satellite.

"Yeah?"

"She lived in fear for a month or two—she did. Taught straight out of the anthology, didn't make up her own shit. But you had to know Dana. She had this way of introducing literature—like, you *lived* it. And she was talking about *Hamlet* one day, and she told me she was losing the kids. This play she thought was just… the be-all and end-all of her subject, and everything in the textbook was dry as dust. And it hit her. 'What the hell am I here for?'"

"What'd she do?" Yoshi asked. Well, Yoshi loved *Hamlet* too.

"She put the text down and said, 'Y'all, what do you think of these friends of Hamlet's? Rosencrantz and Guildenstern?' and her kids just looked at her. And then she said, 'Guys! If *your* friends just told you they were reporting all your shit to *your* stepdad, how happy would *you* be?'"

Yoshi laughed a little. "A point I try to make every year—without the word *shit*."

"Well, this was an inner-city school, Yosh. And most of the kids were entranced. The witch hunters tittered, said, 'Talk about inappropriate!' but you know what Dana told me?"

"What?"

Larx leaned forward. "She told me that *Hamlet* was her cross to die on. If she didn't get this one thing across to her kids, she'd consider herself a failure."

Yoshi took a deep breath and nodded. "If we don't protect these two boys—"

Larx nodded back. "What in the hell are we here for?"

THAT NIGHT he had a talk with Christiana while Olivia was on speakerphone.

"Really?" Olivia asked, but she didn't sound mad. "You ready to do this again, Dad?"

"No," he replied glumly, looking at Christiana. "I'm not. But—"

"But he can't let her win!" Christiana burst out. "Livvie, this chick is... she's *evil*. I mean, she killed *Bruce*!"

"Bruce is *dead*!" Livvie crackled back, horrified. "Why didn't anyone tell me Bruce was dead?" Her voice faded, as if she'd turned her head to talk with someone at her end. "Not Springsteen, asshole, my class's pet snake!"

Larx and Christi caught eyes and snickered in spite of the grimness of the situation, and Olivia's next remark was obviously addressed to them. "We're behind you, Dad," she said softly. When she spoke, Larx could imagine her wrapping the end of her brown hair around her finger like she had as a little girl when she was thinking. "Daddy, uh, how is this going to affect... you know. That thing you haven't told me yet because you're not ready for anyone to know."

"You guys!" he complained, mortified.

"You knew," Christi said, completely unrepentant. "I told you. You knew."

"Yes, but you were supposed to pretend not to until I told you!"

Olivia's rich laughter rolled over the phone, warming Larx in spite of his embarrassment. "Daddy, we're fine with it. *We* approve." Her voice dropped then, the voice of the adult he'd raised. "But does *he* approve?"

"We'll know tomorrow," he said with a sigh. "Every morning, asscrack of dawn."

"And all you do is run?" Olivia asked, the wrinkled nose apparent through her voice alone. "Dad… dude. You've got to fix that."

"Hey, I'm going on a sleepover tomorrow," Christiana said. "Tonight too, if I can swing it. I'm doing my part."

"Good job. I'm proud of you. Now Dad, you need to step up and go get laid."

Larx groaned. "Nobody gave either of you permission to grow up. I didn't sanction this. There will be no meddling with my love life from here on out, do we understand each other?"

He couldn't talk anymore. They were laughing too loud to hear him.

Olivia signed off, and Larx was left in that strangely content quiet of him and his youngest daughter. For a moment he tried to invest himself in his book—a Karen Rose mystery romance—but frankly the lead villain was way too much like his ex-wife. He just couldn't do it. He set his book down and pinched the bridge of his nose.

"Dad, she needs to be stopped," Christi said, like she'd been waiting for him to protest.

"This could have some really shitty consequences for your social life," he said, because that mattered. You make promises to your children—safety, security, food, a future to the best of your ability to provide. Fun if you could manage it, the occasional Happy Meal, toys not *just* on their birthdays or Christmases, and big hugs when they broke their hearts. And if you could possibly help it, you promised to not let your social views destroy your child's chance at a normal, happy childhood.

Larx had already fucked this up once. He really didn't want to do it again.

"My social life is fine," Christi said, complacent. "Me and Schuyler have made out twice. It was sort of awesome. We may make out again. We may even get to third base—but don't tell her parents that. The point is, I don't want Julia Olson up in my face while I'm necking with my girlfriend—or screaming in my face if I break up with her and decide to go for a guy next semester."

Larx tried to hear his own thoughts over the squealing of his brain brakes. He partially succeeded. "You and Schuyler?"

"Yeah. Have you seen her? I mean…." Christi nodded. "Hot. Super hot. I looked up this summer and realized her ass was like… dayum. Anyway, you're not just making it safe for Isaiah and Kellan—"

"I never said their names!" he told her, panicked.

"Dad, please. Don't worry—confidential, just like Uncle Yoshi and Uncle Tane. But see? You're making it safer for them too. You're making it safer for me and Schuyler, 'cause I really wanted to go to homecoming with her but she was too afraid."

"You didn't think to tell me this?" he asked, brain still a little scrambled.

Her bravura disappeared. "Are you okay with it?"

"Of course!" How could he not be? "It's just…." He felt his lower lip wobble. "You're growing so fast."

And this time, instead of rolling her eyes at him like she usually did, she got up and plopped down next to him on the couch, leaning against him while he threw his arm around her shoulders. "I want to be your baby forever," she said, probably just to humor him. He didn't care. He needed humoring, this night in particular.

He kissed her temple. "You will be," he promised, fighting the burn in his eyes.

"I'm not scared," she told him, her voice a little sad. "But I know you are. Don't worry. Nobody has to know."

Larx laughed humorlessly. "Aaron does," he said.

"Is that the part that scares you?"

"Yeah."

LARX WOKE up early, logy from lack of sleep. After trying to nap for an hour, he gave it up and started running early. By the time Aaron came out of his house, Larx had run the loop once and was ready to do it again, just to calm his jitters.

"What's up?" Aaron started stretching while Larx ran in place, trying to keep warm.

"Uh… you remember the Olson kid?"

Aaron listened while he stretched, and then listened as they ran, and then thought silently as they continued to run. With no playing around, no stopping to kiss behind an outbuilding, none of the usual distractions, they were done about twenty minutes early.

Larx paused, waiting for him to say something. Anything. Tell him they should cool it for a while as Larx tried to flush his career down the toilet one more time. Tell him they should forget it entirely. Tell him he was a stupid asshole for letting history repeat itself.

Tell him—

"Baby, come inside. You're exhausted. Let me get you breakfast and drive you home, okay?"

"What?" Larx asked, feeling dumb.

"Breakfast. Coffee. You've been rambling for the entire run." Aaron grabbed his hand and the jitters drained out of his body, replaced by a sense of calm he didn't know he needed.

"I was just… you needed to know," Larx said, certain this had been his motivation.

"*You* needed to know," Aaron said perceptively, pulling Larx through his backyard, past the pool house Larx was desperately jealous of, past an empty dog run, and in through a rather extensive back porch, complete with overhead misters for the sometimes savage heat of the summer.

"I needed to know what? Damn, Deputy, this is a nice place."

Aaron pulled off his hat as they entered. "Caro's parents have money," he said quietly. "They helped with the down payment."

"And you never asked me over to swim? Seven years, Deputy—I'm depressed."

Aaron rolled his eyes. "If I'd seen you in a pair of Speedos, my life would have changed. I wasn't ready for it then."

Oh. "Are you…?" Larx closed his eyes. "Are you…?"

"Ready for it now?" Aaron turned then, while Larx was right on his heels. They were suddenly face-to-face, and hot and sweaty or not, Larx yearned so badly just to fall into his arms and be held. Just a moment, another grown-up assuring him that he was doing his best, even if he wasn't doing it right.

"Are you?"

"Yeah. C'mere."

Oh yeah. Larx melted into his arms, into his wide chest, as they kissed with chilled lips and hot mouths. Larx shivered hard, aware of how cold he'd been since the morning before.

The kiss wasn't sex so much as it was comfort, and Larx had pulled away and was resting his head on Aaron's shoulder before he heard the rustle behind them.

"Uh, Dad?"

Larx startled, but Aaron just tightened his arms around Larx's shoulders. "Kirby, was there something you wanted to know?"

If Larx hadn't been so close to his heart, to feel it pound against his ear, he never would have guessed how much this scared him.

After about three, four million years, Kirby said, "Yeah. Probably lots. But it can wait. Larx, can I talk to your daughter about this?"

Larx laughed for a moment. "Only if you want to know way more about my life than you ever bargained for."

Another eternal, thought-provoking silence. "I'll ask anyway. But don't worry, Dad. I'll… I'm not going to go tell the school or anything. Just… you know."

"I expect the third degree," Aaron said, finally looking over his shoulder. "And I promise. Every question. As honestly as I can."

"But right now I need to go get my backpack together. I hear ya."

Larx straightened up. "I'll run on—"

"We'll have coffee and breakfast ready when you're done. I'll leave early so Larx can get home and change."

"Deal."

Kirby disappeared as promised, and Larx was left with no privacy, no dignity, and no idea what to do next.

"Why'd you do that?" he rasped, voice weak.

"Because now you don't have Kirby as an excuse to pull away."

Larx blinked. "That wasn't why I—"

Aaron turned toward the kitchen, keeping his face averted. "Sure it was. You said it about six times." He strode to the coffee maker and turned it on, then scooped coffee into a filter from a can by the machine. Larx reached his hand out for the carafe, and Aaron gave it to him without thinking. Larx filled it up, still waiting for him to finish that sentence.

Finally, "What? What did I say?"

Aaron finished filling the machine and set the pot on the warmer. "You said 'I get it if you want to bail.'"

Larx took a deep breath and let it out. "You just told your kid."

"Not bailing."

"You shouldn't have—"

"Not bailing," Aaron said, voice hard. "Not bailing. I know what you expected from me, Larx. It's not what's happening. Not. Bailing."

Larx bit his lip and nodded. "Understood. But why? Two weeks—"

"No. Seven years I had to look at you and wonder. Seven years too long. You and me were locked in stone from our first kiss. Just took me until this morning to see it. There's muffin mix in the cupboard. Can you—"

"They'll be done by the time you're done with your shower." Muffin mix, oil, and an egg. Larx could make it in his sleep.

"Good. I'll be down in twenty." Aaron's mouth was compressed flat, a hard line of anger and hurt, and Larx didn't know how to fix it—not with Aaron's boy in his room and school in less than two hours.

"I'm sorry?" Or confused. Sorry worked, though.

"So am I. Sorry you ever thought you had to do this alone." Aaron started for the landing and the stairs then, but he paused as he passed Larx and pressed a hard kiss on Larx's mouth, one that left Larx in no confusion at all.

"Oh," he said stupidly as Aaron pulled back.

"Yeah. That." And Aaron disappeared up the stairs, leaving Larx to pick up the pieces of his brain and start breakfast.

HE HAD warm muffins and coffee ready by the time Aaron came downstairs dressed in his uniform. There was something very dependable and solid about Aaron in khakis with his department-issue jacket and baseball cap. Something that screamed "I will take care of you!"

Larx wasn't sure what to do with that. He'd assumed all of that capability would be spent on Aaron's kids, because that's where it needed to be. He'd had no idea there could be some left over for Larx. He obviously had to reassess the man, because underestimating him had hurt Aaron badly.

"You look good," he said with a half smile. "I didn't used to think uniforms were a thing for me."

"And now?" Aaron bit his lip shyly, and Larx had the curious sensation of being out in the ocean while a giant wave built in front of him. He could either stay where he was, waiting to be obliterated, or he could swim hard, swim fast, breach the wave's crest, and ride it in.

His breath came in fits and bursts in his chest and his mind said, *I can't I can't I can't....*

And then his heart gave a giant throb of *You already are.*

And just like that, he was beyond the scary part, he was on top of the wave and riding the surf in with an exhilaration he'd never felt, not even bungee jumping, not even skydiving, not even in the middle of sex with that one guy he'd really liked right before he got his credential and started dating Alicia.

"Oh my God," he whispered, staring at Aaron and feeling lost and found and hungry, glutting himself on Aaron's bemused face at the same time he was smacking himself for his bollixed timing.

"What?" Aaron said, walking past him to grab his muffin and the aluminum mug Larx had retrieved from the dish rack and filled with coffee.

"I never knew how this felt," Larx said, too stunned to keep his inner monologue actually inside. "I mean I thought this was what you felt when you held your baby for the first time." Because it was suddenly familiar. "But you get a chance with babies. You can win them over. You can be the best dad you can be and hope that does it for them. But you're fully formed. I don't know how to make you feel the same way. This is terrifying."

"Larx?"

"I've got to go," Larx muttered, and then his words filtered down to his brain and he looked at the microwave in the corner of Aaron's white-tiled kitchen. "I really do. I'm the principal, I need to be there before the kids get there. It's the rules."

Larx had never been great with rules, but that one he got.

"Dad, we ready to go? I hung out in my room and texted Christiana—she assures me my world will not end."

"Yeah, come get a muffin and some coffee," Aaron said, sounding not so sure. Suddenly he was in Larx's space, gazing into his eyes, warm fingers on his chin. Larx had always thought Aaron had pretty eyes—blue, like oceans. "Larx, are you okay?"

I just fell in love with you. I'd rather fall off a building. I'm frightened to the pit of my balls.

"Great," Larx rasped. "Peachy. Splendid." He smiled with all his teeth. "Kirby, you said you texted Christi?"

"Yeah. She's weirdly chill about it."

"She's had a while to get used to the idea," Larx admitted. "I came out to them when we moved here. So it's okay if you're sort of weirded out." He looked apologetically at Aaron and took a few steps back. "Feel free to grill me like a cheese sandwich if you need to," he said, some of his equilibrium returning. This is what he did. He talked to kids. He interpreted the world for them. He made it not so scary or confusing as they grew. He could do this.

"Yeah, well, I told Christi I'd be riding to school with you guys—you're both taking the same car today, right?"

"Yeah," Larx said. He took a few more steps away, biting his lip as the gap between him and Aaron grew. "We're at your service, a crash course in gay/straight association, coming up."

"Deal," Kirby said. "I am about to become enlightened."

Larx smiled at him, and Kirby became a real person in the room. "Well, I promise, it's just like science. The more open your mind is, the less it'll hurt."

Kirby laughed and they made it to the car.

The drive to Larx's house via the forestry road was tense and quick, and as they pulled up behind the garden alongside the house, Aaron nodded to Kirby. "Go on inside, son. Are we okay for now?"

"Course. Just 'cause you've gone gay doesn't mean you're not my father."

He slid out of the car, and Aaron laughed, relief showing on his face clear as frost. Larx had a hold of the door handle and was about to make his move when Aaron stopped him with the touch of his hand.

"What?" he asked.

Larx flickered a look at him. "I've got five minutes to shower, shit, and shave, Aaron—I've got to run."

Aaron's grunt of frustration was so classically male that Larx relented a little. He turned in the seat and kissed Aaron's cheek. "I'll be at the school all day," he said quietly. "From seven thirty to the last ember of the bonfire. Any time I see you then, that'll be… like sprinkles on ice cream, okay?"

"I'll show," Aaron said. A brief smile flickered across his lean lips. "But that doesn't mean I can't wait for the smaller one, in your backyard. Especially now that the kids know."

Oh. Wow. "Like a date," Larx said. "Like… like, if Kirby isn't too weird—"

"Sleepover." Aaron grinned. "Damn. Yes. There's a perk! I'd almost forgotten."

Larx started to laugh. "God, we're getting old. Remember when sex was a *priority* and not a perk?" He went to leave and Aaron stopped him again, this time with a kiss. Ah… wine before work, never a good idea.

"Larx?" Aaron said throatily.

"Yeah?" He smelled so good. Clean with some aftershave and leather from his jacket.

"Sex with you is a priority."

Larx smiled and *finally* got out of the SUV.

HE MANAGED the three *S*'s in record time, probably because he'd eaten a bran muffin a half an hour earlier, and he was dressed in jeans and a tie and sport coat, driving the kids in the minivan and heading for the school only five minutes later than usual.

"So," Kirby said as soon as they were on the road, "what are your intentions toward my father?"

"I'm going to kidnap him and brainwipe him until he joins the ranks of the unholy public educators under my sway."

Kirby guffawed. "Okay, it's hard to be weird about this when you are obviously the same smartass teacher I've had for three years of high school. Seriously."

Larx took a deep breath and looked apologetically at Christi, who seemed highly amused by the whole thing. "Kirby, has your father dated *anyone* since your mother passed away? That you know of? Has he introduced *anyone* to you and your sisters and said, 'This is someone important in my life'?"

"No," Kirby said quietly.

"Neither have I, since my divorce."

Christiana patted his arm like she had as a child when he'd been overwhelmed by being the dad. Olivia had done the same thing.

Kirby sighed behind them. "So I wouldn't know about this if it wasn't serious. That's what you're saying?"

Larx shrugged. "I have to worry about my job. So does your dad. It shouldn't be a big deal that way, but it is. So yeah."

"That's fucked-up, pardon me saying," Kirby said after a moment. "I mean, Dad's probably freaking out enough as it is, but... it should be a family thing. Shouldn't be a... a *job* thing."

Larx half laughed. "You are preaching to the preacher here, sir." He pulled into the school parking lot, half-aware that he'd been going a little faster than normal because his body was still on rush.

"So, do I start calling you Dad?"

Larx stopped short as he pulled into the parking space, and both kids broke up laughing. "Christ, no," he snapped. "Even the girls call me Larx."

He parked and killed the ignition, then turned to Kirby with hope. "Are you going to be okay?" he asked. "This was not how your dad meant to tell you. I was sort of freaking out over something and he...."

"He picked making you happy over keeping me in the dark," Kirby said perceptively. "That's… that's Dad. He dealt with my sisters' periods the same way."

"Your dad's the most straightforward guy I've ever met," Larx said, realizing it was true as he said it. "I… I wouldn't want to hurt him for anything."

Kirby grunted. "Okay. I… uh, am still really confused? But mostly I think that's gonna be in my own head for a while. Is that okay?"

"Course. You ready for today's test?"

"Augh!" And it was clear he'd forgotten completely about it.

"You guys go study—Christi, here's my keys. If anyone asks…."

"I stole them from you and you're tied up in a closet with chloroform," she said dutifully. District policy was no kids with keys. Larx's policy was that if he couldn't give his school keys to his daughter, he wouldn't give her car keys or his credit card number either.

"That's my girl." He closed his eyes and sighed. "So, I've got an entire other thing going on this morning. If it spills into class time, I'll send someone in to proctor the exam."

"Wow," Christi said as they got out of the car. "This and the game and the bonfire? It's like you're paying for stuff you did as a kid."

He thought carefully. "Yeah. Ouch. That means it might get way worse."

The kids laughed as they made their way to the classroom, and Larx straightened his tie. Was gonna be a day.

Flame

LARX WAS talking so fast Aaron could barely follow him over the Bluetooth speaker in his vehicle.

"Can you be*lieve* that shit?" he raged. "The school shrink says she's a fucking time bomb, and Heather fucking Perkins says she can cheer the game and participate in the dance and… and oh my God! I was going to cancel the bonfire. I was going to do it, but *no*, Perkins just sucks up to that girl's mother and… holy fucking Jesus, Aaron. Isaiah told her he couldn't take her to the dance over lunch, and both the guys were looking… well, better than they have all week. I don't know what they have planned, but Julia… she just sat there looking all blue-eyed and innocent, and her *mother*…."

Aaron shivered with him in sympathy. He'd met Whitney Olson before. Petite, dark-haired, and blue-eyed, she had at first appeared "adorable." Aaron had been at a sheriff's department fundraiser the Olsons had sponsored, and as they'd stood in line for canapés, he'd watched her interact with several of the town's most prominent citizens.

They'd smiled and told jokes and asked after each other's children.

And to a one, every person who walked up to her and initiated conversation had been afraid.

He'd watched Fred Olson—the owner of the local grocery store and apparently a distant cousin of her husband's—walk up and say, "Heya, Whitney. You'll be relieved to know we remedied that little problem with stocking your favorite wine. Cost us a pretty penny, but, you know, for our favorite customer, it's worth it."

"Oh?" she'd said, looking "adorable" and surprised. "You went to all that trouble for me? I feel so bad about that. I don't even shop in your store that often."

Fred hadn't even blinked, but Aaron had read the waves of homicidal rage boiling off him, and imagined the conversation that preceded this one had been seven shades of awful. And Fred wasn't the only merchant or teacher she'd slighted. Aaron watched as she'd actually approached Larx's friend Nancy Pavelle, and even then, before he and Larx had gotten closer, he'd held his breath.

"Nancy, so good to see you here. I didn't know you came to functions like this."

"Well, my husband and my brother are both policemen down in the city, Whitney. This is our way of making sure our men up here are taken care of."

"Policemen. How wonderful. You know, I was talking to my daughter the other day, and she could not say enough good things about you—"

"That's funny, because when I told her I wasn't changing her grade, every word out of her mouth was of the four-letter variety. I believe I left a message on your phone about that after I gave her detention."

Aaron had been so frightened by the venom in Whitney's stare then that *he'd* stepped back.

"You didn't change that grade?" Whitney said, expression fixed. "Why have you not changed that grade? Julia assures me she's made up the work."

"Your daughter offered me a stolen packet of work in someone else's handwriting, Whitney. And again, I phoned your home, I phoned your cell, and I sent a copy of the referral to your house."

And that's when Aaron had seen the woman get to work. She'd stepped close enough to Nancy that Aaron was a breath away from tackling her to see if she held a weapon. He hadn't been close enough to hear what Whitney had said, but he *had* treasured Nancy's response.

"My brother is open about that part of his past, Mrs. Olson. He's never tried to hide it. His customer base doesn't come from Colton, so telling the world about the substance abuse in his past isn't going to change a goddamned thing about his business. But trying to blackmail me does make me think less of you."

So Aaron was prepared to hear the worst about this woman even before Larx called him up and gave him an earful. But it sure did make Larx's earful a lot scarier.

"And Julia's mother—at one point, she looked at me and said, 'You made me cancel my trip to Tahoe for this?'"

"What did you say?"

"I said, 'Lady, I probably saved you thousands of dollars in damage. Half the school was planning to attend your daughter's little party this weekend, and I bet you would have blamed us for that too!'"

Aaron gasped, impressed by Larx's courage—or foolhardiness. Either one. "And?"

"And Julia shrieked, 'Who told!' which makes her dumber than a box of dog shit, because I didn't even mention the date because it was pure speculation on our parts, and her mother? Her mother said, 'I was aware of that. Do you think the party would have been unsupervised?' And Julia looked like she wanted to cry, because obviously it was supposed to be unsupervised, and now it will be *fully* supervised, and on the one hand, I think that's awesome, but on the other?"

"You don't want her near your school during homecoming."

"Either of them. Isaiah did the breakup during lunch today, publicly, which is good, because—"

"Witnesses," Aaron said, nodding as he turned left on the road that wrapped around nearby Mustang Lake. The rich people—the Olsons and other prominent members of the town—lived in the big houses way over on the north shore, and they usually had their own private security. But there were also cabins out here—some of them occupied, some of them summer or winter rentals—and he liked to keep an eye on things just in case squatters came to live. It was not unheard of, and he had a list of who lived where so he could call if need be.

"But it's bad because—"

"Troll-baiting," Aaron supplied, still thinking having the witnesses was better than not pissing off the already psychotic teenager.

"Yeah. So God knows what she'll do—and you know what? We're not doing her any favors. Her mom just took away her one independent decision, and she looked like she was ready to cry. And now she has to go home and live with that woman? I'd probably be begging for the days when Mommy was gone and I could lay the football team too!"

Aaron had to laugh. It was good to know he was on Larx's list of trusted confidants—and it was easy to tell. Uncensored Larx was like raw whiskey: only for the strong of heart and clearheaded.

"What about your boys?" Aaron asked, scanning from the road to the crystal blue of the lake and back again. There was something floating out there just beyond this next inlet. Aaron parked the car on the deep shoulder, grabbed his radio and his phone, and, still talking to Larx, ventured along the spit of land that bordered the inlet to check it out. It might have been a log, in which case he'd call old Harold, who had a fishing dory and friends with nets. They weren't official Fish and Game, but they liked to patrol the lake and keep it clean of debris that could hurt the folks who used the lake.

"The boys are… well, they looked happy after school," Larx said fretfully. He'd told Aaron he was multitasking—talking while helping to set up the bonfire. Aaron had to trust that the only other people listening to this conversation were teachers, because damn if this boy did not swear like a sailor when he was riled. Aaron sort of liked it—it was as close to a bad boy as he ever wanted to venture, and on Larx it was deadly attractive. "And this is their last football game of the regular season. If they win, they'll make it to state. If they lose, well, Isaiah still has a partial ride to most of the state colleges."

"What about Kellan?"

"I'm seeing about getting him some special ed scholarships. He's got ADHD like fuckin' *whoa*, and given his grades and sports participation, he's a poster boy. But mostly I just want to get the two of them out of here to the college of their choice so they can be whoever the fuck they want."

"Yeah," Aaron said absently. "I think that's a good idea. Uh… oh. Oh crap."

Oh no. He'd seen this before in the water—had worked a few cases like this, actually. The pale form bobbing out there wasn't a log, and it wasn't a fish, and it wasn't an upended boat.

And it wasn't human anymore either.

Fuck.

"Oh crap what?" The sharpness in Larx's voice was reassuring—it meant that for all he had a full plate of his own, he was going to be able to be there for Aaron when he needed someone.

And Aaron would need someone, because this sort of thing was always rough.

"Larx, I'm going to have to call you back. I think we've got a situation here. I'll see you at the game or the bonfire at the very least, okay?"

"Yeah, Aaron. Uh, be careful? Mindful? Whatever?"

Aaron took a deep breath and centered himself on Larx's concern. Because he hadn't had that in a long time. Had, in fact, spent most of his energy reassuring the kids so they didn't ever think about how Daddy's job could be dangerous.

It was nice to have someone worry. He could admit it—especially now.

"Will do, baby. I'll catch you later."

He hung up then and pulled his radio off his belt. "Dispatch, this is Deputy Aaron George calling from the north end of Mustang Lake, about two miles south of Pinto Drive. Do you read me?"

"We got ya, Aaron. What's up?"

"Could you notify Eamon and Cheryl of Search and Rescue? We've got a dead body in the water not far from the highway split, over."

"Oh crap." Angie's voice—roughened by years of smoking and lots of whiskey after hours—grew almost unbearably husky. "How bad is it?"

From just off the edge of the lake, Aaron couldn't see much, especially because the naked, bloated corpse was facedown. But he could see the big missing chunk of bone and matter that should have been the back of the head.

"It's pretty fuckin' bad, Ange. You need to get on the horn ASAP, ya hear?"

"Roger that. Hang tight, Aaron, we've got backup coming."

Aaron signed off and firmed up his resolve—and his stomach. It was time to put on his Kevlar gag reflex and act like a law enforcement officer instead of a besotted suitor.

Dammit.

HE MADE it to the end of the game, arriving just in time to see the Colton Mustangs defeat their sister school, the Tyack Turtles, at a heartbreaking 17-14.

Aaron walked up to where Larx stood, by the home game bleachers this time, and gave him a nod.

Larx nodded back, brown eyes thoughtful. "I heard about the body," he said, voice low. "Bad?"

Aaron nodded, without words. "Details later," he said tersely.

"Loud and clear." Larx kept his eyes focused on the setup for the field goal, but his voice was compassionate.

"How's things here?"

"Tense." He nodded to where the cheerleaders stood at attention, smiles in place, eyes focused on the game. Julia was a carbon copy of her mother, dark hair, blue eyes, charming little cheeks. Her smile was like a death rictus, and Aaron noted there was at least one extra person's worth of space between her and the two girls on either side of her.

"I can see that," Aaron said. "How about the boys?"

Larx's smile showed quiet pride. "Isaiah scored both touchdowns," he said. "Barring injury in the championship games, the two of them should have a good start at the very least."

At that moment Christiana walked by, hand in hand with a tiny blonde waif of a girl who had decided curves.

"Heya, Christi." Aaron tilted his head at her, touching the brim of his hat.

Christi smiled but then looked at her dad anxiously. "Dad, uh, you know Schuyler."

"Hiya, Schuyler—good to see you."

It was like Larx had made his voice extra warm and paternal, and Aaron looked closely at them both to see what was up.

"Hi, Principal Larkin," Schuyler squeaked. "It's uh, it's good to… uh—"

Only Aaron heard his tiny sigh of patience. "I'm so glad to hear you and Christi are dating," Larx said, and Christi met Aaron's surprised eyes with a sardonic expression far beyond her years.

"Oh," he mouthed at her.

"Yup," she mouthed back.

"Really?" Big blue porcelain-doll eyes batted wetly at Larx, and Larx winked at her in return.

"Course, honey. It's all good."

Schuyler smiled nervously, and Christi tugged on her hand. "Christi!" Larx called. "Am I going to see you at the bonfire tonight?"

Christi shook her head. "No—we're taking off after the game—I'll probably spend tonight at her house too!" she called before leading Schuyler up into the bleachers. They sat down looking cozy and sweet, and Aaron tried to wrap his mind around that.

"Really?" he asked, sotto voce.

"Apparently it was Colton's coming-out week," Larx replied, his lips twisted in amusement.

"I didn't get the memo."

"Gotta be on your toes, Deputy. These things are important."

Aaron shot him a fulminating glare, but at that moment, Craig Stevens kicked the field goal in, and the buzzer rang right after, and the two of them had better things to do.

IT TOOK much less time to clear out parents for this one. Larx had to leave Aaron and the other deputies to finish up, though, while he distributed flashlights to the participating staff members and sent everybody along the cross-country trail to the back of the school. They would cross Olson Road and take another trail to the bonfire clearing, where the pile of wood and tinder was waiting to be set ablaze.

Various clubs were selling hot chocolate and cider, the PTSA was selling hot dogs and cookies, and the quarterback and his chosen helpmate would be lighting the fire.

Traditions had their place.

Aaron was one of the folks bringing up the rear, so he had to hustle when the all-call on the radio hit.

"Uh, Larx, deputies, gonna need you guys to escort the team from the path to the bonfire. Can we do that?"

"Any reason why?" Larx's voice came across loud and clear.

"Isaiah and Kellan are, uh, gonna wanna make a sorta statement," Coach Jones said hesitantly. "The, uh, team is behind them, but we may need to make a show of solidarity?"

Aaron knew his eyes got big, and he started to rip through the trail in an effort to find Larx and join the other deputies and staff members before the football team got there.

Larx must have had the same idea, because he was flushed and breathless, waiting for Aaron when he broke into the clearing.

"So," Aaron panted. "You think?"

"I totally do."

"This'll be fun!"

"Oh Jesus," Larx said. "I'm so glad I suspended MacDonald."

"I'm so glad it's you and not Nobili," Aaron breathed. The football team came into the clearing then, and the whole school applauded. They were moving in a huddle with Kellan and Isaiah in the middle, but even with all those bundled-up bodies in the way, Aaron could see the boys were holding hands.

The cheering died down, and the school collectively held its breath, "Sweet Georgia Brown" playing loudly in the silence. Larx walked up to Coach Jones with a wireless mic, and the band cut off abruptly.

Larx whispered into Jones's ear, and the guy closed his eyes for a second and nodded. Okay. They were going to do this right.

"So," Jones said, looking at Larx, who nodded. "Our tradition has it that the high school quarterback lights the senior bonfire, and he gets to pick his helpmate. This year it's Kellan Corker and"— deep breath—"his boyfriend, wide receiver Isaiah Campbell."

For a moment even the crickets were still.

Then Larx, God bless him, started to whistle shrilly and applaud. The football team and high school staff joined him, and then, cued in by the adults around them, the high school students did the same.

They cheered.

They whistled and applauded and shouted "Way to go!" and "Sweet!" and "Congratulations!"

If there were any whispered epithets, any disgusted glances, those were the things that were hidden. The team parted and the boys walked hand in hand up to the bonfire, where Larx stood with a barbecue lighter and a long, thin piece of wood with a twist of paper on the end.

Aaron couldn't hear what Larx said, but Isaiah took the taper from him, and Kellan lit the paper on fire. Together they thrust the starter into the heart of the bonfire and stepped back as it caught.

And then, while the crowd cheered again, they kissed.

Forever locked in Aaron's mind, the silhouette of two boys kissing against the bonfire, old deadwood dying, new love set against the hope of new light.

If only it were that easy.

Larx waited until the kiss was over before walking up and shaking the boys' hands, and he was followed by Yoshi, and Yoshi by Nancy Pavelle. The rest of the staff followed—to a one, even the snotty little pisher who had been helping to ref the game last week.

Aaron looked around, trying to gauge the mood. The band was playing again—"Somewhere Over the Rainbow," because all band kids were apparently sarcastic assholes—and the rest of the kids seemed to have pulled into their cliques. He checked out the cheerleaders, who were running to gossip with the football players—probably about what the boys had said in the locker room and how the whole scene had gone down.

Julia was not among them. She was, in fact, standing in a corner, texting madly on her phone and wiping her eyes carefully with a tissue from her pocket. She had her back turned toward the bonfire completely, and for a moment, Aaron felt bad for her.

She was heartbroken, like any girl. In fact, she was probably in a lot of pain on a daily basis. Whatever had shaped her, the hammer hits must have been pretty brutal, because she seemed to lash out all the time, like a cornered animal.

But like with a cornered animal, any offers of help would be met with fangs and claws, and Aaron only had so much compassion to spare.

Aaron's musings were interrupted when Kirby walked out of the darkness, waving casually to the friends he'd been hanging out with.

"What do you think?" Kirby asked carefully, nodding to where the two boys were still being congratulated by staff and friends.

"I think the world's come a long way," Aaron replied, just as carefully.

"But not far enough." Kirby was good at reading his mind.

Aaron gave his son a troubled look. "I'm sorry. It's been sort of a... a bad day. I would love it if this was it for them. Like in a movie. The bonfire goes up, the crowd goes wild, fireworks, happy ever after, everybody gets a scholarship, hurrah!"

"Doesn't work like that," Kirby said, and Aaron threw his arm over his son's shoulders because his son still let him. If anybody knew that a kiss or a happy family or a beautiful moment was not the end-all of the matter, it would be the kid who'd waited outside in the rain for his mother to come get him on the day when she would never make it.

"I'm concerned is all." And not just for them.

"You want your own happy, right, Dad?"

"Yes," Aaron admitted. "Is that so wrong?"

"No."

God, Aaron was tired. He wasn't sure how Larx was still scuttling around like a rocket-fueled monkey, but Aaron had hauled a body out of the lake today, bloated and fish-eaten. A male by all appearances, wearing his boxer shorts only, and oh yeah, missing his face.

Retrieval had been messy and difficult and identification nearly impossible. They were asking a forensic pathologist to come up from Sacramento to help identify the remains because their coroner had no problem saying, "Nope, I don't have the skills."

Beyond the smell and the animal rot and ugliness of death, Aaron had been saddened by the waste. Suicide? Murder? Whatever—it had been senseless and violent and horrible. He wanted to protect his children from it. He wanted to protect *Larx* from it, and his children too. And that extended to the kids at the bonfire, the stupid, horny, happy, excited teenagers who were looking forward to a future that not even *they* could fathom.

"Dad?" Kirby said into the silence.

Aaron dropped his arm. "Sorry. Just got tired all of a sudden. Go." He made a shooing motion with his fingers. "Go play with the other kids, okay?"

Kirby nodded. "Yeah. Look, I can get home tonight by myself if you need to go back and sleep or something."

Aaron shook his head. "No—I told Larx I'd help him clean up. I'll probably be home after you. But check with me before you go, and I'll do the same."

Kirby nodded and stepped away, and Aaron went to find Larx.

He was surrounded by staff members, all of whom were smiling but none of whom were happy.

"Did you know they were going to do that?" Yoshi asked as Aaron walked up.

"Not a clue," Larx said, sounding like such a choirboy that Aaron had his suspicions.

"You knew it was something, right?" Nancy asked, eyes narrowed, and he shrugged, because she'd obviously hit home.

"Yeah. I knew it was something," Larx said. "I told them to own it or it was going to make their lives miserable. And they did. And now it's our job to have their backs."

"Course," Coach Jones said. He looked at his colleagues and rolled his eyes. "Gotta say, was a little proud to be part of this tonight. Making the school safe. Was like last week when we got all classy. I hope we can keep the good going, right?"

And finally Larx let some of his guard down. "Me too. But you guys know the crap is going to start tomorrow at the dance, and it's going to hit our phones in a big shitload. So, you know, maybe don't check your messages until Monday, 'cause we're going to need to save our strength."

"We should make a *pact*," Nancy said, and they all stuck their hands in the middle, because apparently most teachers were like Larx and hadn't matured since the seventh grade.

Aaron watched them all vow solemnly not to check their voicemail during the weekend before shouting, "*Break!*" into the smoke-scented night. Then they split up to wander the crowd like the good supervisors they were, and no surprise, Larx gravitated to Aaron's side.

Where he belonged.

"So," Aaron murmured, "that was unexpected."

"The break? No. That was just us."

"The full-fledged support."

Larx snorted. "Oh, it was pretty now. Wait until the parents start savaging us like dogs. And the school board is going to have something to say, trust me. No—I know it *looked* like 100 percent support, but if we're lucky, it was 60–40 at the split."

Aaron sucked air through his teeth. "Ouch."

Shrug. "They're scared, Aaron. Change is weird. Always has been. The one thing I do know is that they want what's best for the kids. And when you see something like we saw tonight?" Some of the armor dropped from his voice again. "Well, you think you know what the best thing is. But when you have a bunch of anxious parents screaming in your ear?"

"You start doubting your judgment," Aaron said, getting it. Cops couldn't afford that. There had to be confidence in every action, because the government gave you a gun and assumed you knew what in the hell you were doing with it. Teachers didn't have guns, they had their knowledge of human nature—and the belief that humans made mistakes.

He was suddenly fiercely glad that he was a cop.

"I know you get it," Larx agreed. "Sorry. Just what we do." Then, under the sound of merriment and the band playing Pink's "Just Give Me a Reason," he asked, "How bad was it?"

Aaron shuddered, and even though they couldn't touch, having him there was so... supportive. So warm. He used to come home from work and Caro would pour him a beer and they'd sit and talk about her day. Then she'd ask him, hesitantly, how bad it had been, and he'd gloss it over. But on the real bad days, she'd push, and he'd spill, and just knowing he wasn't in his own head alone with the awfulness had made it bearable.

"We don't have an ID yet," he said softly. "No face. Wasn't a shotgun either—hollow-point .45. Was…." He shuddered.

"Nightmarish," Larx said softly.

And then, to punctuate that thought, a scream shattered the darkness, shattered the hope around them.

Shattered their hearts.

Wildfire

"THE BATHROOMS!" Larx shouted, sprinting toward the edge of the firelight to the back end of the field. He'd had to sign the acquisitions form for three Porta-Johns, and he'd gone all out for the little pedestal with the water basin in front. He'd hung a battery-operated lamp from the pedestal because *he* wouldn't have wanted to be taking a crap back there in the dark, and it was easy to follow that beacon once they left the comforting orange of the fire.

Aaron sprinted at his heels, making sounds that might have been "Let me go first," but these were Larx's kids, and that was so not going to happen.

Larx got to the lamp and saw past it, to a figure struggling under the weight of a big, six-foot-plus limp body.

"Isaiah?"

From behind him, Kellan gave an anguished shriek. "*Zay?*"

Kellan and Aaron were at Larx's heels as he went to help the kid struggling under the body with the ungainly burden.

Joy Bradley was a tiny girl, muscular but short, and as soon as Larx got there to help her with Isaiah's body, she shrugged out from under the weight and left Larx and Aaron to help him to the ground.

He was breathing, but each breath brought a shallow rattle of blood from between his lips. As Larx searched his body for the cause, he found his entire stomach was a big bleeding wound, and that now all of them, Larx, Aaron, and a softly weeping Kellan, were covered in blood.

Kellan knelt at his head, touching his pale face with bloody hands and whispering to him, hoping to hear something back.

Larx looked at the destruction of skin and muscle and viscera and tried not to throw up. He was the grown-up here. His kids needed him.

"Aaron," he rasped, "call the troops. Nancy!" he hollered, and the blessed, blessed woman ran through the crowd, unbuttoning her flannel overshirt as she came. "Nancy, you've got the training, I'm going to get out of your way. Tell me what you need and I'll get it, okay?"

"More flannel for bandages," she stated tersely. "Water. Some to drink if he can. Blankets to keep him warm. One for Kellan too, 'cause the boy looks shocky. That's a start. Go, Larx, *now!*"

Larx had a mission. Oh, thank you, Nancy, he had something to *do*. Yoshi, go get water; Christiana, go get blankets; Kirby, round up flannel shirts and scarves. Everybody give their booty to Larx—he'd give the water to Kellan and have him try to moisten Isaiah's tongue. He'd have Kirby rip the flannel up into bandages and give them to Nancy as fast as he could tear. He'd wrap Kellan in a blanket and leave the boy to his quiet tears, keeping Isaiah calm. He'd move Nancy when the bandages were all placed, and cover Isaiah with a big, fuzzy pink blanket with Minnie Mouse on it, and then kneel by the boy's side and grab his hand, telling him it was all going to be okay, and he'd been brave tonight, and he had such a good future, and Kellan was right there, waiting to share it.

He'd squeeze that hand and make Isaiah squeeze it back until Aaron lifted him bodily off the ground and told him to move because the paramedics were there and it was their job now.

He'd wrap his arms around Kellan's sobbing body and hold him and hold him and hold him, aware that he was crying too, in public, surrounded by his kids, and he couldn't seem to stop.

Aaron stood there, a steadying hand on his shoulder, until Yoshi stepped forward and led Kellan away, telling Larx they were going to the hospital, and to meet them there. Aaron, Larx, and the rest of the teachers began the roundup, making sure kids had rides home or could call their parents. Eamon Mills showed up, his awkwardly buttoned uniform testament to a night spent in bed, probably grateful he was too old to deal with the high school bullshit and shocked and saddened about it now.

Eamon and Aaron conferred briefly and brought Larx into the circle. Aaron had to leave and follow the ambulance, and after a searching glance and a brief nod, he did just that.

Larx had never wanted to follow someone so badly in his life, not even when Alicia had to get a C-section with Christiana and they had Larx leave the room while they made the incision. But he couldn't leave—he was the grown-up. The teachers, the kids—they needed someone familiar, someone kind. The sheriff's department was the authority, the law. Larx was the order.

Still, he was relieved when, just as Eamon began to speak, his pocket buzzed from Aaron.

I'll keep you posted. Hang tight. Text me when you're done there.

"Deputy George?" Sheriff Mills asked.

Larx nodded. "Yessir. Told me he'd keep me posted on Isaiah."

"Well, we appreciate your staying here and making the kids feel safe. Now here's what we're going to do." With that, Eamon told him that he and three of the deputies were going to guard the entrance to the bonfire glade and check the kids out as they left while two others kept the parents out on the school side.

"You need to send a few teachers out front to tell the parents to wait, we're making sure all the kids are safe."

"They won't buy it," Larx said. "You should probably check them out in batches and send them through. Parents will wait if they know kids are coming out."

"That is a very good idea. Okay, then—you send your teacher reps out, my guys will do a visual on the kids as they go out, and we'll let the kids trickle through the walkway to keep the parents from causing a ruckus. I like this plan!"

Eamon clapped his hands together briskly and gave Larx a kind wink, and that was the signal. They went to work.

When they had some order to the madness, Larx and Eamon had a quiet conversation with Joy.

"I just opened the bathroom door," she said brokenly. "I just… he was leaning against it, I think, because when I opened it, he just… fell. Into my arms." She looked at herself woefully, her letterman jacket covered in blood and the pretty green sweater she had on underneath irreparably stained.

"Okay," Larx said, trying not to think about the blood he was wearing like a spilled soda. "Joy, do you remember anyone else in the Porta-John area? I mean, other kids, other adults? Anyone?"

"No, Principal Larkin," Joy said. "I just… he just fell on me, and I couldn't breathe, and I was so afraid I was going to drop him and—"

The poor thing burst into tears.

He texted Nancy to let Joy's parents into the bonfire circle to collect her, and he gave them the district psychologist's number, telling them to call that night and in the morning to make sure she got the message.

He called Becky himself as they walked away, giving her the heads-up and warning her she'd need to plan to be at Colton pretty much all week. Eamon waited patiently until he was done and then started asking Larx questions based on what Joy had said.

"So that girl discovered Isaiah—just opened the Porta-John door and he fell out."

Larx looked over to where two crime scene techs—all the department had—had taped off the bathroom area and the lawn to the bonfire circle. Any evidence brought into the bonfire circle had been trampled beyond identification by the time the department had arrived—Eamon had been the first one to admit it—and there was nothing to be done. It was only thanks to the quick response of the staff that the kids hadn't all fled into the night.

"Yessir," Larx said, in answer. "She screamed, we looked up, and she was trying to hold him up."

"So the person who stabbed him was big enough to throw him back into the john and slam the door."

Larx thought about it and nodded. "Yeah. But strong—not big." He hated thinking about this, but it was important. "The johns aren't raised—Isaiah's belly wound was low on his stomach. It had to be someone not that tall."

Eamon nodded. "Good observation, son. I hear ya. Okay, what angle was he falling out?"

Larx closed his eyes and thought. "Forward. So he'd been leaning against the door until someone opened it."

"Okay. So if it's someone small—with no leverage, like you say—they probably just waited for him to open the door, then got him in the stomach and slammed the door shut again."

"Yeah. We'll have to see what the forensics says, but I'm thinking that may be right." He knew where this was going. Larx and murder mysteries and crime shows—he should write his own book.

"So we're past the point of thinking this had to be a boy because it's such a bloody crime," Eamon said wisely. "Do you have any suspects?"

Larx's skin itched. He yearned for a shower, he yearned for his couch in his comfy little house, and he yearned to hear that his student was going to be okay. "There was a girl causing trouble with the boys," he said. "That's no guarantee she did this, but you may want to take an extra good look as she passes."

"We could go get her right now," Eamon said, because that *would* seem logical if you didn't know the sitch.

"Her mom's Whitney Olson," Larx warned. "Dot your i's, cross your t's, and make sure you have hard evidence before you question her."

"Oh God," Eamon muttered. "This. *This* situation? This boy was gutted like a deer because he dumped her?"

"Eamon, did anybody tell you what Isaiah and Kellan did just before he was found stabbed?"

Larx briefed him quickly, both of them watching as the students moved efficiently through the spotlight searches and disappeared down the path to their waiting parents on the other side.

The parade was interrupted by Julia Olson's shrill bitching as Deputy Parsons nailed her with a Maglite. Larx nodded at Eamon and the older man stepped forward, wielding his own Maglite and speaking to Julia in deep, even tones.

"Little girl, slow and easy now. You need to take your hands out of your pockets."

Larx stared hard at the figure in the lights and his heart stopped. Julia was wearing her cheerleading sweater with a letterman's jacket over it. Both things were white with blue trim. The jacket was thick felt and water retardant.

But Julia's looked like it had been trying to repel black cherry soda instead of water all night, and Larx's stomach grew cold.

"No," she said shrilly. "No, and you idiots are making me late. My mother's waiting for me and—" Her hands moved fitfully in her pockets, like she was clenching something there.

Eamon pulled his weapon.

In his entire life, Larx had never felt such horror. A weapon. On a seventeen-year-old girl. An ugly, *deadly* gun on a tiny little girl.

Who might have a knife in her hand after committing a heinous crime.

"It's just my phone," she sobbed, pulling her hands out with rabbit motions. Later, Larx would be consoled by the fact that if Eamon had been a lesser, more frightened man, he would have shot her, no questions asked, because what she was doing there— that was exactly what law enforcement feared. "See? My phone. My phone, and now my mother is going to sue you. She's going to sue you and—"

"Little girl," Eamon said, weapon still drawn, voice still dangerous, "I'm going to need you to drop the phone and put your hands behind your head."

"It wasn't me," Julia sobbed. "You can't arrest me because I didn't do it. I swear. It wasn't me."

But by now Julia was the target of six bright magnesium beams from the full account of county deputies in the area. And when she held her hands behind her head, they were crusted with bright white pocket lint, sticking to the foulness of dried blood.

Eamon kept the beam trained on Julia while, very slowly, Jim Parks walked over and tightened the cuffs on her thin wrists. When he was done, Eamon pulled a plastic bag out of his pocket and scooped up the phone, wrapping another bag around it and holding it carefully.

As Jim started to read the girl her rights, they heard a high-pitched demand and what sounded like a steamroller crashing through the underbrush.

"How *dare* you!" Whitney Olson snarled. "How *dare* you!" The woman looked worse for her trek through the woods—her fashionable tracksuit was twisted around her body, and her hair hung lank to her shoulders. Julia, upon seeing her, let out a little whimper and, handcuffs and all, sank to the ground, sobbing.

"Mrs. Olson," Eamon intoned, holstering his weapon and turning toward the woman, "I suggest you go call your daughter a lawyer. A criminal lawyer, not a financial one."

"You have no right to detain my daughter. None at all!"

"She's covered in blood," Eamon said in the overly reasonable voice one used when talking to a hysterical child. "A young man was stabbed here by somebody her size, somebody strong but not tall. And your daughter has blood all over her jacket." With that Eamon whistled shrilly, and the two CSIs by the johns looked up. Eamon gestured to one of them and she trotted over, kit in hand.

"I need you to process her jacket and shoes at the very least before we get her to the station. Oh!" Eamon handed her the phone. "And take this as well."

"Yessir. I'll accompany her to the station for the rest of it."

"Thanks, Andrea. Call down to Placer County—they've got labs that we don't. You'll be taking samples down as soon as we get the boy too."

"Not a problem, Eamon." Andrea glared sideways at a fuming Whitney. "Isaiah's one of ours. We'll take care of him."

Julia was led toward the cage lights with Andrea and Colton's one female detective, Julieth Frazier, the better to be processed, and Eamon was left going toe-to-toe with Whitney Olson.

"I'll sue you, Sheriff. I'll sue the school, I'll sue the whole fucking county," Whitney snarled. "This is ridiculous. Half the school was probably covered in blood—I heard that faggot bled like a stuck pig when he got stabbed!"

"I'm sorry?" Larx said, his temper hitting him hard in the gut. "Isaiah Campbell is a student here, and he's fighting for his life, and you need to show some respect!"

"Like you showed when you let two fags make out in front of the bonfire?" she taunted, and Larx's whole body stiffened with violence.

And then Eamon spoke, and Larx was suddenly alert to something more important than his need to actually hit a woman, something he deplored on a regular day.

"How did you know about the boys' kiss?"

Larx's head jerked back at the power of the question, and he saw Whitney stiffen too.

"My daughter texted me," she said with dignity. "Distraught."

Eamon nodded. "Well, we'll check the phone records to make sure."

Whitney sputtered and fumbled for her phone and then stepped out of hearing distance from them—presumably to call her lawyer. Larx realized that for once, he would not be the center of Whitney Olson's anger.

Larx wouldn't be at the sheriff's station at all.

"Eamon, when this is all cleared up, is it all right if I go to the hospital to check on Isaiah?"

Eamon nodded. "Yessir, I think that would be a fine idea."

So Larx had a goal, something to sustain him through the next couple of hours. He also had Kirby, who was in one of the last groups to be searched and who was keeping an intermittent news stream with his father.

"How's it going?" Larx asked as he waited with Kirby's group to be processed.

"Isaiah's in surgery now," Kirby told him. "Apparently his dad was sort of a dick to Kellan. My dad's trying to keep Kellan from losing his shit."

"Aw, hell—has anybody told Kellan's parents where he is?"

Kirby's eyebrow must have been a legacy from his mother, because Larx had never seen that much sarcasm anywhere near Aaron's expression. "Kellan's parents? Begging your pardon, Principal Larx, but you do remember who we're talking about, right?"

Yeah. Oh shit. Kellan's parents might not have come to the hospital if *Kellan* had been the one in surgery.

"Oh damn," Larx muttered. "He's going to need a ride home."

And he couldn't imagine how much that would suck. He looked at Kirby, and he and Aaron's son had a meeting of the minds.

"We should bring him home," Kirby said. He texted furiously for a moment and then looked up at Larx. "He and Christi are friends too."

Larx pulled out his own phone and kept a tight rein on the what-ifs he'd been ruthlessly squashing since Joy's first scream had shattered the night. What if Christi had been there? What if she'd been hurt? What if it had been Kirby in that bathroom? Oh God, what if?

Instead of texting, he called, because he needed to hear his daughter's voice.

"Dad?"

"Christi, hon, I hate to break up your sleepover, but I'm going to need your help. Someone's been hurt."

He explained the sitch in short bursts, being more principal than dad, but he wasn't aware of how much that difference was slipping until he heard Christi, voice fracturing, say, "Oh Daddy. I'm so sorry—yeah. I'm over at Schuyler's—we'll come to the hospital first and then go to our place, okay?"

He had to laugh. He'd had hopes, him and Aaron, together alone.

He should have remembered that part of being a parent was that you were never alone.

"Yeah, hon. That sounds good. Give me an hour or two, though, okay?" He hung up and looked at Kirby. "And since I was your ride to school this morning, I guess you and me are going together."

"D'oh!" Kirby smacked his forehead. "I actually forgot. Geez… this has been the weirdest day!"

Larx chuckled then, a strained sound waiting to break free into hysteria. He pulled himself together and put his hand on the boy's shoulder instead. "It defies the laws of physics, gravity, and the space-time continuum," he affirmed.

And Kirby started laughing, and laughing, and laughing. Larx gave in to his permanent dadness and wrapped his arm around the boy's shoulder until he wiped away tears and caught his breath.

The bonfire was down to the embers by the time they made it to the spotlight search, and Kirby was the last person through. Larx had Kirby wait next to him as he spoke with Eamon one more time.

"I'm going to the hospital if you need me," he said. "And if his parents haven't come to get him, I'll bring Kellan home with me."

"Any reason the boy's parents wouldn't be there to get him?" the sheriff asked perceptively.

"Their son threw two touchdown passes at homecoming and they weren't there," Larx said, dragging a recently cleaned hand through his hair. "And he's pretty sure they're not going to get any warmer when they find out his *boy*friend is in the hospital. I just…." Augh! This was where he got muddy. The line between your children and your kids—where do you draw it? "This has got to be the shittiest night of his life, Eamon. My house is going to have friends and safety. I would like to give him that."

Eamon nodded. "If I don't see you tonight, I'll be by your place bright and early to question him."

Oh God. Thank you for letting this nice man with the flashlight and the gray hair and the solid, solid presence see that this was okay. "Thanks, Eamon."

"I take it I'll see Deputy George there too?"

Larx blinked. "I assumed he'd be going home." Because four kids crying in the living room—who needed the aggravation?

But Sheriff Mills just looked at him, unblinking. "I would prefer to find him at your place drinking coffee in his pajamas, Principal Larkin."

"Uh...."

"Because you've both had something of a day."

"Yeah, well, uh...."

"And I think you both need caring for," Eamon continued implacably. "I like to make sure my deputies have someplace to go when things go to hell. Someplace good."

"That's, uh, yeah. Good idea. Good talk. Sure. Aaro... Deputy George will be at my place. Drinking pajamas in his coffee. Or something. Yes, Sheriff, good idea."

Eamon let out a tired laugh. "Larx?"

"Yes, sir?"

"Go meet your family and go home. We'll take over. I hope the boys are okay. Both of them. You did good tonight—this could have been a multilayered clusterfuck, but it wasn't. Some of that was George, but most of it was you. So, you know. If your school board gives you shit—about any of it? You bring me in. I'll tell them a thing or two about shitty human beings and how you can't always anticipate evil fucking bullshit, okay?"

Larx nodded and wiped his mouth with a shaking hand, suddenly almost undone by the kindness of this authority figure.

"Thanks, Eamon. I'll see you tomorrow."

"See you tomorrow."

Larx and Kirby walked tiredly down the forest path then, and Larx noted that somebody—probably the sheriff's department—had strung lights from the trees before the kids walked back down to see their parents. The thought made him feel protected somehow, like he wasn't alone watching out for them all.

They were reasonably quiet as Larx drove the half hour to the small county hospital. Larx tried not to think about Isaiah in the ambulance, frightened and in pain. Or Kellan fearing for his boyfriend's life.

Funny how people don't always think about the most obvious things until something strikes them just right.

Because right then what Aaron really did for a living hit Larx in the solar plexus.

Maybe it had been seeing Eamon draw his gun on a teenage girl. Or the fact that he was still wearing Isaiah's blood. Maybe it was thinking about Kellan and how frightened he must be, but suddenly Larx was there, in the realization that Aaron wore a weapon, that he was expected to venture into danger.

That one day *Larx* could be in an ambulance, praying to a nameless god for mercy on the boy he loved.

He must have made a sound—or Kirby must have been thinking the same thing—because Aaron's son spoke into the darkness.

"Dad's gotten hurt a couple of times. Once right after my mom died."

"It's like you read my mind," Larx muttered.

Kirby half laughed. "You'd be stupid if you didn't think about it. I mean, Dad likes to play it off like it's not important, but he puts on a gun every morning. He wears Kevlar. And this is gun country up here. So you think about it."

"How'd he get hurt?" Larx asked, almost afraid to ask.

"Got sort of flung at a car," Kirby said. "A few cuts, a few bruises. We stayed with our mom's sister for a while."

"You have an aunt?" Oh, the things Larx did not know.

"Aunt Candace—she comes up for Christmas sometimes. She never married, so, you know, floats around to her parents' or boyfriend's or whatever. She's nice. Would totally approve of you, by the way."

Larx grunted, not sure if the kid was trying to make him feel better or just wanted to get on with the story. "So he got hurt?"

"Yeah. I remember Aunt Candy came to pick me up from school, and I got really upset because, you know, she picked me up when my mom died, and...."

He shuddered hard, and Larx thought he now knew what Kirby would be telling his therapist when he grew up.

"You thought your dad wasn't coming home." His heart ached.

"Yeah. And then Aunt Candy told me that he was fine, and he wanted me not to worry, and it was weird. You know, like one of those hypnotic suggestions?

Because I was *so freaked out* that my dad was hurt, I was like in a really suggestible state. Candy said, 'Dad doesn't want you to worry.' So I just stopped. And now, whenever I get really freaked out about him and what he's doing and whether he's going to come home or not, I remember 'Dad doesn't want you to worry.' I don't know why it works, but it does."

Larx tried it. *Aaron doesn't want me to worry.*

And felt just the same.

"I think it's powerful magic," Larx said regretfully. "But I don't think it's going to work with me."

"Why not?" Kirby asked. "Is it because you're too old?"

Larx grunted, not even offended. "No. I think it worked for you because you felt cared for. Your mom before she died. Her sister. Your father. I think that's like… what's the word? A charm? A…."

"Talisman," Kirby supplied.

"Your English teacher is heinously underpaid," Larx observed. "But yes. A talisman. I don't have one of those yet."

They pulled up in front of the hospital, and Larx found a parking spot. He killed the engine and leaned back in his seat, yawning. The dash clock said 2:30 a.m. God, he wasn't used to going this long on this little sleep. What, did he think he was back in college?

"Larx?" Kirby said softly.

Larx shook himself. "Yeah, sorry. Let's go find your dad."

"Okay. I just… I want you to know something."

Larx worked hard to be in the present. This was important to Aaron's son. "Shoot."

"I hope… I hope my dad can give you the talisman or whatever, to help you not worry. It would be great to have two grown-ups to talk to again. Even if I'm supposed to be grown myself."

Larx smiled at him and slid out of the car. As they walked toward the hospital, he slung his arm around the boy's shoulder, and Kirby didn't object in the slightest.

Heat

ISAIAH'S FATHER was just as tall as his son, with thinning blond hair and muscle that had run to fat, and a drinker's nose.

Pete Campbell wore overalls and a T-shirt to his job as a drywall specialist and never saw any reason to change after work. He wore the overalls and the T-shirt and a denim jacket straight to his son's game, and his wife, a once-lovely, slender woman with surprising height, wore jeans and a pink sweatshirt. When Aaron spoke to her, she would flicker her eyes to her husband before she answered.

Pete's first words—after "What in the fuck did you people do to my son?"—were "And why's this punk kid here?"

"Kellan's Isaiah's friend," Aaron said reasonably. "We thought that when he came out of surgery, he'd want to see him."

"Boy's not family," Pete grunted. "But whatever."

Aaron and Kellan locked grim gazes for a moment before Aaron continued with his job. "Mr. Campbell, we've got people at the bonfire working to find out what happened—"

"You were there! What the hell were you doing?"

"I was talking to the principal next to the bonfire because it was damned cold," Aaron said, hoping to humanize the situation. "And kids were going to use the bathroom. It should have been safe, if a little creepy, and it wasn't. I'm just wondering if Isaiah said anything to you about who might not be happy with him after the football game tonight."

Aaron and Kellan looked at each other again, and Aaron shook his head grimly. This situation had such potential to explode.

"Well, he did tell me he had problems with a girl," Lizzie Campbell said, voice tentative. "He didn't want to take her to homecoming, and she was getting quite insistent."

"Whole thing was stupid," Pete muttered. "A date with a pretty girl—I still don't get why he didn't say yes."

"Because he didn't care about her," Kellan said. "And frankly she was a little crazy." *And he loves me.* Aaron could hear the subtext loud and clear.

"Did he tell you that?" Lizzie Campbell asked, flicking her eyes to her husband before smiling.

"Yes'm," Kellan said. "He did."

"He doesn't tell us anything anymore," she said wistfully. "I guess it's because he's getting older."

"He's afraid of what you'll say," Kellan told her. "He… he's growing into a different person than the two of you. He doesn't think you'll approve."

Pete stopped his pacing and turned toward Kellan with a deliberate slowness. "What in the hell does that mean?"

"It means Isaiah loves me," Kellan said, voice soft but firm. "What Deputy George is trying not to tell you is that me and Isaiah, we came out in front of the whole school at the bonfire tonight. We kissed, and our teachers came to congratulate us and tell us they had our backs. And it was great. But now"—he caught his voice as it tumbled—"now Isaiah's fighting for his life, and we don't know who hurt him. And we have to tell the deputy if anyone would have wanted to hurt him because he… he kissed me in front of the bonfire and the whole world saw…."

Aaron put his arm around the boy's shoulders and just left it there, warm and solid, as Kellan got himself under control and Isaiah's parents caught up to what he'd just said.

"My son did *what*!" Pete yelled, and Aaron stepped right up into his space.

"We're not doing this," he said with all the authority he could muster. "Kellan just told you something hard for you to hear, but you know what? He's right. Isaiah is fighting for his life. When he comes to, you can either be mad at him for being who he is, or you can be glad your son survived. He could *die*. Right now. Do you want him to die without ever really knowing who he was?"

Please oh please oh please….

"He was… is… my son is gay?" Pete asked, stunned. He turned and glared at his wife. "Did you know?"

"No," she whispered, face suddenly gray. Then she turned and glared right back. "How could I? You never let him speak at the damned dinner table! Why do you think he hasn't told us? Everything that comes out of his mouth gets shouted down!"

Pete floundered for a minute. "Lizzie, the boy gets ideas. Going off to college. He's our only son—why would he want to leave?"

"So he could be with me," Kellan whispered, wiping his hand across his eyes. "Because my folks would rather kill me than let me be a fag."

And Lizzie Campbell surprised Aaron then, because she patted Kellan's arm awkwardly and tried to calm him down while Pete just looked on in befuddlement.

"My son has a boyfriend?" he asked, like the sound of the word was foreign on his tongue.

"Yes, sir," Aaron answered calmly. "Yes, he does. Now do you know anyone who might have wanted to hurt him because of that?"

"How could I?" Pete asked, all of the wind suddenly out of his sails. "When I didn't know myself."

He sank down into his chair in a slow avalanche and watched as his wife tried to mother a shy and wretched Kellan, who was picking at the bloodstains on his clothes.

Aaron sighed and flagged down an orderly for a pair of scrubs. He saved the poor kid from the fluttery ministrations of Lizzie Campbell and took him to the shower cubicle down in long-term care. The forensics team had already raked Kellan over—it was time to get the blood off.

"I'll be right outside your door," Aaron promised. "Get washed and I'll see if we can't get you a sweatshirt, and you'll feel a little easier as we wait."

Kellan nodded a quiet thank-you and disappeared, leaving Aaron to text Kirby to get the skinny on what was going down at the bonfire. According to Kirby, Larx was kicking ass and taking names, and Aaron felt a little swell of pride. He was something—clear-thinking, smart, funny even in the direst situations. Aaron thought wistfully that he'd like to see Larx sprawled, naked and sexy, joking in bed.

It was a long night after that. He almost regretted being the guy on the scene, the guy who ended up with Kellan at the hospital, because he wanted to be doing something, anything, besides waiting to see if his son's classmate was going to live.

Kellan got out of the shower, and they went back to the waiting room. Aaron kept texting Kirby, and at some point Kellan fell asleep, his head tilting onto Aaron's shoulder with so much trust Aaron almost couldn't breathe.

These kids trusted them, the adults, to keep them safe. Aaron felt his failure in the marrow of his bones.

He had started to doze off, his dreams flickering between a chilly lakefront and a bloated corpse and a confused orange-lit darkness that covered Larx in blood. New footsteps clattering down the corridor snapped him awake with enough force that Kellan sat up blearily, rubbing at his eyes.

"Deputy George?"

Aaron blinked a couple of times and smiled. Larx's daughter was wearing pink flannel pajamas with kitties and bunnies on them, her letterman jacket, and rainbow sneakers. Her girlfriend was wearing purple fleece bottoms with Snoopy and a Hello Kitty hoodie. Together they were the poster children for adorable, and they were holding two aluminum mugs steaming with what smelled like chocolate, and a plate of fresh muffins.

"Up late baking?" he asked with a wink. He stood up and stretched and accepted the mugs, then handed one to Kellan.

"Dad called up and asked us if we could come hang with Kellan until he was ready to come home with us."

"With you?" Kellan yawned. Christi perched on the chair next to him, looking like a sweet and sleepy bird.

"Yeah. With us. Our living room. You, me, Schuyler, Kirby when he gets here. We'll have a slumber party as soon as we find out Isaiah's all right. You good with that?"

"I don't have to go home?" he asked, plaintive and vulnerable and obviously afraid.

Christi leaned her head on his shoulder and snuggled like a little kid. "Nope," she said, making it sound normal. "Because my dad is *awesome*." She smiled winsomely at Schuyler. "And Schuyler's folks are pretty decent too. They gave us hot chocolate, and since we had some time, we baked muffins. C'mon, eat. I know you didn't get a chance to after the game."

Schuyler sat on Kellan's other side and plied the boy with muffins, and Aaron thought of the miracle of Larx's daughter. Just like her father—spreading common sense and goodwill and genuine generosity.

You could read the man's heart through his children sometimes, and right now his daughter was saying such wonderful things about Larx.

At that moment, the surgeon came through the double doors and became the most important man in the world.

He was covered in blood. It coated his scrubs, it flaked in the mask that hung from his neck, spattered across his clothing in the places it hadn't saturated through.

Just looking at him made Aaron woozy, and he heard a soft moan in time to see Isaiah's mother collapse into her husband's arms. Pete Campbell caught her, held her close, and touched her hair gently like he was comforting an injured bird.

"He's stable," the doctor said, voice coming out in a rush. "But we're not sure we got everything. You'll have a short window to see him before we sedate him with painkillers, because he's going to have a really bumpy night."

He looked out at his audience. "Mr. and Mrs. Campbell? Would you like to go first?"

They looked at each other, and Lizzie Campbell held out her hand. "Kellan?" she asked in a small voice. "Would you like to come with us?"

Kellan nodded and wiped his face, and Aaron gave him a little shove forward. As the three of them followed a nurse through the doors to ICU, Aaron stepped up to the doctor, hating what he had to do next.

But the doctor got it.

"You need to find out who did this, right?"

"Yeah. Anything he can tell us. He got knifed coming out of the john. That's…."

"Sneaky, underhanded, and cowardly," the doctor said with stark anger. He was in his fifties and had what was probably gray hair tucked under his cap.

"That kid had no business in a hospital for anything worse than a torn knee. That thing I just fixed?" He shook his head. "Fucking obscene."

Aaron nodded, out of words. That about nailed it for him. For them all.

"Just let me know when I can speak to him," Aaron said softly. "That would be a big help."

The doctor gave a curt nod and disappeared.

They waited for about five uncomfortable minutes before Kellan and Isaiah's folks stumbled through the door, looking like death. Aaron wanted to comfort Kellan almost more than he wanted to do his job, but Christi Larkin was on it, all over the boy like white on rice. Aaron didn't care how gay Kellan was, he was mostly sure that a pretty girl making a big deal out of you when you felt at your saddest was one of the miracles of life. He left Larx's daughter to her magic and followed the nurse past the double doors.

Modern-day telemetry was usually set so all the beeps and bells and whistles sounded at the nurse's station and not in the patient's room. Aaron sort of missed the regular beeping of those machines, because the quiet respirations that sounded from the room were just not active enough to reassure him.

But Isaiah was conscious as he walked in, breathing carefully through the oxygen catheters taped to his nostrils.

"Sheriff," he mouthed. Well, his insides were mostly taped together with faith and glue. Aaron was pretty sure one of his lungs had been punctured. Breathing was going to hurt—Aaron wasn't going to quibble about titles.

"'Kay, Isaiah," Aaron said, keeping his voice gentle. "You've got limited chances to talk. Let me ask questions and if you can nod your head, do."

Isaiah nodded just enough to see.

"Did you see who did it?"

He shook his head no.

"Well, that would have been too easy."

A slight smile, and Aaron returned it. Brave kid.

"A girl or a boy?" Aaron asked, thinking he'd stick to basics.

Isaiah frowned, a line appearing between his eyebrows. "Girl?"

"Hard to tell?"

"Wearing. Black. On face. Think. I saw. Chest."

He struggled for oxygen for a minute, and Aaron tried to put it together.

"So your attacker was wearing black clothing?"

Isaiah nodded.

"And something black around his face."

Isaiah made a pained wheeze, and Aaron held up a hand.

"Around *her* face, and you know it was a her because she had boobs?" It was a rash guess, but Isaiah didn't have much left in him.

He nodded, looking relieved.

"And you don't know who it was?"

He shook his head, then spoke. "Wasn't. Jule…."

Aaron sucked in a quick breath. "It *wasn't* Julia Olson?"

Isaiah had the most remarkable brown eyes. They didn't flicker or flinch as he shook his head no, and Aaron sighed. He'd gotten the text from Eamon Mills saying they had Julia in custody. This was *not* going to go well.

But that wasn't Isaiah's fault.

"You did good," he said softly. He heard a tread behind him and looked up to see the nurse waiting to lead him back out to the waiting room.

"Kellan?" The boy's voice throbbed with all the things Aaron knew but Isaiah couldn't say.

"Is going to Larx's place for the night. Don't worry. He won't be alone."

Isaiah smiled just a moment before his eyes closed and he fell into a hopefully healing sleep.

Aaron followed the nurse out, texting at light speed, and what he got back didn't reassure him.

We have the girl in custody. She was covered in blood.

Isaiah says it wasn't her.

Odds are good she knows who it was. But you've done your job. Go home with Larx. Long day tomorrow.

Go home with Larx? Aaron stared at his phone, brain working muzzily as he entered the waiting room.

And heard Larx's voice. "Okay, all. Time to shuffle vehicles. Christi and Schuyler in Christi's car. Kirby, here are the keys to the minivan—I know where all the dents are, don't add to 'em if you can help it. Kellan, I'll let you decide who to go with. Everybody ready to go crash on my couches and eat my cereal in the morning?"

There was a general consensus, and then Larx hugged his daughter and her bemused friend in the purple Snoopy pajamas. Kirby stepped forward, a smartassed expression on his face, so Larx hugged him too.

And then he turned to Kellan and held out his arms.

And the boy went, clutching him fiercely.

"He's going to be okay," Larx whispered.

Aaron didn't hear an answer, but he saw Kellan nodding against his chest before finally breaking away.

"Kellan," Lizzie Campbell said, voice hesitant, and the boy looked up. "We'll see you in the morning. Visiting hours are at ten, so, anytime around then."

Kellan gave a brief smile. "Thanks, Mrs. Campbell," he said. "I'll be here."

"Then you'd better go get some sleep," Larx warned, nodding to Kirby, who took his keys like they were fragile gold.

The kids walked away, with Kirby giving his dad a nod as they passed. "See you at Larx's," he said casually, and then they were gone, leaving Aaron all but clinging to the wall in exhaustion.

Larx looked up, just as weary, and smiled, like seeing Aaron had given him some extra strength. "Deputy," he said formally, "I seem to have just given my keys to a feckless teenager. When you're done with your business here, I am going to need a ride."

Aaron was too tired to laugh, but he did manage a smile before he turned to Isaiah's parents. "You two get some rest," he told them, knowing it would be futile. "They'll bring you cots if you ask. That was really nice of you to invite Kellan tomorrow. Here's my card. Text me if you need anything and someone will bring it when they bring Kellan. You keep me posted and I'll do the same, deal?"

They nodded, and Larx appeared next to him, his own business card in his hand. "Same for me." Then he paused to pull a pen out of his shirt pocket and write on the back. "And this is the district psychologist. She's not just for kids. If you folks need to talk to her about anything, you give her a call, okay?"

Pete Campbell's jaw worked. "Our son is gay," he said gruffly, sounding lost.

Larx nodded. "He is. And really brave. And a beautiful football player. And a damned good scientist. And he's an *amazing* stage director, according to Mrs. Graves, the theater teacher."

Lizzie Campbell smiled like she got it. "All the good things that make him up," she said, quiet pride in her voice. Her look to her husband was neither tentative nor frightened. "He's still our boy."

Pete shrugged and then folded her up in his arms, where the two of them had one of those wordless conversations that only a true couple could have.

It was time to go.

Aaron led the way wearily to his SUV, and he held the door as Larx climbed in, and then climbed in himself. He closed the door with a thump against the frosty night air, and it occurred to him that he was, at last, alone with Larx.

For a moment they regarded each other in the quiet dark, Larx's eyes drooping at the corners with tiredness, the planes and hollows of his face stark and tight in the shadows.

Aaron wasn't sure which one of them moved first, but that quick he had Larx pinned against the back of the seat and was devouring him with insatiable hunger.

Aah! He tasted so good—warm and male, and a little like hot chocolate and muffins, but mostly just like strength. And acceptance. And oh God, someone who was there with him at the end of the day, strong and ready for the worst.

Larx groaned, his fingers tugging needily at Aaron's hair, and the two of them battled for a moment over who would control the kiss. And then a wonderful thing happened.

Larx just conceded. Gave in, mouth open as he relaxed against the seat and let Aaron take over in a thorough, methodical ravaging of Larx's mouth, his senses, his self-control. He shoved his hands under Aaron's shirts and kneaded his chest like a cat, pinching nipples once in a while, but mostly just glutting his palms on Aaron's skin.

His touch was like life force, feeding Aaron enough to wake him up, to give him hope, to get him home.

Aaron pulled back and rested his forehead against Larx's, their breathing quick enough to steam the windows.

"What is this about me staying at your place?" he asked.

"Your boss's idea," Larx panted back. "Something about coming by tomorrow and wanting you to be drinking coffee in your pajamas."

Aaron chuckled—a raw sound—and pulled back enough to start the car. "They're going to have to be your pajamas, he knows that, right?"

"Well, apparently he knows something," Larx said pragmatically, "because you don't usually hear that sort of recommendation from an elected public official."

Aaron couldn't help it. His chuckle grew into an actual laugh, and he pulled out of the hospital parking lot, thanking God that he didn't have to go home alone.

THEY BRIEFED each other on the ride, and Aaron paused when they got to Larx's house, pulling in neatly behind the parked minivan.

"Do you see that?" he asked, pointing to the skewed back end of the van. "You gave your keys to a kid who can't park worth shit."

Larx chuckled, his voice raspy and almost gone. "Hey, you're the one who taught him. You might notice Christi's car is parked neat as a bug."

It was too, a little red sedan parked almost razor's-edge even with the side of the carport.

"Your kid is too perfect. I can't believe she's yours."

"Me neither, but shh. I don't want her to go looking for her real dad at this point. It would depress me."

And Aaron had to kiss him again. And again. And again. He was getting hard—which was a pleasant surprise, but not the point.

The point was, he needed reassurance, needed his person, there in his arms, holding on tight, and Larx was not letting go.

Larx needed him too.

But Aaron was kissing slower and slower, and the risk of falling asleep in the front of his car while necking grew greater with every kiss. Finally he pulled back and they both yawned.

"Nice, but time to go be grown-ups again," Larx murmured.

"Speak for yourself. I think grown-ups get sex."

"Eventually. When they're so old they'd rather sleep," Larx said, sounding bitter. Aaron kissed a cheek rough with stubble, and then they climbed out of the car. Larx led the way into the front room, where they both stopped and looked, surprised.

Christi had gotten the big beanbag chairs from her room, and the two that usually lived in Olivia's with the cats, and had spread them over the floor along with blankets. Christi must have given Kirby an old pair of her gym sweats, and Kellan was still in his scrubs, but they were all cuddled among the pillows with each other.

Kids—friends—giving comfort when they could.

Larx squatted near his daughter and shook her gently.

"Dad?"

"We're home. I'll wake Kellan in the morning when the sheriff comes by, but sleep until then, okay?"

"Yeah." She yawned. "Kirby says his dad's staying." She woke up just enough to smile wickedly. "You kids better be dressed when I look in there."

Larx rolled his eyes and tousled her hair. "You are a laugh riot. Go to sleep and save your strength for the comedy show."

She giggled and Larx stood. After leaving the landing light on and turning off the kitchen light, he led the way upstairs to his room.

"Drop your clothes in the hamper," he said quietly as Aaron looked around. A solid wooden bedframe dominated the room, but there was a large matching dresser on the far side. The carpets were plain beige, but one of the walls and trim was hunter green, and the effect was bold—and comfortable. Larx had put some framed prints up—Green Day, Smashing Pumpkins, Nirvana—and Aaron had to laugh, recognizing the music of his twenties.

Aaron did what was asked, so exhausted it didn't occur to him that he was standing in his boxers and T-shirt in front of a man he found attractive until that man threw clothes at his face.

"You get the shower first," Larx said pragmatical-ly, "I'm going to go...." He made a fussy little move-ment with his fingers, indicating his bloodied clothing. "*Soak* everything I'm wearing in cold water and bak-ing soda."

Aaron nodded. "Throw my stuff in the soak too." Floaters were messy. Aaron had deliberately *not* thought about what was on his khakis for hours.

"Yeah." Larx started to undress, and Aaron stood there, staring at him stupidly for a moment, thinking, *C'mon, Larx, let me see your chest.*

Larx stopped as he was pulling his T-shirt up over his head and caught Aaron's eyes.

And smiled goofily, like a teenager. He looked away, biting his lip, and then studied his feet as he kicked off his tennis shoes.

"You're, uh, gonna wanna get in the shower be-fore I fill the sink," he said. "Uh... you know. Water."

"Yeah."

Larx snuck a look at him from under his brow, then went back to looking at his rumpled socks. "We'll uh... you know. It'll happen."

Aaron felt his own neck heat, and his cheeks. "Promise?" he said wistfully.

"Oh yeah." Larx met his eyes then, hunger so blatantly written across his features that even Aaron could see it. "I... oh yeah."

Aaron watched as his chest started to pump, his breathing quickening just at the thought.

"Thank God." And with that he gathered clean clothes and turned toward the adjoining bathroom, figuring everything he'd need would be there.

Well, everything but Larx.

SLIDING INTO Larx's bed, under his green cotton comforter and the extra blanket, was almost surreal in its comfort. Larx's smell—fabric softener, the same soap Aaron had just used, a little bit of sweat—permeated every thread of the weave.

Aaron closed his eyes and soaked it in, right up to the decrepit Siamese cat that curled up behind his head. He woke up a little when Larx—wearing sweats and a T-shirt—turned off the lights and nudged Aaron over so he could climb in. And then it was darkness, and the faint chill of Larx's skin but the warmth of the flesh underneath. Aaron wrapped his arms around that tight, vital body and hugged hard until Larx went boneless against him.

"Alarm," Larx muttered.

"Okay," Aaron said.

Which was why no alarm was set and they were both surprised the next morning when Christi opened the door in her adorable jammies.

"Dad?"

"Wha?" Larx struggled out of Aaron's arms and tumbled out of bed, looking dizzy and disoriented, his dark hair sticking up from his head in spikes, like a porcupine.

"Uh, calm down. We started the coffee. But Sheriff Mills is downstairs eating muffins at our kitchen table."

"Oh," Larx muttered, reaching out and grabbing the end table to steady himself. "Oh. Okay. Muffins. Coffee. Sheriffs. Aaron?"

"Right here," Aaron said, popping out of bed per usual. "Here, let me brush my teeth."

Larx giggled. "There's another man in my bedroom."

Aaron met Christi's amused look. "Not so good with mornings, is he?"

"You see him after two miles. Probably the only reason he remembers your name."

"That is not true," Larx said, sounding indignant. "I remember his name 'cause he's cute!"

Aaron burst out laughing as Christi complained, "Aw, Dad, really?"

"Christi?" Aaron asked, and she rolled her eyes and left, closing the door behind her.

Larx was still standing by the end table, looking dazed, and Aaron walked into his space, cupped his arms through his T-shirt, and rubbed.

"You awake yet?" he asked gently.

"Yeah. Sure. Let me get us sweatshirts. We need to turn on the heater. Do you want socks?"

Aaron kissed him gently and pulled back, waiting to see if his synapses would fire.

Larx just looked at him limpidly, lost as a child. "This is so much not fair," he said after a moment.

"Coffee, Larx. Then let's fix the world."

Larx smiled faintly and pulled away to rifle through his drawers. When they went padding downstairs, they were wearing sweatshirts and thick socks, and Aaron felt like Larx had done his best to protect them both from the day to come.

Flare

USUALLY COFFEE made everything better, but not so much this morning.

"You're letting her go?" Larx asked for the umpteenth time. "She was covered in blood."

"Well, yes, she was," Eamon acknowledged, nursing his own coffee. He looked exhausted, purple pouches under his red-rimmed eyes showing he hadn't been to bed yet. "And that might even make her an accessory. But the boy told George last night and me this morning—his attacker was wearing black, and it may have been a female, but it most definitely wasn't Miss Olson."

"It makes sense, Larx," Aaron said quietly. "She was covered in blood because she *knows* the attacker—but she was wearing white, and her hair was up and heavily sprayed in one of those fake-bun things. Isaiah would have known her."

"But… you can't *compel* her to testify?"

"She's a minor," Eamon said. "And yes, we could send her to juvenile hall on a count of withholding evidence, but that wouldn't get her to talk, would it?"

"Her mother would be up your asses with a Brillo Pad," Larx said dispiritedly. "And her lawyer could argue there's a thousand ways she could have gotten that blood on her that would have nothing to do with knowing the assailant. But…." He shook his head. "So that's it? She just shows up at school on Monday? No harm, no foul?"

Christi had made their coffee—and their hot chocolate—and she had lingered nearby, eavesdropping shamelessly.

Her evil chuckle actually made Larx's coffee congeal in his belly.

"Oh, Daddy. Do you think anyone is going to talk to her now? I mean…." Her sneer was a thing of cold beauty, and Larx didn't like seeing that expression on his baby. "She's a ghost. Isaiah is a hero—she's the bitch who betrayed him."

Larx looked at his daughter helplessly. "Christi, that sounds really… poetic, in a terrifying way, but ugly begets ugly, honey. I don't think—"

"It won't work anyway," Eamon said, voice grim. "The first thing her mother did was demand an HIV test on Isaiah's blood. The second thing she did was demand an emergency board meeting tomorrow night. I don't know if you've checked your messages yet…."

Larx groaned and tore his hand through his hair. "No. My phone's charging upstairs."

"Well, you're going to need more than coffee when you go through those messages. That woman has people all stirred up blaming Kellan here for Isaiah—"

"But—" He flailed his hands, looking at Kellan in horror. Kellan shrugged, pale, dead-eyed, obviously still in shock.

"She's got him painted as a jealous lover, and his parents have…." Eamon looked at him sorrowfully. "Son, are you sure you want to be here for this?"

"They said they don't want a fucking thing to do with their faggot son," Kellan said, voice wooden. "I'll be lucky if they don't burn my clothes."

Eamon let out a sigh. "I rescued some boxes of them, and your yearbooks. It's what I did before I came here."

Kellan barely grunted with the news.

"Christi? Kirby?" Larx said, not hesitating. "If you guys could bring that stuff inside and set it up in the game room? It's got a futon, Kellan, but it's also got some dressers and bookshelves. Feel free to put up posters and stuff. I'll try not to embarrass you too much at school."

"Mr. Larkin?"

Larx caught his eyes. "Son, I'd be grateful if you stayed at least until graduation, if not until we get you situated in a college somewhere. Isaiah and Coach Jones have put a lot of work into you at this point. It'd be a shame to kick that to the curb, you think?"

"Yessir," Kellan said, wiping his eyes with the back of his hand.

"Consider yourself my last chance for a son," he said, trying to lighten the moment.

"I am not chopped liver," Kirby said with dignity, and Larx gasped, meeting Aaron's son's eyes for a whole other reason.

"Twins!" he said brightly, fighting back emotion with everything he had. "Freshly delivered on my doorstep at seventeen years of age. Thank God you're both potty trained. Now go unpack."

The kids all disappeared, and Larx looked at Eamon, feeling somewhat stunned. "So, is there anything else I should know while they're all busy?"

Eamon nodded. "She's going to blame you for letting the gay kids come out. And whatsherface, Heather Perkins, is right on board with that shit, and so's Heather's husband, Carl, and so's her bestest mani/pedi buddy, Sissy Graham."

Larx stared at him, flat-eyed. "That's three of nine people on the school board," he said in disbelief. "How…?"

"You had best get calling folks, Larx. Every teacher you think will come represent you, every parent you have with a kid in the GSA—I know you didn't want the job, but if it's not you, it's going to be someone who doesn't protect those kids like they need you to do. I'm giving a press conference this afternoon. I'll talk about how you ran a tight ship, about how we suspect it was someone sneaking in deliberately from outside, how your quick thinking kept Julia Olson from getting away unquestioned— and yes, I'll mention that little girl's name out loud, and how her mother is obstructing justice. But we need a politician here—I know you loathe the species, but it's time to learn some of their tricks, you understand?"

"But… but tonight's *homecoming*," he said, feeling stupid. His whole day was booked up from three o'clock because he had to supervise decorating the gym.

"Well, do what you can today and pick up the rest of it tomorrow. I'm telling you, if you don't get ahead of this thing, your school is going to the people who would have let a riot happen last week, and personally, I'm not real fond of bigots."

Larx nodded. Play the game. He'd been doing it for seven years, trying to leave those days of just blurting out whatever he felt in public behind him.

If Whitney Olson got her way, his entire school would be a gay-free zone, all in the name of drawing attention away from her daughter's complicity in attempted murder. Larx hated it—and he hated that people could be so easily led.

But he understood it, and knew it was the truth.

"I'll go get my phone," he said. Then he paused. "Uh, Aar—uh, Deputy George, what are you doing today?"

Aaron looked at his boss, who answered. "He is going to get himself a clean uniform—"

"Fuck—the dryer," Larx muttered, and Eamon didn't bother to hide his smile.

"And then he's going to escort Kellan down to the hospital to visit his boyfriend, just like you both promised Isaiah's parents last night. Yes, they told me, they're expecting you. Then he's going to escort the boy back and help you do what you need to."

Larx moaned. "I needed to burn my garden waste tomorrow before the winds kick up and they don't let us burn!"

"I'll get hot dogs and marshmallows on the way back," Aaron promised. "I can stop and feed the chickens and get a change of clothes for the dance and some more for tomorrow."

"You don't want to go to the dance," Larx said weakly.

"I want to see you in a suit," Aaron said. His hand on Larx's shoulder was warm and grounding, and Larx reached across his chest and grabbed it on reflex, just to squeeze. Then he remembered Eamon, and startled.

Eamon smiled gently. "I'm not your enemy here," he said. "But you two—I know it's new. I know you're grown men trying to live good lives. But this town is about to be up in your colon like a fiber-optic network reporting on your morning dump. You need to decide—and I'm talking *today*—what you're going to say publicly about each other. Now I told Deputy George he's my pick for sheriff next year, and that will stand until they pry this job from my cold, dead hands. But Larx, you could lose all sorts of things—including that promise you just made to that boy there—if you let this town get the best of you. So you two talk it out—"

"I'm in," Aaron said implacably. "I'll follow Larx's lead. When he comes out, I'm coming out. Not until then. Not to the press unless he's making the announcement. He's the one who needs to guide the herd. I'm just the dumb muscle behind him."

"Ha-ha. Dumb muscle. It is to laugh," Larx muttered. "Okay, Eamon. Point taken. We'll talk about it—I'll talk to my friends at school, whatever. If I can, I would like to *not* make Isaiah's attack about who I'm sleeping with, though. I would actually *really like to know* who is running around with a big fucking knife making holes in my kids!"

"Or a big gun making holes in nameless guys in the lake," Aaron said, and Larx groaned.

Then he looked at Aaron thoughtfully. "Think they're connected?"

Aaron cocked his head. "No…?" But not like he was sure.

"What would make you think so?" Eamon asked.

Larx shrugged. "I don't know. Just… we're a small town, you know? Every town has its problems, and violence isn't just a city thing, but two violent crimes in one day? What are the odds?"

"But the victimology is all wrong," Aaron said, impressing Larx with the word in spite of his addiction to crime fiction. "I mean, a middle-aged man was shot and dumped, and a teenager was knifed and left for dead. Besides the violence—"

"And how personal the crimes were," Larx said. "I mean, you have to admit, shooting a guy in his face in his underwear was…."

All three men shuddered. Yeah, that was personal.

"And the knife thing was brutal and close," Eamon said, like he was considering it. "You have good instincts, Larx. I don't know if we can link the investigations yet, but I think we can definitely keep our eyes open for possibilities."

Larx nodded and looked at Aaron. "Are you sure they don't need you to knock on doors or something?"

Eamon shook his head. "Nope—we've got the rest of the force canvassing the area. Larx, part of my job is not just solving crimes, it's making sure the town doesn't burn itself to the ground because people are flighty, spastic cattle. You're the heart of that operation right now. Making calls and supervising homecoming are like tactical battles, and Deputy George is your right-hand man."

He stood and Larx stood with him. "Wait a minute, Sheriff Mills, and I'll get you some fifty-fifty in a travel mug."

"Hot chocolate and coffee?" Eamon said wistfully. "That is damned kind of you, Principal Larkin. You have just become my favorite school official ever."

Larx let a smile slip through the grimness of the morning. "Well, I need to practice my skills in the next couple of hours. I'll be sure to add that."

AN HOUR later the kids had unpacked Kellan's clothes and personal items and effectively converted the game room to Kellan's bedroom for as long as he needed a safe place to stay. Christi had gone so far as to break out some gaming posters and some old football posters that Olivia hadn't thrown away from when she'd had a major crush on one of the Green Bay Packers. They put the posters up, and a picture of Isaiah that Kellan had drawn in art, and Larx had fished out his old comforter—this one blue and brown—and the teddy bear Olivia kept on her bed for when she came to visit.

"It's got good love in it," Christi said soberly. "When we first lived here and Olivia and I had nightmares, Larx kept that bear in his bed. We'd crawl into bed with him for that night, and he'd give the bear to us the next night and say it had all his good dreams in it to keep us safe."

Kellan hugged the bear self-consciously. "Did it work?" he asked, like this was important.

"It did," Christi said, nodding at Larx. "We could sleep when that bear was in bed with us—it was Daddy making sure we were loved."

Kellan hugged the bear some more and looked at Larx with naked longing in his green eyes. "I can have it? Really?"

Larx opened his arms, and Kellan rushed in like any kid he'd ever hugged. "Yeah, kid. All yours. Same love there, I promise."

Kellan nodded and set the bear down on the corner of the futon on top of his pillow. He looked past the room then and said, "Do you think Deputy George is ready to go to the hospital yet?"

At that moment the dryer went off, and Larx grimaced. "Give him five minutes—his clothes just finished." Aaron was showing Kirby how to clear the garden and finish building the bonfire, a task the George men had appointed themselves, apparently.

"Uh, Larx?" Kellan asked, looking from Christi to Larx and back.

"Yeah?"

"Uh, Deputy George stayed here last night?"

Oh. "Yeah."

Kellan smiled a little. "Okay. I'll, uh... I'll keep it secret."

"Not for too long," Larx conceded. "It's just... very new."

"It's a good thing." Kellan nodded for emphasis. "Me and Isaiah, we can't be the only ones, you know?"

"I know." Larx clapped his hands to snap them all out of it. "Okay, everybody—I'll go tell Aaron to get dressed and we can get this road on the show!"

Aaron shooed Christi, Schuyler, and Kellan out to the SUV before he went out himself, pausing for a minute to corner Larx in the kitchen.

"What?" Larx asked, his stomach upset with all of the possibilities for shit to be wrong. "Is there something else I don't know? Another windmill to tilt at? Another fucking dragon hiding in the trees?"

"Larx. Hush."

Aaron was getting good at shutting him up with a kiss, and Larx opened to him greedily, needing all of the comfort and want and warmth that Aaron was trying to shove down his tonsils with his persistent tongue.

Aaron came back up for air, and Larx was lost in that little fantasyland where they would actually get time to themselves.

"Larx?" Aaron said into his ear.

"Yeah?"

"I'm coming home with you after the dance tonight. I'll have clothes for tomorrow and Monday with me. Kirby too."

"Wha—?"

"Parents actually never have the house to themselves, you know that, right?"

"But—"

"Everyone thinks we're sleeping together anyway. I'd like to get some sex out of it."

"Aaron, that's no reason to—"

And another bone-melting, cock-hardening, unapologetic kiss.

"That's not why I want to sleep with you," Aaron said, breath coming short.

Larx studied him for a moment. He was so blond and earnest and kind. "It's going to be a real thing," he said. "I mean… you staying the night, we might end up telling the whole town about that."

"Larx, I want to tell the whole *world* about you. I'll be back with hot dogs and marshmallows and overnight bags. We'll have the bonfire tomorrow because we need to do something normal, and we'll deal with the homecoming dance and whatever the town throws at us together."

Larx closed his eyes and let that sink in. "It feels like we've been together my whole life," he confessed weakly. "Like waking up with you is normal. Like working as a team is the way we're supposed to be."

"Then we'll make it so," Aaron promised. One more kiss then, on the forehead, and Larx was left in a quiet house to pretend he was a politician instead of an educator.

If he hadn't had the taste of Aaron on his tongue, the feel of him still lingering under his palms, Larx would have doubted his life had changed.

But it had changed, and it was those changes that gave him the strength for the task ahead.

FIFTY-FIVE PHONE calls and a fuckton of crepe paper streamers later, Larx stood in the school gym, watching Aaron scoop punch and wishing they could have stayed home with Christi, Kellan, and Kirby. (Heh-heh—alliteration! He giggled to himself, which meant that, yes, he really had just adulted himself off the fucking rails.)

"If you don't want the world to know you're in love with the guy, you need to stop staring at him," Nancy said archly.

Larx shook himself, aware he'd allowed his eyes to glaze over in Aaron's direction.

"At this point I could be staring at my cat licking himself and not know," Larx told her, somewhat unfairly. "I don't function well on four hours of sleep." Two days in a row.

"Yeah, I hear you." Nancy yawned, reminding Larx that she'd been there plenty late the night before and that she'd been his second phone call after Yoshi—and she'd been awake already. She had grade school kids, poor thing. Soccer left no rest for the wicked. "And judging by the gossip, you were on the phone all day. How's that going?"

Larx shrugged. Everyone he'd talked to had *voiced* support. "Everyone sounds like they're on the side of not killing the boys with fire. I'm going to hope. So far I've got sixty people coming to the board meeting in support, and I'm calling grade school people tomorrow."

"We already need a bigger room," Nancy observed. "I'll call Jenny Graves tomorrow. We can use the auditorium."

Larx grunted. "I actually called Heather about that tonight, while I was on top of a ladder taping streamers, if you can believe that."

Nancy laughed. "Only you, and yes I can."

Aaron had been there to help, and he'd turned around from moving chairs and about lost his shit. "Goddammit, Principal Larkin, get your ass down on the ground and pretend you're a fucking adult!"

The class president had almost wet herself laughing, because an adult—an *authority figure*—had not just sworn in front of her but had cursed out her principal. Larx finally taped the damned streamer and continued his conversation with Heather.

"So you're not going to change the venue?" he'd asked.

"We see no reason to at this time," she replied smoothly. "The community will know the teachers are there. That's enough."

"It is *not* enough to 'know' they're there when they're in an overflow room. They need to *see* us there, concerned about the attempted murder of one of our students!"

"We just feel the attitude of the teachers could distract from the problem at hand, and if you'll excuse me, I have another call."

He'd stared at his phone then, outraged, and looked up to Lisa, the poor class president, who was still laughing. He'd smiled for her sake, but inside he was sick at heart.

Kids like Lisa wanted to make a positive difference in the world. How did they grow up into people like Heather, who wanted to control the world in an indifferent fist?

Larx smiled at Nancy now, because he was tired of being pissed and hurt, but Nancy saw through him in a second.

"What did she say?" she asked perceptively. She was a stout, ruddy-faced blonde woman who had probably been bubbly and adorable as a teenager. Now she was pleasant and kind—and brilliant and stronger than she looked. But it was easy to underestimate the

Nancy Pavelles of the world, and Larx made an effort to not be one of the poor souls who did just that.

"She's putting us in an overflow room," he said, furious all over again.

"Really?"

"Really."

"Fucking *really*?"

Larx smiled at her, pleased. "Fuckin' really really, hon. We're gonna be squashed in a conference room with a PA system while this bullshit goes down around our ears."

Nancy shook her head. "Nope. First of all, we're getting there early—as many of us as possible."

Larx smiled at her, encouraged already. "Second of all?"

"Well, I'll go first. Nobody listens to me when I speak at these things anyway. And for my two minutes, I'll have the teachers file past from the overflow room. All of them. So the parents *do* know how many people are concerned about what happened to Isaiah and that the board *doesn't* speak for all of us, and Whitney fucking Olson certainly doesn't."

"I like this plan!" he said, pulling some heart from Nancy and her no-bullshit approach. "I like this plan a lot!"

"Good," she said, winking. "Now tell me about you and Deputy George."

Larx glared at her, and she shrugged.

"What?"

"You think maybe this is a bad topic at a school dance?" he asked her pointedly.

She paused and then grimaced. "Dammit. You know what? It shouldn't be. You asked me about my kids, my husband, my parents—why does this not qualify? Debbie Conrad is over there talking about her boyfriend and how maybe this one will actually give oral—"

"Are you serious?"

"She says it's a deal breaker."

"But *kids* can hear her?"

He was starting to dread Nancy's shrugs. "Kids aren't listening—they're all trying to dry-hump on the dance floor."

Larx looked out over the pressing bodies milling to whatever made him feel too old *this* week, and grimaced. "We should probably do a tracer maneuver there at the next song."

Nancy nodded. The "tracer maneuver," as Larx had dubbed it, was to discharge a clot of teachers at one end of the dance floor and have them spread out and wade through the dancers to the other end. Larx was aware that doing this didn't *guarantee* no pregnancies would occur on the dance floor, but one of those every fifteen minutes definitely cut down on the likelihood.

"But in the meantime," Nancy said like they hadn't dropped the subject, "I would really like to know about you and the yummy deputy."

Larx looked around, and pretty much all the kids really *were* at the refreshment table or trying to simulate sex on the dance floor. "It's happening," he said, glad the lights were dimmed so she couldn't see his cheeks pink. "It's a thing. A relationship." *Running together, making out, a hand job, a blowjob, necessary kisses, sleeping overnight, our kids know, our friends know, it's real. It's real. It's real.* "It's real," he said after a deep breath. "I... he keeps promising he's not going anywhere."

Nancy hmmed in her throat. "Good." She touched his shoulder gently. "You've been alone too long."

Larx looked at her drolly. "My socks match, my hair is combed, and I have a tie. Larx is very self-sufficient, thank you."

"Yes, Larx. You're a fucking island. Now go shut Debbie up before the kids start thinking that oral is a marriage proposal."

That was actually a priority.

"SO," AARON asked on the way home, "do you think any of them got pregnant there?"

Larx laughed. "We did our best," he said, feeling sweaty and sticky and grouchy. "I swear, one more trip through the dance floor and I was going to start handing out condoms and telling them to go for it, just be safe."

"Yikes. Your career would end, but at least you'd go out in flames."

Larx leaned back in the seat as Aaron drove. "Yeah, but geez, that music makes me feel old."

"I heard some Linkin Park in there," Aaron observed.

Larx had too. "I wanted to see them dance," he said disconsolately, feeling stupid and idealistic. "Do you know what it would have meant to me in high school, to see two boys dancing at homecoming?"

"Yeah," Aaron agreed. "I do."

"But it was more than that. I wanted to see *them* dance." Larx sighed, remembering that hidden shaft of joy he'd felt when the boys had come out. God, had it only been Thursday? "I wanted to see them have their whole lives together without the closet looming over their heads."

"They still have that."

"Yeah, but now they have *this*," Larx snarled. "And they have this, and now the board is trying to make some woman carving a hole in a boy's stomach into the boy's fault for being gay, and into *our* fault for making it okay. I don't... I mean I *should* understand. I should. 'Hey, we don't get the gay! And we're scared 'cause we're not qualified to deal with knife-wielding psychos! So we're going to confuse the two issues and give everybody a thing to hate! And expect you all to just fucking live with it!' I mean I get the strategy, and I get what they're trying to do, but I just don't get it. Why are they in charge if they're that fucking stupid!"

Aaron's laugh rolled bitterly through the car. "I don't know, Larx. Maybe it's because the smart people fight like hell not to be in the driver's seat, you fucking think?"

"Augh!" Larx covered his face with his hands and fought the urge to kick at Aaron's county-owned vehicle. "This board meeting's going to be a travesty, you know that, right?"

"No, I don't. Because you're going to be there, and I don't know if anyone has told you this, Larx, but you don't suffer fools."

"Gladly?"

"To fucking live."

This surprised a laugh out of him. "You make me sound bloodthirsty. I'm really a very nice man."

"Sure you are."

"I'm pissed. Someone hurt one of my kids."

"I know, baby." Aaron's voice dropped intimately. "And you feel like you're in a pressure cooker. I've been there. Not quite like this, but you remember the—"

"Healey case," Larx said, feeling numb. "I remember." A mom-and-pop pot operation had turned into a shootout with deputies. Five years earlier—Larx remembered. "Maureen was a sophomore then. She was a basket case when that happened. I remember you dropped the kids off at school the next day and you still had the sling." There had been an investigation—six weeks Aaron had been on paid leave while the feds and the county had picked his life apart to see if he had made the wrong decision.

"We saw smoke," Aaron said, voice lost in reverie. "And me and Warren went to investigate. That was all. We called it in, I went first, he stayed behind as backup, and oh my God, fucking psychopaths with Uzis started firing at us. It was insane."

"You were cleared," Larx said, voice hoarse. He knew Aaron had meant to reassure him, but Larx wasn't thinking about the investigation or about Aaron's career. He was thinking about that sling, and about how Aaron had been shot at, and oh my God, he could have been a hole in the world, and Larx would never have known.

"Yeah, but it was uncomfortable. I'm not going to lie. But that's what happens when you take on responsibility, you know?"

"Uh-huh." Larx's head was swimming and he could barely breathe. "You were shot."

"I was fine."

"Shot," Larx said, a full five-ton weight descending on his chest and head just as Aaron pulled into the driveway. "I'm going to get outed to the school board and you could get *shot*!"

"Uh-oh."

Larx dropped his hands and looked out, expecting to see cherry lights or policemen or the house on fire or fucking monsters at this juncture. His adrenaline was dumping so hard into his blood he felt his eyelids throb.

"Uh-oh what? The kids? The kids are okay, right? Oh God. I have another kid. I have *two*. I have a god-damned haiku poem sleeping in my living room, and they think I'm a grown-up! And I'm going to need to out myself to the school board and you could get *shot*!"

Aaron killed the engine abruptly, and while Larx was still thumping back into his seat, he unclicked his seat belt *and* Larx's, putting his head practically in Larx's lap to get to the buckle.

"Larx, baby, calm down."

"Shot!"

"Stop saying that!" Aaron framed his face with chilled palms and just held him, looking into his eyes and breathing meaningfully until Larx took his lead and tried to still his breathing. "Now calm down."

"I'm… I'm…."

"Freaking out. I get it. Deep breaths, Larx. One. Two. Three. How we doing?"

Larx's eyes burned. "It's like my brain's on ran-domizer," he said in horrified wonder. "Twenty things I have to worry about, real things that may happen, and what's floating to the top is five years ago, you got shot. Why is this such a big deal? Except you could have died, and I wouldn't have known you, and oh my God, what would the world be like without you in it?"

Aaron's kiss was not a surprise.

Larx opened his mouth and tried to relax into it, to allow the contact to calm him, and to some extent it worked—but not entirely.

Aaron deepened the kiss, sliding his hands down to cup Larx's jaw, then his neck, and some of the anxiety slipped away—but not the burning eyes, not the swollen throat. Larx shuddered hard, and Aaron pulled away to whisper in his ear.

"Let it out. C'mon, Larx. You don't have to be strong all the time right now."

Larx let out a whine, part yearning, part pure frustration, and he dissolved, allowing his body to slump forward into Aaron's arms. Aaron caught him, tightening his embrace, trapping Larx against his chest, letting him know he was there, he was fine, and that Larx could keep breathing, in and out, one problem at a time.

Larx's shivers subsided, and he became aware of the good things—Aaron's heat through his leather jacket, the smell of sweat and aftershave, the feeling of his stubble-rough cheek against Larx's own.

The rumble of his deep voice as he hummed. Foreigner's "I Want to Know What Love Is." Larx let a whisper of a laugh out.

"Foreigner?"

"God," Aaron rumbled. "I got so tired of pop and hip-hop tonight. I know it makes me old, but I was just *done*."

"Holy crap," Larx muttered. "Right? I could have killed for some Offspring or Green Day or—God, we are so damned old."

"The Killers," Aaron sighed. "Was it so much to ask?"

This time it was a real laugh, not bitter at all. He began to sing "I Want to Know What Love Is," using words and everything, and Aaron pressed Larx's head against his shoulder, and they sang quietly together.

"Sappy song," Larx breathed when they were done with the chorus.

"Got me laid a lot," Aaron confessed.

"Mm. For me it was Tesla's 'Love Song.'"

"Local boys." Aaron sounded like he approved. "Larx, let's go inside. Let's give thanks for the kids, shower—"

"Because oh dear Lord could those kids sweat," Larx swore fervently.

"A-to-the-fuck-men. And let's crawl in bed together and, you know. See what love is."

"Sure." The word was mild, but Larx's heart felt anything but. "Sure," he repeated, reaching up to cup Aaron's cheek. "Anything. Anywhere you are. That's where I'll find it."

"Sure," Aaron whispered against his temple.

A breath. And then another. And then a third, and they could separate long enough to climb out of the SUV.

Out of Control

THE KIDS barely moved as the two of them came in. A half-finished game of Monopoly sat on the coffee table, along with a pizza box and chip bags and soda cans, all pointing to a well-funded pity party for three kids who would not be going to homecoming. Aaron had sort of hoped Kirby would get his courage up and ask a girl—or a boy—this year, but his son was so damned pragmatic. And a little bit shy. Aaron hoped the boy lost his virginity in the semi-anonymity of college, because the small-town thing was inhibiting him in ways Aaron had never anticipated.

But Kirby's sex life was—happily—not Aaron's concern now or, really, ever.

Aaron's sex life was about to dramatically improve.

Aaron lay in Larx's bed up on his elbow and waited for Larx to talk himself from the shower to the bed.

Aaron knew he was done with the shower—it had gone off five minutes ago. He'd heard teeth brushing, a quick pass with the electric razor, and what had to be BO control, and then, just when he thought he'd finally see Larx's chest again, silence.

"Larx?" he asked gently, wondering how much the poor man could take before Aaron had to forget about sex and just sedate him until the board meeting on Monday.

"Yeah?"

"I would really like to see you naked."

That surprised, almost shy half laugh Aaron was getting used to. "I think you have *vastly* overrated this body without clothes."

"Please tell me you're not standing in front of the mirror wondering if you can do this."

"I have gray in my pubes," Larx said, and Aaron stifled a laugh on his bicep. "My *pubes*, Aaron. I haven't looked at them in seven years and they grew gray without me."

Aaron reached out and turned the lamp off. "Put your underwear on, slide in with me, and we'll have sex by braille. There are no gray pubic hairs in braille."

The bathroom light went off, and Aaron scooted over to make room for the man in his underwear. He was a little regretful that he wouldn't get to see Larx's chest again, but as Larx turned in his arms—warm, smooth skin, tightly muscled man—Aaron thought he could live with the loss just this once.

He captured Larx's mouth in a kiss, and those didn't get any worse, so he just kept going. Ah, the kissing got better. Every time, the kisses got better. Fresh breath helped, but this time, so did knowing they weren't going anywhere. They weren't in the car, they weren't outside, they were in a bed, and Aaron continued with the kiss. It grew in momentum until they were locked in a full-on mouth-maul, tongues battling, breath coming short. Larx's hands were insistent on his hips, pulling him forward until they were grinding on each other, a master class of frotting.

Aaron groaned into his mouth and stilled his frantic humping.

"We'll come too soon," he whispered. He rolled then, pinning Larx underneath him, a part of him stirring in excitement when Larx spread his knees and went limp and pliant.

"You have plans?" Larx asked, looking hopeful and, God—trusting. Innocent. Young.

Aaron wanted to give him *everything*. "I sort of want to lick you all over," he said, nipping at Larx's chin. "But you've got to, you know. Tell me what's right, what doesn't work—"

"I washed everything twice," Larx said earnestly. "Tongue everything. You can't go wrong with tongue. Lubrication. Penetration. All good."

"Oh my God!" Aaron laughed. "You are really needy, do you know that?"

"Eight years, Aaron. You are warm, you are"— Larx wiggled his groin against Aaron's throbbing cock—"willing. You even seem to like me. A lot. You have the fucking job."

"And the job fucking you, I hope."

Larx nodded, eyes limpid in the dark, and Aaron kissed him again, running his palms down Larx's arms, the lean knots of muscles at his ribs and his stomach, then down under his shorts.

"Mm…." Larx relaxed more with every caress, and Aaron kissed down his neck, nibbling, liking the greedy moans Larx made when his teeth sank into the skin.

He tasted clean, of course, and spicy, and Aaron licked and nipped his way down to Larx's pecs. He smiled for a moment, because he'd never tasted a flat male nipple before, and he lost himself in suckling the tiny ridge of flesh and tonguing the soft flatness of the areola.

Larx panted, kneading the muscles of Aaron's shoulders before tangling his hands in Aaron's hair.

"That's awesome!" He ground up against Aaron again, and Aaron sucked a little harder. "Great. Fantastic…. God, Aaron, keep moving down, okay?"

Aaron chuckled against his skin and stuck out a pointed tongue. He swept and tickled and nibbled a little more down to the edge of Larx's boxers, pushing the comforter down as he repositioned himself.

"This is excellent," he said, excited as a teenager. "I'm going to taste your penis!"

Larx let out a bark of laughter, and Aaron pulled down his shorts. In the faint light from the window, he could see the thing—the big thing, the thing that many people saw as the difference between heterosexual and homosexual sex.

It was both unimpressive and really fucking amazing.

It lay long, erect, and thin against Larx's abdomen, and the circumcised head was flushed darkly, leaking as it flexed. Aaron licked slowly from the base to the tip, tongue dragging along the veins under the skin.

The surprisingly soft skin.

He grabbed Larx's cock in his fist and stroked, using the same motion that would please himself. Larx's moan gratified him and gave him courage at the same time.

He licked the head, closing his eyes at the taste of precome, at Larx's greedy whine.

Again, and again, the texture of the skin, the sweetness of the pre, the strangled, incoherent begging sounds Larx made—Aaron ground himself against the bed to ease the ache in his own cock.

Larx spread his knees, arching his entire groin up, making it clear he was Aaron's banquet and Aaron could sample as he wanted.

Aaron wanted the whole meal.

He kept his fist wrapped around Larx's cock and kept that delirious pressure against the head with his tongue and palate. With his other hand, he reached for the lubricant he'd snuck out of Larx's dresser. It was there, right by his pillow, exactly where he put it, and he snicked the lid open and dumped some on his fingers.

Multitasking—it was the thing that was really hard to do for yourself. Yeah, Aaron had fingered his own ass in the darkness over the last ten years, and he'd stroked his own cock, but it was the coordination that was hard to manage.

He could *do* that for Larx. Carefully, aware that this could be an intrusion—and that Larx had said it hadn't happened in a while—Aaron slid a single digit past the cave of mystery into the little puckered porthole.

Larx moaned and hunched down, taking his finger in to the second knuckle as Aaron wiggled it around a little, trying to stretch the rim.

"Oh my God.... Aaron... oh God. Not gonna last...." He spurted a little in Aaron's mouth, just to prove it, and Aaron let go of his cock entirely.

Concentrating on his job, he shoved Larx's thighs up until his knees were spread and his ass was splayed open for Aaron to play with.

Ignoring the taste of the lube—which was vaguely salty—Aaron pulled out his finger and swiped his tongue across Larx's pucker, taking heart from the way Larx thrashed, begging breathlessly, that he was doing this right.

"More, Aaron—God—"

"Patience, not your strong suit," Aaron mumbled, licking between words.

"Want you inside me!" Larx begged, and oh! That's what did it. Aaron pushed up, shoving his shorts down and wiping lube over his cockhead before covering Larx's body with his own. Carefully, he positioned his aching erection right at Larx's stretched, lubed entrance.

"Larx, you sure you're ready?" Aaron asked, agonized. This could hurt—he knew that. But he wanted to be inside Larx as much as Larx wanted it.

Larx cupped his neck with unsteady hands. "Please," he whispered. "Please."

Aaron thrust forward slowly, feeling that tight ring of muscle expand around his slickened bell. He studied Larx's expression, but Larx's head was back, his eyes closed, his face slack as he made every effort to accommodate this invasion into the snug haven of his body.

And still he kept pushing, shuddering when the warmth and slickness enveloped his cockhead, kept spreading wider as he pushed inside. Larx shook around him, his limbs pliant, his hands fisting the sheets and releasing in the pulse of the desire that rocked his body.

Oh God. Almost there. Almost there. "Oh yes," Aaron sighed as he nestled firmly in Larx's ass.

Larx shuddered around him. And again. And then he wrapped his legs around Aaron's hips, and—eyes at half-mast, too submissive to even look at Aaron and see him—he begged, "Fuck me now, sweetheart. Please. I need it so bad."

Wow. Just…. Aaron pulled back, feeling the squeeze and glide of that band of muscle, and then he thrust forward, the pressure around his head exquisite. Larx moaned, moving his hands to Aaron's shoulders, and Aaron did it again and again and again.

"Faster!"

"Nungh!"

Faster, harder. Larx was sturdy, strong, body knotty and weathered, a runner, muscular and tough. Aaron rocketed inside him, the slap of his thighs against Larx's backside satisfying and dirty at once.

Larx moaned, eyes drifting closed, and Aaron felt the first convulsion of orgasm rock his body. He looked down just in time to see it, a white ribbon in the darkness, striping Larx's abdomen, painting his chest and the little patch of gray-and-black hair in the center. Larx's limbs shook, and the things that did to Aaron's insides….

It was Aaron's turn to groan, and he muffled the sound in Larx's neck, wanting to lick up his come and taste it but too engaged in the act of *fucking, I'm fucking a man, I'm fucking Larx and he wants it, he came, it's sticky and bitter under my skin* to stop. Larx bucked and keened, lips clamped together in an attempt to keep quiet.

So. Damned. Sexy.

Aaron's orgasm washed hard, tightening his taint and his asshole, pulling his testicles up into achy little balls, clenching his stomach and throbbing through his cock with a giant, almost painful spasm. He bit down on Larx's shoulder and Larx made a deep, throaty, satisfied sound that defied description.

Aaron bit again, his entire body convulsing as his orgasm rocked him hard enough to blacken his vision.

He was coming, ejaculating, shooting his spend *inside Larx's body*.

Larx was sated, half-conscious, beautifully submissive to Aaron in a way Aaron had never imagined, his thighs splayed, his hands patting limply at Aaron's neck as he half sobbed into Larx's ear.

Oh God. Oh God, they'd done it, and it had been beautiful, overwhelming, stunning.

Aaron closed his eyes so tight the tears slipped through, and when Larx tightened his arms around his shoulders, he had no choice but to let go, surrender to the comfort of his lover's body as his lover had surrendered to the invasion of Aaron's flesh.

"Oh Larx," he whispered when he could talk again—could *breathe* again. "That was so very very—"

"Important," Larx said, and the desolation in his voice made Aaron's chest ache.

Oh Larx, you aren't in this alone.

"Important," he seconded, licking a drop of sweat as it ran down Larx's jaw. "Necessary. God…. Larx, I can't live without your body in my bed. Not anymore. You have to know that now."

"Good," Larx whispered, wrapping his arms and legs completely around Aaron's body and shivering hard. Aaron's cock slid out, and Aaron felt the loss of that warmth, that shelter, keenly. "I can't… I can't go back to life before you," he said, voice broken. "I don't know how there was ever a life before you."

They were grown men, nearing fifty, but it didn't feel ludicrous at all. Every touch, every whisper, every shiver between them was brand-new. It wasn't young love—it was worse, bigger, more painful. They'd lost before. They knew the dangers of love. And they fell anyway, whispering each other's name in the dark, their bodies coated in sweat and come, vulnerable to the cold.

Aaron wanted to be the only warmth Larx would ever need, but eventually he pulled the comforter around their shoulders and rolled to his side. Larx pillowed his head on Aaron's bicep, and they touched softly in the protection of their blanket fort, grown lovers, as lost in the dark as children.

AT SIX in the morning, Aaron's phone rang next to the bed. He had to practically crawl over Larx to get it, and Larx barely grunted.

"Eamon?" he asked, voice bleary. He *thought* that was the name on caller ID.

"Deputy? I know I gave you yesterday off while we canvassed the neighborhood and tried to ID the corpse, but something's come up, and we need you."

"Come up?" Oh yes, something *had* come up the night before. It took a minute—Aaron had to shake himself before he realized that the only people who would want to talk about that were him and Larx.

"Yessir. Our canvass team found some blood on one of the docks out here at the lake. It's a private dock—it serves ten of the residences here, and we have warrants to search the grounds and the garages of each of those houses."

Well, that was a big job—but usually one they could leave to the poor deputies who were working that weekend.

"And you need me for this because why?"

"Because one of the names on the list of home-owners was Olson."

And that suddenly, Aaron was wide-awake. "Olson?"

"Whitney and Carl Olson."

"Oh my God." Aaron's side of the bed backed up against the wall, so he made moves to slither out at the bottom. "Have you spoken to either one of them? Their lawyer? Anything?"

"See, that's where you're needed here. This is go-ing to be a complete and total surprise—and if you're here, we can serve three houses at the same time, which means—"

Aaron slid completely down and landed on the ground with a thump. "We can catch them by sur-prise," he said excitedly. "Bright and early, seven in the morning, found the body, found the blood, we can search everyone's house. 'Oh, hey there, Mrs. Olson, we didn't know this was you, fancy that, do you have any idea who was floating in your lake two days ago?'"

Eamon's chuckle was decidedly unfriendly. "That's what I'm saying."

"I'm totally in," Aaron muttered, standing up and shivering. They hadn't turned on the thermostat the night before—Larx was probably one of those heathens who waited until it got *really* cold before he did that, which meant that Aaron was running around naked in a room so chilly he could see his breath. "Just let me get dressed."

"Meet us at the entrance to Mustang Estates," Eamon told him. "I'll bring coffee this time if you promise to bring me some of Larx's fifty-fifty tomorrow."

Aaron paused in the act of pulling boxer shorts from his knapsack. "I'll, uh, tell him," he said, realizing that would mean he'd spent the night at Larx's three nights in a row.

"Is that going to cause a problem?" Eamon asked mildly.

Aaron's cheeks burned, and he shimmied into his boxers as fast as possible while he spoke. "Just trying to find a sleepover rhythm," he mumbled.

"Rhythm? Boy, if you fit into a man's life as easily as you fit into that man's kitchen, your rhythm is that you go to sleep in his bed and you wake up in his bed and you go to sleep in his bed and you wake up in his bed. Jesus, do I have to show you where to put your pecker?"

Aaron flipped his T-shirt over his head. "No, sir," he said, his entire body sweating by now. "We figured that out on our own."

"I am relieved to hear it. Now get your ass in gear and get down here. You've got forty-five minutes."

Eamon signed off, and Aaron pulled his pants on and slid his cell phone in his back pocket. Then he slid his khaki shirt on and clipped on his badge before tucking everything into place and buckling on his holster. His gun had been packed in a locked case in his knapsack, and he pulled it out and snapped it in place with fingers long accustomed to the task.

"I forget," Larx mumbled from the bed, startling him.

Aaron grabbed socks and boots from the bag and went to the edge of the bed, shoving Larx back a little so he could sit down.

"Forget what?" he asked, keeping his voice soft. He wanted to think of Larx warm and sleepy as Aaron got ready to face his day.

"You and the gun." They'd kept the lights off the night before. Larx hadn't been able to obsess about Aaron's scars, but Aaron knew a reckoning was coming.

"Yeah. I have one," Aaron admitted, leaning down to kiss Larx's temple. "I rarely draw it, but it's what I do."

Larx cupped his cheek. "Such a gentle lover," he slurred. "Hard to believe you carry a gun."

Aaron's heart swelled to the point of aching, and he captured Larx's hand and placed a kiss in his palm. "I'll always be your gentle lover," he promised. "My job won't ever change that, okay?"

"Deal." Larx smiled, and his hand slipped down limply. "Where you going?"

"To serve a warrant to the Olson family."

Larx's eyes tried hard to open. "For reals?"

"For really really," Aaron told him. "I'll call you when I'm done, okay? Maybe bring you coffee?"

"Bring yourself, Deputy. No new holes. It's all I ask."

"Well, start the bonfire without me if I can't make it before afternoon," Aaron said—it was only practical. "And maybe let Kirby go get some more clothes if Christi is taking Kellan to the hospital as well."

Larx groaned. "I might as well get up now."

"You absolutely will not!" Aaron laughed, putting his hand on Larx's arm to keep him still. Larx's mouth might have been saying "Get up!" but his muscles were abandoned and limp. "You, my friend, are going to stay here and sleep until at least eight o'clock. I know you've got a day of phone calls and home improvement in front of you, but the least you could do is get enough sleep to get it done."

"You sound all bossy. Just because you topped doesn't make you the boss of me. Wait until *I* top. I will be so sweet and submissive to you the next day, you'll have to check to make sure it was my cock in your ass."

Aaron laughed throatily, not sure if it was the sleep or the man talking but thinking he was funny and uninhibited this way. "I'll definitely know whose cock was in my ass," he whispered next to Larx's ear before nibbling a moment on the lobe. "Now be good and I'll turn on your thermostat before I leave."

Larx groaned in pure hedonism. "You *do* love me."

It wasn't even a question. It was as simple and as real as falling in love with his wife had been. "Of course I do," Aaron whispered into his ear.

And then he kissed Larx on the cheek one more time and slipped away before Larx could realize what he'd said and panic about it. It was no more than the truth.

LESS THAN an hour later, he, Sheriff Mills, and the entire complement of deputies were standing in a huddle near Eamon's unit, waiting for their warrant assignments.

"Everyone know where to go?" Eamon asked, and of course they did.

"Yards, pool houses, outbuildings, garages, cars," Aaron said smartly. "The line is drawn at the door to the house. If we find anything interesting, we get Andrea and Gracie"—he indicated the two forensic investigators—"to collect it and test it for residue. If we find blood, bodies, or weapons, we have probable cause and we can search the house. Did I cover it, boss?"

Eamon nodded. "You make sure you cover *your* asses," he said seriously. "These people are rich. Most of them have lawyers to validate their morning dump, and if you so much as sneeze on their Bentleys, *we'll* be the ones up on charges. Are we clear?"

"Yessir!"

Aaron looked at Warren Coolidge, who was the guy he usually ended up partnered with when they did things like this. "You want me to serve while you poke around a bit?" he asked.

"I understand she's a ripe bitch. You're welcome to her."

Aaron nodded and then remembered Larx's opinion about the two crimes being linked. "Look, keep

your eyes open for *anything*. Clothing, signs of trying
to destroy evidence, hunting knives—"

"But wasn't this guy shot?"

Aaron huffed out a breath. "Two violent crimes in
what? Two, three days?"

Warren was younger than Aaron—pretty, with
blue eyes framed with black lashes, and a full, red
mouth—but he had a content, uninquisitive sort of
mind. Aaron had seen him lots of times without his
shirt, but never, not once, had he felt the urge to follow
him anywhere and beg him not to run in the road. It
was starting to occur to him how much he had enjoyed
Larx's *person*—and not just his pretty, shiny chest.

And finally—*finally*—Warren arrived at the con-
clusion that Larx had beat them all to the day before.

"You think the kid getting stabbed was
connected?"

Aaron shrugged. "It's an idea," he said. He remembered Larx saying that Whitney had arrived late,
out of breath, with wet hair. Mustang Estates was
about twenty minutes from the high school. Fifteen
if you sped like you were covered in blood and didn't
want anyone to see. How long had they waited for the
ambulance? How long had the paramedics worked
on Isaiah before they left the scene? How long had
it taken to round up the kids and start the spotlight
search? Long enough for a woman to run to her car,
drive home and shower, then drive back?

Think… think… think…. Well, it would depend
on where she'd parked her car, wouldn't it?

Aaron remembered seeing Julia in a corner, texting furiously—not to a friend in the crowd.

"George!" Eamon barked, and Aaron pulled his mind to the here and now.

"Yessir, we're moving." Warren had ridden with Eamon, and Aaron gestured for him to get in the car along with Gracie.

His stomach vibrated in anticipation, a thrill of electricity riding him. The last time he'd felt like this, he and Warren were knocking on the door of a mom-and-pop weed operation, and it had been the reason he'd heard the click of the gun before the first shot. Listening to this humming had saved his and Warren's lives that day—he was hoping it would serve them just as well now.

The main house on the Olson estate was nearly half a city block long, but because it was set on a square half mile of property, it looked big but not monstrous.

At least until Aaron powered the SUV unit up over the long concrete driveway to the top of what had once been a small hill.

"The pool, the pool house, the garage—"

"Four-car garage," Warren muttered.

"The yard—"

"How far?" Gracie asked. The house itself had a decent-size yard, fenced in with a wrought-iron masterpiece about four feet high. But beyond that, the property itself stretched back a few acres, and as Aaron pulled up to the guest property on the side of the house and scanned that stretch, he saw the smoke of a recently used fire pit.

"Start with the fire pit," he said grimly. "It's part of the grounds, it counts—"

"And it's a stunning place to try to get rid of evidence," Gracie conceded. "Okay, guys, suit

up—Aaron, here's your gear in case it goes from
search to crime scene." She handed him a small sealed
packet of booties and gloves, as well as an evidence
bag and forceps for the small stuff.

"Wait until after I serve the warrant," Aaron said
dryly, pocketing the gear anyway. His stomach was
buzzing big-time.

He strode up to the door, Warren at his back, while
Gracie continued to the garage, which stretched out on
the other side of the house. She'd wait until his signal,
but the fact was, the warrant didn't require notification
or anybody on the property. This was a courtesy—like
Eamon said, CYA.

He hit the doorbell hard, unsurprised when a
mussed housekeeper answered the door.

"May we speak to the lady of the house?" he
asked politely, and the woman—fortyish, with a lined
and stoic face—darted her eyes to the upstairs and
back.

"She's not well at the moment," she said quietly.
"What can I do for you?"

Aaron pulled out the copy of the warrant Whitney
would need to give to her lawyer. "Could you give this
to Mrs. Olson and tell her we're instituting a search of
her grounds, her garage, and all of the outbuildings on
her premises? We'll need the garage door opened, and
if that doesn't happen within a reasonable time, we'll
have to force it open, and I can't promise it will be
pretty. According to that warrant, if we find probable
cause in any of the outside part, we can turn our focus
to the inside part, so she needs to know that too."

God, let it be outside, he thought from a strictly
pragmatic point of view. He'd hate to be in charge of

searching this place—the odds of missing something
small in a venue this large were staggering.

The woman took the paper with an almost rab-
bit-like movement, as though she was used to dodging
angry words a lot, and then she nodded at Aaron in
fear. "I'll give this to her," she said. "But she won't
be happy."

At that moment, Aaron caught a rustling from the
corner of his vision, and he looked up in time to see
the edge of a filmy white nightgown disappear from
his vision.

"Mrs. Olson?" he called, taking a step inside.
"Mrs. Olson? We're searching your property right
now, and that of your neighbors. There's a possibility
of a dangerous fugitive on the grounds or about this
area, if I might have a moment of your—"

"*Fuck off!*" Whitney shrilled, and Aaron shook
his head.

"Well, then," he muttered. "I guess she'll call her
lawyer."

He nodded at the poor housekeeper, who was going to have a *very* unhappy morning, and walked out,
closing the door behind him. He strode toward Gracie,
and they crossed in front of the wide expanse of the
garage. They were in the middle of the second door
when Aaron heard the unmistakable sound of a perfor-
mance engine revving hard from a cold start—and it
was coming from behind the door they were passing.
He grabbed Gracie's arm instinctively and hauled at
her hard, both of them clearing the edge of the second
door as it exploded out behind them. Aaron kept running, pulling Gracie to her feet when she would have
stumbled, and he turned in time to see Julia Olson,

her face contorted in fear, as she backed that gigantic vehicle down the hill. She swung the car around at the bottom of the hill, her touch on the wheel so inexpert that she almost dumped it over between the angle and the speed.

She made the spin, though, and took off, leaving Aaron and Gracie with their chests pumping in and out, both of them shaking with the adrenaline bleed.

"Well," Aaron said, looking at the remains of the fractured door in the driveway, "at least we don't have to ask them to let us in."

"Uh, Aaron?" Gracie asked, eyes big. "Did that look like a car you'd give a teenager?"

"Nope," he muttered, taking a few steps toward the inside of the garage. Sure enough, a bright blue Kia Sportage sat, pristine, at the far end. "In fact, that looked like the kind of car an adult would tell her kid to drive off the premises to hide evidence."

He pulled out his radio. "Sheriff Mills, this is Deputy George, can you read me?"

"What do you got, Deputy?"

"I've got Julia Olson taking off in her mother's car, so freaked out she took the garage door with her."

"Well, that was unexpected."

"You are telling me."

"I think that might get us a probable cause. You sit tight and we'll send B group in with you for the premises search, and we'll see what we can do."

"Yessir. You may want to put out an APB across the county for a black Lincoln Navigator with the following plates—"

"You got the plates?"

"Yessir, I did."

"I'm having my wife bake you some more cookies, Deputy, because that was damned quick thinking."

Aaron met amused eyes with Gracie as she made gagging motions with her index finger. "That would be much appreciated, Sheriff Mills. Thank you kindly."

He rang off and shook his head. "Are we ready to start the garage now?"

Gracie made gagging motions again. "I can't believe you get excited when that man rewards you with cookies."

Aaron laughed and figured he was safe with Gracie, mother of two and raging liberal. "I came out to him and he still wants me to have his job," he said mildly. "I'll even take home her coffee cake."

Gracie looked amused. "Yeah, and let Larx put it down the garbage disposal," she snorted.

Oh. "You know about Larx?"

Gracie shrugged. "Dropped my kid off at the dance last night and saw you two talking," she said with a little smile. "I'm a trained observer, Deputy, but I wasn't going to say anything if you weren't."

Aaron thought about Larx, warm and sleepy when he'd left the bed that morning, and felt an unexpected surge of satisfaction at that. People saw them and thought they belonged together. Not "go figure," not "stranger things."

"Well, one of us has a scary job where coming out could shake people up," he said meaningfully.

"Yeah, and the other one of you is in law enforcement."

He laughed then and had a thought. "Here, let me get in there and turn on the light for you, and we'll start searching. But first I need to call Larx."

Home Fires Burning

So much for sleeping in.

The call from Aaron came at seven thirty in the morning—it wasn't the first call he'd gotten, although it was the one guaranteed to wake him out of that "screening the calls" fugue state that grown-ups could enter when they didn't want to get up.

"You're okay, right? What happened?"

"Fine," Aaron said, his voice so deliberately laid-back Larx had to wonder what happened. "I was just wondering—the Olson girl took off in her mother's car just as we got here. Do you have any idea where the kids might park—any lovers' lanes I haven't heard of, any haunts where a kid who's got no friends at the moment would chill out and hide?"

Larx sat up in bed and sucked in a breath. His ass was a little sore—muscles a little stretched, a little used, all points south a bit tender. He wriggled as he sat, and the tenderness became sensitivity, and whee! Just like that he was ready to go again.

At forty-seven. Go figure.

He had to work at focusing on what Aaron had asked him about. "Uh, there's a pullout off Olson Road. It's sort of overgrown—used to be a forestry service track, but it's what we used to get all the chairs and shit to the bonfire, because you can pull a car closer and come in from the north side instead of the east side where the footpath is."

Aaron's rough chuckle told Larx he'd said something important. "You are sheer genius," he told Larx. "I hadn't thought of that one. It's like you can read my mind."

"Can you read mine?" Larx asked lasciviously, and this time Aaron's laugh grew positively filthy.

"We'll play that game after the kids are asleep," he promised. "And I've got to go so we can be done and I can get home to you."

"Okay," Larx yawned. "Love you—be careful." And just like that, he was wide-awake. "Oh my God."

"I already said it," Aaron told him. "So you can't freak out. Love you too. Back later."

The click on the other end of the phone left Larx floundering, lost in what they'd both said, all of it, while Larx's body still tingled from their lovemaking the night before.

Oh God. He'd said it. He meant it. How could he possibly have meant it? It had been—*Forever. Weeks. Months.* They'd known each other for years.

He meant it. There was no time before Aaron. If he didn't have two beautiful daughters, he wouldn't believe any such time existed.

An odd feeling, this—not something he'd felt with Alicia. Not something he'd felt with *any* lover. When he'd been a kid fucking anything that moved, he'd thought love didn't happen. Love was too painful. What human being would actually let themselves in for that sort of loss? And then he'd held Olivia, and Christiana, and he'd known love was real, it was powerful, and the creatures we bestowed it upon were fragile and human.

With Alicia he'd experienced contentment, but he'd thought that was all a couple would have—you couldn't *choose* to love another adult human being the way he'd been compelled to love his two tiny daughters.

But you could. He *did*. He chose to let this feeling in, chose to let Aaron take over his heart just like Larx had let him into his body.

Those fucking-around years—the lube-and-condom years, the "what was this person's name again?" years—hadn't prepared him for the night before.

Hadn't prepared him for this moment right now.

His name was Aaron.

OF COURSE even epiphanies about love had to yield to taking a shower and answering the slew of calls coming through.

And then returning more.

Yoshi called at ten while Larx was outside, talking on the phone and finishing the final bits of stripping the garden. The weather had gotten chilly since two weeks earlier, and Larx was in jeans and a sweatshirt, wearing gloves to keep his cold fingers from stinging as he pulled plants from the ground.

"Yes, I'm freaking out," Larx said. "Yes, it's going to be a clusterfuck. Yes, Heather Perkins is a complete twat. Is there anything we haven't covered here, Yosh?"

"What are you doing?"

"Getting the burn pile ready. I'm taking the kids to the hospital in half an hour, and after visiting, we're coming back to roast hot dogs and marshmallows. Because I need to clear my yard, dammit!"

"Fine. I'll be there with soy dogs."

"That's blasphemous."

"Soy dogs, Larx, soy dogs. Something not awful for you!"

"That will give me gas when I've finally got someone willing to sleep with me? Thanks a lot, Yosh. I thought you were my friend."

"Wait—go back to that other part again?"

"I don't kiss and tell."

"But do you fuck and write it in an exposé?"

Larx laughed. "Not that either. But it's real, Yosh. I hope it is. I'm a little bit, uh… you know."

"Gone."

"Think so."

"I'll tell Tane. He keeps telling me your aura was incomplete—he'll be happy."

Larx didn't want to talk about Tane, thin and intense and taciturn—he never could figure out how cheerful, sarcastic Yoshi could live day in and day out with Tane Pavelle, but he figured as long as Yoshi stayed cheerful and sarcastic, it had to be all good, right?

"I'm happy he's happy," Larx said diplomatically. "Why are you coming here with a meat-like abomination?"

"Because," Yoshi said, sounding like an irritated child. "Because I need you to not do anything stupid tomorrow, and I'm hoping by coming and participating in your weird Samhain ritual bonfire, you'll listen to me when I talk."

"I always listen to you when you talk," Larx said, confused. True, Yoshi couldn't ground Larx the way Aaron—unexpectedly—could, but Larx would have gotten fired at least three times if he hadn't listened to Yoshi's commonsense advice.

"Sure, but you don't always do what I say, and we need that to happen this time out."

Larx sighed. "I was hoping it would just be because you wanted my company and we were friends," he said, feeling melancholy and betrayed.

"We *are* friends. I love your company. More specifically, I would like to keep working with you for the next twenty to thirty years."

"In thirty years I'll be too old to have a prostate. Let's settle for twenty-five." But in thirty years, if they took good care of each other, maybe he and Aaron would still be around. That was heartening.

"Only if you never mention your prostate again for the next twenty-five years."

"Deal."

"I'll be there at three. I'll bring Nancy with me—"

"Not Tane?" Larx was trying to be a good friend.

"This whole discussion makes Tane crazy. He can't believe it's even coming up, and he gets weird and his art gets weird and we start having goat people with swords coming out of the kiln. Do you know there's a glaze that perfectly simulates old dripping blood?"

"Gnarly."

"I'm too young to even know what that means."

"God, fetus, get off the phone so I can talk to Coach Jones, who is calling me right now."

"Fine, geezer. Later."

Larx switched over. "Hey, Andy. How's the wife?"

"She says if I get fired over this, she's going to make me sleep on the couch."

Oh God. "I'm sorry—"

"I told her if she kicks me out to the couch, I'm getting a divorce, period, because I didn't sign on to blame kids for getting stabbed in the stomach."

"Oh, damn. Thanks, Andy—"

"She said I was really sexy and commanding when I was standing up for my principles. We had the best sex of my life. I think we made a baby."

"And that was too much information."

"I blame you. I'll see you tomorrow, Larx. I'll be there early for the meeting, but you'd better not get me fucking fired. I'm gonna have a kid to support."

Larx laughed in bemusement and took the next call. This one was from MacDonald's father, who thought Isaiah should have died and gone to hell.

Larx was done laughing by the time that conversation finished. And he was more determined than ever to listen to Yoshi—but not to yield to the idea that they were defenseless punching bags of hysterical parents either.

Dammit, the world had changed. This town needed to change with it.

ISAIAH WAS pale, flushed and feverish, when they arrived. Larx kicked Christi and Kirby out after a quick hello, and he sat quietly as Kellan told him about their homecoming pity party and about how quiet it was at Larx's place.

"No Mom yelling?" Isaiah asked softly.

Kellan shook his head. "No Dad…." The boys looked at each other meaningfully, and Larx knew about all those things in Kellan's life that no one could prove but that were happening anyway.

"Thanks, Larx," Isaiah said, eyes never leaving Kellan's. "It's good he's safe."

"We're happy to have him," Larx said sincerely. "It was getting too quiet with just Christi and me."

"And Deputy George," Kellan said slyly.

Larx had to smile. "And Deputy George," he conceded. "But that's new."

"Wait. What'd I miss?"

Larx felt his face heat, unable to do a damned thing about it.

"Larx is *gay*," Kellan said, lowering his voice and looking both ways like they were sitting in the quad. "And so is Kirby's dad. They're *together*."

The look Isaiah gave him was so full of shining worship that Larx felt a little ill. He wasn't out. He wasn't proud. The only reason he and Aaron hadn't lived and died in Colton without ever knowing they were meant for each other was that Aaron—who'd had no active physical knowledge of his sexuality—had been braver than Larx about his heart.

"You're dating?" he breathed.

Larx nodded. "Something like that." They'd tried. Aaron had bought him hot dogs at a football game. Larx had made him coffee in the morning. "It's pretty new."

Isaiah's happy glow faded a bit. "So… you know. Not coming out? Not—"

"When we're ready," Larx said. "Just like you two. I've already *done* the dramatic coming out, Isaiah. I almost lost my girls. I promised them I'd never let who *I* was hurt them again. That's why I'm so glad for the two of you. You have a freedom now—a strength—that I never had."

"But what about…?" Isaiah bit his lip.

"The board meeting," Kellan said, looking at Larx worriedly. "They're not going to make it… you know. Illegal to be gay, are they?"

Larx shook his head. "Guys, you did nothing wrong. And me and as many teachers as I can drag in by the hair are going to show up to tell them that." He grimaced. "Isaiah, what happened to you was awful and scary. People always want to find a reason—a thing they can point to and say, 'This awful and scary thing will never happen to me!' So boom! Guess what?"

"It's being gay," Isaiah said, nodding.

"It's not fair. It's not right. It's not *logical*, but people are—"

"Dumb, panicky animals and you know it," Kellan quoted.

"Tommy Lee Jones said it best," Larx agreed. "It's my job to keep them from bolting and trampling the innocent bystanders. That's what I'll be doing tomorrow night."

"You can't do that if you scream 'I'm the boogeyman,' can you?" Isaiah said, his breath fading so that *boogeyman* was barely a word.

"No," Larx told him. "I wish I could. If I could make this… this… fucking *idiocy* go away by ripping off my shirt and revealing the big rainbow *G* on my chest, I'd be first in line. I tried that once. It wasn't the way to go."

The boys nodded like they understood—but Larx didn't. He kept thinking about seven years of living like his sexuality was an old drug dependency, something that had hurt his girls, something that he couldn't let touch them again.

Would the town—the *board*—be any more accepting of kids like Isaiah and Kellan if Larx had just worn his rainbow sweater and told the world to fucking deal?

"No," Yoshi said later, as they were roasting hot dogs on sticks. Yoshi's damned soy dogs kept falling off into the fire, and he was very gingerly trying to keep the last dog in the pack on the two prongs with a third stick to help it.

An evil, evil part of Larx hoped the dog would fall in, fry, and leave Yoshi to face the privation of all-beef hot dogs dripping grease the way God intended.

"No?" Larx asked curiously. "You don't think I should have just been out and proud and—"

"They would have taken away your children," Yoshi said brutally. "Seven years ago? This town? You would have gotten laid once or twice, someone would

have talked, and it would be the first hearing all over
again."

Larx started to shiver all over. "For Christ's sake,
Yoshi. Do you even—?" He'd told Yoshi about how
bad it had gotten for his kids—Olivia's hair, head lice,
no food for days, no baths. Would that really have
happened again?

"That's what I'm saying. It's getting better now,
and maybe this is the time to come out. But not seven
years ago. Not for your family. Don't second-guess
yourself, Larx. You did what you had to in order to
protect your children, and nobody's going to hold that
against you."

Larx looked up at the kids, all of them grouped on
the other side of the fire, showing Nancy how to keep
the dogs near the embers so they could cook slow and
not just burn on the outside. Kirby fit in so well here.
Larx knew the kid was probably dying to sleep in his
own room, in his own bed, but right now the chaos
of the three of them—Christi's sarcasm, Kellan's quiet humor, Kirby's stoic goodwill…. He could look at
them with some joy. These young people made him
happy.

"I need to protect these children too," he said.
"Kellan—nobody protected him growing up."

Yoshi grunted. You knew—when a kid was being
yelled at too much, flinched too much in school, you
knew. But if it wasn't bruises, the county couldn't do
squat. "We tried," he said. "You've made school a safe
place for him. It was the best you could do."

"We need to make it stick," Larx said with some
conviction.

"We do. Which means *you* need to not be poster child for gay. You can't fall on your sword and die here, Larx. It's not going to help. You need to be the guy leading the troops. I'd lead the troops, but nobody follows me. Ever. I could have the last rowboat on the *Titanic* and people would be like, 'No! You are a strange Asian man, and I'd rather take my chances in the water!' But *you* they'd follow."

Larx nodded soberly. "They would too follow you."

"They would pitch me out of the fucking boat," Yoshi said with some conviction. "The only reason the kids follow me is that I bribe them with stickers. You heard me—*stickers*. They're almost grown-ups, and their future hangs on stupid sticker sheets with Hello fucking Kitty. No. I'm the soldier that needs to fall on the sword."

"Hello Kitty? Really?" Larx grinned at him. "I would have thought *Young Justice* at the very least."

"Don't fuck with me and my show, Larx. I'm serious here. You be calm and talk everybody to death. It's what you were born for."

Nancy had edged over into their conversation. "Don't fight it, Larx," she said, laughing softly. "You're our fearless leader and you know it."

"I hate you both. Edna's coming, right? And Mara?" They were the union reps, and since their contracts didn't include any protection if a teacher voiced an opinion counter to the district's, having your site union rep in the audience could be very helpful.

"They'll be there early, like us. We should have about thirty, forty people there early enough for the big room, Larx. Don't worry—half the room will be hostile idiots, but the other half will be teachers on our side. And I'll make sure everybody knows that almost every teacher in the district is in the overflow room."

Larx shifted uncomfortably. "Uh, Nancy? How many *teachers* are going to be hostile idiots?"

Nancy stopped short. "I... you know? I hadn't even thought of that."

"There's no rule that says you can't teach in California if you think the spectrum is an abomination," Larx said, remembering the administrators who had thrown him under the bus. "Maybe we should...."

Nancy nodded. "Yeah. You know what? I'll coordinate with the principals at the other schools, just so we have an idea. If there's a religious fundamentalist who's going to speak out, we can at least know who they are."

Larx pulled his own hot dog out of the fire and used the bun in his hand to capture it so he didn't burn his fingers.

"Fucking groovy," he muttered. He gazed at the bonfire moodily, shifting on restless feet. They'd held off the bonfire until five, but Aaron hadn't been able to get back in time—something about finding evidence that could break the case and promising details later. The mystery reader in Larx wanted to concentrate on the new evidence, the clues, the finding the murderer in Colton.

The grown-up in him knew he had to actually deal with the job he *had* as opposed to the one he'd always sort of fancied until he remembered that he hated authority and never wanted to touch a gun ever.

"Here, I'm going to go get ketchup," he muttered to Yoshi and Nancy, then left them to plot the Battle of

Colton Gay High—which is what he'd been calling it
to Yoshi, just to watch him sputter.

He walked around the blaze to the little table
that held all the ingredients of dinner and dessert and
prepped his dog, then added a paper bowl of some of
the potato soup Kirby had spent the afternoon making. He claimed it was a family recipe, but Larx had
watched the kid work, and there had been more magic
than recipe there. Larx fully approved, and he balanced
the bowl on top of the plate, getting ready to juggle his
way back to either the kids or the grown-ups.

He paused, though, gazing at the fire.

Such a simple thing, the clearing away of the
old stuff, the burning to make way for the new. Comfort and danger all wrapped up in one big, glowing,
hypnotic ball. Larx stared into the flames against the
darkness, letting the comfort seep in, suddenly keenly
aware he hadn't had enough sleep in *days*.

He opened his mouth and yawned, almost losing
his precariously balanced dinner in the process.

"Here," Aaron said over his shoulder, rescuing
the soup and stabilizing the hot dog. "I'll eat the soup,
you eat the hot dog, and then you can eat soup, and I
can roast my own."

He stood right over Larx's shoulder, and Larx
leaned back into him, comforted and warmed. "Deal.
You're late, Deputy—it's nearly seven."

Aaron yawned. "I know it. Sorry—I stopped at
my house to feed the chickens and collect the eggs."

Larx felt bad. "You should probably stay at your
house tomorrow night," he said. "Take care of business and shit."

Aaron whined softly, leaning his temple against Larx's. "But I want to debrief after the big meeting!"

Larx sighed. "Adulting is hard. Sorry, Deputy. Them's the breaks."

"I'll drive you to the meeting," Aaron said firmly. "That way we can debrief, and we might even get to make out in the car afterward. That'll be something."

"I'm going from work so I can get there early," Larx said, laughing.

"Goddammit!" Aaron snapped, his optimism apparently fading. Then: "No—wait. You and the kids take one car tomorrow, they can come home, and you and I can take the SUV to the meeting. See? I *will* get my Larx time, I *will*!"

Larx loved him so much in that moment, he almost didn't have any more banter left in his swollen, achy chest.

Almost.

"That's excellent. I live for being tongued and groped in a car in front of my own home. Someday I might even get knocked up and married, Pa!"

Aaron laughed—and then smacked him on the back of the head. "Brat."

"You only say that because I—"

Aaron put his free hand over Larx's mouth. "Don't say it," he ordered, and Larx grinned behind the warmth of his hand. And then stuck out his tongue and licked the palm.

Aaron's body sort of melted in an effort to get closer to him, and Larx licked again. Aaron moved his hand and replaced it with his lips, and for a brief moment, Larx got to kiss the man he loved in front of a crackling bonfire, content and steady to the core of his soul.

"Oh, would you two knock that crap off!" Yoshi complained. "You're making me sick!"

"Sorry, Yoshi," Larx said dutifully. Aaron jerked backward, obviously remembering they had an audience.

"Sorry, Mr. Nakamoto," Aaron said, looking somewhat abashed.

Yoshi chortled. "Oh my God, Larx! He's adorable! He's still treating us like teachers!"

"Oh! Quick! Do my name!" Nancy said excitedly. "Call me Mrs. Pavelle. I'll tell my husband—it'll make his day!"

Aaron laughed wickedly. "Sure, but then you both have to swear for me. C'mon, Larx says the staff room sounds like fishwives and truckers—I'm dying here, someone drop the F-bomb!"

The kids were paying attention by now, and that set them off laughing uproariously, and suddenly Yoshi and Nancy weren't so smug. The laughter died down eventually, and so did the fire. The kids broke out the s'mores, and Larx ate one and wondered when his heart would stop thundering from the damned sugar rush. Apparently the kids all crashed at the same time, because they all went inside to shower for school the next day while the adults stayed out to worry.

Yoshi and Nancy talked about all the things they were worried about, and Aaron listened to every word, all of the things Larx hadn't been telling him because Larx hadn't wanted to burden the guy charged with finding the real culprit and not the scapegoat the district was trying to create.

Larx listened and didn't add much, feeling strangely detached from the drama. He'd stressed all day—for the last two days, really. His body, short on sleep, high on anxiety, simply shut down, leaving a calm, empty space inside him where he sat cross-legged, watched the action, and refused to speculate.

While they were talking—and Aaron was throwing in some valid observations about the members of the board that Larx wouldn't have thought of himself—Larx started gathering buckets of water to surround the fire pit with, now that it was down to embers.

He wanted the ash and the debris cleared out. He wanted the fire pit scraped clean and the cold ashes buried in his garden, to make the growing good again. All of this... detritus the world carried, from old hatreds and prejudices, he wanted it burned away and gone, and a long, quiet, cold period to recover from the horrible things people could do to each other.

He wanted the seeds of what he and Aaron had planted in the last few weeks to grow in the dark and fertile soil of their rich and varied pasts.

But he couldn't do that while everybody was talking about the board meeting.

Finally, they'd exhausted themselves and the fire was so low that they were all shivering in the chill of autumn. It was October now, and next month there would be snow.

"Are we ready?" he asked, once everybody was anchored around the pit with their water buckets. "Remember, the wind is heading that way." He pointed northeast, and Aaron made a point to get out of the way of the smoke currently drifting in that direction.

"So try to make sure we keep the fire from jumping that way with too much water force, 'kay?"

"Can we do this and go home? I'm freezing my ass off!" Yoshi complained.

"Can we do this and go home?" Nancy echoed. "If he goes home and bitches, Tane bitches at me."

"God, you guys—so selfish," Larx chided. "I thought we were all about the greater good!"

"The greater good is tomorrow," Nancy said soberly. "I could see you processing it all, Larx. Don't worry. Keep your head and don't lose your temper. All we can do is tell them the truth as we know it, and hope they're smart enough to listen."

"I hate depending on other people's common sense," Larx muttered, feeling that truth deep in his bones. "But okay. C'mon, guys. One, two, three—"

They poured water into the fire pit, stepping back when it steamed, and again and some more, until the embers were all sodden. All that remained was the coldness of the stars, spread out over their heads like a giant cookie, cut into shape by the shadows of the trees.

AARON SHOWERED first while Larx checked on the kids. He spent a moment with each kid before he locked up and went upstairs.

"So," he asked seriously, "you doing okay with two brothers you didn't know you had?"

Christi thought about it, scratching Trigger's head by habit. "I like it this way," she said seriously. "I'll be sad to see Kirby go home tomorrow. He says he has to—laundry, chickens, keeping the dust away—but, you know." She shrugged. "You and me by ourselves was nice, Dad, but this is a big family again. I like it."

Larx kissed the top of her head and gave Trigger a pet too. "That's because you have a generous soul," he said seriously. "And yeah. You know—you've got one more year of high school after this one, but maybe Kirby and Kellan will be around for a lot of that. I like that too." He laughed a little, feeling silly. "I like that I'm looking after 'kids.' Maybe it's all the years in the classroom, but I'm more comfy when there's more than one."

She laughed too, and he shut off her light and closed the door.

Kellan was worried about Isaiah—and about going back to school. Larx reassured him that Christi and Kirby were in most of his classes, and that Isaiah's parents had been saying good things—not only *to* Kellan, but *about* Kellan. A small piece in the local paper had come out on Sunday. In a phone interview, Lizzie and Pete Campbell had said they were relieved their son appeared on the mend, and glad he was seeing such a nice boy. There had been no shock about the boys coming out, no surprise at Kellan's presence in their lives—the piece had, in fact, been reassuring. The paper was treating this like what it was: a crime against a boy, not a crime because of his sexuality.

The approach had settled Kellan as well, as did Trixie, who had chosen Kellan as her designated human by curling up on his pillow. Larx bid him good night, and just as he was closing the door, Kellan spoke up.

"Larx?"

"Yeah?"

"Uh… you said I could stay as long as I wanted. Uh… if Isaiah and I don't go to college next year, because, you know, recovery and stuff... does that include—"

The extra year this boy needed to learn how to grow up and feel safe? "Course. Meant what I said, Kellan. As long as you need."

"Thanks, Larx."

Two down, and Kirby to go.

Larx was all set with the speech—he had it planned out in his head. *So, sorry about the insta-family, bet you'll be happy to spend a couple of nights in your own room, right?*

But when he opened the door, Kirby turned to him with a smile.

"I like this room—Olivia's, right?"

"Yeah. She didn't do girlie." She'd done country blue, navy blue, rose, and maroon. Was almost gender neutral, right down to the curtains.

"It's not a bad room. She'll probably want it back when she comes for Christmas, right?"

Larx smiled. "She and Christi will probably spend the whole time in Christi's room gossiping. Why do you ask?"

Kirby rolled over on the bed, lying across it with his sweat-socked feet dangling off the end. He was wearing basic boy's sweats and sitting nose-to-nose with the torti kitty, and he made Larx wish for a son all over again.

"This weekend—I mean, I don't want to say it was fun, because what happened to Isaiah was awful. But... having people in the house? I like that."

Larx had to laugh. "Christi said almost the same thing."

Kirby grinned. "I bet I could build a chicken coop next weekend. Kellan could help me."

Larx looked at him drolly. "Wherever would we get chickens?"

"I know a place," Kirby said, nodding, and Larx had to laugh.

"Kirby, I love having you. The big family thing—can't say it's not a turn-on for me. But you and your dad need to talk, and so do your sisters. It's not just my call."

Kirby looked suddenly sober. "Okay. I get that. But... but when you two are all in? Remember that we *like* each other. And it's lonely in the house by myself."

Larx's chest swelled a little. "Kirby, you are welcome here *any*time. If your dad and I don't work out, you are *still* welcome here to eat or hang out while he's working. I know he'd agree."

Kirby grinned. "You guys'll work out. I mean, like you said. Ten years, and he hasn't been serious enough about anyone to even introduce me? You guys made out in front of us tonight. I'm thinking it's a lock."

Larx laughed a little and bid him good night, because that was a good thought to go out on.

Aaron was already in bed, reading messages on his phone and frowning, and Larx stripped, thinking he'd need to do more laundry the next day.

"If you leave some stuff here," he said thoughtfully, "you *and* Kirby, it would be easier to stay the night on a whim."

"Yeah?" Aaron asked, looking up from his phone.

"Your son wanted to build me a chicken coop. I think your chickens would be very confused."

"They'd get over it." Aaron's chest was almost impossibly broad when it was bare. Larx found himself staring at his tiny pink nipples, T-shirt hovering over the hamper. Maybe they should leave the light on tonight?

"I like you here," Larx admitted, now concentrating on the curly blond hair on Aaron's pecs. It had been soft under his fingers. He'd forgotten men's chest hair was so soft—or maybe none of the men he'd banged before Alicia had been old enough for chest hair. "But I don't want you to do anything hasty."

"Nothing irreversible about a chicken coop," Aaron said, winking.

"Your house has a pool," Larx said, startled enough by the wink to look into his eyes. "You ever think maybe we should move into your house instead?"

"No." Aaron shook his head. "Because you're not there."

Larx smiled and felt it spreading all over, his cheeks, his neck, his chest, his nipples, down his stomach to his groin….

"You are getting wood," Aaron said, his amusement never fading. "Now go shower, because I'd like to do something about that."

World's quickest shower.

Larx got out just after the thermostat timer clicked off, and he scrambled into bed, shivering. Aaron pushed Delilah off and rolled over for what was probably going to be a kiss if Larx's mouth hadn't gotten in the way.

"The cats."

"Wha—?"

"They each picked a new human. It was weird."

"Larx, are you stalling?"

Larx closed his eyes and rubbed his hands along Aaron's bare chest, his libido picking up right where it left off. "No," he murmured. "No, just sharing."

Aaron chuckled softly. "We can share afterward." He captured Larx's hand and brought it to the front of his boxers.

"Oh!" Larx squeezed his erection, which was adamant and wet at the end. "Ready?"

"I want to see if it's as good the second time," Aaron whispered, licking Larx's lips softly.

"Better," Larx promised. He abandoned thoughts of cats and board meetings and making sure the kids were okay. Aaron was here in his bed, and he wanted *Larx*, again. It was time to make Larx okay.

This wasn't the first time, full of nerves and "oh, what does this button do?" moments. Aaron knew what that button did, and they both had to be up in the morning, and they couldn't afford whips, chains, and that carefully hoarded stash of basic sexual aids Larx kept in his end-table drawer. There were teenagers asleep down the hallway, and their breaths had to stay quiet, their moans silent against their hands, the bedsprings unabused.

Larx took the initiative tonight, kissing down Aaron's chest first, licking his collarbone, edging with his teeth. He let his hands wander as he sucked on Aaron's nipples, soft, then with some tongue play, and then hard with teeth.

Aaron sucked in his breath and tugged at Larx's hair urgently until Larx got a little bit nippy. The hand in Larx's hair jerked hard, and Larx peered at Aaron with mischievous eyes.

"Ouch," Aaron mouthed at the same time he arched against Larx's hand.

Larx regarded him steadily, massaging his erection through his shorts. "And?" he whispered, squeezing and stroking at once.

"And I'll come in my pants if you don't get a move on!"

Larx chuckled and started nuzzling his way down Aaron's chest. "Get the lube," he ordered between licks, and Aaron surprised him by *immediately* fumbling for his hand.

Larx turned his head and grinned, holding the small bottle up as evidence. "Getting a little eager, Deputy?"

"On a timeline, Principal," Aaron hissed, thrusting against Larx's hand with more urgency.

Larx chuckled and kissed down Aaron's abundant happy trail, smoothing his fingers along the soft blond hair. Aaron's whimper spurred him lower, and he got a chance to meet Aaron's cock again, from the other end.

It was just as awesome head-on.

Larx stripped Aaron's shorts and devoured, leaving the teasing for another time. Girthy with thick veins, it was almost bigger than the circle of Larx's fist. Larx hummed in his throat, happy to see it again, and licked the head boldly. Aaron gasped and Larx took it into his mouth, letting it stretch his lips as he pushed his head down, swallowing. Aaron might not realize it, but his member was reasonably impressive. Larx was old enough not to fetishize dick mass, but he was also boy enough to be grateful for what he got.

What he was getting was more than a mouthful, hard and sensitive, and sucking it was an even bigger turn-on than he remembered.

He moaned, grinding his groin into the bed, and then, keeping Aaron's cock in his mouth, he responded to the tap on his back. He lifted up on his knees and scooted his backside over so Aaron's caressing hand had easy access. As he concentrated on his own task, Aaron was stripping off Larx's shorts and sliding his palms over Larx's backside, cupping his thighs, teasing his crease, and then, oh thank you God, squeezing his cock, long and slow, skating his thumb in the precome at his head.

Larx moaned, thighs shaking, and realized he really didn't have a lot of time to screw around. With the hand *not* wrapped around Aaron's base, he snicked the top of the lube open and dumped some on his fingers. Aaron fumbled the bottle from his hand and hopefully closed it, while Larx slid his hand behind him and, helped by Aaron's palm separating his cheeks, slid his slippery fingers into his own asshole, stretching quickly, deliriously, body shaking from arousal.

Aaron gave a little whine below him and his cock stiffened, spurting more pre into Larx's mouth.

Larx couldn't wait anymore—didn't *want* to wait anymore. With a grunt of reluctance, he let that beautiful cock slide out from between his lips and swung his body around so he was straddling, squirming his body until he felt Aaron prodding his entrance.

Aaron's eyes were wide open, fixed on Larx's face. "You are pretty damned tricky," he breathed hoarsely.

Larx craved too badly to grin. He reached back to hold Aaron's cock right where he needed it, and as soon as his fingers found Aaron's shaft, Aaron thrust up.

Larx slid down.

Gah! Just as good as the night before, Aaron thick and awesome, giant, filling him. His cock expanded, lodged to the root, until all the stress, the unnecessary things in Larx, disappeared, evaporated, leaving room for nothing but Aaron's flesh in Larx's body, his soul consumed by their joining.

Aaron grunted, digging his fingers into Larx's thighs while Larx just sat there, impaled and shaking, body too full for his brain to function.

"Larx!" Aaron begged, tortured.

Larx rocked forward, letting him slide out a little, and then leaned back, burying him again. It worked, oh God it worked, but it made a tremendous amount of noise on Larx's old bed, his knees popping into the springs the way his body *hadn't* the night before.

They both froze, an agony of arousal shaking through their combined bodies, coupled with the simultaneous thought of "Crap, did we wake the kids?"

"Larx," Aaron hissed. "Hold still!" And then he clamped his hands on Larx's hips and did what he did best.

Took over.

He braced his feet on the mattress and then arched his hips up, filling Larx even further, and then down, pulling out. His stomach and core flexed under Larx's hands as he moved, slowly, faster, harder, *oh God harder*, and Larx struggled to stay still, to not simply flounder, filled with his shaft and dying with pleasure. Aaron's eyes pinned him in place. His hard hands anchored Larx, forcing him to take it until his head fell back, his mouth opening slackly, and he let it wash through him, wave after wave, with every thrust.

"Oh…." He shuddered, his cock smacking lightly against Aaron's abdomen. He needed. He needed. Something there….

Aaron moved one of his hands from Larx's hip to Larx's own hand, thrusting it toward Larx's crotch.

Oh. Oh yeah.

Larx wrapped his hand around his cock and started to stroke, desperate, because his body was going to explode. He was full to his skin with that amazing, wonderful, fantastic, *gigantic* extension of his lover.

He never lost control of his voice, but his panting was frantic and unformed. As he felt the beginnings of a wrenching orgasm start at his thighs, his taint, and ripple up his balls and his cock and his spine and his core, he fell forward, catching his weight on one hand. He buried his face against Aaron's shoulder, groaning, and his cock erupted between them both, spattering hot and wet. He clung there limply as Aaron's thrusts lost cohesion, and with a roar he muffled in Larx's neck, he held Larx's hips and tried to shove himself into Larx's ass.

Larx moaned softly, opening himself, stretched, dilated, dripping in come, and tried to take all of him, wanting his whole body inside so Aaron was safely captured, along with Larx's heart.

The shaking eventually stilled, and Larx straightened his cramped legs, sliding to the side and ignoring the mess that seeped from his stretched behind.

"We'll change the sheets tomorrow," he mumbled into Aaron's shoulder, and Aaron laughed weakly.

"That got better," he said, sounding gobsmacked.

"Not just me, then?"

"No, seriously, Larx. That got better."

Larx chuckled. "That got better from twenty
years ago," he said in wonder. "I mean, I thought sex
peaked in college."

"I think that's a myth we tell young people so
they don't suspect their parents are doing it," Aaron
said, sounding serious.

Larx couldn't be serious—he was *euphoric*.
"That's genius. Sheer genius. Just tell the kids we're
not having sex, we're communing deeply. They'll buy
it, right?"

Aaron chuckled with him, finally moving to recover their underwear.

And a sweatshirt.

"I can't sleep on your bare chest?" Larx
complained.

"You can if you turn the thermostat up," Aaron
told him. "I love you, but I'm going to get blue balls if
you keep it this cold in here."

Larx grunted. "Fuck. Hold on a minute." Still in
his boxer shorts, he padded out of the bedroom, struggling briefly with the turn lock on the door handle before he disappeared. He came back, and as he opened
the door, the heater kicked in.

Aaron grinned at him happily and took off the
sweatshirt.

Larx shook his head. "When we moved in," he
explained, "I was... well, beyond broke. I had just
enough money left over from my settlement for a
down payment, and the rest was the job and some
scrimping and saving—especially to keep the college
funds alive. So I made it a game with the girls—what
could we do without."

"Heat," Aaron said in sudden understanding.

Larx nodded and climbed into bed with him, turning off the lamp. They'd made love in the light this time. Aaron's beautiful, powerful body was going to be dancing behind his eyes for days.

"We'd have a contest to see how long we could go without heat. The more days past October we went, the more cookies I'd buy after school."

Aaron laughed. "Oh, weren't you crafty."

"Parenthood. Teaches you things."

Aaron nuzzled his hair, pulling the blankets around their shoulders—he'd turned the heat on, but not high. "Single parenthood teaches you more things."

"It's the hardest," Larx agreed, snuggling. His body ached again, tingling from climax and really amazing sex, but this full-body contact—it was tremendous. God, he didn't want to give this up. Ever.

"I was not aware of how much my wife did," Aaron muttered. "I mean, we always worked as a team, right? She did the house, I did the yard. She was there after school for them, I took them out on my weekend off so she could have a breather. We had date night and one day for the whole family. It was… I mean we worked hard at it to make sure we were both there."

"I'm jealous," Larx said frankly. "It sounds…." He swallowed. Like what he'd always wanted and had never had.

"It's what I want with you," Aaron said, kissing the top of his head. "I know we only have them for a little while longer. I don't know if I'd relive the baby years if I could. But I love not doing it alone. I love that Kirby has someone to talk to when I'm not there. I love that you took a boy from your class in because your heart is that big. I… I don't think your house will ever be empty, Larx. I just want to be in it too."

Larx hummed. "Yeah. Fine. Share my life. 'Cause that's not going to be the most fucking romantic thing anyone has said to me ever."

Aaron held him tighter, and the moment turned golden. Aaron's grip relaxed in a few heartbeats, and Larx caught it—that instant when his breathing deepened and he was just about to snore.

But Larx hadn't asked his questions yet.

"Wait—Aaron, wake up!"

Aaron snorted and struggled to sit up. "Wha? What is it? The kids? You need a dog!"

A dog? "Sure, Aaron. Get me a puppy for Christmas. Just make sure it won't eat the cats. Delilah won't put up with foolishness." Larx put a restraining hand on his chest and he settled down. "But you didn't tell me about the damned investigation. I was waiting for everyone else to go to sleep, and then *you* almost went to sleep."

"Oh!" Aaron slid to his side and propped his head on his hand. "That's right. And it was something I wanted to tell you. But, you know—"

"Totally secret." Larx mirrored his position, and suddenly they weren't in afterglow anymore, they were the Hardy Boys, only sleeping in the same bed in their boxers.

"Right." Aaron's teeth glinted in the dark, and he reached out and ran his hand down Larx's shoulder, cupping his bicep. Larx melted a little. Okay. Maybe not the Hardy Boys. "So, for starters, Julia Olson is on the run. She took off in her mom's SUV—"

"Not her car?" Larx knew it—a little electric blue Sportage. The girl had lorded it over her fellow students since she'd gotten it the year before.

"No—and that's suspicious. Whitney heard us serving the warrant, and about five minutes later, Julia comes blasting out of the garage—didn't even stop to raise the door. Gracie and I had to hustle to get out of the way—"

Larx's heart stopped. "She almost *ran you over?*"

"Not to speak of," Aaron said glibly, and Larx's eyes narrowed as he thought of all the ways getting hit by an SUV would be very much to speak of. But Aaron kept talking and Larx almost forgot about his worry. "But see? That's the thing. Because she did that scaryassed thing, we could search the house. And when we got there, I said we should start searching in the fire pit, because—"

"Perfect place to get rid of evidence," Larx said, enthralled and thinking about the blaze that had so mesmerized him that night.

"Exactly. So because Julia flew the coop so spectacularly, we had CSIs inside the house too. And the thing is, both fireplaces had this weird residue—something thicker than paper and wood, something that needed an accelerant to burn."

Larx couldn't have moved right then if someone had set *him* on fire. "*And!*"

"And in the outside pit, we found this ball of fabric. Like someone had rolled up, say, a black pair of wool trousers and sweater and tried to burn it."

"Wool doesn't burn," Larx said, because he taught chemistry and knew this.

"Exactly. It needs an accelerant. But she'd rolled them up—"

"Because she was panicking!" Because of course she'd been panicking—she'd been needed back to take care of her kid.

"We think she tried to burn it in the fireplace inside first while she showered. Then she got home and realized it wasn't burning, and took it outside with some gasoline to finish the job."

"But the polyester fibers—if the pants were a blend, they would have melted—"

"Locking the wool inside," Aaron said, smiling. "The CSIs are hoping there's enough there to confirm blood."

"Huhn," Larx pondered. "If her kid had paid attention in my class, she probably just would have thrown them in the washer with half a bottle of bleach. That's really the smarter thing to do."

Aaron grinned in the dark and kissed his nose playfully. "And that is why we're glad you only use your Larx powers for good," he said. "You'd make a much better criminal than Whitney Olson."

Larx sobered. "Is she really a criminal? Have you arrested her?"

"No." Aaron shook his head. "We need to test for blood, and her lawyer is going to challenge the warrants—and he doesn't have a legal leg to stand on, but he's got one made of money, and that might work too. So we don't have a lock, or an arrest. And Julia is still in the wind, and that…."

"That's bad," Larx said softly, thinking about Christi alone and freaked out. "I mean… I haven't thought well of the kid, but…."

"But she's a kid," Aaron said.

"And if she knows her mom tried to kill Isaiah…." Larx frowned. "But wait—weren't you serving the warrant for something entirely different?"

Aaron grimaced. "Yeah. We were hoping we'd get some evidence on that floater I found Friday."

Larx groaned. "God, Aaron—didn't you tell me once you mostly checked up on fishing permits and teenagers getting impregnated in the woods?"

Aaron's laughter was rich, even in the hush of the darkened bedroom. "Well, yeah," he conceded. "But sometimes it gets interesting."

Larx laughed softly, and they talked some more. Not about the case or Isaiah, but about students Larx had taught or cases Aaron had worked—getting-to-know-you conversation, mostly.

Except Larx felt like he'd known Aaron his entire life. This just felt like catching up, really. In the best sort of way.

Sodden Ashes

IT SHOULD have been a perfect day.

It had started off warm and snuggly, Larx lying next to him on his stomach, both fists tucked under his chin. At their age, sleep didn't make them young or innocent—it just made them look at rest. Larx was so rarely at rest—restless brain always working; active, sturdy body always doing something. Gardening, running, cooking, stoking a fire, petting a cat, talking to kids, turning a group of confused strangers into a family.

Making love.

Larx wasn't just a man—he was practically a force of nature. Aaron had been caught in the pull of his turbulent winds since he'd first seen him without a shirt and realized that there was a human under that pleasant community member.

The alarm went off and Larx opened his eyes, squinting, looking confused, smiling shyly—and then rolled off the bed and popped to his feet, scrambling for sweats and his running shoes long before Aaron suspected he was actually awake.

Aaron was *very* awake as they slipped quietly out the door and into the frosty air. Larx was quiet for their first two miles on the track, and then, as they drew near the back of Aaron's house, he grunted.

"What?" Aaron asked, hoping it was safe to talk to him now.

"I used to get all excited when I saw your house, 'cause, you know, 'Aaron's there!' Now it's just another house, but I get to go home with you. I mean, this is better, but I'm still trying to figure out where to get my rush."

Aaron chuckled. "Maybe when you see my SUV in the driveway or when I get home early from night shift."

"You work night shifts?"

"Sometimes. I used to leave the kids after they went to bed and get home in time to take everybody to school."

Larx grunted again, and for a moment, Aaron thought it was because he still wasn't very awake.

"Aaron, did Caroline have trouble with your job?" he asked soberly.

Aaron tried to kick his brain in the direction Larx's had just gone. "No," he answered, thinking about it. "I... I don't know. I told her it was going to be okay and she believed me."

"I'm not that trusting," Larx muttered.

Oh no. "Is this going to be a problem?" Aaron asked, legitimately spooked.

Larx looked at him, his feet doing that same dancy thing he'd done on that first day, the one that kept him upright when he wasn't watching where he was going.

"No," he said after a moment and bit his lip. "I'm going to get used to it."

Aaron actually stopped, because he couldn't make his feet go anywhere without his eyes to guide him. "That's it?" he asked, sort of gobsmacked.

Larx turned around, jogging in place. "That's what?"

"You're going to get used to it?"

Larx squinted at him. "It scares me shitless, okay? But I'm not going to ask you to quit. You obviously love your job. You're good at it. You loved someone for ten? Twelve—?"

"Fourteen," Aaron said quietly. "Fourteen years."

Larx nodded. "Exactly. There's no fucking guarantees. You know that. I know that. You make me happy now—I'm too goddamned old to be throwing something this good away because I'm afraid. What in the hell— I'm a big pouty baby who needs my fucking way?"

Aaron smiled at him then and started running again, mostly to keep warm. They resumed their path down the track, and he said, "Remember, we need to cut this a little shorter than usual."

Larx grunted. "It's a good thing I just decided not to be a big pouty baby."

"I'll get there," Aaron panted. "But not today."

"Me too," Larx said, and Aaron had a sudden shaft of gratitude. Thank God for grown-up lovers who recognized what they couldn't fix in other people and endeavored to fix in themselves.

"I try to call," Aaron told him. "Or text. Or sema-phore. I do it with Kirby—make sure I'm on time or that I've told him. I'll put you in the loop."

"Thank you," Larx said humbly. "That's considerate."

They pushed on, Larx reaching that pace that made Aaron haul ass after him, but the conversation sat hard on Aaron's shoulders.

Because instead of reassuring Aaron that Larx could handle the risk, it had reminded Aaron that now he *had* something to risk.

And like Larx, he was going to need a little time to get used to that.

When he got to work that morning, the sober re-minder of the risks of trusting fate had put him into… well, not so much a funk, but scrambled and unfocused.

Aaron *forced* himself to fill out the paperwork for their search and seizure the day before, but restless-ness was an itch up his spine, and he could hardly sit still.

Warren was sitting in the desk next to his, and every time Aaron stood up, sat down again, and sighed, he shot an irritated glance Aaron's way. "Je-sus, George, what in the hell?"

Aaron scowled at him. "There's something itch-ing at me," he muttered. "It's like… like Christmas, but the opposite of that. Something's building."

Was this just one of the stages of having a part-ner? Had Caroline done this when he'd gotten out of college and gone into law enforcement? Had he just not noticed? Had he been too arrogant, too assured that the world always dished out happy endings to ever anticipate Caro going before him?

So many things you depended on, took for granted, when you had someone in your life—

"Wait," Aaron said, standing up and looking for Eamon.

Eamon was walking by, looking restless and irritated himself.

"Eamon?"

"Deputy?"

"Where in the fuck is her husband?"

Eamon's eyes widened. "Whitney Olson's?"

"That's the one. We've talked to her kid, her lawyers *plural*—but you know who hasn't been called in now that his daughter is on the run and his wife is under house arrest?"

"Carl Olson," Eamon said.

It hit them both at the same time.

"Oh my God." Aaron picked up his desk phone and dialed the coroner. "I'll tell Gary, and you tell forensics to go get some of Carl's DNA from the house. We might know who our floater is."

EVEN WITH DNA evidence, it took longer to confirm an identity than most people assumed. Aaron, Warren, and Eamon were running down Carl Olson's financials, trying to figure out where he'd been and if he was still there, when Aaron looked up at the clock.

"Son of a fucking bitch!" he snarled. "Eamon, I've got to get the hell out of here."

"Your boy going to bat for the school?" Eamon asked laconically, and Aaron pulled on his hat and his jacket and gloves. It was dark outside and nippy to boot.

"Yeah. He's getting there early, but if I don't see how it goes, I'll feel like crap!"

"I'll be right behind you," Eamon said, waving him on.

Aaron hustled out the door, hoping he could get to the district office in time to find a spot.

He parked illegally, putting the cherry light on top to pretend he was on duty, and hustled into the squat, circa '95 district office. He walked through the normally monitored front entrance and toward the back, where the board meetings were usually held. He had to wade through people, all of them milling for the back overflow hallway, to get to the meeting room itself.

He walked to the entrance of the meeting room, and Kirby thrust a program at him and scowled. "Way to represent, Dad. Do you want to go back to eating my cooking?"

Aaron scowled back. "I texted him on the way. Shit came up."

But Kirby did *not* look happy, so Aaron figured he'd better try to get in Larx's good graces ASAP. He stuck his head in the room and Larx caught his eye almost immediately, pointing an imperious finger to the vacant spot next to him. Well, it was a madhouse— Aaron had never seen so many people there. Larx'd probably had to draw blood in order to keep Aaron a spot.

He scooted in, took his place on the end, and looked down the row at the list of grim and furious teachers lined up.

"Check your agenda," Larx said tightly, and Aaron's heart sank.

He scanned through the photocopy and grunted.

First thing on the agenda was revisiting the need for the GSA.

Second thing on the agenda was a discussion of how Larx had handled the night of the bonfire.

Third thing on the agenda was how to apportion the funds raised by the GSA for a scholarship should the GSA be disbanded.

This did not bode well for the first and second thing on the agenda.

"Okay, then," Aaron said, standing up.

"Where are you going?"

"To speak for local law enforcement—"

"Your friend Percy already signed up." Larx looked sourly to where the duty-deserting slacker was sitting in a suit, looking proud as punch.

"Tough," Aaron said, heading for the podium. He got there just in time to grab the clipboard and scratch out Percy's name and place his own. They were still down on the roster—maybe twentieth to speak—but Aaron was damned if he was going to let someone like Percy have a say when the asshole hadn't even *been* there for the stabbing.

He signed his name and made direct eye contact with Percy just as the gavel sounded, and he hustled back to his seat.

Heather Perkins was a squat little woman who had apparently not gotten the memo that helmet hair was no longer in fashion. Her friend Cissy wore the full-on waterfall/iron-throne cut that seemed to mark chic motherhood these days, and both of them streaked their brown hair blonde. Heather's husband was a colorless little man who slumped next to her and looked sorrowful and confused during school board meetings. The rest of the board consisted of a junior high principal who worked in the adjacent Placer district but lived in Colton; a member of the rotary club, Gordon Chandler; a member of the Colton Chamber of Commerce and Whitney Olson's distant cousin; the student body president—a kid Kirby had abhorred as a snack-stealing suck-up; and three people Aaron couldn't have picked out of a lineup.

He had the feeling it wouldn't matter. This was mostly Heather and Gordon's show.

Heather called the meeting to order, and the first thing she did was violate the order she'd set.

"So I understand a member of the Colton County Sheriff's Department is here to brief us on the events of Friday?" She smiled at Percy Hardesty, and Aaron stood up.

"Indeed so, Madam Chairperson," Aaron said briskly. "Given that I was there during the events of the bonfire and an active part of two pertinent investigations, I think both Sheriff Mills and Deputy Hardesty will agree that I can take it from here."

Percy scowled, looking around the room like he wanted to cry, and Aaron didn't give a crap. As far as he knew, the guy had gotten to the scene of the bonfire about a half an hour before the last teacher left. He'd seen the report—Percy had been there to clean up the crime scene.

Heather looked at him in surprise, her fine-point eyebrows arching. "Uh, sure, Deputy George, if you're sure Sheriff Mills would ap—"

"He does," Eamon said from the doorway. "I don't know why you'd want to listen to Percy. He wasn't there anyway."

Heather nodded grimly, and Aaron proceeded to the podium. He gave a terse and pithy version of events, from the moment Joy had screamed.

"But Deputy George," Heather said in confusion, "if you were there, didn't you see the... the incident at the bonfire?"

Aaron was ready for this. "I saw two boys, supported by their staff and student body, come out honestly, like men, and share a kiss. It was brave on their part, but it wasn't an 'incident.' They were congratulated by their teachers and their peers, and frankly we're not sure it had anything to do with what happened next. Isaiah is a busy boy by all accounts—football, drama, AP classes. The anger that fueled a crime like this could have come from any place *besides* his sexuality, especially with a staff that kept the bullying down to a minimum."

"Well, thank you, Deputy George. We'll be sure to take that under advisement—"

"While you're doing that, you should also know that we've served a warrant to a person of interest. We are unsure of this person's motives. Please be aware that this may or may not be a hate crime. If it is, treating the object of this person's hatred as a guilty party can only make this situation worse. If it isn't, you have created an opportunity for bigotry where none existed before. Isaiah and Kellan did nothing wrong—this next item here, the disbanding of the GSA? That can only make things worse."

Heather gaped at him, and he asked to be excused.

"Well, then," she said, trying to get her composure back. "Our next speaker is Mrs. Nancy Pavelle."

Nancy was sitting on the other side of Yoshi, and she stood and spoke clearly from her seat. "Okay, folks," she said, her voice like a crystal freight train— clear and strong and unmistakable. "First of all, I would like all employees of the Colton Unified School District who support Principal Larkin and Vice Principal Nakamoto to stand up." They paused and let that happen. "Now for those of you from the parent community who are here thinking that the teachers you see in the auditorium are the only voices here, I would like everybody who supports Larx and Yoshi but who was forced to wait in the overflow room due to board member shortsightedness to please file in past the podium and back out to your little cave of exile, okay?"

She must have had a runner waiting with a signal, because it happened so quickly. The parade of teachers started, in through the side door of the meeting room, down past the podium, and up through the main entrance. The teachers started out quiet, glaring at the board meaningfully, but then their uniform footsteps took on a hollow, march-like tempo.

Some smartass started to chant.

"Larx! Larx! Larx! Larx! Larx!"

Aaron looked at Larx in surprise, and Larx was squeezing his eyes shut like he could make it stop.

"They love you!" Aaron chided under the rhythm of the chanting.

"I'd better not fuck this up," Larx muttered.

On and on, until Heather Perkins nailed her table with her little gavel. "Enough! Enough!" But the line of teachers continued. "Dammit, Nancy, you only get two minutes to speak!"

"Well, you should have put us in the theater auditorium," Nancy retorted over the shouting. "Like
we asked, so the community could see that we've got
Larx's back."

Heather scowled, but the parade went on, ending
thirty seconds later when the last irritated teacher disappeared. A barrage of applause erupted from outside
the meeting room, and Nancy smiled graciously.

"Your floor, Madam Chairwoman. Now you
know."

"Well, now," Heather said, glaring at her husband
like the last three minutes had been his fault. "Now
that we are aware of how many teachers are here, is
there a parent who would like to speak on the matter
of the GSA?"

"I would!" bellowed a voice, and Aaron looked
back to the corner of the room.

And groaned.

"Yup," Larx muttered. "All that wonderful pos-
turing, and it's about to be ripped to shreds by Billy
MacDonald."

Aaron could barely listen to the man. He rambled,
his arguments made no sense, and he must have said
the word *faggots* six times without getting silenced
by Heather's wretched gavel. When he was done, the
audience gave him a scatter of applause, but mostly
he was greeted with an icy silence. Aaron studied the
faces around him as he strutted back to his seat.

"You know," he said quietly in Larx's ear, "I think
he might have done more harm than good."

Larx looked around and shrugged. "No one wants
to admit they're on his side," he said philosophically.
"Wait—it's coming."

Sure enough, the next parent was college educated, the leader of the local book club, a Sunday school teacher. She did *not* use the word *faggot*.

She just asked if, perhaps, giving the students a Gay-Straight Alliance didn't give kids the option of being gay when they might not think of it themselves. Weren't they just creating their own gay community when one didn't really need to exist?

This woman got applauded.

So did the father who worried about what kind of sex his daughter would learn about if she attended those meetings with her friends.

And the chamber of commerce member who was afraid of the "crowd" they'd attract if their high school was known as a gay-friendly kind of place.

By the time the next five speakers were done, Aaron felt sick to his stomach.

Then Heather called on Andy Jones, the football coach.

"If you please, Madam Chairperson," he said, standing up but not coming to the podium. "Me and the next four teachers on your list have agreed to give our time to Larx, who's going to tell you why all that stuff you guys just said was crap and why you're only hurting your kids."

The room erupted into cheering—and it was echoed by the crowd down the hall.

Heather finally got to bang her little gavel again.

"So, Principal Larkin, you have ten minutes—"

"Twelve," Larx said. "I'm on your list too."

"Fourteen!" called a timid-looking woman in the front. "I'm way down on the list, and if Larx speaks for me, we can go home earlier."

There was some general laughter then, and some scattered applause.

As Larx made his way to the podium, Aaron's stomach lightened up, and he felt hope.

Everything Larx said made so much sense.

He started with the nice Sunday school teacher and pointed out that kids were born gay or bi or trans or straight—and that giving them a safe place to talk about who they were did more than just make them feel good, it kept the bullies away, because the LGBTQ kids knew they weren't alone.

He told the father worried about his daughter learning about sex that they weren't authorized to even talk about sex—they just wanted to make the kids growing up with the same crushes everyone else had to feel safe. (A simple roll of his eyes told Aaron that he thought kids should be talked to straight-up about sex without adult sugarcoating, but since not all the parents could read Larx's eye roll, Aaron figured they were safe.)

With the chamber of commerce member, he almost lost his cool. "Harry, you sell handmade quilts and seasoned-wood faux antiques. If you don't think a third of your customer base is gay, you're not an awesome businessman." There was some laughter at that, and some gasps as well, and then he grimaced and remembered himself. "Look, that was stereotyping, and I apologize. But the fact is, much of our commerce comes from the gay community, whether you want to recognize it or not. We sell high-end arts and crafts—not a lot of discount stores here, you guys. If you start turning away the LGBTQ community, a lot of you should probably close up shop, and if you want to make money off their business, you should maybe think about not pretending they don't exist. That means not ignoring the children who need this organization in their schools, because that's just hypocrisy right there, and I'm not a fan."

So his first nine minutes were spent refuting the people who had spoken before, and when he got to his last five, he looked exhausted.

"Okay, folks. I've spent a good chunk of my time explaining to you why a GSA is necessary—which is something I had to do to institute the club in the first place. But I think we need to talk about what's really going on here. Two boys kissed in front of a bonfire. For those of you who haven't chaperoned a dance or a bonfire or a football game, well, you should know that kids kissing happens all the time. We have to make an exhaustive effort to make sure no kids get knocked up *on the dance floor* at homecoming, and if you think that's disgraceful, well, then we sure could use your help chaperoning the dances, because the teachers are outnumbered. If the act of violence hadn't been perpetrated on an out football player, we wouldn't be here. But Isaiah got hurt, and the whole community was shocked, and they were looking for a scapegoat.

"Guess what? The kid was gay and you found your reason. So a whole lot of you are here because you think if we don't have any gay or trans people, all our kids will be safe. I am sorry to tell you this, but there are *always* gay and trans people. Giving them no place to go only makes them feel alone, isolated, and unhappy. Our kids would be so much *less safe* if the kids who felt different from the rest of the world were deprived of a place and a time to meet.

"Blaming Isaiah for getting blindsided and stabbed is cowardly. Every person here who is saying, 'Well, if he hadn't been… you know… *gay*' is trying to blame one of the best kids I've ever known for his own attempted murder. I thought better of this town, I really did, but if that's why you're here—to blame Isaiah for getting hurt because he kissed a boy in public—then you need to say this to yourself. Look in the mirror and say, 'I am a coward, because I'd rather blame an innocent kid for my fear of gay and trans people than face my fear and grow.' Everyone here who wants to kill this program—to tell our LGBTQ kids that they have no place to go—is a coward."

For a moment there was silence—and then deafening applause.

Aaron stood up, the teachers stood up, and for just a moment, there was glorious, supportive pandemonium.

Heather pounded it into submission, of course, and when she was done, she spoke directly to Larx—which was not protocol at all, but her color was high and her lips were compressed into a flat line of bright red lipstick, and she looked like she'd swallowed a giant bug.

"Principal Larkin, I do not like the insinuation that I am a coward or that the members of the board have a hidden agenda in trying to remove this potentially harmful program—"

"No, Madam Chairwoman, your agenda is quite clear. You would like the children you don't approve of to be shoved out of sight and out of mind, where they can suffer with their doubts and fears in silence."

It was a beautiful line. Aaron's breath caught in his chest, and he stared at Larx for a moment, just filled with pride. The rest of the assembly gasped too, because there was no comeback to that. It was the absolute truth, and voting the program out of existence based on the events at the bonfire would have proven it.

"Wow, Larx, you sound like you know a lot about it. Are you a fucking faggot too?"

God *damn* Billy MacDonald!

Larx, surprised and pissed off, turned toward him with his mouth open in a snarl. Aaron wanted to groan. No. God, no—*Larx, not this way. C'mon, man, don't say it, don't let them change the dialogue. You have them on the ropes!*

"I am," Yoshi said clearly from Aaron's left. "I am gay, and Larx is my friend—does that mean he is unable to speak for me as well as for our kids?"

Larx stared at Yoshi in a combination of shock and irritation.

"Goddammit, Yoshi," he muttered. The microphone missed it, but those who knew Larx—they picked up every syllable.

Aaron turned to Yoshi with big eyes, and Larx's best friend looked blandly back.

"What are they going to do?" Yoshi asked. "Fire me?"

But the shock rippling through the meeting room was not promising.

"We got a faggot working at the school?" Billy shouted. "Fucking pervert!"

Larx turned furiously to Heather. "Where's your gavel now, Madam Chairwoman? This is your ally? Really?"

Heather belatedly called the meeting to order, and just as she was calling on the next speaker, Larx said, "And I still have three minutes to go."

"Continue on, Principal Larkin." Aaron was surprised ice crystals didn't form when she spoke.

"Just remember, people," Larx said, turning his back on the board itself, "if you are voting to overturn the GSA or to seek retaliation on Yo—Vice Principal Nakamoto—you are letting Billy MacDonald speak for you. Think carefully about that, because it means you're choosing your prejudices over student welfare, and yes, that makes you a bad person. You have taken your fear and focused it on students you assume have no voice. Bullying is the worst of humanity, and you have let it come to roost in this room." He turned back to Heather.

"We're supposed to be the grown-ups here. I taught today, and all I heard, all day, were wishes from the kids that Isaiah was well. Kellan Corker was afraid to go to visit Isaiah in the hospital that night because Isaiah hadn't come out to his parents, and it's true, Isaiah's parents were surprised to find out their son was gay—but they spoke to a reporter and told the world that their love outweighed their shock or their fear, and that the love extended to their son's boyfriend. Kellan was afraid to go to school, because oh my God, what if the students were going to be horrible to him. But—and this is partly because my staff did such an awesome job of making sure those kids were welcomed and loved, but also because our kids are tremendous—Kellan was loved. He was hugged by friends and straight football teammates and even kids he'd never really talked to, all of them telling him how proud they were of him and how much they wanted Isaiah to be better. So this young man faced his fears and discovered the world was better than one act of violence. We filled a car with stuffed animals and cards and flowers to take to Isaiah—because apparently your kids *do* know what love is, even if some of the people in this room do not." He spat that last line at Heather, who flinched.

"And *now* my fourteen minutes are up."

It took ten minutes for Heather to tap order into the room with her little gavel.

AARON WAS stoked on the way to Larx's house. "Oh my God, you were amazing!" he gushed. He could not remember being more proud of another person in his entire life. "I'm just boggled—you were so awesome!"

Larx smiled wanly. "You were pretty awesome yourself—smart thinking taking the podium from Percy. I was hoping you would, but I didn't even have to ask."

"Yeah, well, Eamon backed me on it, which was damned awesome." Aaron hesitated, because he hadn't mentioned this to Larx before. "He wants me to run for sheriff next year. And I think he wants me to do it out."

Larx frowned. "Really?"

Aaron shrugged. "I mean, I told him I was"—oh, this was a little embarrassing—"thinking about dating. A man. And he told me that was fine, he'd still back me. But he's been... almost fatherly, like he's encouraging a dowry match or something. It's... weird. Anyway, he surprised me, showing up tonight. I'm glad he did, but I was not expecting it."

"It was kind of him," Larx said distractedly. Then: "Kirby got home okay, right? I didn't realize he was passing out flyers for the student council."

"Yeah," Aaron said, wondering what was up. "He texted me about fifteen minutes before we got out of there. Said he was going to bed early but I should wake him up when I got home."

Larx made an affirmative sound. "Good. I'll miss you guys tonight, but I hope you get some rest."

Aaron grunted in irritation. About five hundred yards away was a turnout into a forestry road, with a fence and a cattle guard to keep out trespassers. Instead of passing it by, he took it, then went left into the open space forged by cars using the spot to turn around. The result was a hidey-hole, out of sight from the traffic of the highway, tucked back among the trees. Aaron was almost sorry he was an adult—as a teenager, he would have been here with his girlfriends in a hot second.

"Okay, Larx. Spill."

Larx looked around, startled, as though surprised to see they weren't at his house yet. "Spill what?"

"What's wrong?"

Larx sighed and turned around in his seat. He'd kicked off his dress shoes, and now he undid his seat belt and put his feet on the center console, wrapping his arms around his knees. He looked like a teenager himself in the dark, and Aaron sort of wished he'd turned the other way instead, and laid his head on Aaron's chest.

"I think Yoshi is going to get put on leave," he said after a moment.

"I'm sorry?"

"The human resources administrator was there—he's in Heather's pocket. I saw them talking, looking at Yoshi—it's how they work, Aaron. In secret. Nobody talks about it—they just pull you in early in the morning, read you a letter about what a pervert you are, and then put you on paid leave."

Aaron sucked in a breath. "Oh," he said softly. "That's how they do it."

Larx scrubbed at his face with both hands. "And Yoshi knows it—I talked with him before I left. He's going back to the school to write up a list of things on his plate and a note for the sub of his one class."

"How come you both teach classes—you don't have to, right?"

Larx shrugged and turned his head, looking out the windshield. "Not necessary, no. But we both spent years building up the AP program. It costs money, and convincing people to devote a class so kids can take a test takes some doing. My first class took the test and about 20 percent passed it, because kids have to be prepped for years. Last year's class had a 65 percent pass rate. Not stellar, no, but—"

"A lot of work," Aaron said, understanding.

"He doesn't want to let the AP English class die," Larx said, voice small. "He's leaving months' worth of lesson plans and practice tests." He leaned his head back against the window. "So tired," he mumbled. "Don't know how I'm supposed to do my job without Yoshi."

Aaron looked at him wordlessly. Oh. This is what Larx looked like when he stopped moving. It was a sad thing—a sort of violation of nature.

"Any way to get him back?" Aaron asked, voice quiet.

Larx shrugged. "Depends on how good our union lawyer is. Usually they're sort of amazing, but sometimes... I just ended up in the rubber room for a year and a half."

"What's that mean?"

"No talking to anyone from your old school, no going to the press, no trying to find another job—just sit at home, take your money, and wait for your lawyer to settle so you can decide if teaching is really what you want to do with your life." Larx's voice had gone bitter, and Aaron remembered him talking about this. A year and a half Larx had been suspended in limbo, watching his daughters be mistreated, not able to teach, not able to talk to any of his old friends, angry at himself for a thing he'd done with the best of intentions.

In that moment, Aaron felt that time in his bones. "We'll do something about getting him back—if they do take him." Aaron brightened. "We could just be borrowing trouble."

Larx nodded, eyes still closed. "I know. I just... I feel like such a chickenshit. It's like he threw himself on the grenade or something."

"Larx," Aaron said, frustrated. "I was *begging* you not to do it, in my head. I don't care if anyone knows—I mean, I don't. I want to tell the world. I want to call the girls and tell them, 'Hey, I'm in love, and I want to move in with him, and I know it's sudden, but it's real!' We could be a sitcom family—it would be great. But tonight? If you'd done it tonight, you wouldn't be going back to the school to fight for

Yoshi tomorrow. And sometimes that's all you've got. Once Billy threw that bomb, if Heather wasn't going to defuse it, it had to explode somewhere. Yoshi knew it. He took the hit so you could get him back."

Larx nodded and rested his cheek on his knees. "Yeah. I know."

So defeated.

Aaron undid his own belt. "C'mere," he ordered.

Larx peered at him through the darkness.

"No, I don't want a blowjob. I just want to hold you. C'mere."

Larx's shoulders shook in what was probably a laugh, but he scrambled over the seat until he was leaning into Aaron's arms over the driver's console. It was probably not comfortable in the least, but he was lying with his head on Aaron's chest, and that's really all Aaron wanted.

"Do you know," Aaron said conversationally, "when my wife died, her parents assumed I'd give them custody of the kids."

Larx scowled up at him. "That's weird."

"Not so much. She's from the Midwest, and I guess it's a common assumption there. Fathers don't raise children."

Larx scowled. "Yeah, that's frustrating. I got that when I moved up here. The girls got a lot of 'Why aren't you with your mom?' It's like the Y chromosome makes us incapable."

"And then there's people like Billy MacDonald who try to prove it. But that's not what I'm saying."

"What are you saying?" He was gazing up at Aaron with such trust.

Aaron was going to tell him about when he'd nearly broken faith with everything he'd ever believed in about love. "I... for a week I took them up on it. For a week they gathered the kids' belongings and kept them at the hotel, and I came home every night and drank. And then, on like, the fifth night, I woke up in the girls' room, delirious, fucking out of my mind. I'd dreamed that they were down a well and calling for me, and I was just walking away."

Larx made a hurt sound, and Aaron shrugged.

"I called up the in-laws the next day and told them no. I was coming to get the kids that afternoon, and all their stuff, and Caro's sister—"

"Aunt Candy?" Larx asked. He must have been talking to Kirby.

"Yeah. Aunt Candy—she came with me and brought her boyfriend's truck. We loaded up the kids, and I took them back home. Because there's losses you have to take and losses you don't have to take. Caro was dead—I had to fucking deal. But losing the kids hurt just as bad, and that I could control."

Larx nodded and straightened, kissing him gently before he put himself back into his seat. "The e-brake was trying to geld me," he said in apology. "But I hear you. I don't have to take Yoshi lying down."

"No. And you don't have to take it alone either. I'm here, Larx. I'm...." Could you really say it too often? "I love you."

Larx's smile was a little more animated. "Thanks, cowboy. I love you too."

Aaron dropped him off in front of his house with a long kiss, and wished heartily for some time alone. "I would *really* like to just bend you over and fuck you until the headboard banged against the wall, do you know what I'm saying?"

Larx laughed, the defeat gone from his voice and from the strong line of his shoulders. "I could totally live with that," he said earnestly, kissing Aaron one last time. "Running tomorrow, ri—"

He froze, his pocket buzzing.

His shoulders drooped again as he looked at the text.

"No run tomorrow," he said flatly. "Yoshi has a meeting with HR and his union rep before class. We have to be there at six thirty."

"In the morning?" Aaron squeaked, appalled.

"Yes, Aaron, in the morning," Larx responded with no humor at all. "Because that way Yoshi can be out of the parking lot before the kids see the big horrible pedophile who's been working his ass off to serve his community for the last six years."

"Aargh!" Aaron pounded his steering wheel and then glared at Larx. "*You* get some fucking sleep, you hear? And figure out a way to fucking stop this. It's what you're good at, Larx. Doing what's best for the kids and getting your own damned way."

Larx nodded soberly, touched Aaron's cheek, and slid out of the car. Aaron watched him go, his gut churning with anger and helplessness. He wanted to be with Larx—*needed* to be with him.

But goddammit, Kirby needed him to come home.

Larx got to the porch and turned on the outside light—and shooed Aaron on. Because he had two kids of his own under his roof. Aaron got it.

But he didn't like it one bit.

Wildfire Blaze

LARX SAT in his office, numb.

It was like he'd had a Magic 8 Ball, he'd predicted how the scene had played out so well. Yoshi stood up at the end of the meeting and shook his head, and Larx gaped at him, feeling like his arm had been sliced off.

"Don't look helpless at me, Larx," Yoshi said sharply. "You're the one getting me out of this mess. You're fucking genius at getting people to do what you want—get going! Chop-chop!"

Larx narrowed his eyes. "Chop-chop?"

"I'm Asian. I can say it."

"I will beat you when I get you back here. Soap in a sock—they'll never see a bruise."

Yoshi laughed in spite of the fact that his eyes were shiny and red-rimmed and in spite of the union rep trying hard to usher him away. "You do whatever you want with me when you get me back—but you're gonna get me back, asshole. You'll never live with yourself if you don't."

And then he was gone, and Larx was left with Fred Embree, trying not to flip the guy off.

"For the record, I think it's highly doubtful the school board will allow Mr. Nakamoto to negotiate for his job back—"

Larx snapped. "Get the fuck out of my office. They'll get him back when their entire district threatens to quit, because they don't have the *balls* to explain to the union why they put him on leave in the first place. Now go. *Go.* I don't have fucking time for you!"

Fred left, glaring, and Larx narrowly avoided sticking out his tongue. He was so fucking *furious* he could hardly speak.

He spent five minutes pounding his desk with his fist, and ten minutes ranting to Nancy over the phone as she sat in her office, trying to prepare for her day.

"Larx—*Larx!*" she hollered finally. "Look, we'll have an emergency staff meeting after school, and we can get people to sign a petition. We threaten to quit. Whatever. We'll brainstorm. Yoshi's well loved, and 90 percent of us think this is bullshit. They can't lose 90 percent of us. It's fucking November, for sweet Christ's sake. Who in their right mind is going to move halfway between bumfuck Truckee and Ta-hell right before the goddamned snows? They'll have to bus the kids to Placer County because they're fucking idiots—I will go to the goddamned media before that happens, okay?"

Larx grunted. "The media," he said, perking up. "That's an option too."

"See? And Yoshi's got protection—there are gay rights legal groups that can add some lawyer power.

We can fix this, Larx. I'll call Tane, you call Edna with the union—we're not helpless."

That had been what Aaron had said.

Yoshi had damned near banked his career on it.

Larx wasn't helpless.

He could fix this.

But still, he had to find a teacher willing to take over Yoshi's zero-period class, and when that was over, he trudged into his own class, trying hard to remember what they were doing.

Oh. Oh hell yeah. They were writing up their lab reports from their experiments the day before. Thank God. No lectures, no lab supervision—just go from table to table and help whoever needed him.

He could do that in his sleep, which was a good thing, because once again it had been a late, restless night and a shitty, crotch-of-dawn morning.

And he missed his goddamned run.

He'd be able to wander around the classroom and work off some extra energy. Fantastic. As long as he didn't dwell on how sad it was that this was the best news he'd heard since…

Well, since Aaron kissed him weeks ago.

Okay.

Aaron. Loved him. He was going to have a big family again.

Perspective, Larx thought, grabbing his briefcase a little tighter and soldiering on into his room. It was always good to have.

"OKAY, SO he's still using his credit card?" Eamon said, looking at Aaron in concern.

Aaron nodded, nibbling his lip. "Actually, at that nice little resort outside of town. The room is paid up until tomorrow, and there are charges regularly at the restaurant."

Eamon looked at the list of charges Aaron had just gotten from the credit bureau. "Someone's getting the free continental breakfast," he speculated. "Anything else?"

"I sent Warren and Percy out to bring in whomever is in Room 32," Aaron said grimly. "And checked in with the people at the Olson house, making sure Whitney hasn't flown the coop. By all accounts, you can hear her screeching from the curb."

"You've been a busy bee," Eamon said mildly. "Any reason you were here so early?"

Aaron grunted. "Had to go home last night," he confided. "Larx got called into an early meeting about his vice principal."

"Oh no," Eamon said, pinching the bridge of his nose. "They didn't really do what I think they did?"

"He texted me about ten minutes ago. The staff is gathering together to figure out how to fix it. He's pissed."

Aaron ached for him at the same time he fiercely missed his company in the mornings. He'd taken a short run, but it just wasn't as much fun without Larx. Kirby had fed the chickens and collected the eggs, and then, without a word, they'd both packed overnight bags.

"Last night sucked," Kirby said with a grunt. "I don't even want to talk to people all the time. It's just good to know they're in the house."

"So, chicken coop weekend?" Aaron said with a sad little smile.

Kirby looked at him and shrugged. "If it doesn't work, we move back. They don't have a lot of computer room—I may end up coming here to study. But…." Kirby looked around the house. "I know it's stupid, but I miss the crap out of Maureen."

"Not Tiffany?" Aaron asked, sort of hating himself for letting that happen.

"Fine. Sure. Maybe Tiffany." Kirby met Aaron's eyes then. "Look, Dad? I'm eighteen in January. If it turns out that being a stepbrother isn't my thing, I can move back here and be all hermity and mean. I'm not worried about me. I'm not worried about you not loving me anymore. I guess I should be. Kids at school whine about their stepparents all the time. But I'm not. I'll be okay. But you and Larx—you're… happy. Kids worry about growing up and being happy. You're happy. I don't think it can be a bad thing, you know?"

Aaron thought about the night before, when Larx had been small and sad and human, not his bigger-than-life Larx self at all. And how Aaron had needed to choose Kirby.

Kirby was saying he didn't have to choose.

"How much is this going to cost me at Christmas?" Aaron asked suspiciously.

Kirby grinned. "I already have Maureen's old car. I'll have to come up with something really good."

"I'll talk to him," Aaron said, suddenly sober. "I mean, it's been a quick five days."

Kirby counted on his fingers and then grimaced. "Oh my God, is that all it's been? Okay. Fine. You can have a whole week. Jeez, it's not like you're going to live that long anyway!"

Aaron scooped a throw pillow from the couch and threw it at his head. And then hugged him hard, because God, who wouldn't give thanks for a kid like that?

And now, standing in the squad room, wishing hard for a snack since he'd gotten there an hour early, he was starting to see how this getting-to-work-early thing might pay off.

"Well, I'd be pissed too," Eamon said, breaking into his thoughts. "I don't know what people are thinking right now."

Larx did. "They're thinking that Whitney Olson is bad news," Aaron said shortly. "And she was complaining about the gay kids, so that's where we'll put our attention."

Eamon gave an evil chuckle and scratched the graying hair under his cap. "I think they should be thinking that Whitney Olson is a murderer, and maybe they should find another team."

At that point, Warren and Percy burst through the doors of processing, an unhandcuffed woman standing between them. She was in her late thirties, not a stunning woman, but well cared for. Thick, straight brown hair, a wide-hipped build that she obviously kept in check with exercise and probably a strict diet. The most remarkable thing about her was her eyes, wide and brown and direct, and she spotted Eamon and Aaron as soon as she walked in.

"I'm sorry," she said, the model of composure. "Are you two in charge?"

"He is," Aaron said, pointing to his boss. "But I follow his orders." He ignored Eamon's gentle snort. "I'm sorry to interrupt your morning, uh—"

"Lori Anne," she said quietly. "Lori Anne Beresford. Does this have anything to do with Carl?"

"Carl Olson?" Aaron asked carefully, looking at Eamon.

"Yes, sir. I'm…." And for the first time she seemed to lose her poise. "I'm the skank whore," she said in apology. "The homewrecker. Carl was going to leave his wife and we were going to run off together, you see?"

Aaron struggled for breath. "Really?"

"Yeah. I know. It's a soap opera." She shifted from foot to foot, looking uncomfortable and worried at the same time. "But he went to talk to his wife and maybe get his daughter to come with us, and he hasn't come back." She swallowed, and Aaron saw that her clasped hands were white, and her jaw was tense enough to send a vein throbbing in her forehead.

"When did you last see him?" Aaron asked.

"Thursday morning," she said. "Around eleven o'clock. He was going to check his daughter out of school and then go talk to his wife."

Aaron's brain started working overtime. They'd checked some of the local hidey-holes for Whitney Olson's car, but there were just too many of them to comb through in two days. Even Colton's recently developed suburbs featured three- or four-acre yards, most of them with big-assed trees in the middle. Hiding a car, or a seventeen-year-old kid, was easier in a small town than most people assumed.

"I'll call the attendance office," Aaron said briskly, pulling out his phone. "Let's see if she got there."

He had his phone in his hand when it buzzed, and he was surprised to see it was one of the extensions of the high school.

"It's like they read my mind," he mumbled. "Deputy George," he answered. "How can I help you?"

In his entire life, he could only remember his vision turning icy, crystal blue once—when he'd gotten the call that his wife had died.

And now, listening to Nancy, it was twice.

LARX BIT back a yawn and listed the requirements for an A+ lab on the whiteboard. "Okay, all," he said, turning around. "I know it's not the most exciting class in the world, but I'll rent the circus next week. For now, it's time to buckle down and write up your labs for yesterday's experiment. Yesterday was fun, today is not so much. If you want I can put in my old people's music and we can chill."

"Can we listen to our own?" Michelle asked from the back.

Of course.

Larx had never been a stickler for rules like this one. If the kids were listening to *Larx* at the appropriate time, he didn't mind if they listened to something else when they were working quietly.

"Yeah, why not. Remember, if I can hear it as I'm walking back and forth, it's too damned loud, okay? Your hearing may be the first thing to go, but you don't have to chase it out with whatever crap you kids are listening to now."

The kids laughed a little, and everybody pulled out their books, their notes, and their writing utensils. Normally a day like today would be the perfect time to grade something, but Larx headed for his desk with every intent of getting on his computer and cooking up a plan. An appeal to the media first—because Heather might go there if he didn't, and they couldn't afford to have public opinion against them—then an appeal to the teachers, and then a plausible petition, as well as a plausible action to take if they didn't reinstate Yoshi. He had lots of things on his list that had nothing whatsoever to do with the kids in the room. For the first time, he was starting to see why he might have to let go of this class, eventually—but not now. Right now, he really needed the basic purity of teaching to give him faith for the fight ahead.

When he got to his desk, he turned around one last time to make sure they really were doing what he'd asked of them, and that's when he saw her coming in through the door in the back of the room.

He opened his mouth to say her name, but then he noticed everything at once.

Her clothes were a mess—dirty, sweat-stained, askew. It looked like she'd run out of the house in her pajamas and a sweatshirt and had been living in them for the past two days. He could smell her from the door, like she'd had to pee in the woods and had maybe caught the hem of her pajama pants once or twice.

Her hair—usually impeccable—was in a tumbling, greasy topknot that tangled around her ears and fell in her eyes.

Her miserable, red-rimmed, darting, panicky eyes.

In her hands she carried a black Sig Sauer. Larx only knew what one looked like because he'd had to

take a gang seminar back when he worked in Sacramento, and it was America's favorite handgun.

"Julia?" he asked courteously, walking up the
aisle between the tables to talk to her. Christiana and
Kirby sat in the front. *Don't hurry, but pass them, pass
them, pass them, pause, look the girl in the eye. Tap
Kirby on the shoulder. Gesture behind your back. Go.
Go. Go.*

"Julia?" he said again, voice gentle. "People are
looking for you. Would you like me to take you to
them?"

"You'd like that, wouldn't you?" she snarled,
still cradling the gun. From the corner of his eye, he
watched as his daughter and Aaron's son stood up
slowly and walked toward the door.

"Well, like I said. Worried. Can you tell me where
you've been for the last few days?" The next group
of kids to his left stood up in a rush, and he gestured,
keeping his movements small. And keeping his eyes
locked on Julia, who seemed fixated on him as well.

"In my car," she sniffled, because that made
everything clear. "And I didn't know where to go.
Everybody knows me." She looked up at Larx and
pushed her hair out of her eyes. "I couldn't even go
to McDonald's."

"So you must be hungry?" He took a step to his
left, and Kellan was in the next row. He very quietly
got up and left. Larx could hear the rustle of papers, of
pens, as kids put their stuff down and got up to leave.
They all seemed to be taking their cue from Kirby and
Christi, bless them all, but Larx wasn't going to count
on anything until the girl put down the *big, ugly gun*.

"I'm so hungry," she sighed.

Larx looked down at Christi's backpack—she packed herself a lunch every morning. "Uh, I can get you a PB&J if you want," he said politely. "Here—" He held his hands out and knelt for a moment. "Uh, going to unzip the pack, okay?" He showed her the inside of the backpack—which was a disaster of assignments she'd gotten back already and hadn't filed—and pulled out the ridiculously cute Hello Kitty lunchbox she'd reclaimed from a pile of donations to Goodwill. "See? Food."

He unzipped the lunch box, grateful that her attention had been focused intensely on him when he saw the last of the kids disappear out the door.

He handed Christi's lunch to Julia and glanced up at the doorway in time to see Christiana stick her face back in the doorway, looking at him in agony.

He shook his head slightly and mouthed, "Love you," at his daughter before turning back to the girl with the gun.

Julia had torn through the sandwich, and he handed her the apple slices automatically. While she ate, she held the gun sideways, pointed toward the wall, her arms pulled up to her stomach while she ducked her head and ate from her hands like a raccoon.

"Julia," Larx said, keeping his voice even, "where did you get that?"

"This?" She gestured casually with it, the muzzle pointing up toward her face, then out toward Larx's chest, then back to the side. "This? My mother gave me this. Isn't that awesome? I… I didn't even know we had it until…." Her voice broke and the apple slices fell down. Larx pushed Christi's bag of tiny Oreos into her hand, already opened, and she cradled the bag against her stomach with her gun hand and used the other hand to lift them dispiritedly to her mouth.

"Until when?" Larx asked softly.

"Dad was...." Julia stopped, stared straight into space, and said, "I don't want to talk about that."

Her eyes were flat and dead, and Larx watched as she tightened her hand on the gun.

"We don't have to talk about anything you don't want to," he said fervently. "What... what *do* you want to talk about, Julia?"

"I... everyone says what a great teacher you are. I... what a good guy you are. But you never liked me. How come?"

"You tried to blackmail me for a better grade," he said, wondering if this was one of those times in his life he really should have lied.

"I wanted an A," she said, munching. "Why wouldn't you give me an A?"

"Because you hadn't turned in the work or passed the tests," he said. Sweat trickled down his spine. "Did you... uh, were you planning to make that class up? It was, uh, two years ago, but I think I could find my materials—"

She scowled at him. "No," she muttered. "That's stupid. Just... tell me something. When my mom met with you and got pissed because you wouldn't change my grade, what did you think?"

"Julia," he asked after his heart thudded in his throat, and he tried, once again, to figure out if the truth was going to get him killed, "what is this about?"

She slipped, made eye contact, and then looked past him again. Her jaw locked and her chin trembled, but she kept her voice flat. "My mother," she said soft-ly, "is not a nice person."

He took a big breath. "No," he agreed. "Not from my end."

"But she always fought for me," Julia said, eyes still vacant. "Kids would talk about how their parents didn't trust them, didn't care. Mom always fought for me."

"You do what you can for your kids," Larx said, searching past her, making sure Christiana, Kirby, and Kellan were all staying well clear of this room.

"But my dad…." Julia's body gave a hard shud-der, and her hand tightened on the gun. Larx heard the click of the safety disengaging, and his water dropped into his bladder with a giant *whumpf*.

"What about him?" Larx asked softly. He knew. He'd known in his gut from the beginning, but he'd had no words.

"He came back to fight for me," she said, and her eyes stayed flat. But they also filled with tears. "And he was changing, and packing. Told me to change and pack too. And I was in my room, looking around, wondering if he'd laugh at me if I brought… this big stupid bear. He used to buy me all these big stuffed animals. Even… my car. A big one in the front of my car. And… and Mom came home."

Tears dropped from Julia's eyes, through the grime on her face, and mixed with the snot on her lip. Larx remembered the way his girls used to cry with their whole bodies, like their hearts would come apart because their little persons shook so hard, and the chill knife in his bowels twisted.

"Julia, maybe you want to put down the—"

Julia brought the side of the gun to her head and pressed like she was trying to grind out the memory with her fist and forgot the gun was there. "They were fighting, and then he got so scared. And I looked out my door and she was backing him out… in his underwear!"

She didn't move her hand, but she looked at Larx in agony, the ugly black pistol hard against her forehead. "His *underwear*, Mr. Larkin! She won't even let me out of the house in a miniskirt!"

Julia shook her head then and started gesticulating wildly, the gun pointing everywhere. Larx watched it with wide eyes, waiting for her to wind down.

"I don't know what happened after that," she gasped, the weight of the gun pulling on her exhausted, undernourished body. "*I don't know! You can't make me tell!*"

"Of course not," he said, and he heard his voice shake. "I won't make you tell. Not right now. Julia, do you think I could have the—"

"And I didn't ask." Her gun hand calmed down, and she brought it up against her stomach again, muzzle pointing up past her shoulder this time so she could hold the Oreos and continue to eat.

"I understand," he said, throat dry. He did too. Her mother killed her father on the end of the dock. She knew it. She'd maybe even seen it. And then she'd come back to school, which, just like it had been for Kellan, was a place of safety. And the boy she'd wanted hadn't wanted her back. And the other kids had laughed at her, maybe—or maybe she just wanted Mom to do something. That was her pattern, to call her mom.

"And I told my mom at the bonfire that night, the boy didn't want me. I had the dress, I had this whole stupid date picked out, and he… he'd rather kiss a boy. And my mom…." Julia's breath caught. "I don't know what she did," she said, voice finally breaking. "I don't. I didn't see… I can't think about it. She was there. She ran by me and hugged me and told me it would all be okay, and I didn't see the blood, I swear I didn't see the blood until they pulled a gun on me and I almost wet my pants!"

She was beginning to crumble, the gun swinging loosely from her fingers. Larx put his hands out slowly.

"Julia," he said quietly. "Hon. That thing, it must be so terribly heavy right now. You've been carrying it for such a long, long time. You want to give it to me? And we'll get you some clothes, and a bath, and some food, and a place to sleep, and someone to talk to, and—"

He made his voice soothing, hypnotic, and even as he stretched out his arms, he watched warily as her hand drooped, the gun sagging out of her fingers, and he reached for it with one hand while he wrapped his other arm around her shoulders.

He saw it falling and made a grab for it so it wouldn't hit the floor.

He heard her scream in his ear just as the sound of the shot rang out through the classroom.

AARON AND Eamon got to the school in time to see the milling kids being shepherded by Nancy Pavelle. Aaron sought out Larx's room, back to the left of the administration building, and saw the open door just in time to spot Christi running away from the room, wiping her face on her sweater.

Eamon disdained the curb, the sidewalk, and the quad grass and used the SUV's torque to get them up and into the middle of the quad. He parked right next to a familiar battered-looking Navigator squatting in the middle of the grass, and Aaron tried to keep his heart beating.

They'd been looking for that vehicle, and here it was, at the school to greet them.

Nancy ushered the kids closer to the admin building to give them some room, and Aaron wondered which kid had gone to get her—it had been a good move.

Kirby spotted his father first and grabbed Kellan's arm and Christi's hand, and in a moment Aaron was the center of their frightened, hysterical chatter, and hard-pressed to put some semblance of order to the kids while icy fingers of fear ripped all the strength from his body.

"Enough!" he snapped and opened his arms for Christi, reliable, practical Christiana, who melted against him with a whimper. "Now someone tell me what happened and where Larx is!"

"We were working," Kirby said, looking at Kellan, who nodded. "And the room was quiet, and he saw her coming in. He met her in the middle of the aisle and just…."

"Wiggled his fingers," Kellan said with a small shrug, "like he was shooing us away."

"We looked up and saw the gun and just went," Kirby said.

"I thought he'd come with us!" Christi wailed into Aaron's shirt, and Aaron held her, and then he reached out his other arm for Kirby. Kirby dragged Kellan, and for a moment they huddled, paralyzed, while Aaron tried to put his fear in a little box so he could function.

Larx. Larx was in that room with a desperate girl. Who had a gun.

Eamon had sent Warren and Percy to go arrest Whitney, but what was going on in that classroom might be over way before then.

Aaron backed up a bit and caught everybody's eyes. "You three, stay here. Right here. Let me take care of it. I'm getting the other kids out of the quad and to safety, okay?"

They looked at him and nodded, and he strode away, Eamon at his side.

"Nancy," he said, "can we get these kids out of the quad?"

"Yeah, sure," she muttered, looking like she was barely keeping it together. "I can get them to my room. But you've got twenty minutes, maybe less, before the bell rings. Normally I'd have Yoshi call over the intercom, because besides the kids he's the only one who knows how to use it—"

"Kirby!" Aaron barked, pulling his son away from the SUV. "You know how to use the intercom?" He remembered Kirby talking about his stint as an office TA.

"Yeah?"

"You need to help Mrs. Pavelle talk to everybody *besides* Larx's room. Can you do that?"

Kirby appeared to think about it. "Maybe," he said, thinking. "Okay, yeah. I can do that."

"Okay," Aaron said, trying hard to think. "We don't want them all in one place. We don't want them milling about. Tell them to go to their homeroom immediately. Go!" They took off, but before they'd even turned around, he was on to the next thing. "Eamon?"

"Yes, Deputy?" Eamon asked mildly.

Aaron ignored the sarcasm. He'd learned a lot by watching Larx do big group logistics, and he was trying to think just like him. "Do we have backup?"

Eamon looked up in time to see a second unit pull up, siren blazing. He pulled his hand across his throat immediately, and the noise cut off.

"Roadblock the drop-off points," Aaron said, head swimming. "Have them take down student names and send the kids home. Some of the kids are already here, and we can't fix that. Some of them walk or ride bikes or drive, and we can't fix that. But we can stop anybody else from turning into the driveway and dropping their kids off into chaos. Tell them to call the attendance office as soon as they can so we know the kid's safe, but start that right the hell now."

"Read you," Eamon said, and then he saluted smartly and trotted down to meet the other two deputies to have them block the main entrance with the SUV.

Aaron looked up and saw that Nancy had put another teacher in charge of herding Larx's class to her room, picking up any kids she could find on the way. The quad was much clearer now, and he still had fifteen minutes to go.

He reached into his SUV, behind the seat, and pulled out his Kevlar.

"Here," he said to Kellan, "hold this." He took off his jacket and put the vest on, making sure his own weapon was clear. He glanced at Kellan holding the jacket to his chest and shivering and said, "You can put it on, son. I'm not going to need it for a few."

"That looks *so scary* in real life," Kellan told him with a wobble in his voice.

Aaron smiled grimly and ruffled his hair. "It'll be okay." He touched Christiana's cheek with his knuckle. "Both of you. We have to have faith."

He had to. He'd thought his faith had been destroyed, decimated by his wife's death, the things he'd seen on his job, raising his children single-handedly, and feeling like he failed more often than he succeeded. But he'd fallen in love—he and Larx had made love, and his body felt brand-new at over forty-eight, and his heart felt bright and shiny, and he just needed some fucking faith.

He smiled at them and told them to sit tight. "I mean it," he said soberly. "Wait until I give the all clear, okay?"

Eamon came trotting up at that moment, and Aaron looked to the school's entrance to see the roadblock in place just in time to hear Nancy over the intercom.

"All students, report to their homeroom immediately. Do not linger in the quad. Go now."

And that took care of the rest of the lingerers. The kids were safe behind the SUV, and it was time to get closer to Larx.

"Boy, are you going to wait for me?" Eamon muttered, reaching into his side of the vehicle. He threw his jacket onto the driver's side before securing the door, and he was fastening the Velcro as he caught up with Aaron, weapon drawn and pointed downward, as he approached the still-open door to Larx's classroom.

"Let me take point," Eamon commanded softly, and Aaron's common sense kicked in just in time, before he could run in like a goddamned cowboy.

Eamon could think through this better. He didn't have any high-school-aged kids. His lover wasn't in there facing a gun. Eamon would have the clearer head, and Aaron needed to trust him as Eamon had just trusted Aaron to keep the kids safe.

"I don't know what she did!" Julia wailed. "I don't. I didn't see… I can't think about it!" Aaron and Eamon exchanged grim glances. Oh yeah. They'd figured out what she'd seen on the way over. They took position at the door, Eamon against the wall, Aaron against the open door. Eamon glanced in first, and then Aaron, and Aaron felt his heart stall.

Julia was standing, back toward the door, and Larx was… oh God. Two feet away. She gestured as she spoke, and they got glimpses of the inexpertly held gun flailing in time with her emotions.

Then Larx started talking, and Aaron blessed him. His voice was low and soothing, and they both watched as he reached… reached… reached….

The gun fell and went off, firing randomly up at an angle. Julia screamed and Larx finished his hug, falling into her a little at the same time. Eamon rushed through the door, wrapping his arms around her as she went limp and sobbing, while Aaron went for Larx.

Who was squinting at Aaron fuzzily, one hand coated in blood while he stared at a deep gouge in his arm. "Holy crap," he muttered. "She shot me!"

"Larx?" Aaron said, wondering how he could talk if his heart hadn't started beating yet. "Larx, you okay?"

Larx looked at him and tried a smile. "I could use some fuckin' sleep," he said distinctly.

Aaron nodded, holstering his weapon. "I know, baby. C'mere. We'll get you home." Larx didn't even flinch as Aaron pulled him into a very careful embrace.

"I'm so glad to see you," Larx whispered against his shoulder, his voice shaky. "I was so afraid—"

"Yeah," Aaron told him, reassured by his warmth and his quick breaths against Aaron's neck. "Me too. Let's get you outside, okay? The kids need to see you."

"Paramedics would be a great idea too," Eamon said tartly, putting his own weapon away. He'd cuffed Julia from the front, but he also had a protective arm around her shoulders. "I'll get her to the deputies to take to the station. You stay and take care of your family. I'll deal with the press, because I can't believe those assholes aren't here yet. And you have an appalling number of teenagers to tend to."

Aaron let out a laugh that wasn't quite sane. "Yeah. That."

He looked at the floor and saw the gun, still smoking, and holstered his own weapon. Then he picked the damned thing up in his gloved hand and clicked the safety on. He put it in his left hand while he wrapped his right arm over Larx's shoulder, thinking of evidence bags and lockboxes so he didn't have to think about how this wound, this moment, had been a near miss—and a big hint from the universe not to take anything for granted.

The paramedics were up on the curb by the time they got outside, and Aaron steered Larx to sit down on the tailgate to be doctored. Larx winced when they cut through his shirt and his sport coat. "I don't have many of those," he muttered. Then he saw Christi approaching and he smiled.

"Hey, Christi-lulu-belle. How're we doing?"

She gave a wobbly smile and then threw herself into his arms and fell apart while the EMTs worked.

Aaron talked quietly to the boys, reassuring them both and making sure they could get close enough to Larx to see he'd be okay. When the medic had Larx sufficiently drugged and bandaged, Eamon approached.

"Boys, I hate to break this to you, but they have a really cozy shot of the two of you leaving the building. If Larx hadn't been bleeding, it would look like a date photo. Larx, I think you're going to need to talk to the press. Follow my lead."

Larx nodded. "Yessir," he said, smiling brightly. "Christi, let me up."

He nodded a little shakily and shed what was left of his sport coat, looking woefully at the sleeve the EMT had butchered. The EMT—a calm, capable woman who treated Larx like she knew him—glared back.

"Larx, you should be going to the hospital," she said patiently. "I know how you feel about following rules, but you're going to want a painkiller and some antibiotics, and I can't give you any of that."

"You did too," Larx muttered. "You just gave me a painkiller."

"I gave you a *shot*, not a prescription. And I gave you a tetanus and an antibiotic shot. You're going to want more."

Larx grimaced. "Really, Mary-Beth? Can't I go home and sleep and take some Advil?"

"Mr. Larkin, you can do anything you want to, but I'm telling you, you're going to wake up in a world of hurt if you don't go to the hospital!"

"Just give me something to sign," Larx muttered. "Sorry, darlin', I'm proud you took my class and ran with it, but I've got way too much to do here."

She looked at him doubtfully even as she was reaching for a clipboard—one that probably had AMA papers on it.

"The kids'll be home to take care of him," Aaron said quietly. "And they'll call me if he gets bad."

She sighed and took the clipboard back. "Well, it's good to know someone's watching out for him. Geez, Mr. Larkin, you totally need a keeper!"

Larx grinned what was probably his best, most evil teacher grin, and she shook her head like he was a naughty child. With a sigh, Larx stood, and Aaron gestured to Kellan for his jacket.

Larx took it, looking a little dazed, and then he paused and smiled impishly. "Why, Deputy, if the whole town sees me in your jacket, won't they know we're going steady?"

"Course they will," Aaron shot back. "That's the point." He helped Larx slide his arm in. "Hiding the bloody bandage has nothing to do with it."

"Not a thing," Larx agreed through gritted teeth.

Aaron could see the sweat beading on his forehead, and he kissed Larx's temple, done with being careful. "C'mon, love," he said quietly. "We can get this done."

"Yeah, sure." Larx turned a game smile at Aaron and then shored it up a little for the kids. "C'mon, guys, let's all go watch your principal pass out on live TV. It'll be a hoot!"

Together they soldiered to the front of the school, where Eamon was being interviewed by an earnest on-location reporter from a local affiliate.

Eamon had done meet-the-press before. He spoke briefly and succinctly about how a girl whose mother was wanted for questioning in two violent crimes had come into the school looking for sanctuary.

"But the student was armed?" Marissa Schroeder, rookie reporter at large, asked, sounding confused.

"She had the gun her mother asked her to hide," Eamon said cagily, "but from everything we know, she had no intention of using it."

"Didn't the gun go off?" Marissa asked. She was woefully underdressed for October in the mountains, and Aaron wished someone would go get the poor woman a coat to put over her black blazer and red skirt.

"It was accidental—she was giving the gun to her principal, Mr. Larkin, when she dropped it, and it fired. People forget—guns are dangerous things, particularly in the hands of people who haven't been taught how to use them. This little girl was tired, distraught, and desperate. She went to a place she felt safe. She'd been told to protect the gun, so she took that too. This was scary, no doubt about it, but don't make it anything it isn't, because there's enough awfulness in the world without that."

"Well, thank you, Sheriff Mills." She turned toward the camera in obvious dismissal. "And next we have Principal Lyman Larkin, who was the teacher in the room when the student walked in. Principal Larkin, what can you tell us about this near tragedy?"

"Handguns are dangerous and we shouldn't give them to children?" Larx said, as though puzzled the woman needed to hear the obvious.

"Is there anything else?" Marissa rooted a little desperately.

Eamon glared at Larx, and Aaron saw the light-bulb go on.

"School is a sanctuary, Marissa," Larx stated. (*Lyman Larkin*, Aaron thought giddily. Finally he knew. No wonder he was Larx.) "This student was in pain, and she came to someone she thought she could trust. I talked her into putting the gun down, and it went off accidentally—which hurt, I won't pretend it didn't. But I think the larger thing here is that students—even desperate ones on the run from the law—want to feel safe at school."

Beautiful, Larx. Now come on, junior rookie reporter with too much blonde hair.

And she did them proud. "Do you feel anyone was at fault for this incident? Is there anything anyone could have done to keep this student from coming onto the campus armed?"

"Since you asked, our school board spent last night distracting both the sheriff's investigation and the community from finding the student in question, instead focusing the blame for a violent crime on the sexual orientation of the victim. This morning—right now, in fact—I could really use my vice principal on campus to help with student crisis management, but he was removed for objecting to the school board's actions. The kid coming into my classroom with a gun had absolutely nothing to do with either of these things. This campus would have been a lot safer if we had focused on helping students instead of finding ways to *not* help the ones the school board doesn't understand."

Marissa Schroeder's big blue eyes grew bigger and rounder as Larx spoke. "That is really unfortunate," she said sincerely. "What do you think this community should learn from this incident?"

Larx frowned, and Aaron could tell he'd had his limit. "Be more afraid of the people with the guns and spend less time worrying about who's kissing whom," he said shortly. "Give me a day or two and I might come up with something more profound."

Marissa turned back toward the camera, and Aaron spotted the wobble in Larx's knees before he went down entirely. He stepped in and got Larx around the waist and started to guide him away from the camera and the noise. He was waylaid by the tiny blonde blue-eyed reporter, who started to follow them across the quad in her high heels.

"Deputy? Is Principal Larkin okay?"

"He's fine," Aaron said, grimacing at the mic in his face. "He needs some food and some rest and some antibiotics and he'll be dandy."

"What can you tell us about Principal Larkin's state of mind before the incident this morning?"

"I'm still here," Larx snapped around Aaron. "And I was pissed off. My vice principal had been dragged away for no damned good reason, and my whole damned town wanted to kill gay people with fire. Now go away!"

"Easy, easy," Aaron muttered as they came to the squad car. The kids were leaning against the passenger's side, away from the forensics team currently going over the inside of Julia Olson's SUV.

"Christi, where's his car? I'm going to send him home with you three—"

"No school today?" Kirby asked. He'd come trotting back from the attendance office right as Larx had gone up for his interview.

"School's out for summer!" Larx sang irreverently, and Aaron gave the camera a meaningful look.

"Well, we've got no principal," Kellan quipped, and the kids, bless them, took over.

Aaron turned toward the reporter as they hustled Larx to his minivan, and just looked at her until the kids were out of earshot and she covered her microphone.

"What do you need from us?" he asked quietly.

"You two looked awfully cozy for a deputy sheriff and a principal," she said without subtlety.

Aaron kept his gaze level. "Did you hear nothing he just said? The entire school board was distracted by questions like this—the entire *town* was distracted by it—and that girl was wandering around, desperate for help, until she came here with a gun on campus. Can we maybe stop focusing on who's kissing who—"

"Whom," she supplied, so grave and sincere he wanted to smack her.

"Could you just maybe leave us alone to do our jobs?" he asked, his heart sore because his job was going to require that he stay at the school and help sort out the mess, and what he wanted to do was go home and sort out Larx.

She grimaced. "Fine. I will make you a deal." She reached into the pocket of her blazer and pulled out a card, and then grabbed the pen from her blazer. "This is me," she said, circling her name. "I also do online pieces for a couple of websites you might have heard about." She wrote the titles on the back and waited until his eyebrows went up. Yeah, he recognized them—both sites were extremely civil-rights friendly. "I've got footage of the two of you that about breaks my heart it's so sweet. I'm not going to release it to the network without your permission, because that would be wrong, but in return, I want you to contact me in the next month for an exclusive."

"What if we can't!" he protested. "His job—"

"I get it. But if he gets his VI back, I want you to at least contact me and let me know why you can't."

God, she looked little and fuzzy, but she was apparently tenacious.

"Why us?"

At that moment, of all things, the bell rang. A student body at about half capacity started to straggle out of rooms, probably to their next class, and Aaron realized he was going to be in charge of getting the kids home and helping Nancy put together a phone message. And when that was done, he'd need to start his end of the paperwork on Julia Olson.

Marissa kept her steely blue gaze locked on Aaron. "Because you're important. You're being positive and active in your community. You're raising a family. People need to see that."

Aaron grunted. "Nobody wants to see that," he muttered. "Look, I've got to do my job."

"Please," she said, her hand on his sleeve. "Please—I'll cut this to make your guy look like a rock-star martyr—just think about being the poster family for what real love looks like."

"I haven't even moved in," Aaron muttered.

Marissa rolled her eyes. "What in the hell are you waiting for? Man, life is short and you never know what'll happen next."

She turned around and clipped away, her cameraman at her heels, and Aaron waved to Eamon and Nancy, who had just come out of the admin building.

"How's Larx?" Nancy asked briskly.

"Falling down," Aaron replied. "I sent him home with the kids, and he didn't object. I've got some painkillers I can bring him later."

Nancy let out a grunt. "Well, sir, I'm going to need someone's help getting kids home, so if one of you could stay—"

"*Can* you get them home?" Aaron asked.

"Yes—in fact, we programmed a home call that went out about five minutes ago. We're going to need to plan student pickup and checkout, but I got permission from the district to treat this like a snow day, so the kids can go as soon as we have parent contact. We should probably have them all cleared out in two hours."

"Well, then," Eamon said, looking at Aaron, "that's going to be your duty, and as soon as it's done, we need you at the office." He nodded. "Nancy, you make sure to abuse my boy to the fullest extent of the law."

"Yessir," Nancy replied smartly. "C'mon, Aaron—let's go take care of Larx's kids."

Seeding

THE PAINKILLERS the EMTs had given Larx must have been TKO strength, because the kids put him to bed as soon as they got back to the house. He woke up around four, aching and disoriented, surprised to see Aaron at the foot of the bed, throwing his uniform into the hamper while he slid on sweats.

"You're home already?" he said, squinting in the darkness.

"Stay right there," Aaron said, coming to sit on the edge of the bed. "Here." A bottle of Vicodin and a bottle of water sat on the end table, and Larx struggled to sit up.

"Where'd the codeine come from?" he asked, holding out his hand. Aaron put one in his palm and handed him the water to wash it down.

"My last dentist appointment," Aaron admitted. Fretfully, he pushed the hair away from Larx's temples. "Since you opted out of the hospital visit, I thought I'd share."

"Decent of you," Larx said, still tired after sleeping for most of the day. He yawned. "Don't you get home at six?"

"Well, Yoshi arrived at the school around noon to finish clearing out kids and dealing with parents, so that freed me up to go help Eamon. He sent me home at four because he said I was too worried about you to work right. I figure he was mostly correct about that."

Larx moaned and fell back against the bed. His arm was on fire, and his body felt achy and feverish. "If I was in the movies, I'd still be on the run taking down bad guys."

"Real life sucks enough," Aaron agreed, putting his hand on Larx's forehead. "Yeah, you feel a little warm. Give me your health card. I'll call your doc for antibiotics."

"Ugh. Fine. It's in my wallet, which is—"

"In your pants, next to the bed," Aaron said, smiling a little.

"Yoshi's really back?" Larx asked, knowing he sounded plaintive and not caring.

"He is. He wants me to tell you that getting shot was not what he meant by getting him back. I told him to take whatever help he could get."

Larx had to laugh. "You *so* get me and Yoshi."

Aaron nodded soberly and cupped his cheek. "I do. And I'm glad he's back. But…."

His voice was cracking, and Larx put out his good arm. "You were worried."

Larx wrapped his arm around those broad shoulders while Aaron rested his cheek on Larx's chest. For a moment all was quiet in the room, and then Larx felt Aaron's shoulders heave and shudder, heard the constricted breathing of a man trying hard not to come unglued. An insistent wetness seeped through Larx's shirt, and he realized with a shock that he'd never held another man as he cried.

He tightened his grip and hung on, giving in to the hot burn behind his eyes.

The storm passed, and Aaron's breaths grew deep and even as he struggled to get hold of himself. When he spoke, though, his voice was thick and clogged.

"I was not okay with what happened today," he said. "You are not supposed to be the one in danger. I lost someone already, Larx. I don't… what am I supposed to do if I lose you?"

Larx bit back the obvious retort of "Welcome to my world." Instead he said, "You do what you've always done. You raise your kids. You raise chickens. You protect people and shit. You…." He swallowed. "You find someone else and you start again."

"No," Aaron whispered, burrowing against him, holding him tight. "No finding someone else. Took me ten years after Caroline. I can't do this one more time."

Larx let out a semihysterical laugh. "Yeah, well, I only just got you. Take care of what's mine, 'kay?"

Aaron peered up at him in the darkness, face ravaged by tears and stress. Larx pulled that thick blond hair back from his forehead. Lucky bastard—there was some silver in there, but you'd never know it. It was just all pale hair. "I am yours," he said gruffly. "I'm building a chicken coop here this weekend. Kirby and I'll move in."

"Your daughters!" Larx half laughed, but he wanted them there too.

"God*dammit*!"

Larx couldn't help the laugh that escaped. "We'll figure it out," he said softly. "As long as you stay tonight."

"And tomorrow." Aaron came up and gave him a sloppy, salty kiss.

"And maybe the weekend too," Larx said when they came up for air.

"Sure."

The quiet then was profound enough that Larx almost fell asleep, but his phone started buzzing. He glanced at it and groaned.

"Yoshi?" Aaron asked, smiling.

"Doesn't he know my texting arm is wounded?" The Vicodin had kicked in, so Larx was feeling decidedly floaty, but he was aware that his arm was a swollen mass of abused muscle.

"Yeah. Well, you pick up the phone and call him. I'll go get something started for dinner."

Larx closed his eyes. "D'oh! For the life of me I can't think of a damned thing to make."

"We've got eggs, cheese, and veggies," Aaron soothed. "Omelets work every time."

He started to stand, and Larx paused him by cupping his jaw. "I just found you," he said soberly. "I'm not planning to go anywhere for a while."

"I'm not taking a single damned chance," Aaron told him, expression bleak. Well, he'd spent ten years getting over that wound—seeing the same blade swing so close wasn't going to be easy.

"Deal," Larx agreed. His phone buzzed again, and Aaron stood up.

"Talk to Yoshi," he said, wiping his face on his shoulder.

"Hey—"

"Space," Aaron rasped. "Need space or I can't deal with the kids."

Larx nodded and sighed.

And picked up his phone and ignored the texts and called.

"You got shot, you prick."

"Love you too, Yoshi."

"No, seriously. I told you to get me back, I didn't tell you to get shot and pass out on the news."

Larx groaned. "Oh God—you saw the *news*?"

Yoshi's laughter sounded like an evil gnome. "Oh, Larx—*everybody* saw the news. Fred Embree called me sounding like he'd eaten a bug. I heard Heather almost swallowed her own goddamned tongue. The superintendent saw it and apparently served new assholes for lunch. It was be-yoo-ti-ful!" he crowed.

"You're welcome?"

"Yeah, I was welcome, thank you. By the way, your deputy missed looking gay for you by a hair. You need to either come out of the closet or club him over the head and lock him in one."

Larx laughed, holding his good hand across his stomach. "I think it will have to be out. I don't know—should I tell anyone?"

"Harvey Hassbender," Yoshi said seriously. "The superintendent. He called me right after Fred and sounded contrite as fuck."

"If he was so contrite, why wasn't he at the damned board meeting?" Larx muttered.

"Apparently he spent the last week at a workshop for high school inclusion," Yoshi said, sounding smug. "Some asshole called the DO and told them the principal did a great job at the game a couple of weeks ago and that maybe the entire district should take some classes so all the other schools learn from him."

"Whee! I thought Vicodin was a good drug *before* you started talking rainbows and fairy tales!" Larx was almost at full-on giggle by now.

"Stop it. I'm being serious—your old school buddy called up and praised you. Apparently Hassbender got back after being gone for five days and realized his district was falling apart. He was not pleased."

"He should try getting shot. That'll *really* put a crimp in his diaper."

"Larx, I'm telling you that you can come out. You can talk about your boyfriend in front of other teachers. You can tell people your plans at the district meeting. You can say things like 'That's my boyfriend's kid' at ACADECA. You can be out—and the next time two kids want to kiss in front of a bonfire, nobody's going to give a ripe shit."

Larx caught his breath.

"That's, uh…." He forced himself to breathe again. "That's intoxicating," he said humbly. "And I'll probably take you up on it." Focus on real details, the day-to-day—it's how Larx had lived his life from the moment Olivia had been conceived. "He wants to move in. Like right now."

"You okay with that?"

Larx closed his eyes and thought about that moment when the noise deafened him, before he felt the actual pain and knew he'd live. "All I saw… the gun went off and all I saw was him."

Yoshi's voice grew soft. "That's a yes, isn't it?"

"Yeah."

"Then what's the problem?"

Larx sighed. "I think I have a fever." This was true—the floaty feeling wasn't going away, and he kept kicking off his blankets. "And his daughters might not like me."

"Tough," Yoshi said. "About the daughters. The fever thing is the direct result of not going to the doctor's and having them irrigate the damned wound. Yes, Mary-Beth came by and gave me an earful. She told me you were an amazing teacher and probably an awesome principal, but she'd never realized before how irritating you could be when someone tried to tell you what to do."

Larx was forced to laugh. "Ungrateful brat. She's right, but I helped her study—she should have more respect."

"She would have had more respect if you'd *gone to the doctor's*. As it is, I think I get to run your school for another day."

Larx grunted. "Don't do anything nuts like, you know, buy more books or hire an AP teacher for your class."

"Your class, stupid. You're the one who thinks he's Superman."

"Oh ha-ha. I'll send Christi with lesson plans. Don't let that asshole Ryan fuck up my kids."

"I make no promises. You should have gone—"

"I get it, I get it! You know, if I'd gone to the doctor's, they would have made me stay home another day anyway. This way it's my own bed."

Yoshi made a frustrated sound. "You are the most exasperating man I've ever met. You got *shot* and you turn it to your own advantage. It's like a fucking *superpower*."

Larx half laughed, and then he had the most horrific thought. "Oh God. Yoshi—the news. Did they show my name?"

Yoshi's cackle made Larx doubt seven years of solid friendship. "Yeah, Lyman, they did. Best part of my day, I'm fuckin' telling you. Now get off the phone with me and heal. We need you back here by Friday."

Larx tried to think. If it was Tuesday now, then…. "What's on Friday?"

"You are. We're having an assembly. Hassbender is talking, you're talking—everybody's talking except Yoshi, who will happily be going back to being second fiddle to you assholes who make all the good quotes."

"I may shoot my other arm to avoid this," Larx said, but he was definitely only kidding. He'd run away first.

"Don't you dare. We're having press too. Hassbender wants to be a poster child for inclusion—it's a thing."

"You guys are pretty tight. Does Tane approve?"

"He already puts up with your mangy ass. I'm sure he's thrilled I'm finally kissing up to someone who can do my career some good."

Larx laughed some more, and his head hurt. "Yoshi, as much fun as this is—"

"Yeah, sure. Thanks for getting shot for me, ass-hole. Next time you get my job back, make sure you're here to suffer with me."

"That's a promise."

Yoshi hung up, and Larx closed his eyes against the headache and the floating. He'd get better—he knew he would. But nobody could argue that his world hadn't changed in a big way. He just needed to wake up at some point and recognize that he'd changed with it.

TWO MILDLY uncomfortable days later, Larx had kicked the fever and was back to trying to cook for everybody when they got home.

Kirby called his dad *in the kitchen* and begged him to bring home takeout because Larx was going to poison them with vegetables, wine, and parmesan cheese. Aaron told his son to suck it up, Larx loved them all, and they should trust him.

Larx chuckled evilly and added more cheap wine to the sauce. "Vegetables, young man, they make the digestive tract run."

"So does hamburger," Kirby replied sourly.

Christi cackled in the background. Kellan just kept putting plates on the table, his demeanor sub-dued. Larx hadn't had a moment to talk to him, but something had happened that day that had pulled the boy into a dark gray funk.

"Here," Kirby said, handing Larx the phone. "Stop trying to get minors drunk and talk to my dad."

"The alcohol cooks off!" Larx said, offended, be-fore talking into the phone. "Hello, are you afraid I'm poisoning us with vegetables too?"

"Since your daughters both lived this long, I'm going to say no. You shouldn't be out of bed. I told you I'd bring takeout."

Larx blew a raspberry. "I was bored. Delilah kept patting my cheek to make sure I wasn't dead."

"Whose opinion matters more? Mine or the cat's?"

"I've known her longer. Without her, the field mice would have taken over years ago."

"Then what are those other deadbeats for? Are you raising them to eat?"

Larx laughed, but Aaron sounded strained. "Christi, could you take over?" he called and wandered into the living room. Truth was, he'd been on his feet cleaning the house and cooking, and yes, he'd run a fever for two days, and he wasn't a kid anymore. Kids could just pop up like nothing had happened. Grown-ups usually needed a day of sleep to recover from being sick. Fucking kids—they had no idea.

With a grunt, he settled down into the recliner.

"What's wrong?"

"Wow."

"Wow what?"

"Caroline used to do that too. It's uncanny."

Larx figured he'd get used to the comparisons with the late Caroline—she was Aaron's only other long-term relationship. But right now it felt a little like a slap in the nads.

"Ouch. Is there something I should know, Deputy? I was making plans for fresh eggs. Do I need to change that?"

Aaron's sigh gusted over the earpiece. "No. But you'd better make plans to pour hot water into their feed, or no eggs for us."

"What's wrong?"

"Whitney's lawyer cut a deal. Manslaughter and assault, down from murder in the first and attempted murder. She'll get ten years, probably parole in five. She's already got her attorney looking for a book deal, and her kid's going to live with the grandparents in another country. It's just…."

Larx thought of Isaiah, who would be in physical therapy for another year. "Not fair," he said with feeling. "And in five years, you and me need to remember our Kevlar union suits."

"I understand they're real crotch-biters, by the way."

Larx's laugh sounded bitter, even to his own ears. "Okay. Well, that's five years. If you keep bringing home pizza and hamburgers, we might not even last that long."

"I'd better learn to live with veggies—at least Whitney will kill us quick."

Larx took a big breath, and then another one. "I don't feel forty-seven," he said apologetically. "When I look in the mirror, I'm surprised you like me, because I remember being so much hotter than this."

Aaron's throaty laughter was aloe and lidocaine on a sunburn. "It's a good thing I didn't see you when you were younger and hotter, then," he said sincerely. "Because I love my kids. This was a good path. Not easy, but good."

Larx closed his eyes, the quiet of the living room soothing. He was right, of course. Any path that led to them, right here, this moment, was the only path they could have followed.

"I have to go talk at an assembly tomorrow," he said, because it had been bothering him all day.

"You do that all the time," Aaron said, but his voice was gentle, and Larx figured he probably knew where this was going.

"The kids said enough students saw you and me together that they're getting asked questions."

"Well, baby, I think you need to answer them."

He sounded okay with it.

Larx closed his eyes. "Yeah."

He didn't remember turning the phone off, but he must have. He didn't wake up until Aaron came in with a plate of food for him and one for himself.

The veggie Alfredo turned out great, and their quiet dinner, away from the kids, was even better.

That night, though, as Larx was toddling to bed—early, but feeling like tomorrow he'd be up to full strength—he stopped in Kellan's room last.

The boy was crying.

Larx sat down on the side of his bed and stroked his hair back from his face, the same gentle way he'd do with Christi.

And just like with Christi, Kellan broke.

"My folks haven't called," he said, voice congested.

"I figured."

"I didn't expect them to—I mean...." He grimaced. "They didn't even protest. I thought... I thought they'd fight for me, just a little. But...."

Larx had met his father once, at freshman orientation. A small, mean, flat-eyed man, he'd spat tobacco juice on the sidewalk, looked around, and told Kellan he was on his goddamned own.

"Parents are sort of hit or miss," he said, trying for truthful. "But that doesn't mean you're not a good kid."

"I just...." Kellan wiped his face on his shoulder. "Isaiah, he's going to Sacramento on Saturday. He's going to be there for *months*. And he told me...." Oh no. Larx knew what was coming, because it was something he would have done himself. "He told me that we were still friends, but that... that...."

"It would be better if you broke up?" Larx asked, because he could tell—it hurt too much to say.

Kellan nodded, face buried in his pillow, and Larx rubbed circles on his back.

"He doesn't want me either," he choked.

"No... no." Larx repeated it over and over again until the boy could talk.

"How do you know?" he finally asked, congested and bitter.

"Because he's an honorable man," Larx said, knowing that sort of bitterness. "He wants you to be free while he's busy healing. He doesn't want you to be tied down to him. He wants you to heal too."

"*I'm* not the one who got stabbed!" Kellan snarled, pounding his pillow.

Larx wrapped his good arm around the boy's shoulders and rested his chin in his hair. Such a good boy—still so much in need of parenting. "No," he said. "But you still got hurt."

"So he hurts me some more?"

Another storm of weeping shook him, and Larx waited for this one to pass too.

"Kellan?" he asked when it was over.

"Yeah?"

"He said you were friends, right?"

"Forever."

"You know what friends do?" Larx couldn't have, not at this age. But Kellan was smarter, stronger, more faithful than Larx had been.

Less angry.

"What?"

"They write letters. Real letters. Not email, but letters. And they don't care if they get responses or not. They just keep writing."

"But...." Kellan turned a tearstained face to him. "Even if he doesn't answer?"

"Do you think Isaiah could read your letters to him and not treasure them?" Larx asked quietly.

Kellan's mouth parted. "No," he said after a moment.

"And if you change your mind and you realize you need your freedom too—"

"I've been a friend." He nodded. "I... I can know in my heart that I loved my friend with all I had."

Larx smiled. "You're such a good boy," he said sincerely. "So good. I'm so proud of you."

Kellan hid his face, and Larx figured he'd had enough. "Night, Kellan."

"Night, Larx. You ready for tomorrow?"

"As I'll ever be."

It would have to be enough.

LARX WAS yawning nonstop by the time he crawled next to Aaron. Aaron groaned and turned sideways, pulling Larx's back against his front, being the big spoon because he *was* the big spoon.

"Not that this isn't nice," Larx grumbled, "but we had sex. We actually had sex. In this bed. I was getting used to that."

Aaron nuzzled the back of his neck. "Me too. But you're dead on your feet. What are we, kids?"

"It's not fair," Larx whined. "When I was twenty, I got into a motorcycle accident, ripped the hell out of my back, broke my arm, got a third-degree burn on my ankle, and I was getting laid two days later because why the fuck not?"

"Larx?"

"What?"

"That doesn't make me feel any better."

"I haven't ridden since the girls were born."

"You are missing the goddamned point." Aaron pulled him closer.

"What's the point?" Larx grumbled, the passion that had driven his little speech draining out of him like sand.

Aaron slid his hand down Larx's tummy and under his shorts, fondling his privates, which were as sleepy as he was. "The point is I'm holding you. I want to hold you forever. That's the point."

"Don't you have to call your daughters?"

Aaron groaned. "I told Maureen—she was thrilled for us."

"What about Tiffany?"

Aaron's muscles went soft, defeated. "She was… skeptical. I texted and said I wanted to call her, and she said not to bother because I called Maureen first. And she said she didn't want to hear anything about it when she came for Christmas."

Larx would have turned in his arms, but that would have put him on his bad arm. "So what are you going to do?"

"I assume I'll drive her to the old house for Christmas, and then Kirby and I will come home," he said shortly. "She doesn't have to hear a thing about it if the two of us aren't there."

Larx couldn't help it. He laughed. "You, sir, are a master at dealing with tantrums. I am most impressed."

"She's being a brat," Aaron grumbled. "She's not even here—why does she get to boss me around?"

He laughed some more. "Which is, I'm sure, what she's saying to all of her friends right now. This is precious."

"Whatever."

Larx turned his head as far as it would go. "Kiss me, at the very least. It's necessary."

Aaron pushed up and captured his mouth in a sweet, all-consuming kiss. "Like breathing," he whispered. "Go to sleep, Lyman—"

Oh God. "You heard?"

"Oh my God, yes. Now go to sleep. Tomorrow's going to be a big day."

"Can you be there?" Larx felt pathetic about asking.

And apparently Aaron felt sad about saying no. "Sorry, baby. If you come out about me, Eamon is going to be fielding a lot of calls about his pick for next sheriff. I should probably be there."

"Yeah. Okay." Well, he'd been alone and strong for a lot of years. At least now he'd have someone to tell.

"If I can be there, I will," Aaron promised. "Now go to sleep, Ly—"

"Only if you call me Larx. Forever. Forget you heard that name. Ever. Promise."

Aaron's deep chuckle assured him of no such thing. "Night, Larx. Sweet dreams."

"Night, Deputy. Dreams are sweeter after sex."

"Don't pout. Love you."

And that was what it came down to, wasn't it? "Love you too. Night."

LARX WENT in to teach the next morning and was greeted by a standing ovation from his students—and flowers and letters of thank-you from their parents. Larx took a moment to read some of the letters. Many of them mentioned Aaron.

We understand you and Deputy George are dating. As long as he keeps our kid's favorite teacher safe, that's okay.

We're so glad you found someone. Please don't feel the need to hide from us.

Even if you're gay, you're the best principal this school has ever had.

"Even?" Larx muttered to himself. "*Even if?* Really?"

"What are you whining about?" Yoshi asked, coming into his office. "And who died?"

Larx had asked Kellan and Kirby for help moving the flowers in. "I did. Almost. Apparently it was enough to make up for being gay."

"Not to me. You still owe me for being shot, you bastard."

Larx laughed and drank in the sight of Yoshi looking tired but composed in a bold blue sweater and a red tie. "Isn't your boyfriend an artist? Shouldn't you dress better than that?"

"Like he'd tell me what to wear." Yoshi sank down into his seat across from Larx's. "Oh my God, I'd forgotten how comfortable this seat is. You're welcome to that one, it sucks."

Larx's seat was, in fact, one of the few posh things he'd ever owned or asked for. It had been sort of a bribe from the DO, and he settled into it like a cat into its favorite cushion.

"So what's imperative that I sign, call about, or fight for?" Larx asked reluctantly. Ugh—there was so much bureaucracy with this damned job!

Yoshi pushed the clipboard in his hands across the desk. "Red is urgent, blue can wait until Monday. Hassbender is eating lunch with us—don't plan on doing any work while he's there. Nancy and I have hall monitoring and lunch duty, and I am under strict instructions to get your fat ass out of your chair and home by five thirty."

Larx regarded him with deep suspicion. "I'm dying, aren't I? You all lied. There was secret poison on that bullet and I am dying. My day is never this light."

Yoshi rolled his eyes. "No. You are not dying. It took me, Nancy, and Edna three days to get your schedule this light, so don't make fun of us."

"Why? Why would you do this?" He was deeply touched—tearful, even. He couldn't seem to get a handle on what it meant to him that he not return to be inundated with paperwork and phone calls and a deep submersion into all the parts of his job he hated most.

"Oh, get a hold of yourself. We just…." Yoshi looked away, his attempt at disgust not matching the vulnerable curve of his chin. "You just did something really awesome. Lots of awesome things, actually. You worked your ass off this last week—if you hadn't gotten shot, you would have gotten sick anyway. Wasn't just the three of us—everybody pitched in to make this place go. I mean, for a guy who's so reluctant to be the grown-up, Larx, you hauled this district—this town even—into the twenty-first century by the frickin' ear. Don't make me say that again, by the way. I am way too uncomfortable with that much emotion."

"So noted," Larx said, blushing probably all the way to his toes. "Thank you, Yosh. This was really nice."

"Don't get shot again, asshole. That needs to be a rule."

"It was just a graze," Larx said. "Wanna see?" They had actually changed the bandage on it that morning—and it had hurt like hell—but Larx was enough of a fifteen-year-old boy to want to gross people out with his war wounds.

Yoshi had apparently never been that boy. "Don't make me regret the last three days," he said with a flat stare.

"Okay, fine. I'll try to be done with all my shit before whatsisface—"

"Hassbender."

"Hassbender gets here."

"He's bringing lunch because I told him you never do."

Larx actually grinned. "Aaron packed me a lunch this morning. It's got"—he shuddered—"*bologna* in it. Having someone bring me lunch is the best thing I've ever heard." Aaron's idea of a simple healthy lunch was way, way different than Larx's. Just one of the many small happy wrinkles of coupledom.

"He's going to the teriyaki place in town."

Larx arched his eyebrows. "It's a good thing I like that too."

"I consider it a fortunate accident. Now get to work. I'm going to go wander the halls and make them safe for people over eighteen."

Larx nodded, content. "Thanks, Yoshi."

"Yeah, well. We were worried. We miss you. Don't fucking do it again."

"*That's* a deal."

HARVEY HASSBENDER looked like the bad-guy administrator in every high school movie ever made. He was round, with cheery red cheeks and the thinnest comb-over Larx had ever seen. He also had a deep, resonant voice and an infectious laugh, and by the time lunch was over, Larx wondered if this was what having a favorite uncle felt like.

It was disconcerting, because Larx usually resented any and all authority, but the old superintendent had left after Duke Nobili, and apparently Harvey had been a trade up.

"I'm so glad we had a chance to do this," Harvey said as Larx cleaned up the lunch detritus. "I had planned to have a long meeting with each of my principals after I was hired, but first there was paperwork, then there was that whole facility issue in the grammar school out near Mustang—"

"I heard about that," Larx told him, because it had dominated the local news. The school had been built ten years earlier, and the contractor had built nothing to code. The facility had been falling down, and the

old super had ditched the problem right in Hassbender's lap. "That was a mess."

Harvey rolled his eyes. "Still *is* a mess," he cor-
rected. "But see? I was hired at the end of August,
right after school had started, and we haven't even had
a meeting. I'm surprised you could even remember
my name!"

Yoshi and Larx both laughed too loud, and Harvey's grimace silenced them.

"You couldn't remember my name, could you."

"I remember it now that you've bought me
lunch," Larx said, batting his eyelashes.

Harvey's marvelous laugh rang out, and Larx did
something rash and foolhardy and right.

"So about this afternoon," he said, quietly enough
to sober up the room.

"Yes?"

"I don't plan to bring it up, but I'm not going to
dodge the issue either—"

"Does this have anything to do with you and Deputy George?"

Larx swallowed. "Does everybody know?"

Harvey shrugged. "Apparently when the deputy
ran in to get you, the kids saw you together. It didn't
take a rocket scientist. And I was surprised when I got
the first phone call, but I told them what I told the last
phone call."

"And what was that, sir?" Larx's mouth was dry.

"That your personal life is your business, but that
if you decided to take out an ad in the paper, it still
wouldn't change the quality of the man who had put
his life on the line to get his kids out of danger."

Oh. "That's… that's kind of you. And stand-up too. Our kids have been getting questions at school—"

"Kids? Does this include the boy you took into your home?"

Larx nodded. "Kellan. He was one of the boys at the bonfire, and his parents…."

Harvey let out an exasperated grunt. "Assholes. But go on."

"They're getting questions, and I'm assuming I'll get the same questions when I'm giving my little talk today."

"You answer them as you are most comfortable doing, Principal Larkin. I have every confidence you'll do a good job."

Larx grimaced. "Well, first, you can call me Larx— my own boyfriend didn't know my first name, so feel free. Second, you *did* see me on the news, didn't you?"

Harvey Hassbender chuckled deep in his throat. "You said we should keep handguns away from teen-agers. I am not averse to that in any way."

The bell rang, calling students to assembly, and Larx took a deep breath. "I'm most grateful," he said. "Alrighty, then—let's go include."

THE ASSEMBLY started with Harvey talking to the kids about what diversity and inclusion really meant. He had a slideshow—a little dated, perhaps, but it gave the kids the idea that their student population was not the *only* population. It showed the "hidden" diversity of students with disabilities, students who were born in ethnically diverse households, and the inadvertent ways these students could be harmed by careless words. It moved on to the LGBTQ population, and Larx figured that by the time that segment showed up, the kids were bored into submission, because he heard none of the discomfort he'd expected.

Or maybe his original assessment had been right—the kids were on the internet enough to have some natural insight into the variations of the world.

Either way, by the time the slideshow was over, the kids were anxious for some interaction, and that was where Larx came in.

He was unprepared, though, for the round of applause when he stood up.

"Well, thank you," he said when some of it had died down. "It's nice to know I'm appreciated."

The seven hundred or so kids calmed down a little, and Larx got down to business.

"So, first of all, it's good to be back—and I'm glad you guys were happy to see me. But what we just saw is pretty important, and I'm wondering if any of *you* had any questions for *me*?"

The first kid with his hand up asked the big one. "Are you gay for Kirby's dad?"

Larx grimaced. "Bisexual, people—it's a thing. And yes, Deputy George and I are seeing each other. Any other questions?"

"Is that legal?"

Great. Who let Curtis MacDonald speak? "In this state, yes." Wonderful.

"Wait a minute," said Christi, and Larx grimaced. "You mean it's *not* legal in other states?"

The entire student body gasped, and suddenly Larx saw why what he was doing was important. He was an educator, in his bones.

Larx, it's time to educate.

By the time he was done speaking, he'd covered gay rights, gay bashing, Stonewall, Orlando. He'd covered students being bullied to death, adults being complicit, and gay homeless teens. He'd covered Don't Ask, Don't Tell, Million Moms, and being gay in other countries.

And not once had he needed to silence a kid or reprimand someone for being rude.

The kids were right there with him, wanting to know more.

And he'd remembered all over again how he'd raised his girls and why being honest with kids was the best weapon in his parenting arsenal.

He was still talking when the final bell rang, and he felt wrung out, exhausted from leading a conversation for nearly an hour and having the responsibility of representing his community on his shoulders for the entire time.

"And I guess that's it," he said as the bell finished ringing. "And I'd like to thank you all—I didn't expect this, any of this, to happen today. But I've always said that students are the reason I'm here, and that our kids at this high school, they're our future. You guys—you have the makings of a wonderful future, and I have never been prouder of my students than I have been today. You all have a good weekend, you hear?"

This time he didn't stop the applause—he had to leave the auditorium because he'd promised Yoshi he'd do parking lot duty.

He was out there for an hour, because the kids wouldn't stop coming up to him and telling him thank you.

By the time Aaron came to pick him and the kids up at five thirty, he was fast asleep at his desk.

New Growth

AARON MANAGED to get some dinner into him before he fell asleep again at eight o'clock. There were no football games, no school activities, and Aaron spent a quiet night with three teenagers, watching horror movies until twelve o'clock at night.

He found out that Christi was a bloodthirsty little vixen, Kirby was truly susceptible to the jump scare, and Kellan tended to hide his face for 90 percent of the movie. When the kids went to bed, each one dragged a signature cat with them—and Aaron realized how tight this past week had really made the little group.

They were family already.

As he locked up Larx's snug little house—and made sure the thermostat was somewhere above freezing—he wondered about that. No fighting? No drama? When did the real teenagers come out? But then, each kid had known loss. Each kid had their family, their security, yanked away. That could make kids a lot more afraid of having their lives disrupted. And it could make a kid a lot more grateful for what he or she had.

Aaron figured he'd take a page from their book. He wouldn't take their peaceful little existence for granted—but he would be grateful that at the end of a long week of worry, the three of them had screamed and laughed at a stupid movie with shitty special effects.

It was the best he could do.

As he crawled into bed next to a sleepy Larx, he figured it was good enough.

HE WOKE early—he'd never been able to sleep in—and for a few moments just lay there, head propped on his hand, watching Larx sleep. Or so he thought.

"That's really creepy," Larx mumbled. "I was dreaming about being Billy Pilgrim and humping a porn star while aliens watched."

Aaron's eyes widened and the last vestiges of sleep fled like cowardly mice. "What porn star?" he asked, scandalized.

Larx laughed evilly. "Oh, the things I have to show you on my computer."

"No. Absolutely not. I didn't do porn when I was married, didn't do it when I was single, won't do it now."

And now *Larx's* eyes widened, a little reddish but very aware. "Well, that's just disappointing. It's a flaw. I've finally found a flaw. Doesn't like porn. However shall we get along now?"

Aaron chuckled and kissed him, pulling back to
cup his face, smooth a thumb over his irrepressible
smile. "We'll have to have so much sex you don't
even miss porn," he said decisively.

Larx's eyes narrowed with mischief. "You just
sealed your doom, Deputy—you have no idea how
much sex it would take me to forget about sex!"

Aaron laughed softly and kissed him again, and
again, and just when things were getting *truly* interesting, Larx arching insistently against Aaron's hand, little pleading noises coming from his throat, the sound
of voices raised in quarrel penetrated from downstairs.

"Augh!" Larx fell back against the pillow. "What
are they doing up?"

"I have no idea." Aaron rolled out of bed and
struggled into his sweats. "But I'll find out."

He trotted downstairs in time to hear Christiana
snap, "No, you can't. Now go put your stuff back,
you're just being stupid!"

"This makes perfect sense!" Kellan replied,
sounding a little desperate. "I move down to Sacramento with him—I catch a ride with his parents and
get a job down there and—"

"And don't graduate from high school and don't
have a family for Thanksgiving and break my dad's
heart because he wants you to be happy!"

Oh.

"But don't you understand?" Kellan demanded
just as Aaron rounded the corner. "He's leaving. He's
leaving, and he's the only person who's ever given a
shit about me, and I'll just be stuck here in this little
fucking town and—"

Aaron put his hand on the boy's shoulder. "Leave the family that's starting to care for you very much," he said quietly. "I thought you and Larx had a plan for this?"

Kellan turned a miserable face up to him. "But I tried," he wailed. "I tried. I can't write a good letter. I... nothing I say sounds good. He's going to get these letters that are supposed to be the... the... windows to my soul and my soul is gonna be *shit*."

"No, that's not true." Aaron pressed the boy's face against his side. "None of it. You'll get better with words as you practice, son, but nothing about you says your soul is shit. And it's not going to get any better if you run away to Sacramento and drop out of school. How's Isaiah supposed to relax and get better if he's worried about you?"

"I just...." Kellan looked wildly around the kitchen. "I don't know how to do all this—you all are so nice to me, but how long's it going to last?"

"I dunno," Christi said like she was taking him seriously. "Olivia's twenty—she came home this summer and Dad cooked her waffles five days a week. I'd say you've got at least three, four years of it. What's to lose?"

Aaron laughed. "I understand the contract has a lifetime guarantee," he said. "With addendums for weddings and children." He thought of Tiffany and grimaced. "The language gets a little fuzzy if you turn into a total and complete asshole, but I assume you still have rights and privileges then too."

Kellan looked away from both of them. "I'm just...." His voice failed.

"Afraid," Aaron said gruffly. "Because the future is uncertain. Trust me, Kellan. Nobody knows that better than the people in this room. Or"—he grimaced, because the odds of Kirby being up for this conversation were the odds of Larx not wanting to go running on Monday—"in this house. You're here, and you're safe, and you've got room to grow up. Now grow up, son, and go write your boyfriend his first letter."

Kellan groaned and rested his head on both hands. "How did you know—"

"Because I'd panic if I had to write a letter too," he said honestly, God. Put how he felt about Larx into words? "It's fucking terrifying. Now go suc up and get it done."

With a sigh that shook the world, the boy dragged his sorry ass up and slunk out of the kitchen, bringing his half-packed duffel bag with him.

Christiana waited until he was out of earshot to beam brightly at Aaron. "Nicely handled, sir. You fit right in here."

Aaron chuckled and looked around the kitchen, which appeared to be in a state of organized chaos. "Why, thank you. Would you like some help?"

She showed all her teeth. "Set the table? I was just about to pour the mix into the waffle iron. Blueberry waffles, coming up."

Aaron let out a decadent groan. "Christi, I adore you, but you're going to make me fat."

She shrugged. "Larx won't care. He'll make you run longer."

Aaron groaned again. "I thought you liked me!"

"I do. Now set the table, sir. You asked."

He realized she had started calling him *sir* instead of *Deputy George* or *Aaron*. How could he not do a damned thing she asked of him? Like Larx, Aaron was a sucker for a daughter who cared.

LARX CAME down to eat, freshly showered, and he brought Kirby with him. Aaron had heard him chivvying the boy from the top of the stairs.

"Well, do you like waffles?"

"Not as much as sleep!"

"Do you like to eat?"

"Geez, Larx—"

"That's what I thought. Now wake up!"

However Larx managed it, they all made it, and all lingered around the breakfast table over juice and coffee and light, fluffy blueberry waffles that made Aaron a wee bit jealous of how Larx had learned how to cook, even if his girls had needed to teach him.

Larx was nibbling at the last waffle, tearing pieces off it while it still sat on the plate. "So, gang," he said, thinking, "I know Kellan wanted to go to the hospital and say goodbye to Isaiah, and I think we should go with him—"

Aaron grimaced apologetically. "Bills, Larx. I've got some sorting to do—" The past two weeks hadn't left him a lot of time to do grown-up shit, and there was no excuse today.

"Yeah, I hear you. I have the same things. How about…." He looked up at the kids, his lips curving into an almost devious smile. "How about you guys drop me off after the visit and go into Auburn or Meadow Vista for a movie? If you get me back around twelve, that's two hours in, the movie, two hours back—you'll be home right before dark."

It was such an unexpected treat—and judging by the hunger on their faces, so very, very needed.

Aaron could see it—the three of them free from adults and out of this tiny, claustrophobic town. Even Kellan, who would probably cry all the way there, was going to have something to do besides mourn that his best friend—his first crush—was leaving him behind.

Christi leaped up and kissed Larx on the cheek. "For *that*," she chirped, "I'll even do dishes!"

"Nope," Larx laughed, standing. "My turn to do dishes. You guys go get ready."

Aaron gave a sigh of relief. "Oh wow. I might actually get bills done without everybody here!"

Larx's eyes grew big, and then it looked like he intentionally made his face blank. "Sure," he said. "You count on that. But maybe go get your stuff and get started now."

Aaron took one last drag of coffee and nodded. "I'm gonna go up and shower, then take off."

"You're bringing your bills here, right?" Larx asked, sounding unduly anxious.

"Oh yeah. Let me feed the chickens, air out the house. I should be working on them before you get back."

Larx glowed at him like this was the best gift Aaron could possibly give, and Aaron smiled back.

In hindsight he'd recognize that he was possibly the dumbest man ever to walk the earth.

HE WAS hard at work at Larx's kitchen table when he heard Larx in the driveway telling the kids to drive carefully after probably handing Christi his entire chunk of disposable income for the month.

Larx strolled inside, stopping to pet old Delilah, who was lying in a sunspot right next to the glass insert in the entryway. "Still hard at work?" he asked.

Aaron grunted. He hated math. He hated paperwork. He hated his checkbook. All of it— All. Of. It.— bore the brunt of his undying hatred.

Larx disappeared up the stairs, and Aaron concentrated on the next column in his ledger.

Right up until he felt Larx's fingers carding through his hair, grasping, yanking, and Larx's tongue lining the shell of his ear.

"I need you to stand up," Larx whispered in his ear, and Aaron's eyelids fluttered down just as his cock stiffened up.

"Okay," he rasped, carefully sidestepping all his paperwork and putting himself at Larx's mercy. "Where we goin'?"

"The couch." Larx steered him carefully, but his hand never let up pressure on Aaron's scalp, and Aaron's whole body tingled. It hit him then. The kids would be gone for *hours*. Hours.

Aaron was not always bright—he could admit that sometimes. "You *planned* this!" he gasped as he stopped, the couch at his crotch.

Larx's low chuckle rewarded him, and Larx plastered his (bare? Was he *bare*?) front to Aaron's back, anchoring himself with a hand at Aaron's belt. Very deliberately he nibbled on the side of Aaron's neck, and Aaron almost bent over then and there.

Larx moved his other hand, and two objects appeared in Aaron's peripheral vision, resting on a towel

on the back of the couch. One of them was a bottle of
lubricant, and the other was something Aaron hadn't
seen before. He straightened, wanting to examine it.

"Where do you think you're going?" Larx
laughed.

"Is that a…?"

"World's smallest butt plug?" Larx asked, clev-
er fingers making quick work of Aaron's belt. "Yes."
He tugged at Aaron's shirts, and Aaron sucked in his
stomach and raised his arms, giving Larx easy access.

"What's that fo… ah…." Larx *was* bare. From
the waist up, at the very least. And his chest pressing
against Aaron's back made Aaron's whole body weak.
Oh my God. A *week*.

"We haven't done this in a *week*!" he realized,
and even his hands broke into a needy, horny sweat.

"I am *saying*!" Larx burst out, his breath sending shivers down Aaron's spine as he kissed. "Why
is that?"

He reached the small of Aaron's back and those
busy hands were at work again, undoing his fly and
shucking his jeans to his ankles, then helping Aaron
step out of his tennis shoes and socks. Aaron started
to turn around, wanting to take Larx into his arms, to
be naked together, but Larx had plans, seductive ones,
and Aaron was suddenly lost in the feel of masculine
hands running up his calves, cupping the backs of his
thighs, running up the front, just barely missing the
big bundle of toys in the center.

"You were hurt," Aaron mumbled as Larx stood
up, pressing against him. He *was* naked, his cock hard
and unmistakable and dripping, even, as it pushed into
Aaron's left cheek.

Larx held him hard, arms under Aaron's and around his chest, the rasp of the gauze wrapped around his bicep and shoulder inconvenient but not unwieldy. "Not the last two days," he said, arching his hips again.

"You were tired," Aaron tried again, and Larx pinched his nipples hard enough to sting. "Ouch!"

"Tell the truth!"

Oh.

"You were hurt," he said again, but not with the defensive edge. Some of the arousal seeped out of his body, naked in Larx's living room, and he was left with the knowledge he'd been trying to fight since Tuesday. "I… I was so scared. I… didn't want to hurt you."

Larx planted a reassuring row of kisses across his shoulders. "I'm here," he whispered. "I'm here, and I'm fine."

"That wound…." Aaron didn't want to talk about all of it, about the terror of having your partner, your other half, the first and third beats of your heart, suddenly yanked out of your life.

But Larx knew. Larx read minds for a living. He paused again, resting his cheek against Aaron's neck. "I'm here *today*. It's the only promise I can make. You get that, right?"

Aaron nodded, thinking his heart was suddenly too sore for sex. Then Larx smoothed his hand slowly from the base of his neck down his spine, lighting a fire under his nerve endings with every inch. When he got to the small of Aaron's back, he pushed with the flat of his other hand against Aaron's shoulder blades until he was bent over, clutching the couch under his chest, his ass out in invitation.

It was as vulnerable as he'd ever felt in his entire life.

Larx lowered his face to Aaron's, and Aaron turned his head so they were eye to eye. "Do you trust me?" Larx asked seriously. "If you don't yet, it's okay. We'll trade places—you'll take me over the couch and it'll be great. But if you do, I'll make it good, Aaron. I swear. Just trust me, here. Can you do that?"

Aaron's mouth went dry. *Do you know what you're asking?*

But of course he knew. He'd trusted too. He'd had the rug yanked out from under his feet. But he still trusted Aaron not to do that.

"Yes," Aaron graveled. "I trust you."

Larx's lazy, sleepy, sexy-confident smile actually made Aaron's cock throb.

"Good," he said and took Aaron's mouth in a long, drugging, urgent kiss. Aaron groaned, knees going a little wobbly, and Larx chuckled before breaking away. He went back to Aaron's neck—that was really starting to turn Aaron's key—and kissed a line down his spine, down again but quicker this time. When he got to Aaron's backside, he squatted and started massaging Aaron's cheeks.

"You've got a great ass," Larx said, kissing him just inside the crease. "I mean, I know we're supposed to be over stuff like that, but I really do like it. It wouldn't be a deal breaker or anything if you just had a couple of bony yabs sticking out, but I seriously worship your behind."

He never stopped squishing, kneading, separating, smoothing his thumbs down Aaron's crease, along the insides of his thighs. He paused and Aaron heard a sucking, popping sound, and then his finger, wet and slippery with spit, traced down again.

Rubbed his pucker, which made Aaron gasp and tingle.

Rubbed it again.

Got it wet again and rubbed it some more.

Aaron moaned against the couch, remembering performing this act and hungering for just this reaction from Larx.

Now he understood.

Larx penetrated him with one finger, the other hand continuing that insidious massage. Aaron gasped and wiggled, the discomfort giving quickly way to an achy sort of pleasure. He expected another finger then, but Larx stood up, still stretching, and drizzled lube on the blue plug.

"What're—"

"Sh—your knees are gonna go, and mine aren't twenty anymore."

Aaron gasped at the coolness of the lube and then sort of whimpered when Larx removed his finger. That had felt so very good—

Oh!

The plug was smooth and slick, and Aaron tightened around it, clenching, relaxing, clenching. It was invasive, a little thicker than one finger but not as thick as two, and just long enough to tease his prostate.

Larx laughed, shoving the plug forward and smacking Aaron's cheek. "Clench and stay clenched or it's going to fall out," he warned.

Aaron pulled in a breath, and Larx helped him stand up before walking him—very slowly—around the couch.

Every step made his limbs tremble more, made his arousal ramp higher. Larx would slide his hand back every few steps and tap the thing into place, which made Aaron want to cry. Oh—so unfair. So… oh God.

He was shaking by the time Larx spread the towel on the battered corduroy couch and helped him lie down, ass on the towel, one knee propped up and the other spread wide while he rested his foot on the floor.

He had a sudden awful thought.

"Movies?" he said, making sure.

Larx nodded and bit his lip hopefully. "Swear."

"Okay—let's do this thing."

And then Larx did the best thing, which was sink into the couch with him, knees between Aaron's spread thighs, cover Aaron's wide, pale body with his own wiry, strong one, and kiss Aaron hard, insistently, with all the passion in his soul.

Aaron kissed back, wrapping his arms around Larx's shoulders and crushing him tight. His body shook with arousal and invasion, but also with need to have Larx skin to skin. *God*, Aaron needed him, needed *this*, needed the reassurance of flesh and bone, of body and blood in his arms.

Larx broke off the kiss for a moment and slid off the couch so he could kneel at Aaron's side. He brushed Aaron's hair from his temple and pulled him into another kiss.

"We're going to play for a minute," he said softly, breathing like he was restraining himself. "I'm gonna play with the back and you're gonna play with the front, okay?"

Aaron barely kept back his laugh. Of all the times for Larx's teacher voice to emerge….

Then Larx took one of Aaron's hands and wrapped it around Aaron's throbbing cock. He moaned breathily, and Larx whispered in his ear. "Wait for me, then do whatever you need to there, 'kay?"

Aaron nodded, stroking slowly, strongly, just to keep himself grounded and on the couch. Very carefully, Larx reached between his asscheeks and slid the plug out.

Aaron sighed with the relief, and then… oh, he clenched against nothing, wanting so hard, so bad. Larx fumbled with a little bit of lube, and then one finger breached Aaron's ass again.

Aaron moaned in relief, squatting down, wanting more, and Larx rewarded him with another finger.

"Oh God, yes," he groaned as Larx began pumping two fingers back and forth. Aaron's cock throbbed in his hand, and he added the other hand, just to steady himself. He had control there, and it helped him, grounded him, as Larx added one more finger and blew his mind.

"Aah…." His voice shook, a deep vibrato grunt, and Larx laughed softly, lowering his head to engulf the bell of Aaron's cock in his mouth.

Aaron shook so much his teeth chattered, and he came, spurting hard into Larx's mouth. Larx swallowed again and again while Aaron's fist tightened and stroked, and still Larx's fingers kept moving inside Aaron's ass.

When Aaron's climax stilled, they stayed there—invading, stretching, and oh God, arousing enough to keep Aaron hard.

Larx took his mouth again, hot and dripping with come, and Aaron fell into the kiss, the decadence and earthiness that was sex and Larx and their bodies twining in sweat and heart and spend.

"You ready?" Larx asked, spreading his three fingers a little, just to the point of pain.

"Oh God," Aaron moaned, needing him inside.

"You're ready, right?" Larx taunted his backside again.

"All of you," Aaron rasped. "I need all of you."

Larx pulled his fingers out and wiped them on the towel and then scrambled up on the couch between Aaron's knees.

"All of me," Larx vowed, easing into Aaron's ass.

"Too gentle," Aaron pleaded. "All, now, hard."

Larx paused to smile. "Oh yeah."

The first thrust into Aaron's body lit up every nerve ending like a chemical flare, so bright it was painful.

"*Larx!*" Aaron howled, and Larx rocked back, made ready for the next thrust.

"Louder," he whispered wickedly, and suddenly the sheer carnality of being fucked naked into the couch in the middle of the day was just as amazing as the eroticism of being, oh hell, as loud as he fucking wanted.

"Fuck me!" Aaron shouted, freed and shaking with arousal again. "Hard! God, hard!"

"Damned straight," Larx crowed, following up with a flurry, a solid rabbit-pistoning of Larx's hips thrusting his cock into Aaron's ass with precision and speed.

Aaron couldn't scream enough, couldn't groan, couldn't shout enough.

They were alone, naked, two people in the world, and Larx, *his* Larx, his lover, his partner, his companion, was inside him, filling his empty places, taking control of Aaron's body like Aaron couldn't have a pulse without him.

He wouldn't.

The terrible frenzy reached its maximum, and Aaron started to tremble, his ass aching, his cock swollen and primed once again.

"Oh God, Larx, baby, I need you with me!"

Larx shook terribly, his arms giving out as he fell against Aaron, body slick with sweat, hips rutting furiously as he groaned his climax into Aaron's shoulder.

Aaron's orgasm detonated in the pit of his groin, a force-ten explosion rippling out, taking over his limbs, washing his vision black and white and black again, rattling his heart in his ribs, the marrow in his bones.

The sound he made into Larx's neck was barely human, and the echoes were still dying when both of them collapsed, limp as flags of surrender.

Heartbeat, breath, Larx's breath, Larx's heartbeat, Larx's skin.

Their heartbeats. Their breath. Their skin.

Them, together, still joined. Larx peppering his face with little kisses, nuzzling his neck. The thunder of their heartbeats passing like a summer storm.

"Larx?"

"Yeah?"

"I think you killed me."

"Heh-heh-heh-heh…."

"You're not even a little sorry, are you?"

"No. Give me a sec and I'll get up so we can shower, and I can kill you again."

"Heh-heh-heh-heh…." He stared up into Larx's faintly dusty ceiling fan, which was lit gold by the sun coming in through the sliding glass door.

He'd had good moments, beautiful moments, wife and children and family moments.

He knew what happiness felt like, the kind that filled a man up and made his eyes burn, made his soul sure this was the path he was meant for.

Moments exactly like this one, with the man he loved in his arms.

THEY HAD to move eventually. The feeling of come leaking from his behind made Aaron a little panicky until Larx used the towel to wipe it up.

"Handy, that," Aaron said, looking around for his shorts.

Larx shook his head. "Move it to the showers, I'll get your clothes," he chided. "I'll be right there."

He was too, joining Aaron in the warm water as Aaron stood, dazed, trying to pull back into himself.

"Stop," Larx said, soaping his chest. "You'll hit earth soon enough. Float until you don't need to."

Aaron blinked and looked at him, trying to formulate a question. "What now?" was the best he could manage.

"Today?" Larx kissed his cheek and moved to soaping his back and stretched, slippery backside. "Today you go back to bills when you can, and I work on some of my own, and the kids get home, and dinner, and…."

"I mean all of it," Aaron reiterated. Words. He had been fucked almost wordless. He had no idea it was even possible.

Larx cupped his cheeks. "I understand someone was going to make me a chicken coop," he said winsomely. "So we could live in my small house like one big happy family."

Aaron smiled, the floaty feeling drifting away and leaving contentment and promise in its wake. "I like this idea," he said, kissing Larx because how could he not? "This is your best idea."

"You like that?" Larx whispered. "That's good, Deputy. 'Cause it was your idea, and I'm saying yes."

"You are a smart man."

Larx grinned.

They were going to have such a life together. Aaron had plans.

Epilogue: Sprouts

PLANS HE followed. The chicken coop came first, him and Kellan and Kirby swearing in the cold sunshine of October, trying to beat the long tree shadows before they had to call it a day. It took them longer than a weekend, because a chicken coop had to be a chicken *mansion*, someplace insulated and wired to the house, if you lived in the snow. Aaron's coop at the other house had a door that opened and closed with a light sensor, and he had to back-order one, because letting the chickens in and out was a pain in the ass.

It was early November before they moved in for real, and by then their schedules and just plain life had forced to spend enough nights apart that every night without Larx in his arms felt like a hardship, something not to be borne.

Kellan wrote a letter a week, and while the first one might have been short and awkward, Aaron

noticed that the subsequent letters got longer and Kellan began to shake himself out of his sadness.

Of course, getting his first letter from Isaiah
helped, and after retreating to his room and crying for
a bit, he came back and read the less personal parts to
the family.

And then the time came for Aaron to put up or
shut up.

The tenacious little reporter contacted him in early November, and with some reluctance, he and Larx
gave her a brief, heavily edited statement. They used
assumed names and kept all pictures of the kids out of
it, but they talked about starting over again so close to
fifty, and they talked about their jobs, and they talked
about the could-have-happened that had haunted them
both.

Marissa Schroeder told them that they got scads
and scads of fan mail when the piece went live, but
neither of them looked. As Larx said, it felt like they
were talking about somebody else. Their own lives
were so prosaic, so very, very normal.

And their disappointment was normal when none
of the girls came home for Thanksgiving—they were
all too involved in school, in finals, in the lives they
were forging for themselves. Aaron took it in stride.
The week before, while Larx and the kids were home
cleaning and cooking, he was getting frequent texts
from Maureen showing him how she and her friends
were getting ready to improvise their own feast. Tiffany hadn't said much beyond *Not coming for Thanksgiving*, but with Maureen, at least, he felt like his baby
wasn't alone.

The morning before turkey day they woke up to six inches of snow—and no Delilah on their bed like she usually was. Larx ran downstairs, concerned, and found her curled up in front of the glass insert, catching the cold light of the new snow. She'd passed quietly, without fuss, truly content as only cats could be.

Larx had wept then, openly and like a child, before the kids were awake to see. Aaron crouched next to him as he petted the ragged fur, and looped an arm over Larx's shoulders, feeling useless. He hadn't been great at Caro's tears either, but as Larx began to talk about the old cat, what she'd meant to his family, how she'd been his daughters' symbol of hope and normalcy during a really difficult time, Aaron found himself making rash promises about dogs and dog pens and Christmas and anything, oh, please, Larx, anything but feel happy again!

Larx had finally let out a strangled laugh and turned his tear-warped face to Aaron. "It's okay, Deputy—men cry. It doesn't always have to mean we're broken."

Aaron shook his head and wiped his eyes with his palms. "A dog," he said, nodding. "A big stupid dog. For Christmas. Just let me get you a dog."

"Sure." Larx used the sleeve of his sweatshirt to catch Aaron's tears. "A dog. Whatever you need."

"A dog," Aaron said staunchly, his own voice choked. He'd promised.

The kids came down eventually, and they mourned. Larx dug a hole in the garden, grateful the snow was new enough that the ground wasn't completely frozen. Christiana sobbed so hard Aaron was afraid her slender body would shake apart, and he and the boys stood and watched them grieve together.

It felt only right.

That night Aaron got home from work in time to hear Larx's conversation with Olivia, and he was genuinely concerned.

He'd expected tears, but her voice rose and fell shrilly, almost hysterically, and as Aaron walked into their bedroom, he caught the look of worry in Larx's eyes as he calmed her down. Finally she hung up, still weeping, and Larx collapsed backward across the bed.

Aaron flopped on his stomach perpendicular to him, nuzzling the top of his head. "That was rough."

"She's not sounding…." Larx sighed. "She's sounding off. Not… not centered. Her mom—her hormones really fucked up her brain chemistry, you know? I always thought, you know, maybe if I'd caught it first, if I'd realized how much pain she was in before the whole school thing blew up—"

"You didn't make her attitude, Larx. You didn't make her turn on her kids." Aaron tried not to get angry or short, because the more he knew about Larx and his girls, the more he realized what a truly good father he was.

"Yeah. But Olivia—her voice just keeps hitting those pitches, you know?"

Aaron nodded. He'd heard it too. "It was rough news."

Larx turned shiny eyes toward him. "It was. I know you don't get—"

"Don't apologize," Aaron said gruffly. "You're hurt. It's…." He thought about the events in October, how hard Larx had worked to make everything okay for all of them. "It's the one time you let me see that it really hurt."

Larx shrugged. "Well, if you can't trust Deputy George to make it right…."

Aaron smiled and kissed the top of his head. "How hard has Principal Larkin been working today? Are you ready to cook some more or—"

"Ugh…." Larx rolled over to his stomach. "God. Stuffing… pies… sweet potatoes… gravy…. Aaron, make it stop!"

"Or I'll go hunt and kill a pizza!"

Larx's smile was totally worth having to drive out in the cold again. "Oh, Deputy, you *do* love me!"

"Don't ever doubt it."

APPARENTLY LARX didn't doubt him. Not once, not at all, not a little bit.

Thanksgiving was everything Aaron had ever loved about the holiday. No worry about gifts— family was the only gift he needed. And he had it in spades. Larx and the kids cooked enough food for six families—on purpose, actually. Thursday morning, while Aaron worked his shift, Larx and the kids were working at the county food bank, dishing dinners for folks who'd had a rough year. That night Aaron insisted on doing dishes while his industrious do-gooders sprawled in front of the television, belching and prodding each other with their toes.

That last thing was a game the teenagers had cooked up to annoy the fuck out of any adult within earshot. Aaron didn't understand the rules, but it made him wish beating was back in style as a parenting tool. Whining—oh dear God, the whining!

But once he'd sprawled out on the couch, Larx's feet in his lap, and started his umpteenth viewing of *The Martian*, he could even overlook the whining.

For the past ten years, his entire focus during the holidays had been to make them okay for his kids. This year his boyfriend and his kids had made it okay for *him*. There was not enough gratitude in the world.

But gratitude was not enough to make all the things right.

A WEEK before Christmas, Aaron and Kirby drove all the way down to Sacramento to pick up Maureen and Tiffany at the airport. They were coming in on different flights, arriving within a half an hour, and Aaron's stomach was in knots.

"Has she said anything to you?" he asked Kirby for the fifteenth time.

"Just that she's ready for you to be over your stupidity," Kirby said, still offended. "Dad, I don't get it. I don't. I… you're happy. *I'm* happy. It's stupid how weird she is about it. I spent yesterday texting the word *bi* to her."

Aaron had to laugh. "Just 'bi'?"

"Yeah. I'm like, 'bi,' and she's like, 'stop it,' and I'm like, 'bi,' and she's like, 'don't be stupid,' and I'm like, 'bi, it's a thing,' and she's like, 'It's Daddy's mid-life crisis.'"

"She *said* that?" Aaron was a little pissed. "Mid-life crisis?"

"I said she was stupid!"

"It's not fair!" Neither was venting to your almost-eighteen-year-old, but Aaron was over this bullshit.

"Ten years!"

"I know, Dad."

"Ten years, and you kids—you were the center of my world."

"Yeah, Dad. I know."

"And you still are," he said, deflating.

"Dad!" Kirby said, his voice gentle—a lot like Larx's, actually. "Dad, look. You get to be happy. You do. You know I believe that, and not just because I don't have to cook anymore.

"These last months have been awesome." And suddenly Kirby sounded seven again, a little lost, trying to be Aaron's little man. "Dad, do you know how much it sucked waiting for you to come home? Even with the girls home, it sucked. Because if anything happened to you, I'd be alone. I don't want to live with Grandma and Grandpa. I don't want to live with Maureen. I feel *safe* like we are. I even…." He sighed. "I want to go to junior college next year. Is that bad? I'm *happy*. I'm safe. I don't want to leave it all behind. Not yet."

Aaron smiled, his heart easing. "That would be fine," he said. "That would be *great*. I'm not ready for my last kid to leave yet."

"Well, Christi's got two more years, and I think Kellan's gonna stick around for a bit. You're eyeballs-deep in kids for a while."

"Let's just hope I can survive the ones who've already moved out."

Aaron could see them standing together at pickup A. Maureen looked like her mother—small, brown-eyed, freckled, hints of red in her dark blonde hair. Tiffany looked like Aaron—tall, with full hips and a generous chest and blue eyes.

But Aaron couldn't remember ever scowling so much, not even right after his wife had died, when he'd felt like every day had been a fight to find the good in the world.

He left the car in Park and got out, greeting Maureen first for a great big bear hug. She laughed and kissed his cheek and called him Daddy like she had as a little girl. Bright like a spark or an ember, Maureen had been almost independently cheerful, fay and dancing.

It wasn't until she skipped off to hug Kirby that he realized how much she reminded him of Larx.

Which left him facing his eldest, and he did his best, holding his arms open. "Tiff?"

"Hi, Dad," she said stiffly, allowing herself to be hugged but not reciprocating. "Are we going home?"

"You and Maureen are staying at the house," Aaron replied equably. He winked at Maureen. "Unless you guys want to sleep on the pillows or the couch, which is fine too." He turned to Tiffany and finished with "We opened the place up, cleaned out the fireplace, turned on the power, and stocked. You should be really comfortable there."

It had taken the lot of them an entire day of their precious winter vacation, and not one of them had complained, not even Kellan, who by all rights didn't have to do jack to make Aaron's daughters happy.

"So you're just going to leave us there?" Tiff snapped. "Thanks a lot, Dad."

"Sounds awesome!" Maureen chirped, glaring at her older sister. "I mean, Christmas Eve at your place, we can have the other place to ourselves." She smiled ingratiatingly. "Tiff, Dad said he moved the chicken coop. We don't even have to feed the damned birds!"

Tiffany rolled her eyes—and then took the front of the SUV, where she maintained an icy silence until Aaron stopped for gas in Citrus Heights.

"Tiff, how 'bout you get in the back and give your sister a chance." Maureen had been trying to have a conversation for the whole trip, but Tiffany had replied monosyllabically and Aaron had needed to pay attention to the road on occasion. In the end Maureen and Kirby had chatted happily, but Aaron wanted equal time.

"One more chance to get rid of me," Tiffany muttered.

"No, hon. Just want Maureen to feel welcome too."

"Whatever."

Aaron sighed. "I'm going to go get some coffee. Anyone want some?"

Maureen and Kirby wanted hot chocolate. Tiffany wanted nothing.

Whatever.

When Aaron got back from the gas station, Tiffany was talking animatedly on the phone and Maureen was arguing with her at the same time. Aaron didn't hear what the in-person argument was about, and Tiffany hung up as soon as he drew near.

They got in the car and got back on the freeway when Tiff interrupted Maureen's excited monologue about her lower division biology class and how happy she was to be moving into upper division science at MIT to say, "Dad, you can just drop me off at the train station in Colfax. Grandma and Grandpa bought me a ticket. I can catch another train to San Francisco and fly out to Illinois by tomorrow."

Aaron saw red. "Uh, no," he said shortly. "Colfax is forty-five minutes out of our way, I've got people waiting for us with dinner, and if you want to get the hell out of Dodge and go crying to Grandma and Grandpa, you're going to have to find your own transport from Colton to the train station, because I'm not doing it."

"Daddy! You can't expect me to stay in the same house as you and your... your *boy toy*. It's just too gross!"

"Which part of 'you guys can stay in your old rooms while Kirby and I go back to our home' do you not understand?"

"The part where you didn't even *ask* me if this was okay!"

Aaron crossed his eyes, and Maureen snickered. He winked at her and kept driving, hating himself a little for how easy it was for him to get along with his younger two children, and how hard it was with his oldest.

"This isn't your decision," he said after a deep breath. "I'm a grown-up, Tiffany. I asked Kirby—"

"Kirby begged him," Kirby interjected. "Because you two heifers left and it was lonely. It's not lonely anymore."

"You don't even know what you're saying yes to," Tiffany said scornfully. "You're a *child*."

"And you're a bitch," Kirby snapped.

"Kirby!" Oh God—Aaron wasn't happy with her, but he didn't want the names to start either.

"No, Dad. Listen to her—she whined to Grandma and Grandpa about your gay love nest like the bigot she is. You didn't raise us like that. Mom didn't raise us like that. Half of Aunt Candy's friends are gay."

"I'm not a bigot! It's just… it's *different* when it's your father!"

"Oh Jesus."

"Tiff, are you hearing yourself?"

"God, Tiff, you're so *stupid*."

Aaron, Maureen, and Kirby all took a deep breath at the same time.

"I'm happy," Aaron said, voice shaking a little with hurt. "I'm sorry you don't care about that or want it, but your brother and I are happy. Like I said, you can stay at the house. Kirby and I are going home to dinner. Maureen, you're welcome at any time."

He caught his oldest daughter's eyes in the rear-view mirror. "Tiff, if you're going to come over to try to hurt my feelings, or Larx's, or Kellan's or Christi's, I'd just as soon you find your own way out of town."

And that was the end of conversation for a while.

OLIVIA LOOKED so much like Lila it made Larx's throat hurt. Now that her chin was a little softer and that thinness some teenagers suffered through had rounded out, just like Christi with the dark hair and dark eyes, she was the spitting image of Larx's late sister.

"Are you sure?" he asked, rubbing his chest. Bull-dozer, the mastiff puppy Aaron had brought back from a rescue center the week before, chewed on his slipper laces. He gave up on discipline for a moment and let the damned dog do whatever it wanted.

"Daddy…." Her chin wobbled and she wiped her eyes. "Positive. I told you, I saw a doctor and every-thing. Just… don't be too mad, okay?"

Larx shook his head and opened his arms. "Not mad, sweetie. Not mad at all."

Well, as far as news bombs went, Olivia had been swift and merciful. She'd tumbled through the door, threw presents for everyone—including Kellan, Kirby, and Aaron—under the tree, and then sat down over hot chocolate and rocked Larx's world.

Right now as he held her and they both cried a little, he tried to come up with words.

I'm sorry. I made the same mistake. I guess it's catching.

I'm sorry. I knew you'd grown up. I thought we'd talked about this.

I'm sorry. You're still my little girl and I want to hunt down the bastard responsible and—

"Daddy, I gotta go pee," Olivia said, dark eyes still swimming, dark hair a flyaway mess around her head.

"Yeah. Sure. Go do that." He watched in exasperation as Dozer followed her. Because of course the dog would take to Olivia best. Didn't everybody?

Their exit left Larx slumped at the table, trying to assimilate the news.

At that moment, Aaron and his kids burst in the front door.

Two of his kids.

Larx tried to pull himself together. Aaron looked hurt and frustrated and sad. God. Parenthood—wasn't always sunshine and roses, was it?

"Larx!" Maureen said, genuinely happy to see him. He welcomed her hug, unsurprised, since she'd hugged pretty much her entire graduating class *and* her teachers.

"Hey, George-mau-er," he said, glad they'd had a rapport. "I see you brought your stuff—you up for the couch?"

Maureen rolled her eyes as Aaron and Kirby hefted two suitcases up the stairs. "Better than the company at Cold-Corner Mansion," she muttered. "I hope the power goes off and her tits freeze."

Ouch.

"I should, uh, probably talk to your father," Larx said delicately.

Maureen kissed his cheek. "I thought it would be weird," she said frankly. "But you're still my old science teacher, and I'm glad I'm here."

Oh thank God, two of Aaron's kids really were just like their father.

He made his way up the stairs, passing Kirby, who gave him a playful sock in the arm, and found Aaron in their room, taking off his boots and putting on fleece-lined leather moccasins Larx had gotten him as an early Christmas present so he didn't spend all winter sick.

With a sigh, he sat down next to his friend, his lover, his companion, and slouched into the mattress.

"So…," he started.

"My oldest daughter is horrible," Aaron said, voice shaking with anger. "She's going to pout at the house until her grandparents fly out and rescue her from our den of iniquity." With a heartsick smile, he turned toward Larx. "How was your day?"

Larx's mouth twisted. "Olivia's pregnant."

Aaron's comically widened eyes were almost worth telling him the news. "I beg your pardon?"

"Her cat died, she was alone on Thanksgiving, and she went out and did someone stupid. Doctor says she's due mid-August."

"Oh dear God."

"She's going back to school for next semester, but she wants to move back here for the first two years of the baby's life." She had it all planned out. Most responsible he'd heard her in her entire life.

"We're going to be grandpas?" Aaron asked, still shocked.

And that's when Larx knew.

Knew deep in his bones.

Knew that thing he'd figured out somewhere in his time as a parent and had mastered now that he was living his second family.

It was going to be okay.

Wouldn't be easy—but it would still be okay.

Because Aaron had said "we."

The only end of the race in life was literally the end of the life. Other people, family, friends, career—there would always be hurdles. But Larx had someone next to him to help him over the high ones and who would need help himself.

And the challenges, the stresses, the pain of watching their older children repeat their parents' mistakes, or possibly make bigger ones of their own—those weren't ever going away.

But Larx and Aaron could face them with a little more surety.

Because they were "we."

"Yeah," Larx said happily. "*We're* going to be grandpas."

His eyes burned, and he leaned his head on Aaron's shoulder while Aaron wrapped an arm around his waist.

"You'll be great at it," Aaron said softly.

"You'll be better."

He tasted salt in their kiss, but just like life, their life, it was still achingly sweet.

KEEP READING FOR AN
EXCLUSIVE EXCERPT FROM

CROCUS

AMY LANE

Crocus

Bonfires: Book Two

Saying "I love you" doesn't guarantee peace or a happy ending.

High school principal "Larx" Larkin was pretty sure he'd hit the jackpot when Deputy Sheriff Aaron George moved in with him, merging their two families as seamlessly as the chaos around them could possibly allow.

But when Larx's pregnant daughter comes home unexpectedly and two of Larx's students are put in danger, their tentative beginning comes crashing down around their ears.

Larx thought he was okay with the dangers of Aaron's job, and Aaron thought he was okay with Larx's daughter—who is *not* okay—but when their worst fears are almost realized, it puts their hearts and their lives to the test. Larx and Aaron have never wanted anything as badly as they want a life together. Will they be able to make it work when the world is working hard to keep them apart?

Clouds over the Sun

"OLIVIA?"

Larx regarded his oldest daughter with surprise. She'd been planning to come home at the end of the spring semester to deal with her pregnancy, it was true, but—

"Sorry, Daddy," she said, her lower lip trembling. Oh God. Her eyes, limpid brown pools on the happiest of days, were shiny and filling with tears even as she stood on his porch.

"Come in," he ushered belatedly. "It's cold out there!" February in Colton, up in the Sierra Mountains, was snow season. "How did you even get—"

Olivia turned and waved, then gathered her suitcases and came inside, shivering in shirtsleeves. The unfamiliar SUV in the driveway backed out, and Larx was left with his daughter and what appeared to be everything she'd taken to her dorm in August.

Stunned, he started moving bags into the house. His hair—still wet from the shower—became brittle in the chill. He was dressed in sweats and a hooded sweatshirt, the better to tuck into masses of weekend paperwork without interruption.

Which was where he'd been when his oldest daughter once again decided to turn his life upside down.

"You're moving back home," he said, stating the obvious.

"Yeah." She turned to him apologetically. "Dad, just leave those in the foyer—"

"So everybody can trip on them? No—I'll take them to your room."

Her piquant little face screwed up into a grimace. "I was hoping… you know. Remember when Aaron's daughters came for Christmas, and they stayed at his house since he moved in here?"

Larx gaped at her. "That is making one hell of an assumption."

Larx and Aaron had gotten together during a tumultuous autumn—but the relationship and the love had stuck, and stuck hard. Aaron and his son, Kirby, had moved into Larx's little house right before Thanksgiving, building a super special space-age chicken coop for their beloved birds. Aaron and Kirby's house was about five miles away on conventional roads, but only about two miles by the forestry service track that ran behind both properties. Aaron's daughters had stayed there over Christmas—one under extreme duress—but for the most part Aaron checked on the place once a week to start the heater and make sure nothing leaked and (Larx suspected) to read his phone in the bathroom in complete peace since there were only two bathrooms in Larx's house and five people living there.

Yes, it was vacant.

Yes, it was available.

But it was *Aaron's*, and Larx was just so damned grateful to have Aaron in his life that he didn't want to impose.

But then, thinking about having one more person using the bathroom in the mornings—one who, by all accounts, was suffering terribly from morning sickness—felt like a burden Larx's crowded little house shouldn't be made to bear. It had been hard enough over the Christmas break, but this was… forever?

"Daddy!"

"We'll ask him," Larx said, numb.

"Where is he?" she asked brightly, turning around and walking backward.

"He's at work today—"

"The boys?"

"Kirby took Kellan to go visit Isaiah. Watch out for the—"

By the grace of God, Olivia avoided Toby, who'd picked that moment to dart across the room. Toby, always a skittish sort of cat, disappeared behind the entertainment center, where she'd probably stay for the next two days.

"How are Kellan and Isaiah doing?" Olivia asked, turning around to negotiate the furniture.

"Still broken up," Larx said shortly. Kellan, the boy Larx had taken into his home in October, had been heartbroken. But Isaiah, who had sustained a brutal knife wound, was busy recovering—both physically and emotionally—and Larx could see how he'd be reluctant to share the darkness in his heart with the boy he loved.

That didn't mean Larx didn't hurt, every day, picking up the pieces.

But Aaron's youngest—Kirby—had adopted Kellan as a brother pretty much from the beginning. He'd been the one to make Kellan keep sending letters, and to explain how having hope for a friendship was so much better than being a bitter, snarling asshole because he was in pain.

Kirby's words. Larx had been hampered by his own compassion—or that's what Aaron told him after Kirby had gone off in Kellan's face and snapped the boy out of his funk.

"Aw, Dad, that's too bad," Olivia said softly. For a moment her attention was focused on something besides her own problems, and her brown eyes showed kindness and sorrow. "I know you were rooting for them."

"They're still friends," Larx said, trying to keep his own opinion out of it. His own opinion was that they were still very much in love. "But, honey, you haven't said—"

"Where's Christiana?"

"At her friend's house, so she can whine about her girlfriend and eat ice cream."

"She didn't break up, did she? She would have texted me!"

Larx had always been proud of how close his girls were—but at this point he sort of wished that closeness swung both ways, because Christiana should have told him her sister was coming home!

"No. Jessica was feeling neglected since Christi started dating Schuyler. This is sort of friend time."

Olivia's relentless movement stopped. Her expression closed down, and she bit her lower lip. "That's nice," she said hollowly. "That's... really mature, actually. You know. So, uh, Christiana."

She started backing away from him, once again not watching where she was going.

"Livvy, what's wrong? Shit, Livvy! Don't trip over the—"

And she did. She tripped over the half-grown shepherd/retriever mix sprawled between the kitchen and the living room. Dozer startled and leaped up, barking his head off.

Olivia screamed, fell backward on her ass, and burst into tears.

Larx scrubbed his face with his hand and leaned forward to give her a hand up. "Honey," he said, hefting her to her feet. "Why don't we start at the beginning?"

The beginning, apparently, was born in a relentless shower of tears. It took him an hour—an uncomfortable, unhappy hour, during which time he made her hot chocolate, gave her space while he made her lunch, stacked her boxes in the hall, and took her overnight bag to Christiana's bedroom, where she'd slept when she'd been home for Christmas, and then held her and rocked her and actually sang to her to calm her down.

By the time she'd calmed down enough to maybe, perhaps, tell him what was going on, she fell immediately asleep, facedown on the couch while he was stroking her back.

Larx was in his empty house with his despondent daughter and a table full of paperwork he'd *just* started an hour before.

And a brain that wouldn't stop buzzing.

Olivia had zoomed into the house at the beginning of Christmas break too. She'd zoomed into the house, run to the bathroom, hugged everybody, petted the dog, sat down at the table, and told Larx she was pregnant.

Larx had hugged her and cried and told Aaron, pretty much in that order.

And Aaron had taken it like a champion. No freaking out about how Olivia wasn't the most stable bee in the bonnet, no wondering what they were going to do after she had the baby and they might end up being responsible for it while they helped Olivia juggle her school schedule—nothing.

Just "Oh—we're going to be grandparents."

And Larx, reeling from the news himself, had been counting his blessings every day.

He would be doing something hard, yes—but he'd be doing it with a helpmate, and damn, after all those years of both of them going it alone, that seemed like such a blessing.

But the more Larx talked to Olivia, the more she texted him constantly throughout his day, the more concerned he got. He couldn't put his finger on the source of his worry—he didn't have a name for it.

All he knew was that every time he tried to pin her down on a plan for the next year, she either cried or ran away, or, worse, got hysterical and angry on the phone and hung up. As long as he'd been parenting, he'd prided himself and his girls on their ability to talk to each other, to work out any problem, to discuss things rationally.

Rational had not been on Olivia's plate since Christmas. Hell, if Larx thought hard about it, since even before that.

Larx didn't know much about mental health issues, but what he did know made him want to take her to the nearest psych ward for an evaluation. But every time he tried to bring it up—something along the lines of "You're getting a little, uh, extreme in the mood department, honey," she lost it—anger, tears, or simply avoidance—and now she'd avoided herself right back home, where three more people lived than had been living when she left.

Larx sat in the sudden silence of his little house in Colton, California, and tried to put his own breath into perspective. Not too loud, not too soft, just there.

That's what he needed to be as a father right now. He hoped.

Because otherwise he was as lost as his butterfly daughter, and he didn't have a Larx to turn to.

HE STOOD with a sigh and walked into the kitchen, thinking more coffee was in order. He'd brought home an entire stack of behavioral referrals that needed his signature and some sort of follow-up, as well as minutes from the last board meeting that he wanted to add remarks to, and he was in the middle of trying to reorder textbooks, which was harder than it sounded.

America's textbook industry was still very much dominated by Texas, and Larx was damned if he would okay a science textbook that spent more time on creationism than evolution, because he had a brain.

And because his students' brains were still developing, and he would really very much appreciate it if they didn't develop into complete idiocy under his watch.

Ugh. What was the world thinking?

He'd been looking forward to six or so hours to catch up on his paperwork. The boys, Christiana, Aaron—they were all due back in the late afternoon, when they would make dinner together and play cards and maybe fall asleep in front of a movie as a family, and Larx had planned to enjoy that too.

He had, in fact, been dreaming about some time leaning against Aaron George's solid chest for the past week. Both of them had been busy—heinously busy, in fact.

The last time they'd tried to have sex, Larx had fallen asleep with his hand on Aaron's solid erection and his head on Aaron's shoulder.

For the first time in nearly ten years, they both had somebody in bed and in their lives whom they loved and wanted to be with, and that was as good as sex got?

No. Absolutely not.

Larx was not going to let this stand.

Or he hadn't been, until Olivia had danced in through the front door with all her stuff and moved her ass back onto his couch before he was ready for it.

With a sigh, he put his elbows up on his ginormous stack of paperwork and buried his face in his hands.

His phone, sitting on the table next to him, buzzed, and he was damned grateful.

Hello, Principal—are you being a good boy and getting your work done?

Larx groaned. *Sort of. Olivia showed up on the doorstep this morning.* Oh hell. He didn't even want to *ask* Aaron about using his house.

Is she visiting for the weekend?

No.

The phone rang. "Are you kidding me?"

"Sorry, Aaron." He sighed and sipped his tepid coffee, then took a deep breath. "I don't know what's going on. She came in talking a mile a minute, tripped over the dog—"

"Is Dozer okay?"

Larx had to laugh. "Your dog is fine, Aaron."

"He's your dog," Aaron protested weakly. Yes, the puppy had been a gift for Larx when his oldest cat passed away, but Aaron—big, solid, strong—had apparently been waiting for Dozer for most of his life.

Larx wasn't going to argue that the dog was definitely Aaron's, but it was true. Dozer—a mixed breed somewhere between a Labrador retriever and a German shepherd—was fine with Larx, answered to him just as well as he did Aaron, appreciated the hell out of the full food bowl, gave plenty of sloppy, happy kisses, and pranced about on spindly legs and feet the size of dinner plates.

But when Aaron came home, Larx watched the dog melt, roll to his back, offer up his tummy in supplication, and beg for pets.

Larx couldn't object or be jealous—he felt the same way. Except Larx wanted Aaron to pet more than his belly.

"That dog's your soul mate from another life," Larx said now, scratching Dozer behind the ears.

"Yes, you are. Yes, you are. But you can't have him. He's mine."

"Wow. Just wow."

Larx chuckled, because the distraction had been welcome, but now... now grown-up things. "She's asleep on the couch," he said softly. "Aaron... she's not sounding...." He took a big breath. His ex-wife had suffered from depression after a miscarriage, and he remembered coming home from work bringing dinner once so she didn't have to cook or clean up because she'd been so sad. She'd yelled at him—didn't he think she was capable of cleaning her own kitchen? Then she'd burst into tears for an hour, while Larx had fed the girls and tried to calm her down.

It had been like standing on the deck of a ship in a storm—and Larx had that same feeling now, with his daughter, when his children had always been the source of peace in his heart.

"Pregnancy?" Aaron asked hesitantly. They were so new. Larx hadn't spoken about Alicia more than a handful of times. Nobody talked about depression or mental illness.

Nobody knew what to say.

"Yeah." Larx didn't want to talk about it right now. He just couldn't.

"Baby...." Aaron's voice dropped, and considering Larx had gotten him at work, where he had to be all tough and manly and shit, that meant he was worried.

"Later," Larx said gruffly. "Just not, you know...."

"When the whole world can hear. I get it." Aaron blew out a breath and then took the subject down a surprising path. "Larx, do you have a student named Candace Furman?"

Larx stared at the paperwork in his hand, shuffling back to where he was right before Olivia had knocked.

"Yeah. Not one of mine, but… huh." He reached over to his laptop and accessed the school's portal site. "Hm…."

"That's informative. Want to tell me what you're looking at?"

"It's sort of privileged, Deputy. Want to tell me why you need to know?"

Aaron's grunt told him he was being annoying, but Larx couldn't help it. He didn't want to just divulge information on a kid if it wasn't necessary. It went against everything he'd ever stood for as a rebellious adolescent.

"I just got…. It was weird. We got a domestic call to her house—her parents answer, and it's all great. 'No, Officer, we have no idea why somebody would call in screaming or a fight in the snow.' We take a look inside, house is okay—but really clean."

"Like somebody just swept up all the pieces of all the things?" Larx hazarded.

"Yeah. Either that or just… unhealthily antiseptic. And Candace and her sister—"

"Shelley," Larx supplied since he had the file open on his computer.

"Yeah. Anyway—the girls are fine. 'Yessir. Nossir. It's all okay, sir.' But they've both got these… like, girl masks on?"

"Makeup?" Larx said, trying to picture it.

"No… like… face goop. Like… whatwazit? Mrs. Doubtfire stuck her face in the cake 'cause she didn't have her makeup on?"

It took Larx a minute to process all that. "A facial," he said, blinking hard because the movie was that old, and the antitrans messaging had been so strong that Larx forgot he too had been part of America who'd laughed their asses off at a man in a dress with flammable boobs.

"Yeah. That. And that shit could be hiding anything, right? Their eyes were red, but then, for all I know the facial goop did that. So I'm not sure if they're hiding shiners or if their neighbors just got hold of some bad weed—"

"Did you knock on their door?" Larx asked. Between him and Aaron, they really did know most of the town. "Who's their neighbor?"

"Couple of brothers," Aaron said thoughtfully. "Just moved at Christmas. Youngest one goes to Colton High—"

"Jaime Benitez," Larx said promptly. "Junior." He pressed the right link and there was the master schedule. "He and Candace are in some classes together."

Aaron grunted. "Well, the older brother had been lighting up pretty hard—but it doesn't seem like Jaime's the type to indulge."

"You didn't bust them?" Larx asked curiously. He'd done his share of weed in college—but Aaron had been off fighting and bleeding for his country when Larx was in college. This was something they'd never talked about.

"Hell," Aaron muttered. "Unless they're growing to distribute, it's mostly legal. Not for minors, of course, but both boys were functional, polite, and their eyes were clear. Roberto—who's twenty-one, by the way—actually produced a prescription for anxiety without being asked. I could have made a stink about it, but I couldn't see the point."

"I love you so hard," Larx breathed. "Seriously. I can't think of a sexual favor good enough for you. I'll have to make something up."

"I'm sorry?"

Larx couldn't articulate it. It wasn't that he'd smoke it now unless it was prescribed, and he didn't want his kids—or his students—indulging without cause. But something about knowing Aaron, for all his law-and-order propensities, didn't push rules just for the sake of there being rules made Larx even prouder of him.

"Just you're a good guy. Jaime Benitez is getting good grades. He's part of the local service clubs, including one where he tutors eighth graders in trouble. Nice boy."

"In your class?" Aaron wanted to know.

"Senior year, like Kirby. Christiana is sort of—"

"Special," Aaron said fondly. "Yeah. I know."

Well, Larx's youngest was the girl with the flower—her brightness and sparkle was coupled with a quiet good sense. Irresistible. She was also razor-sharp, which was why she was taking Larx's class in her junior year.

"So what about Candace?" Aaron prompted.

Larx sighed. "She's... well, she *was* a straight-A student, but no involvement in anything."

"Nothing?"

Aaron might well be surprised. It was a small school in a small town. Activity involvement wasn't mandatory, but if a kid wanted any sort of social life, being part of a club or a sport was pretty much the only thing going on after school.

"No—that's odd. And that's probably why I can't place her. Her sister's in grade school, so I wouldn't know her. But Candace is just… not involved."

"Was," Aaron prompted, and Larx rested his chin on his fist and looked woefully at his paperwork. Ye gods, the pile wasn't getting any smaller.

"Yeah. *Was* getting straight As. Is no longer. Is veering off into C and D territory. And I have in front of me, waiting for a signature, her very first referral for behavior."

He stared at it, wondering how the pieces fit.

"What'd she do?" Aaron asked patiently.

"Well, it says she got to class late and then ran out a few minutes after the bell rang. It was her first-period class, and when she came back—looking pale—the teacher asked if she was okay. Apparently she laughed hysterically and told the teacher to fuck off."

"Uh…."

Larx sighed. "Yeah. That's why I'm up to my eyeballs in paperwork, Aaron—so I can look for kids like this and ask them what happened. I'm on it."

"That's my boy," Aaron praised softly. "Good. Keep me in the loop, okay? I don't know if the girls were being abused, and frankly I didn't have enough evidence to so much as make them wash their faces. I don't know the story behind the boys living together without parents, and I don't know why one of them would be anxious enough to get a prescription for a ton of weed. These are things I would like to know before I go venturing in there with CPS and the DEA to make sure everything is kosher, you understand?"

"Got it, Deputy." Larx looked at both kids' files again and wondered at the puzzle. "Aaron, I'm serious. You're a good man. These kids—there's pieces missing here. Yanking them away from their homes, dragging them into the fray—I'm not sure if that's the best thing here."

Larx was starting to know Aaron's grunts—this one was the respectful disagreement grunt. "Some stuff needs to see light, Mr. Larkin," he chided gently. "If something's festering in that girl's life, it's our job to make sure she's okay."

Of course.

"Roger that." Larx tilted his head back and pinched the bridge of his nose.

"Have you eaten?" Aaron asked.

"Uh…." He'd gotten a sandwich for Olivia, but he'd put off getting his own.

"Eat, Principal. Work on your paperwork. And maybe take a nap on the couch before I get there. Save up your strength." He gave a chuckle that was absolutely filthy. "You're going to need it."

Larx whined. "But… but Olivia—"

"If hearing us have sex gives her reason to move out, more's the better," Aaron intoned darkly.

Oh shit. "She… uh… she sort of hinted… never mind."

"My house. Yes. We'll move her tomorrow."

Larx groaned and rested his forehead on the paperwork on the table. "God. You're the perfect man. Where's the rub? Where's the flaw? There's got to be something here that makes me want to smack you—where is it?"

"Mmm…."

Oh yeah. That conversation they *weren't* having because of all the conversations they *were*.

"Understood." Larx sighed. "I'll see you when you get home."

"Eat, dammit."

Larx smiled, reassured. "Sure. Take care of what's mine."

"Always do."

"Love you."

"Thanks for the info."

Aaron signed off, and Larx's text pinged thirty seconds later.

Love you too.

Yup. Too good to be true.

Larx's worry about his daughter—and about Aaron's input into the situation—doubled down in his chest.

Please, Olivia—please. Don't make me choose between you two. Please.

AMY LANE is a mother of two grown kids, two half-grown kids, two small dogs, and half-a-clowder of cats. A compulsive knitter who writes because she can't silence the voices in her head, she adores fur-babies, knitting socks, and hawt menz, and she dislikes moths, cat boxes, and knuckleheaded macspazzmatrons. She is rarely found cooking, cleaning, or doing domestic chores, but she has been known to knit up an emergency hat/blanket/pair of socks for any occasion whatsoever or sometimes for no reason at all. Her award-winning writing has three flavors: twisty-purple alternative universe, angsty-orange contemporary, and sunshine-yellow happy. By necessity, she has learned to type like the wind. She's been married for twenty-five-plus years to her beloved Mate and still believes in Twu Wuv, with a capital Twu and a capital Wuv, and she doesn't see any reason at all for that to change.

Website: www.greenshill.com
Blog: www.writerslane.blogspot.com
Email: amylane@greenshill.com
Facebook:www.facebook.com/amy.lane.167
Twitter: @amymaclane

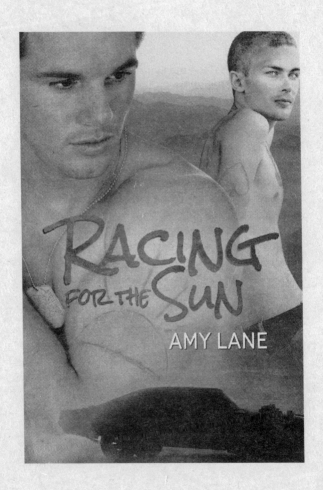

RACING
FOR THE SUN

AMY LANE

"I'll do anything."

Staff Sergeant Jasper "Ace" Atchison takes one look at Private Sonny Daye and knows that every word on paper about him is pure, unadulterated bullshit. But Sonny is desperate, and although Ace isn't going to take him up on his offer of "anything," that doesn't mean he isn't tempted.

Instead, Ace takes Sonny under his wing, protecting him when they're in the service and making plans with him when they get out. Together, they're going to own a garage and build race cars and make their fortune hurtling faster than light across the desert. Together, they're going to rewrite the past, make Sonny Daye a whole and happy person, and put the ghosts in Ace's heart to rest.

But not even Sonny can build a car fast enough to escape the ghosts of the past. When Sonny's ghosts drive them down and run their plans off the road, Ace finds out exactly what he's made of. Maybe Sonny was the one to promise Ace anything, but there is nothing under the sun Ace won't do to keep Sonny safe from harm.

www. dreamspinnerpress.com

Guess who's swimming in the
same pond...

FISH
OUT OF
WATER
Amy Lane

PI Jackson Rivers grew up on the mean streets of Del Paso Heights—and he doesn't trust cops, even though he was one. When the man he thinks of as his brother is accused of killing a police officer in an obviously doctored crime, Jackson will move heaven and earth to keep Kaden and his family safe.

Defense attorney Ellery Cramer grew up with the proverbial silver spoon in his mouth, but that hasn't stopped him from crushing on street-smart, swaggering Jackson Rivers for the past six years. But when Jackson asks for his help defending Kaden Cameron, Ellery is out of his depth—and not just with guarded, prickly Jackson. Kaden wasn't just framed, he was framed by crooked cops, and the conspiracy goes higher than Ellery dares reach—and deep into Jackson's troubled past.

Both men are soon enmeshed in the mystery of who killed the cop in the minimart, and engaged in a race against time to clear Kaden's name. But when the mystery is solved and the bullets stop flying, they'll have to deal with their personal complications… and an attraction that's spiraled out of control.

www. dreamspinnerpress.com

There's blood in the water and death in the air...

RED FISH,
DEAD
FISH

Amy Lane

"Deliciously tense . . .
a satisfying mix of sweet
angst and steamy suspense."
KAREN ROSE,
NYT Bestselling Author

They must work together to stop a psychopath—
and save each other.

Two months ago Jackson Rivers got shot while
trying to save Ellery Cramer's life. Not only is Jackson still suffering from his wounds, the triggerman remains at large—and the body count is mounting.

Jackson and Ellery have been trying to track down
Tim Owens since Jackson got out of the hospital, but
Owens's time as a member of the department makes
the DA reluctant to turn over any stones. When Owens
starts going after people Jackson knows, Ellery's instincts hit red alert. Hurt in a scuffle with drug-dealing
squatters and trying damned hard not to grieve for a
childhood spent in hell, Jackson is weak and vulnerable when Owens strikes.

Jackson gets away, but the fallout from the encounter might kill him. It's not doing Ellery any favors either. When a police detective is abducted—and
Jackson and Ellery hold the key to finding her—Ellery
finds out exactly what he's made of. He's not the corporate shark who believes in winning at all costs; he's
the frightened lover trying to keep the man he cares
for from self-destructing in his own valor.

www. dreamspinnerpress.com

Some lovers are as familiar as the family pet.

FAMILIAR
ANGEL

Amy Lane

"Fantastic...a transcendent
love story that will sweep you
off your feet."
CINDY DEES,
NYT and *USA Today*
Bestselling Author

One hundred and forty years ago, Harry, Edward, and Francis met an angel, a demon, and a sorceress while escaping imprisonment and worse! They emerged with a new family—and shapeshifting powers beyond their wildest dreams.

Now Harry and his brothers use their sorcery to rescue those enslaved in human trafficking—but Harry's not doing so well. Pining for Suriel the angel has driven him to take more and more risks until his family desperately asks Suriel for an intervention.

In order for Suriel to escape the bindings of heaven, he needs to be sure enough of his love to fight to be with Harry. Back when they first met, Harry was feral and angry, and he didn't know enough about love for Suriel to justify that risk. Can Suriel trust in Harry enough now to break his bonds of service for the boy who has loved his Familiar Angel for nearly a century and a half?

www. dreamspinnerpress.com